NELL'S WEST

ERIN ELDRIDGE

NELL'S WEST
by
Erin Eldridge

Copyright © Erin Eldridge 2022
Cover Copyright © Kitty Honeycutt (Ravenswood Publishing)
Published by White Stag
(An Imprint of Ravenswood Publishing)

WHITE STAG

Ravenswood Publishing
1275 Baptist Chapel Rd.
Autryville, NC 28318
http://www.ravenswoodpublishing.com
Email: RavenswoodPublishing@gmail.com

Paperback orders can be placed through Amazon
http://www.amazon.com

Printed in the United States of America
First Edition
10 9 8 7 6 5 4 3 2 1

ISBN-13: 9798821898012

For my Irish grandmother, Mary Kennedy, who loved to read a Western. She had four sons and three daughters. One daughter was named Ellen (Nell).

PROLOGUE

"Gimme that gun, bitch!"

Nell held the pistol steady, sighted along the barrel and squeezed the trigger, hitting her target with exemplary accuracy, in the groin, his tumescent penis providing a good focal point, as it were, aroused as he'd foretold by the slap he'd just given her across her left cheek, the stinging effects of which drew water from her eye. Not her sighting eye, unluckily for him. His own ferrety, bloodshot eyes bulging in disbelief, he doubled over, screaming and clutching at the crotch of his grubby, sweat-stained long johns, blood spurting through his fingers. The gunshot and the screams transformed the ruckus in the bar below to a dramatically contrasting silence, and then Nell heard footsteps pounding on the stair treads as responders climbed towards the room. She had mere seconds to get away.

Thrusting the gun into the waistband of her petticoat, she snatched up her erstwhile customer's money pouch from where he'd placed it on the bureau, thrust it down her cleavage, and ran to the open window. Lithe as a cat, she slipped over the sill and on to the narrow verandah that fronted the saloon's top storey. Peering over the railing, she made out several horses tethered below. Glancing back over her shoulder, she saw the door to the room being flung open, a hulking figure filling the frame, his menacing bulk backlit by the passageway lamps – it had to be Jarrow. He'd have a struggle following her through the narrow window. On the floor, her tormentor was writhing about like a scalded snake, his initial bloodcurdling screams fading to sobbing whimpers. Jarrow spotted her, stepped over her convulsing victim, and advanced, fists ominously clenched, a gurgle of rage surging up from his throat like fire from a dragon's bowels. For a split second Nell considered putting a bullet in Jarrow, too, but dismissed the thought, however tempting, almost as quickly. She needed to escape, and fast. Reaching up she tore the cheap pearl choker from her neck and flung it away as a final act of defiance.

Nell climbed on to the railing, gripping with her bare feet, took a deep breath, and jumped. It would have been outstanding if she'd landed in the saddle, any saddle, like a hero in a penny dreadful, but her descent was far from elegant or precise. She glanced off one startled horse, dozing like the others, striking it on the nose before she landed on her backside in the mud beside it, and the beast reared up, neighing wildly. At least the soft mud had broken her fall a little. Nell scrambled to her feet to avoid the flying hooves and wisely

2

chose the animal two mounts away, which was not as spooked, regarding her more with curiosity than fright, nickering its surprise as she unfastened the reins from the hitching post, and leaped into the saddle.

"Yee ha!" Jerking its head viciously around to face the street, Nell dug her hard little heels into the horse's flanks, and the animal lunged forwards willingly, doubtless relieved at the change of weight on its back from hefty male to a slip of a girl. As they raced away into the night, Nell heard the commotion of outrage behind her, and a couple of bullets whined past her head. Then they reached the outskirts of the town and the darkness swallowed them up, the horse stretching out into a steady gallop as its muscles warmed. Nell leaned forwards in the saddle, urging it on with tongue clicks and flicks of the reins. She grinned, blonde hair streaming out behind her as the few remaining pins in it flew away. Her short-lived career as a whore was over. Her career as an outlaw had just begun: guilty of (probably, given the way the bastard was bleeding) murder, guilty of common theft (pistol and money), guilty of horse theft. And this newly fledged villain was clad only in her underwear; very muddy underwear at that.

CHAPTER ONE

Iowa, seven years earlier, autumn 1851

Nell placed the basket of eggs she'd just collected on the kitchen table, wiping her nose on the back of her hand. "Eight this morning, Ma," she announced with a pleased grin. Looking after the chickens was her foremost chore, and she felt justifiably proud when they laid well. Here was the satisfying proof of her diligent husbandry – a clutch of large brown eggs. Tending the vegetable garden was one of her chores, too, especially now that Mam couldn't bend easily anymore.

A young woman turned around from the wood stove, where she was flipping over sizzling strips of bacon in a cast iron pan. "Good girl, Nellie. Bring me two. Pappy will be in for his breakfast any minute." Her face was flushed from the heat of the stove, and she tucked away a stray strand of dark hair as she smiled down at her daughter. "Want to break them into the pan for me?" she asked, as the child stopped before the stove, holding an egg in each hand, bits of cack and feathers still sticking to the shells. "Don't get no muck in there, though."

Nell nodded, clamping her small tongue between her front teeth to aid her concentration as she broke first one, then the other egg into the pan, smiling up at her mother when her contribution to Pap's breakfast was successfully accomplished, the eggs sizzling in the bacon grease.

"Well done. Didn't break a one of 'em." Priscilla opened the warmer hatch and removed a bowl of corn mush, placing it on the table, which was set for breakfast, along with a pitcher of milk and a cup. "Wash your hands now, and then eat up. I don't want you late for school." As Nell hastened to obey, she called after her, "Want me to cat your braids? An' lace up them boots! How many times I got to tell you?"

"Yes, Mam." Nell dropped first on to one knee then the other, yanking the laces of each boot into tautened compliance before tying them nimbly into bows and proceeding outside.

While Nell was washing her hands at the pump, Pap darted around the side of the farmhouse and ambushed her, carrying her back inside underneath one arm, squealing and giggling. He pulled out a chair and planted her in front of her breakfast before sidling up to his wife, absorbed in her cooking, and wrapping his arms around her from behind, tenderly stroking her pregnant belly with one hand.

"How's the two of you this mornin'?"

His wife thrust her face up to his, and they kissed lingeringly, making a soft 'mmm' sound.

"Ewww! Stop that!" Nell squirmed, blushing with delight at her parents' open display of affection.

"How'd you think *you* got here?" asked Pap, grinning at her, and laughing as his wife playfully slapped him, frowning her disapproval.

"Nathan! Hush now! Sit down and I'll fetch over your fixins."

Pap planted a resounding kiss on her cheek before sauntering to the table to join his daughter. "Hey, slow down on that mush, or you'll give yourself a bellyache!"

His wife placed his breakfast on the table in front of him, and both Nathan and Nell reacted with alarm as she gave a high-pitched little squeak, recoiling away as if an unseen hand had jerked her backwards.

Nathan leaped to his feet. "Priscilla! What's wrong?" Both he and Nell visibly sagged as they saw that, although she had her arms crossed over her swollen abdomen, she was giggling. "That babby! Every time I get near the table edge, he knows it an' kicks out like a mule, an' it's the strangest feelin'. Has me hoppin' back like a rabbit every time." She gave a delighted little shudder.

Nathan sat down slowly. "I thought the child was fixin' to come out, Prissy, the way you acted." He gulped down a big swig of coffee to steady his nerves and blew out his breath, raising both eyebrows as he looked across the table at a chuckling Nell.

"Not likely," Priscilla patted her spooked husband's shoulder. "Three weeks to go, by my reckoning. I carried Nell right through. No reason to think this one'll be any different." She jerked her chin in Nell's direction. "You be off, now, missy."

"Yes, Mam. I'll ride into town after school with the extra eggs an' butter, if you want."

"Thank you, Nellie."

Nell took her dishes to the washboard and picked up her lunch pail, which was an old syrup bucket, kissed her parents in turn, and skipped to the door. Outside, she stood on the porch for a moment, closed her eyes, and savoured the feeling of the early morning sun's fragile warmth on her face. She sighed. It was going to be another beautiful day. Life was good. Glancing back, she saw Mam sitting down opposite Pap as he tucked into his breakfast, lifting the coffee cup to her lips and smiling as she watched her man do justice to her cooking. Nell closed her eyes again, indulging in the warm glow of security she always enjoyed, seeing them together. Then she heard Jimmy calling to her from the stile over the fence on the other side of the field, their customary morning meeting place, and her eyes snapped open.

ERIN ELDRIDGE

"I'm comin'!" Nell raced down the steps and off across the field, pigtails flying.

****

"Mornin', Nell."

"Mornin', Jimmy."

They fell in alongside each other with an ease born of long acquaintance, and Jimmy wordlessly relieved Nell of her lunch pail, carrying it for her as he did on every school day. Nell liked that. It made her feel special, confirmed that he was her beau. Jimmy was thirteen years old to Nell's eleven, and very protective of her. It grieved Nell that Jimmy had no lunch pail of his own, but he never complained. He was due to finish school soon, and Nell knew she'd miss him sorely.

Jimmy and Nell had known each other since they were knee-high to grasshoppers, as the saying goes, because they lived on neighbouring farms, and they were as close as siblings, with an overlay of boy-girl attraction, strolling to and from school together every day, perfectly at ease in each other's company. Jimmy was an only child, too, but his pappy was much more demanding of him than Nell's father was of her when it came to doing the chores, him being such a loyal son and a willing worker who never complained. He often fell asleep in class as a result of his workload, and, sometimes, missed days altogether because his pa needed him to

8

help out at home, especially during spring and autumn. Their teacher, Mr. Cosgrove, was an understanding man, indulging Jimmy's naps without rebuking him because he was a good student, whip smart and hungry for learning. It wasn't uncommon to have a few children in the class sleeping at the same time, especially on a warm afternoon. Mr. Cosgrove largely indulged these naps as being needed for growing young bodies – and brains.

"How's your mam?" asked Jimmy as they walked.

"She's fine, big as a pickling barrel; just a few weeks to go now." Nell aimed a kick at a tempting stone, sending it skittering away. "Oh, Jimmy, I just cain't wait 'til that baby's born. It's a boy, I know it is. I'm gonna take such good care of him, love him to death. He's gonna grow up big an' strong, be helpin' Pap out on the farm in no time."

"He sure will. You got a name for him?"

"I want him to be called Jesse."

"That's a good name. Do your folks like it."

"They will," said Nell confidently.

Nell glanced sideways at Jimmy. His mother, a wiry, thin-lipped woman with hard, piercing blue eyes, was not known for her maternal largesse. She seemed indifferent to Jimmy at the best of times. "Do you wish your mam could have another baby?"

Jimmy pursed his lips. "I guess." He chuckled. "Leastways, I'd have someone else to share the load with an' gripe to."

9

Nell ran an appraising eye over him. He sure was skinny. Everyone knew Hal Hochstedder was hard on his son, and Nell had seen bruises on Jimmy from time to time. They could have happened innocently, and Jimmy was tight-lipped, but she knew the truth, even though Mam had sternly insisted you shouldn't jump to conclusions when she'd mentioned this to her, along with the information that Jimmy was the only kid who came to school without any victuals. However, Mam, who was kindness personified, often slipped an extra treat or two into Nell's lunch pail on the understanding that she could share them with Jimmy, who always devoured the offerings gratefully. Other kids shared food with him, too, and Mr. Cosgrove regularly slipped many a lunch Jimmy's way, perhaps an apple a student had brought him, or a pie a mother had baked him, making an excuse like, "I can't manage this as well as what my dear wife has packed for me, and wasting food is a sin." Everyone contributed in ways that preserved Jimmy's dignity.

Nell hoped that one day Jimmy would be able to get away from his tyrant of a father and his neglectful mother. Mr. Cosgrove, who always patiently helped the boy to catch up on work he'd missed labouring, insisted Jimmy could really make something of himself. For Nell's part, she couldn't understand anyone not loving Jimmy to bits. He was so sweet and gentle, and nice-looking, too, with his wavy brown hair and a smattering of gold dust freckles across his comely features. All the girls were sweet on him, but Nell knew his heart belonged to her.

Her musings were interrupted by the distant clangour of the school bell ringing, and both children began to lope towards the sound, Jimmy with his long, spidery legs easily outstripping Nell, looking back at her over his shoulder and laughing, her lunch pail dangling from the end of one gangly outstretched arm.

"Jimmy! Wait for me!"

****

The day at school passed in a familiar routine. There was some excitement, though, which momentarily alleviated the humdrum nature of the predictable sequence of lessons when, during a quiet moment of copying from the board, Sid Newberry slipped a frog down the back of Sadie Pettigrew's dress. Mr. Cosgrove regained control amidst all the laughter and shrieking with his usual mix of firm but calm child wrangling and stood Sid in the corner with his back to the class for the rest of the afternoon, eyes watering after receiving six lashes from his teacher's hickory stick. Sadie was invited to come sit at the teacher's desk until her tears abated and her equilibrium was restored. The rather dazed frog was returned to the nearby pond.

For the last half hour, the pupils took turns reading aloud to their peers from copies of the new farming catalogue, which Nell always enjoyed as a break from the Bible and McGuffey Readers. She wasn't bookish as such; not like Jimmy, who regularly borrowed books from Mr. Cosgrove and avidly devoured them in secret places where his father wouldn't catch him. Then the bell rang, and, after bidding their teacher farewell, all the kids poured out into the sunshine for the journey home. Nell walked happily alongside Jimmy, still chuckling over the frog incident. She couldn't help feeling a bit smug about Sadie's distress because she didn't like her. She had a tendency to put on airs and graces because her father's farm was the biggest spread in the district.

"Poor Sadie sure hollered when that frog went down her dress."

Jimmy nodded, lips pursed thoughtfully. "I think Sid is sweet on Sadie."

Nell stopped abruptly, looking at him wide-eyed. "Whaaat? She's gonna hate him now, for sure!"

Jimmy winked. "Wait and see. He sure got her attention, anyways. Took his punishment like a man, too."

Nell drew herself up to full height, sticking her nose in the air. "Any boy did that to me to get my attention, I'd punch him on the nose."

"Maybe first up, but then you'd be lookin' at him, and he'd be lookin' at you, and afore you knows it, you'd be sweethearts." He stuck his own nose in the air, manner confidently superior. "I *seen* it."

Nell studied him with narrowed eyes as she mulled over this questionable insight. Was Jimmy possibly wiser in the world of inter-gender relations than she was? He *was* older than she. Eventually, she made a snorting sound. "If Sadie Pettigrew becomes Sid Newberry's girl, then I'll bake you a cherry pie, all to yourself."

Jimmy grinned. "You're on. But what's my forfeit if I'm wrong?"

Nell pursed her lips, studying him. "I'll think of somethin', maybe getting' you to do some chore I don't like much."

"Tell me tomorrow. Nothin' too messy now. I better be right about those two." Jimmy started to skip away backwards. "Come on! I'll race you to the stile!"

He loped away on his long, skinny legs and Nell scampered after him. "No fair! You got a head start! Hold up! Who did you mean when you said you '*seen* it'?"

****

Nell was panting, a sheen of perspiration highlighting her cheekbones, by the time she caught up to Jimmy. "Tell me who you seen, Jimmy." Her small chest heaved with exertion. "Don't you tease me none." She swatted his nearest shoulder crossly.

Jimmy did not answer. He was standing with one foot on the lower step of the stile, leaning forwards slightly, a hand shading his eyes as he peered in the direction of the farmhouse.

"Ain't that Doc Lindstrom's buggy?"

Nell stepped forwards, squinting. Her sharp eyes instantly recognised the doctor's conveyance and his ribby bay mare standing in the shafts in the shade of the large hackberry tree to the left of the farmhouse verandah. "Yes, I reckon it is." Her eyes flew open and she gripped Jimmy's forearm. "The baby! He must've come early! Oh, Jimmy, Mam's having the baby!"

"Steady on, Nell. It's maybe just a social call, or Doc's checkin' on her 'cos her time's close."

Elbowing a startled Jimmy out of the way, Nell was up and over the stile in a flash, racing away towards home with renewed energy and a whoop of joy.

"Your lunch pail!" Jimmy shouted after her. Then realising there was no chance of her turning back, he shrugged, leaped over the stile himself and loped after her.

****

Nell raced up the steps and burst into the kitchen, pulling up short as she instantly realised that something was dreadfully wrong, an icy worm of fear writhing up from her belly. Her cosy farmhouse home felt completely different: cold, sinister, drained of what was good. Pappy was seated at the table, holding his head in his hands. He didn't raise it to look at her. Doc Lindstrom sat opposite him, his shirtsleeves rolled up well past his elbows, shoulders stooped dejectedly. Each man had a tumbler of whiskey in front of him, the half empty bottle sitting in the middle of the table. The doctor's head jerked up as Nell entered and he rose to intercept her, a weak smile lighting his drawn features. The long surgical apron he was wearing was stained with blood.

Nell recoiled in horror, almost bumping into Jimmy, who was by now right behind her, standing very still. He delicately slid the lunch pail on to a corner of the table. "Where's Mam?" whispered Nell.

The doctor placed both hands on her shoulders. "Nell, you must be strong now and help your father."

"Where's *Mam*?" Nell shrilled. Then she wrested herself from the doctor's grasp and charged across the kitchen, wrenching open the door to her parents' bedroom. The sight that greeted her shattered her childhood on the instant. Allegra Harwood, the local midwife, sat on a chair beside the bed, hands folded in her lap. She half rose, lips parted, but then sank back on to the chair in silence, lowering her reddened eyes.

Mam lay on her back on the coverlet, wearing her best dress, her limbs neatly arranged like an effigy atop a tomb. Her lovely dark hair flowed either side of her face, which was pale as milk. Nell's gaze moved to the small swaddled bundle that lay curled within the embrace of her mother's right arm. Both gone? It couldn't be. She was surely in the grip of some hideous nightmare and would snap awake any second. "Mam?" Her own voice sounded disembodied and far away. She moved closer to the bed and its tragic burden, tears beginning to flow.

"I'm so sorry, Nell." Doctor Lindstrom spoke behind her. "Your father found her when he came up for his dinner. She'd haemorrhaged – was bleeding badly. Nathan fetched the midwife and sent Zebulon for me. By the time I got here it was too late." He placed a hand on Nell's shoulder. "The baby is a little boy."

A deep, shuddering sob shook Nell's frame, and she crossed the room on wobbly legs to drop with a thud on to her knees beside the bed. Slowly she raised one arm, reaching over to place a trembling hand on Mam's, where they rested one on top of the other, her slim fingers bare except for her heavy gold wedding ring. *So* cold. She recoiled in horror from this unmistakeable chill of death. How could those hands, which had always felt so warm whenever they touched or caressed her, now feel like ice? Then she looked at her little brother, whose tiny, mottled face was just visible within the swathe of quilt that enveloped him, the quilt Mam had made to cover him in his crib, but was now his shroud. He looked so peaceful and perfect, as if he were only sleeping, and Nell repressed a strong urge to prod him a little, to wake him up so she could see what colour his eyes were. How could the strong little boy that kicked the table edge just that morning now be cold and dead? She lowered her face on to Mam's shoulder and wept, wracking sobs jerking her small body like a string puppet. She was vaguely aware of Jimmy kneeling beside her, his arm around her shoulders, his voice soft in her ear.

"I'm here, Nell. You still got a brother. I ain't leavin' you, ever."

16

****

The days that followed passed in a blur for Nell. She and Pappy seemed unable to comfort each other, both numb with grief as they were, and sidestepped around each other as they prepared to farewell their loved ones. They had no immediate family on hand, but neighbours, friends, members of their church congregation rallied with an efficiency born of long acquaintance with the brutal suddenness and prevalence of death in the times and place they inhabited. The undertaker carried out his work with speed and sensitivity, confirming the details of the funeral with the minister, who ensured that the church service, interment, and subsequent wake went off without a hitch. Priscilla and her infant son, whom the minister had hastily baptised as Jesse Nathan Washburn, were duly laid to rest in the same coffin in the little parish churchyard, buried in the shadow of a yew tree of such a dark hue of green that it was almost black.

As Nell, holding tight to Jimmy's hand, watched the coffin being lowered into the gaping cavity of the freshly-dug grave, she had internalised a valuable lesson: never take anything in life for granted, because life can change on the spin of a dime.

CHAPTER TWO

Six months later, winter

Nell stared at her hairbrush. There was an awful lot of hair in it again, long blonde wisps trapped between the bristles. Looking into the mirror, she raised a tentative hand to her head, picked up a strand of hair, and gave it a sharp tug. It came away easily and painlessly in her fingers, a sizeable clump, dull yellow and straw-like in texture. Nell tore away the hair trapped in the brush, rolled the whole into a ball, replaced the brush on the dresser, and made her way to the kitchen. Opening the damper, she lifted the front plate on the stove and thrust the crushed mass into the red coals, watching it flare briefly before slamming the plate back in place. Then she crossed to the row of coat hooks by the door, plucked her thick woollen hat from its peg and pulled it down hard over her ears, furiously tucking any stray strands of hair up under its rim. She'd been wearing a headscarf for some time since she first noticed her loosened hair, and it hadn't drawn any attention if, say, visitors came to the house, because it was common headgear for women going about their work as a means to prevent dust and dirt fouling their tresses. Mam had always worn one at home. Pap wouldn't have noticed anything, not in his present state. Now, it was time for more concealing headgear, and with it being winter she could get away with it. Unacquainted with physical manifestations of profound grief, Nell didn't know why her beautiful hair was falling out, and she didn't have time to dwell on it. From now on, she'd just keep it covered.

Returning to the stove, she shoved a couple of billets of wood into the firebox, fetched eggs, a flitch of bacon, bread, and butter from the pie safe, and set about making breakfast for herself and her father. Hopefully, he'd eat something this morning.

On cue, Pappy came out of his room, shuffling groggily and scratching at his crotch while he rubbed his eyes with a balled fist. Nell frowned. She hated the slovenly way he got about these days in his long johns, unshaven, reeking of cheap corn mash moonshine and frequently hung over. He was still young, only twenty-eight, and nice looking before he'd let himself go. She watched him as he made it to the table, gripping the back of a chair to steady himself, before he jerked it out and collapsed on to it, slumped forwards, hands nursing his head.

"Coffee," he murmured.

Nell made a noise of disgust loud enough for him to hear, and then set about making a pot of strong coffee. Pappy never budged all the while she was preparing breakfast, only flinching a little when she slammed his mug of coffee down in front of him, following it with the thud of a plate laden with bacon and eggs and a clatter of cutlery deliberately dropped from a height. He looked up then, regarding her with soulful, bloodshot eyes. Nell's nostrils twitched as they registered the sour smell of his unwashed body.

"I'm sorry, Nell." Then his eyes narrowed. "Why you wearing your cady at the table?"

Nell sat down to her own breakfast, stabbing her fork towards his plate. "You better eat all that up, starting now, 'cos I didn't make it just for the fun."

Pappy nodded, like a chastised child. "Thank you, Nell." He took a long swallow of coffee and then picked up his cutlery with the slowness of an old man, the utensils wobbling in his shaking fingers as he poised them above his breakfast. For a moment, he sat immobile, staring vacantly at his food, and then he slowly lowered the knife and fork, dropping them either side of his plate. Once more, he raised his head to regard her sorrowfully. "I cain't eat it, Nell. I'm like to throw up if I try." To emphasise the point, he made a retching sound into his fist.

Nell leaned over the table, snatched his plate away, took it to the stove, and thrust it into the warmer hatch, which she slammed shut with unnecessary force. As she returned to her own half-eaten breakfast she snapped, "Maybe you'll feel like it later. We cain't afford waste. Drink your coffee, leastways. I made plenty." She sighed. "If you leave out your flannels I'll wash them."

Pappy nodded obediently, lifting the mug with both hands to steady it. He glanced over at the hearth. "Why ain't the fire lit?"

"I ain't got time, that's why."

"It's cold in here."

"Stove's goin'. It ain't the cold that gives you the shakes."

By the time Nell had washed up the breakfast things, fed the fire box again, and was coated up ready to head off outside to her chores, Pappy had returned to bed, lying sprawled face down on the comforter, snoring rhythmically. The brown, salt-glazed whiskey jug lay empty on its side next to the bed. Nell grimaced resignedly, gently pulled the comforter up over him, picked up the jug, and pulled the door to, mentally bracing herself for another lonely day, digging deep to find the strength to face the snow-blanketed world outside.

****

The snow was not deep, for which fact Nell gave silent thanks as she trudged towards the barn armed with egg basket and milk pail.

The winter had been a mild one, but Pap had ignored his usual seasonal tasks like mending tools and checking implements in preparedness for the approaching busy spring period. Nell thought of Jimmy and her friends at school, tossing snowballs at each other before retreating into the warmth of the classroom with its cosy potbelly stove radiating heat to every corner. Weather permitting, there was always good attendance at school over winter because the kids' workloads were lighter at that time of the year. Not hers, though. She'd given up school right after Mam died, having had to grow up fast, taking over the running of the homestead and minding her broken father. She was only twelve-years-old, but she knew how to take care of things. All homesteading mothers taught their daughters how to cook, clean, run a home, tend a garden from the time they were old enough to totter about a kitchen, and Mam had been no exception. These were the skills essential to a woman's survival and that of her family in a harsh and unforgiving world where the fragility of life frequently forced youngsters like Nell to assume responsibilities ideally considered beyond their tender years. She might have had some help if things had worked out, but they'd had to let Zebulon Waller, the elderly Negro who'd always helped out around the place, go, since Pa drank his wages, and he had his own family to feed and care for. Both Priscilla and Nathan had been only children, so there were no aunts and uncles to provide support, and her grandparents had all passed. Grandpa Washburn, who had founded the farm, had lived with them until his recent death, and Nell missed the wise old man deeply.

Nell glanced over at the woodpile. At least they had enough wood to see them through the winter, thanks to Jed Witherspoon and his two strapping sons, Zachary and Joshua, who had cut and chopped and hewed diligently to ensure their stack was sufficient, refusing to take any payment in cash or kind. It was the homesteading code to help your neighbour out in bad times because you never knew when you might need their help in return, and Nathan and Priscilla had been well liked as decent, kind folk. It was by now common knowledge in the community as well that Nell was shouldering a considerable burden for one of relatively tender years, and people kept a discreet but vigilant eye on her, especially the women of the church charity committee and Reverend Jameson. But everyone's lives were equally busy, times were hard, and distance, especially in winter, was not conducive to regular neighbourly visits. Nell knew that most of the time she just had to grit her teeth and try and get on with things.

She opened the barn doors to be greeted by a chorus of grunts, bleats, whinnying, and mooing. Nell put down her basket and pail, exchanged her coat for the old cover-all she kept on a hook by the stalls, took a deep breath, and set to work. She had milked the cow and was doling out feed to the animals when a figure appeared in silhouette in the doorway. No mistaking that slender, gangling figure. Nell finished pouring grain into the horse's trough and broke into a grin as she straightened up.

"Jimmy!"

"Hi, Nell." Jimmy advanced into the barn. "What do you want me to do first?"

"Can you make a start on mucking out?"

"Sure." Jimmy took the shovel off its peg and set to work. This was not an uncommon occurrence, and Nell turned her back, swallowing hard before she resumed her work.

****

Nell and Jimmy worked tirelessly, and it was dinnertime when they made their way back to the house. Aware of Jimmy's adolescent male lack of co-ordination, frequently expressed as clumsy gaffes, Nell carried the basket of eggs while he carried the pail of milk. Better spilt milk than smashed eggs, she reasoned. Jimmy had gotten so tall and skinny that he no longer seemed able to keep track of where he began and where he left off. His coat was thin and his pants ended well short of his ankles, giving him a neglected air. He had no warm hat either, she noted. Nell suspected the bruises she often spotted on his body, despite his best attempts to conceal them, were the result of retribution meted out by his short-tempered father when Jimmy unwittingly messed up. If his pa found out he was skipping school to help her, he'd probably give him a larruping, not because his pa valued learning; because he was just mean and possessive of Jimmy as his own personal helot.

"You shoulda been in school," observed Nell, hoping Jimmy would understand she was being protective rather than ungrateful. "I don't want you missin' your learnin'. You gotta think of your future."

Jimmy adopted a ministerial air. "Mr. Cosgrove says there's more to learnin' than just books. He calls it 'the school of life'. Besides," he grinned, "I gotta do my forfeit, remember? Sadie hates Sid somethin' fierce still."

Nell smiled, then laughed drily. "I guess that's my schooling now." She waved an arm to encompass the farm and environs. "This is my classroom." She touched his arm. " I believe you did your forfeit many times over. I'm mighty obliged."

"It won't always be like this, Nell," said Jimmy, his face serious as they climbed the steps to the porch. He put down the pail, turning to face her. "You *will* come back to school, I know it."

Nell shrugged. She couldn't attend school at the moment anyway, not the way she looked with her balding head. "It don't matter, none. I already know my letters and numbers. That's more'n some young'uns get. Anyways, come in for hot soup. I got a nice pot of corn and sweet potato chowder on the back of the stove. Please," she added, seeing his hesitation.

Jimmy nodded. "Thanks."

They sat down side by side on one of the two bench seats on the verandah and removed their boots, carrying them inside, along with their respective foodstuffs, to dry out by the stove. Nell took the pail off Jimmy and jerked her chin towards the table.

"Gimme your coat. Have a seat and I'll dish up."

While Nell hung their coats on the row of pegs by the door, Jimmy pulled out a chair and sat down at the dining table. He looked over at Nell curiously, wondering why she hadn't removed her hat indoors. Watching her standing at the stove, stoking the embers, it was painfully apparent how much weight she'd lost.

When the soup was piping hot and bubbling, Nell broke a fresh egg into each of two bowls and ladled a generous serving of chowder over them. That's how Mam had taught her to do it, to enrich the soup and boost its food value. She placed a steaming bowl in front of Jimmy, and then fetched spoons and a platter with bread and butter before sitting down opposite him with her own meal. Jimmy inhaled deeply.

"Hmmm. Smells awful good, Nell."

"It's one of Pap's favourites," she answered, stirring her bowl to break up the coddled egg. "Well, used to be. He don't eat much of anything lately, just pours that hooch he gets from old Milt Hickson down his throat, spendin' money we ain't got."

"Moonshine whiskey? That's the devil's gutrot. Won't do him no good, Nell." Jimmy hunched over his soup, spooning it down eagerly. They were both of them famished as well as cold to their cores.

"Ain't that the truth?" Nell shook her head helplessly, then frowned. "Lookit, I'm forgettin' my manners. Help yourself to bread."

"Thanks."

As Jimmy reached for a slab of bread, the door behind Nell opened and Nathan stood, paused in the frame, swaying slightly and blinking owlishly at the two diners. Nell turned her head.

"We got company, Pap," she said evenly. "You ain't decent."

Jimmy lowered his eyes so as not to stare. He was deeply shocked by the dishevelled state of Nell's father, whom he had not seen for quite a while, although it was common knowledge he'd turned drunk and become a good-for-nothing.

"Oh, it's only Jimmy." Nathan waved a hand as he wobbled over to the table and sat down with a jolt, noisily scraping the chair legs forwards. "You don't care how I look, do you Jimmy?"

Jimmy reddened, then shrugged. Nell glared at Pap.

"You got some of that mush for me?"

"It's chowder. You finish your breakfast?"

No answer.

Nell flung back her chair, took another bowl from the sideboard, filled it, stabbed a spoon into it, and thumped it down in front of Pap with such force that some slopped over the edge on to the table. He appeared not to notice, and began to slurp noisily, hunched over his bowl, elbows resting on the table, looking like a hobo in a soup kitchen. One hand reached over and seized a piece of bread, which he dunked in the soup before devouring messily. Nell squirmed, her embarrassment obvious.

By this time, Jimmy had emptied his bowl and Nell replenished it without asking. Nathan finished his, too, and pushed the bowl away, belching noisily before turning in his seat to look at his daughter, an expression of distaste on his face.

"Why you wearing that hat at the table again? What's happened to your manners?"

Nell thrust her small chin forwards. She looked him up and down with calculated disgust. "You gonna preach to me 'bout *manners*?"

"Don't you sass me, girl. Always yammering at your father, no respect." He pointed a finger at her. "You forgot the Fourth Commandment, girl? You got a real bad attitude these days."

"And you got no attitude at all! Wallowing like a hog in your self-pity and leaving all the work to me! Why would I respect a stinkin' drunk? Thank the Lord Mam can't see you, or she'd die twice over from heartbreak and shame! Sloth's a sin, too!"

Jimmy, taken aback himself by Nell's vehemence, saw Nathan tense, his right fist balling up, and he half rose in his chair, sickened by the thought that her father was about to strike Nell. He was used to blows, but he didn't think you should strike a girl. Instead

28

Nathan's hand unfurled, snaked out, and whipped the woollen hat from Nell's head, throwing it across the room. Her own hand flew up reflexively in a vain attempt to pre-empt him, but too late. Jimmy sat down again. He and Nathan stared at Nell in silence. Her lustrous blonde locks, so thick and wavy they always made Jimmy want to run his fingers through them, were all but gone, the previously luxuriant volume reduced to sad wispy remnants amongst islands of exposed scalp. Nell made as if to rise but then sagged and sat still, looking from one to the other, lips set in a tight line. Nathan rose slowly to his feet and stood close to his daughter, staring with a shocked expression at her head, which was more scaly bald patches than anything else, sprouting a few random tufts of blond hair. The most recent loss trailed in sad little strands from the discarded hat, some of it doubtless wrenched out by her father.

"Oh, my lord. What happened, darling?"

Nell crossed her arms defensively, turning away from him. "It's gone. Been like that a while now. Guess you finished it off." Nell was relieved to have her shame revealed. She no longer cared. Her eyes met Jimmy's, and the pity she saw there cut deep.

Pappy dropped to his knees beside her chair, making a choking noise, tears streaming down his face. Nell turned her head to stare at him, shocked. He hadn't cried once since Mam died, not even at the funeral. He put his arms around her and clasped her to him so hard she could hardly breathe. At first Nell resisted, but then found

29

herself crying, too. They clung to each other, both repeating the word 'sorry' over and over. The grief that had divided them for so long was shared at last.

Jimmy took his bowl to the servery, retrieved Nell's hat, placing it on the table beside her, grabbed boots and jacket and snuck out without a word.

CHAPTER THREE

Nell sat quietly in front of the blazing fireplace, a cloth draped around her shoulders, while Pappy carefully snipped the trailing wisps of her remaining hair until he had achieved a kind of short-cropped, pudding bowl uniformity. She gripped the hand mirror she was using to scrutinise her father's progress in imposing some sort of order on the disaster that had befallen her crowning glory. He seemed to be doing quite well.

When Nathan was satisfied with his barbering, he fetched an enamel basin filled with warm water, dunked a cloth, and tenderly bathed her head all over. Finally, he massaged in some rosemary oil from a bottle that had belonged to his wife, one of the many natural remedies she'd made from her kitchen garden. The musky aroma stirred bittersweet memories for Nell. She knew Pap would feel it, too. Priscilla had frequently massaged his neck and shoulders with the oil after a hard day's work.

Pap cleared his throat. "Folks say a raw onion rubbed into the scalp is good, but I don't think you'd be partial to that." He chuckled.

"I'd be a nosegay after an onion rub, right enough."

Pappy squeezed her shoulder. "You're still my beautiful girl. Nothing can change that."

Nell looked over her shoulder, smiling up at him. "Thanks, Pappy. If we're done, I'll clean up and get supper on." She slid the cloth from her shoulders carefully, scrunching it up to trap the hair trimmings, which she shook into the fire.

Nathan, still in his long johns, gave a sheepish grin. "I guess I got time to clean myself up."

"You mean it?" Nell couldn't conceal her delight.

"You're right, Nell. Priscilla would be downright ashamed of me. Her memory deserves better."

"Oh, Pap." Nell's smile was radiant. "Shall I fill the tub?"

"You better believe it."

****

Nell had a dressed rabbit she'd shot the day before hanging in the pie safe, and now, with renewed enthusiasm, she converted it into a tasty stew using the receipt Mam had taught her, while Pappy performed his ablutions. Supper served, she sat to his right at the table, stealing glances at him as she ate, unable to stop smiling at his transformation. He had bathed, washed his hair, which had grown quite long, and shaved before putting on fresh clothes and joining her at the table. He was a handsome, well-built young man, broad-shouldered, with thick fair hair and deep blue eyes. Mam had told Nell she'd met him at a church social and it was love at first sight for both of them. He'd lost weight, his cheekbones prominent and his trousers noticeably looser, so Nell was pleased to see him tucking into the rabbit stew with enthusiasm. After two big helpings, he pushed his plate away and rose to fetch his pipe and tobacco pouch from the sideboard before returning to the table.

As he filled the bowl of the pipe with the fragrant tobacco, tamping it in with his thumb, he said softly, "Things will be different around here from now on, Nell."

"Different?"

"Yep. No more slacking on my part. Spring's nearly here, and I've been shirking my jobs. Time I caught up a bit."

"I can help as much as you want."

Pappy crossed to the hearth and used a spill to light his pipe before returning to the table, drawing deeply, and puffing smoke from the corner of his mouth. Nell watched him keenly.

"Nope. You already done enough." He reached over and stroked her thin face. "You and me, we're all we got now. We'll pull together."

"An' no more hooch?"

"No more hooch. I ain't claiming I'll be perfect from now on, but I'm sure gonna try not to let you down again."

Nell felt as if a dead weight had been lifted off her chest. "I'll fetch us some coffee."

They lingered on at the table in affable silence, sipping their coffee, Pappy enjoying his pipe, until Nell rose and headed to the door, lifting her coat off its peg.

"Where you going?"

"Gotta check the stock."

Pappy stood up, shaking his head. "I'll do that. Fetch me the lantern. You clean up here and then rest."

Left alone, Nell sat on at the table a little longer, pondering the events of the day. The loss of her hair had been traumatic, but it had also brought Pappy back to her. Spring was coming, and with it renewed hope that life for her and her father might get better, that they might be able to put tragedy behind them, find peace with each other, and move on with their lives.

****

Two Years Later

Nell watched Pappy pushing his stew listlessly around his plate for some moments before he shoved it aside. Then she frowned when he picked up the bottle of whiskey to refill his glass.

34

"Supper not to your likin'? We can pick and choose so, can't we?"

Her father sighed. "Don't scold me none, Nellie. Leave me be." He took a swig and hunched over his glass, the very picture of abject misery.

"That stuff'll just strip your tripe, Pap. You need food in your belly. Besides," she added, "I made it the way you favour, with lots of mustard."

Her tone was gentle, wheedling. She'd given up warring with him some time ago. Pap sighed again, put down his glass, and pulled his plate towards him. With a marked lack of enthusiasm, he began to spoon down his cold stew, swallowing with some effort. After a few mouthfuls, he pushed the plate aside again. Nell rose and began to clear the table. As she reached for his plate, Nathan laid a hand on her arm.

"Sit a spell, Nellie. I want to talk to you."

Nell put the dishes down and slid back on to her chair, watching him apprehensively. He wasn't much of a one for talking these days. "Yes?" she said, by way of encouragement.

Nathan refilled his glass and took a sip, wiped his lips with the back of a hand, and looked his daughter in the eye.

"I want to sell up here and move on. I want to go to Oregon and make a fresh start. The government will give me one hundred and sixty acres of prime land in the Willamette. All I have to do is farm it for four years and it's mine. With what I get for this place, I can set up a good spread." He sipped again. His daughter's face gave nothing away. "Well, what do you think?"

The first thing that struck Nell was the lack of the pronouns 'we' 'our' 'us'. The second thing that struck her was the set of Pappy's jaw, which intimated low tolerance for dissent. Fortifying himself with moonshine whiskey doubtless strengthened his resolve.

"Why you askin' me, Pap? Sounds like you already made up your mind." She crossed her thin arms over her chest and scowled at him.

Nathan shook his head. His eyelids were drooping, his voice slurring faintly. Same as every night, now. "No. No I want you to have your say, Nellie. It's a big move, a long journey. We'd be leaving behind everything we know. It's important to me what you think."

Nell sighed, unfolded her arms, and leaned forwards, hands clasped in front of her. "Pap, I know things have been tough since Mam died, and nature hasn't been on our side, either, with two hard years and not much to show for it." She almost choked on the words. She was really thinking, *And you drinking your way through what little we do have.* "But your father, Granddad Jacob, he brought you here from Indiana, he built this place with his bare hands and he toiled to make something good here. You goin' to just up and leave

36

all that behind? Things can get better for us; I know it. We just have to hold on."

She jumped as her father reared up on to his feet, violently shoving his chair back, and wobbling unsteadily. He thumped his empty glass down on the table and snatched up the bottle, which was about one third full. "You don't need to teach me the family history! I know what my pa did, and maybe he was stronger than me, and maybe he had family back then to help him, too! We got no family here now except each other. I'm a drunk and you're a little girl who works like a slave day in and day out. Look at you, always in dirty dungarees, never see you in a dress no more! Where'd my pretty girl go? You're like a damned boy!" He paused, taking a deep breath. "I want to go, Nell, my heart's set on it. I want to leave all the sadness and hardship behind and be better than I am." He swayed a little, his voice breaking. "I know I can be better if I just get away." He waved the bottle around his head. "Everything here reminds me of her. We ain't had no luck since she died." A belch jerked his skinny frame. "I want to go."

He lurched off towards the bedroom, clutching his bottle to his chest like a lover. As he fumbled the door shut behind him, Nell sat staring straight ahead, the hot tears that had welled up at his words spilling down her cheeks, while she made no sound. Mostly, she cried inside, the familiar wad of sorrow and exhaustion congealed into one big ache in the middle of her chest, but now she released them both, lowering her head slowly on to her folded arms, felled by a deep weariness for her life as it was.

Nell sat sobbing quietly for a long time before she abruptly straightened up, wiped her eyes on the hem of her shirt, and got unsteadily to her feet. What was it Mam used to say? Oh, yes: 'This won't buy the baby a dress nor pay for the one it's wearing'. She smiled, gathered the dirty crockery and cutlery, and headed to the washtub. "Looks like we're goin' to Oregon," she murmured as she placed the dishes into the tub. "Beulah Land, here we come."

Pouring hot water from the kettle over the dishes, she added, "That's if Pap hasn't forgotten all about the idea, come breakfast time."

****

Leaning on the top railing of the fence, Nell rested her chin on her folded arms. Jimmy stood beside her, one boot propped on the bottom rail, hands in his pockets. They were watching the small number of runty little shoats rootle about in the earth of their pen, grunting softly and getting fractious with each other.

"That's all that's left," said Nell. "I think the hogs dyin' off is what finished Pap, broke his spirit. He always raised good hogs." She sighed. "He says when Mam died all his luck left with her. He met up with some old fur trapper was stayin' over at Milt Hickson's place, an' he was tellin' anyone who'd listen a bunch of high falutin' stories about the Promised Land of the West, where the soil's so fertile you can grow two crops a year. Now he's got the Oregon fever real bad. Dead set on goin' to see the elephant."

Jimmy nodded. Nell knew full well that neighbouring farmers had their own theories as to why Pap's hogs had died, and neglect was foremost among them, the same reason for his crop failures. Nathan had pretty much exhausted his neighbours' goodwill. Jimmy knew all this, of course, but he would never say it to her, though. Instead, he said, "I'm real sorry, Nell."

She twisted her head to look up at him. He was so damn tall now having a conversation with him gave her a crick in the neck. "What for? It ain't your fault."

Jimmy waved an encompassing arm. "No I mean for all of it. You sure had a bad run, but mostly I'm sorry you're going to leave." His voice cracked a little as he said the last words.

Nell watched him closely, observing the muscle that ticked in his lower jaw. She placed a hand on his arm. "I'll write to you, promise, and you'll write back, won't you?"

"Of course I will." He smiled down at her, his adam's apple jerking convulsively. "Maybe I'll go west myself before much longer."

"Really?" Nell straightened up. "Oh, that would be wonderful!" She turned away abruptly so he couldn't see her face. "I'm gonna miss you so much."

Jimmy closed the gap between them, sliding his arm around her shoulders and squeezing gently. "Remember what we promised each other, when we was just little kids?"

Nell nodded. "I never forgot." She smiled up at him. "We promised that one day we was goin' to marry. I remember it was when we were catchin' polliwogs in the crick, and you wove me a little ring out of grass. That was such a nice day." She spun towards him, pressing herself into his lean young body, gripping him hard, and Jimmy wrapped his arms around her, resting his dark head on top of her fair one. Her hair had grown back, but increased volume hadn't meant increased length. It was still short like a boy's, and Jimmy, always so kind, said he liked it that way. They remained thus for some time, listening to each other's breathing, eyes closed as they committed the moment to memory.

"Jimmy, can you promise me one more thing?"

"Anything, Nell. Anything."

"Will you tend Mam and the babby's grave?"

"I'll keep it just the way you do."

Nell looked up at him, lips parted invitingly, and Jimmy lowered his head to kiss her lingeringly. "I love you, Nell."

She pressed her face into his chest, inhaling his adolescent male warmth, innervated by the rush of tenderness she felt towards him. "I love you, too, Jimmy. I always have. I always will."

Jimmy sighed, making little side-to-side swaying movements as he held her.

CHAPTER FOUR

Council Bluffs, Iowa, April 1853

Nell sat hunched on the wagon seat, gripping its edges either side of her thighs, slack-jawed and staring around at the scene that confronted her. She had never seen so many wagons, oxen, horses, mules, people, in her life, let alone a whole tent city, bustling with settlers who, like her and Pap, were hell-bent on starting a new life by heading west. The air was thick with the smell of livestock, smoke, food cooking, over-loaded outhouses, and unwashed humanity.

"Jumpin' jehoshaphat, Pa. This place is busy! An' it stinks!"

Pap was too busy negotiating the wagon and team through the congestion to answer. He followed the well-worn wagon ruts into the town, but in truth had little idea where he was going. A pack of dogs and some rag-tag children ran after the newcomers, shouting, whistling, and yapping, making the horses toss their heads and roll their eyes. Still feeling pretty raw, her emotions close to the surface after what had been a distressingly painful leave-taking from friends, neighbours, and especially her beloved Jimmy, Nell was in no mood for catcalls or barking directed her way. She swivelled in her seat and cut loose with some choice expletives that stopped several of the kids in their tracks, a couple of the dogs, too. That got Pap's attention.

"Hey, missy, don't you be cussing like a mule skinner! I'll wash your mouth out for you! What'll people think I'm bringin' in here? They's jus' bein' friendly. Good lord, girl, you are ornery as hell these days."

Nell scowled at him, and snorted at this outburst of paternal indignation. She'd like to see him try to wash her mouth out. He'd almost certainly need bandaging afterwards. She didn't give a hoot what people thought about her, or anything else for that matter, and she didn't want friends. She felt brutally deracinated from her old familiar way of life, however hard, cruelly severed from everything she held dear, like her mother's and baby brother's grave, and right now she felt like killing something, starting with Pap. These homicidal thoughts were fortunately deflected as a beefy, red-faced man emerged from a small wooden building beside the road and came huffing towards them waving an arm.

"Halt! Pull up!"

The man negotiated the ruts with practiced agility, hopping over the ridges with a nimbleness that belied his bulk, and approached Pap's side of the wagon, which had lurched to a stop as commanded, the horses stamping and snorting. The man grinned up at Pap, extending a hand, which Nathan shook firmly.

"Nathan Washburn. Pleased to meet you."

"And you. Name's Isaiah Piebenger, appointed to keep some kinda order here. How was your journey?"

"Not too bad. Less mud than we was anticipatin'."

Mr. Piebenger nodded. "Well, I'll show you where you and your boy can pitch camp. There's a small fee, which most folk pay by the week. If you stay less time than that, you'll be refunded."

Nell bristled. *Boy? Boy?* Pap gave her a helpless look and shrugged. As if to add insult to injury, a small voice piped up to Nell's right.

"What's your name, sonny?"

Nell whipped around, eyes narrowing as she glowered down at the small cluster of children that had crowded curiously around the new arrivals, the freckle-faced lad to the forefront of the group clearly the interrogator.

"None of your business, half-pint." She flung out an arm. "Skedaddle!"

Nell felt a sense of satisfaction as the kids scarpered. Looking after them, she sighed. She must look like a boy to anyone sizing her up, after all. She was wearing a faded blue flannel shirt under dungarees, and her feet were clad in far from feminine boots. Her hair, still short-cropped, was all but hidden under a brown felt hat, while her wistful, elfin features could have suited either gender. She hadn't even menstruated yet. Nell compressed her lips. Well, let them all think she was a boy. It was no doubt easier that way, not having to explain her short hair or adoption of boys' clothing. Not having to tear open old wounds that were still far from healed. She gripped the edge of the seat as Pap clicked his tongue, urging the horses on, and the wagon lurched forwards to follow in the wake of Mr. Piebenger.

****

The township of Council Bluffs had evolved a slick, reliable infrastructure to support the dreamers heading west. Indeed, its economy was largely dependent on supplying the settlers with all the paraphernalia they needed for the dangerous two thousand mile, six-month journey. The emigrants stayed long enough in tent city or boarding houses in the town while they accumulated all the goods they needed for their great trek westwards. Nell and Pap needed to do some refitting on their farm wagon to make it more travel worthy, source their food supplies, and swap their horses for oxen, which were eminently more suited to the wide prairies. Pap had sold the farm for $2,000, a fair price considering he'd allowed it to run down somewhat, but they'd had to pay off some debts, too, and needed to

45

husband their remaining cash carefully if they were to get a good spread in the Willamette Valley, so they wouldn't be patronising any boarding establishments. Nathan had carefully packed all the money they owned in the world into a money belt Nell had crafted for him, and which he wore diagonally across his body, under his clothing. Nell had done such a good job that its presence was indiscernible.

Pap had taken on a new lease of life from the moment they'd sold the farm and commenced their journey, had noticeably reduced his drinking, had a better appetite, and was looking stronger, physically, already. This transformation had convinced Nell to put her own misgivings aside, bury deep her own sadness over the wrench of departure from all she held dear and embrace this new adventure, which had clearly made her father happier than he had been in a long time. Didn't mean she couldn't still be a bear with a sore head on occasions, though. Pap was pretty patient with her mood swings these days.

Mr. Piebenger stopped beside a relatively free patch of turf shaded by a large tree, waving his arms in dramatic fashion to indicate that this was where he wanted them to locate for a while, and Pap manoeuvred the wagon and horses, already excited as they sensed journey's end, on to their allotted piece of sward before calling 'Whoa!" pulling hard on the reins, and applying the wagon's brake. He looked over at Nell and grinned.

"We made it, sweetheart. We made it to our jumping off point."

Bone weary, achingly homesick, Nell opened her mouth to reply, then hesitated. The expression of pure delight on her father's face forced her to stifle the sarcastic retort that was going to be her response to this self-evident truth. Instead, she took a deep breath and said sweetly, "We did, Pap. We're a good team." Her reward was seeing a film of tears web Nathan's eyes before he quickly blinked them away.

Mr. Piebenger pointed out facilities like grazing, wells, and outhouses before accepting a week's fee, shaking Pap's hand, and hurrying away in anticipation of greeting the next arrivals.

First priority for Nell and her father now was caring for the animals, who had brought them thus far without a hitch, and which they would now swap for a sturdy yoke or two of oxen, which were slower but much better suited to heavy wagons and rough prairie grazing. The horses stamped and snorted, tossing their heads as they anticipated unharnessing, feed, water, and, most importantly, rest, after what had been a long time on the road. Nell jumped down and went to stand between them, making soothing noises, stroking and fondling them to calm them down before their release. Once they'd quieted, she helped Pap to unharness them, grain and water them, and hobble them on the prairie close by to graze happily with other families' livestock. When that was done, she organised some lunch for Pap and herself, and they ate off a cloth sitting on a groundsheet Nell spread out under the tree. As they chewed their bread and cheese in convivial silence, they both gazed around, taking in their new environs. Nell washed down a mouthful of food with a swig of water from the canteen, wiped her lips with the back of her hand, and turned to Nathan.

"Well, looks like we're not the only idiots on God's good earth."

Nathan snorted with mirth, in spite of himself. "I can always rely on you to rise to the moment, eh, Nell?" He reached over and patted her cheek. "This is a smart move, trust me."

"Hmmph!" Nell was studying a cluster of tents directly opposite them, which bespoke something of a family concern. The largest tent had a table and chairs set out in front of it, and there were various domestic items stacked neatly around, a cooking fire with a black cauldron suspended above it smouldering nearby. Clothes flapped in the breeze on an improvised clothesline strung from the tent to a sturdy pole. Nell jerked her chin towards this impressive set-up. "They sure got themselves organised well over there."

Pap nodded. "Looks like quite a big group."

At that moment, a young woman emerged from the tent to stand in the sunshine, adjusting her pinafore and smoothing her skirts as she gazed about her. The moment she saw them, recognising newcomers, she smiled, tentatively lifting one hand to give a little wave. Pap instantly forgot his manners, swallowed the mouthful he was chewing with an audible gulp, and stared without moving or blinking. Nell took up the slack and waved back, not exactly smiling, but managing a peremptory nod of the head. The simple white calico dress and blue pinafore the woman wore did nothing to disguise the fact that she had a comely figure. She also had a very pretty face and a superb crown of deep auburn hair that tumbled to her shoulders and shone like burnished copper in the sunshine. It felt like a loss when she extinguished it with the slatted bonnet that had been dangling at her waist.

An elder woman, with pinned-up hair of a similar, albeit faded, hue emerged from the tent behind the girl, who turned to address her. The elder woman shaded her eyes to peer over at Pap and Nell, said something to the girl by way of reply, and then strode purposefully towards the new arrivals, the girl following her lead. Nell and Pap dropped their food, leaping to their feet together, Nathan whipping off his hat.

As soon as she was close enough, the woman thrust out a hand. "Welcome. I'm Lucinda Haddon and this is my daughter, Sabrina."

Pap hastily wiped his hands on his shirtfront and pressed her offered hand, smiling at Sabrina over her shoulder. "Thank you. Pleased to meet you both. I'm Nathan Washburn and this here's my daughter, Nell." He gave her a gentle shove forward. Nell felt instant irritation. She was not in the mood for company, but Mam had been a stickler for good manners and so now she retrieved hers.

"Good day," murmured Nell, slowly removing her hat and making a curt bob. She looked down, bracing herself for the likely titters and expressions of surprise that were bound to follow.

"We're so pleased to meet you, Nell."

Nell raised her eyes to meet those of the two women. Both were smiling at her, and there was no trace of derision or curiosity in their expressions. Sabrina's deep blue eyes conveyed a warmth and friendliness that made Nell gag on a sudden surge of emotion in the back of her throat, taking her by surprise. She thrust her hat back on her head, clearing her throat. "Pleased to meet you, ladies."

The stock conversation ensued: where were they from, how long had they been travelling, how many in their party, and so on.

"Just the two of us," Pap replied in answer to the latter question. He shifted awkwardly. "My wife, Nell's mother, passed away in Iowa three years ago." He nodded towards their visitors' encampment. "Looks like you got quite a big clan there."

Lucinda nodded. "Mostly family, but a few friends, too." She glanced down at the half-eaten remains of their lunch. "Anyway, I'm sorry we interrupted your lunch and you'll be needing to set up your tent an' all, so we'll leave you in peace." She turned to leave, then paused. "Say, why don't you both come on over and have supper with us tonight? It won't be anything fancy but we can fill you up."

"Why, we'd be most thankful, wouldn't we, Nell?"

"Yessir," murmured Nell.

"That's settled then." Lucinda beamed. "Sabrina will come give you a call when it's ready."

As the two women walked away, Sabrina turned her head and flashed Pap a sweet parting smile, over one small shoulder. Nell registered this blatant flirtation, then glanced sideways at her father, who was casting lingering looks after the visitors, especially one, fingering the brim of his hat, and simpering like a smitten youth. She felt a spontaneous rush of compassion for him. He was still young, just thirty-three, and so he needed a good woman, not just a crabby daughter, by his side. He was good-looking, too, no denying that, and this fact certainly hadn't escaped Sabrina, Nell thought wryly. Pap had kindly blue eyes, lustrous, wavy blond hair inherited from a Swedish mother and nicely formed features. He also had a good build: six feet tall, broad shoulders, slim waist and hips, and long, muscular legs. Maybe it was time, Nell thought wistfully. Priscilla would have wanted him to be happy, and life went on, impelled by its own stubborn force, even if you'd become rather indifferent to its relentlessly plodding progress.

****

After their newfound friends had departed, Nell and Pap finished eating, rested briefly, and then got to work on their campsite. They put up their tent over the groundsheet and laid out their bedrolls, then tackled the setting up of their campfire, using wood from one of the stacks dotted about the encampment and a flint and steel to

51

strike a spark. Once that was burning away steadily, Nell made an apple buckle in the camp oven as a contribution towards the supper they'd kindly been invited to share. While it was cooking, she washed her and Pap's dirty clothes in water drawn from the creek nearby, using a wooden tub and washboard, and strung up a line to dry them on. Then, as dusk set in, they lit their candle lanterns and washed up in a pail of water to make themselves presentable for company. Pap donned a clean shirt, but Nell stalwartly refused to change. Either they took her as she was, or they left her be. Pap knew better than to argue with her. The only concessions she made were a thorough wash of face, neck and hands, and leaving her hat behind.

Never a fan of whiskers, Pap shaved carefully in front of their small mirror that he'd attached to the tree, before sprinkling water on his hair and running a comb through it. Nell kept a sly eye on his ablutions with an aching heart, and when he finally turned to her to ask her if he would do, she said, "You look so handsome, Pap, fit to break hearts is all I can say."

Nathan flushed with pleasure. "Thank you, Nell. You look mighty nice yourself."

Nell snorted. "Well, at least they didn't have conniptions when you said I was a girl. Maybe their kin will, though."

Her father assumed a serious air. "I think they're right nice folks, Nell. They maybe will ask us to join their party on the trail, an' that will be dandy, since we have no one. Let's try and make a good impression."

Nell broke into a grin. She poked him sharply in the ribs, making him double up.

"Hey!"

"We both know who you're trying to impress, Nathan Washburn." Nell gave him a theatrical once-over, rubbing her chin and frowning for effect, snapped his suspenders into perfect alignment, and smoothed his collar.

Pap regarded her seriously. "Would that be a bad thing, Nellie?" he asked softly. "Wanting to impress – a young lady?"

Nell placed a hand on his arm, looking up at him earnestly. They'd grown so close, and although their relationship could be fiery at times, they were always totally honest and open with each other, more like siblings than father/daughter since there was, after all, only eighteen years between them. "No, Pap. It would be a good thing."

"So I'd have your blessing?"

Nell pushed him gently in the direction of the Haddons' campsite. "You have. Now, get on over there an' start courtin'." She chuckled. "Hope you haven't forgotten how. I just have to fetch the buckle."

"We're supposed to wait for the invite. Least, that's what Lucinda said."

Right on cue, a soft female voice saw them both turn together, as Sabrina stepped into the pool of lamplight. "Evenin' to you both. Supper's 'bout to be served." She looked up at Nathan from under dark, luxuriant lashes, and he stood rooted to the spot smiling down at her. Some serious eye flirtation commenced, Nell noted.

"Oh lawdy," she muttered under her breath, rolling her eyes. "Just fetching my apples," she announced loudly, to bring them back to the present moment. "Shoulda cooled by now. You two go on ahead."

Pap smiled at her over his shoulder as he and Sabrina set off together towards the Haddon camp. Peering around the tree trunk, Nell watched them as they both strolled with deliberate slowness, pausing to exchange conversation, milking these few moments with just the two of them, however brief, and she smiled. "Good luck, Pap," she whispered.

Nell smoored the fire, collected the buckle, and followed her father.

****

Nell held the buckle in front of her like a protective barrier as she approached the Haddons' camp. Neither she nor Pap were used to socialising, not having done so for some time. She'd gone to a couple of friendship quiltings before they'd departed home, but she'd felt shy and awkward and been relieved when it was all done with, especially the tearful hugs, kisses, and emotional farewells, which she found utterly draining. She took a deep breath as she stepped out of the gloom into combined lamp and firelight. Sabrina came straight to her side to greet her and relieve her of the apple buckle, ushering her towards the table around which the family and Pap were ranged, enjoying a pre-dinner drink. Pap's glass of whiskey seemed barely touched, Nell noted with relief, and she was handed a sarsaparilla as she took her seat next to him. As she sat down glancing nervously around her, Sabrina stood behind her, hands resting on the top of her chair, and announced, "This is Nathan's girl, Nell. Nell, you met my mama already. The man to her right is my papa, Henry, and that handsome young fellow opposite you is my baby brother, Noah."

Noah grimaced. "You're not that much older than me, sis."

Everyone chuckled, and Nell, keeping her eyes lowered, acknowledged each expression of welcome directed to her with a curt nod of the head and murmured thanks. When she finally looked up, Noah was smiling at her in a way that lit up his deep brown eyes, and she managed a tremulous smile in return. He was a nice looking youth of about fifteen or sixteen, she guessed, with the same thick auburn hair as his sister. Both children obviously favoured their mother, as Mr. Haddon had a shock of sandy coloured hair and bore no resemblance to either of his offspring.

Introductions over, Nell braced herself for the inevitable queries about her androgynous appearance, but they never came. After some further polite conversation, supper was served, a hearty beef stew with fried potatoes and dumplings, each generous portion garnished with a slab of buttered bread for mopping up the juices. Nell tried to remember her manners, be ladylike, and not wolf down the delicious food, but when Lucinda offered her seconds, she couldn't refuse. After cleaning up the second generous portion, she felt dreamily replete, as well as more comfortable with her hosts, and happier than she had felt in a long time. If Sabrina had had a hand in cooking this superb supper, then Pap was on to a good thing. Sipping her sarsaparilla, she sat back, content to listen to the men talking about the approaching great adventure, and what items constituted the essentials one should bring along.

"You have to watch out for the swindlers," stated Henry, holding his glass aloft for emphasis. "Some of 'em would convince you to buy a grand peeanny to take along. Folks end up dumping stuff they never needed in the first place all along the trail, once the oxen get tired and feed's short. Same hornswogglers go out, pick it all up and sell it again. They use their shills to convince the greenhorns they need this and that, taking advantage of honest folk."

Everyone murmured agreement, expressions sober. "There'll always be those who have no conscience about cheating decent, God-fearing folk," Lucinda pronounced in conclusion. "Now, let's all have some of that splendid apple buckle Nell made for us. I got some fresh cream will go just fine with it."

"Apple buckle's my favourite," said Noah, flashing Nell his bone-warming grin, and she flushed with pleasure.

Pap, seated to her left and at right angles to Sabrina, who had the opposite end of the table to Henry, was lost in quiet conversation with the young woman. In fact, it escaped no one's attention that they were oblivious to everything except each other. Pap had barely touched his whiskey, Nell noted. He was just too absorbed in making a good impression on Sabrina, whose glowing skin and sparkling eyes indicated that she was more than receptive. She was good with the flirting, Nell thought wryly. Hopefully, she was not a shallow heartbreaker.

After coffee, Lucinda rose to clear the cups away, an indication that the evening was over and it was time for all of them to seek their beds. Nell registered her father's joy when Henry put the seal on this happy occasion by asking Nathan if he and Nell would like to join their party of four families and six wagons.

"You'd be most welcome. We're just waiting on one more family to join us, and then we'll go. Do you think you can be ready in about three days?"

"You can rely on us. We'll be ready, won't we, Nell?"

"You can count on it, Pap." Nell was pleased that Pap had got his wish, and they were safer in a supportive group, too. The Haddons seemed like a nice family, so hopefully the rest of their party were the same.

Henry Haddon extended a hand and Pap shook it warmly. "I'll arrange for you and Nell to meet the others. Welcome aboard."

Nell and Pap expressed their appreciation for what had been a lovely evening, said their farewells – Pap lingering over his parting from Sabrina, Nell noted – and made their way back to their campsite arm in arm for support through the darkness that was softened with fire and lamplight from the many campers. Nell smiled as she recalled Noah's last words to her: "See you tomorrow, Nell." She wished she'd mustered something intelligent by way of a reply, instead of just nodding awkwardly. Not to worry. He'd probably have forgotten all about her by tomorrow, anyway.

They carried out their bedtime routine, checking the horses, the fire, the wagon, before they retired to the tent and settled down to sleep in their bedrolls, which Nell had made. Each consisted of several layers of cosy quilts and blankets with a rubberised outer layer to ward off damp. Pap gave a contented sigh as he settled into his.

"They's nice folks. You happy 'bout travelling with them, Nell?"

"Sure, Pap. It'll be good to have company and some support if we have trouble –not that we will," she added hastily. "I think they know what they're doin'."

"Yes, that's my feelin', too." Nathan squirmed himself into a comfortable position, making satisfied little grunting noises.

Nell opened her mouth to say something teasing about Sabrina, but then bit down on it. Happiness, having something to look forward to had been in short supply for both of them, and she was damned if she was going to do or say anything that might risk poisoning this sweet well-spring of hope. She closed her eyes and allowed her thin limbs to relax. Let the cynicism and bitterness go for the moment. What would be would be.

CHAPTER FIVE

The morning dawned bright and clear. Nathan rose first to tend to the stock. Nell got the fire going and made a batch of biscuits to go with the fried bacon, using the scrapings from the bacon along with a little milk and flour to make Mormon gravy, which Pap loved. A youngster had come by on his rounds earlier selling milk, eggs, and butter, and Nell had purchased all three. Pap always allowed her money for housekeeping, which she spent frugally. It seemed the right morning to enjoy a special treat. She wished she had some sausage to add to the gravy and to her father's delight. Maybe the youngster would be able to forage some for her to use next time.

Nell roasted coffee beans, ground them, added them to the pot of boiling water, and by the time Pap returned from seeing to the horses breakfast was ready. Nell served the food on to tin plates, placing a fork on each.

"Smells great, Nellie," enthused Pap as he settled himself on one of their two camp stools, rubbing his hands together.

Nell passed him his loaded plate, placed their cups of coffee to hand on the upturned washtub, and they settled down to enjoyment of the food in contented silence. In the mornings, they were like a well-oiled machine. By the end of the day, things could be a little different when they were both tired and the goodwill was prone to unravelling. When that happened, they both withdrew to their own space until they could tolerate each other again. They locked horns often, but there was no sulking afterwards. Pap always dismissed any rancour with a favourite expression: "Sufficient unto the day is the evil thereof."

A "Halloooo!" from across the way made both their heads swivel to see Sabrina waving to them from in front of her own family's campfire, and Pap's face lit up like a jack o' lantern as he waved back. Sabrina waved, too, and then bent to her tasks. Pap applied himself to mopping up bacon grease with a biscuit, assuming a nonchalant air, fully aware that Nell was staring at him.

"You really like her, don't you?"

Pap squirmed a little, took a swig of his coffee, put the cup down, and settled back on his stool, chin thrust slightly forwards, and not looking at anyone or anything in particular. Nell recognised the signs. He was about to say something meaningful.

"Sometimes, you meet a certain person and you know right away you're going to like them, get on just fine with them. You can talk to them and they listen, the talkin' is free and easy, and you feel like you've known them a lot longer, kind of known them all your life instead of just a short time." He looked into Nell's large blue eyes. "That's how it was when I met your ma. I never thought I'd feel that way again. Do you follow me, Nell?"

Nell wiped her fingers on the bib of her dungarees, and smiled at her father. "I do, Pap, and like I already said you have my blessing. Mam would give you her blessing, too. It's been four years. High time you got hitched again."

Nathan looked startled. "Well, that's gettin' a bit ahead of things, Nellie. I only just got acquainted."

Nell wiped her mouth on the back of her hand and stood up with a sigh. "Life's short, Pap. Don't dally is my advice. Any half blind fool can see the pair of you is smitten with each other. Sometimes, things are just meant to be. Serendipity." She marched over to the washing up pail she'd prepared and dropped her plate in. Pap sat very still for a moment, studying her back as she dropped on to her haunches and commenced to swab her dishes.

"I love you, Nellie."

Without turning around, Nell said, "I love you, too, Pap. Soon's you're done there, we'll make a plan."

Nathan felt the tears start to his eyes as he looked at her thin frame, the curve of her nubby spine under her worn old shirt, the sad little froth of almost white hair above her spindly neck. Even on their worst days in the four years since they'd lost Priscilla, Nell had always subtly but determinedly forced him to confront each of those days, to be part of a fragile little team that spat in the eye of a hard, pitiless world, with the same relentless morning mantra. "C'mon, Pap, we'll make a plan."

He swiped at his eyes. "Comin', Nell."

****

Nell chewed the end of her pencil stub, flicking over the pages of the foxed, dog-eared journal that rested on her lap, and which had originally belonged to her mother for the keeping of farm records. Nell had taken over that chore, along with all the others, after Mam died. Since she and Pap had commenced their journey, however, it had become a combination of personal diary and practical register. Now she chose a clean page, carefully wrote the date at the top, and began to make a list of the foodstuffs and other items she and Pap would need for their epic two thousand mile journey, beginning with 'Flour 400lb'. The ten-cent guidebook she'd been eagerly studying, *The National Wagon Road Guide*, lay on the ground beside her. Pap sat next to her on his campstool, forearms resting on his thighs, hands clasped in front of him, waiting for her to speak. He was not 'good with letters', as he put it, so Nell was in charge of all the bookkeeping and recording, a role she took seriously.

She glanced up and smiled at him. "Four hundred pounds of flour, Pap. That sound about right? I'm goin' by the guidebook. It advises two hundred pounds per person. Our supplies gotta last four to six months."

Pap nodded. "I guess that's right then." By his own admission, he wasn't good with numbers, either, and as for working out how much food they'd need for a journey like this, well, it made his head hurt.

Nell licked the end of the pencil and continued writing, reading each item out for Pap so he didn't feel excluded. She knew he was sensitive about his lack of literacy. He'd been taken out of school even earlier than her to help his own father on the farm and had never been a keen scholar to start with. It was Priscilla who discreetly handled all the reading and writing required to run their spread of eighty acres. Now, he relied on Nell. It bothered him that she'd had to grow up so much, so fast, way beyond her years, and she was whip smart at everything, not like him. It was Nell who'd kept him alive, kept him going. She was his rock. Where did her courage and indomitable spirit come from? She put him to shame.

"Bacon, an' it's gotta be stored in bran to stop it gettin' spoiled. Beans, rice, sorghum molasses, saleratus, cornmeal – I can store eggs in that – salt, coffee, sugar, lard, hard tack, dried fruit, salt beef an' jerky –" Nell paused. "Should we get us a milch cow, Pap? We're gonna need milk and butter an' I can sell the extra. Help us pay our share for the guide an' scouts, an' the agreed sum for the Haddon party's welfare fund. I got some soap, but we'll need more.

And what about airtights? Too pricey, maybe." Without waiting for any reply, she sailed on. "An' we can forage, accordin' to the guidebook; berries, greens, wild onions and garlic, sage hens, rabbits, fish and the like. Says here hunters can get big game, too, like buffalo an' antelope. You're a great shot, Pap. You'll get us fresh meat for sure."

Nathan stood, smiling at the compliment, and placed a hand on her shoulder. "You finish making your list, Nellie. Write down any extras. We can always cross stuff off. I'm goin' to check my tools. Leastways, we already have those. Henry gave me the name of a good emporium, so we'll head over there after noon. We have to be mindful of the weight, keep it under 2000lb, or we're just goin' to tire our oxen to death before we ever reach the Willamette."

Nell nodded. "Sure, Pap." Like her father, she was aware that their Murphy farm wagon they'd brought with them to defray expenses was not large, the bed measuring a compact ten feet by four, and they already had quite a bit in it. It still had to be fitted out with five to seven hickory bows, which had in turn to support a waterproofed canvas cover. Aware they would have to make several river-crossings on their odyssey, they'd already waterproofed the box with tar. She sighed. There was a lot to do, and they had to be ready to go when the Haddons made the call. As soon as the strong, nourishing prairie grass was six inches long and the mud was hardening, the wagons would roll. Nell returned to her list, murmuring as she wrote: "Some shirts, beads, blankets and tobacco to trade with any Indians we meet, an' cloth for makin' and mendin' our clothes."

****

The following days were hectic for Nell and her father as they prepared for their epic journey. Nell had really enjoyed their forays into town, taking in all the sights and sounds, the hustle and bustle, the mud, the stench and the noise, especially the incessant hammering from blacksmith's forges, and helping Pap to haggle for the best bargains. For his part, he was amazed at the way she handled people and the shrewdness with which she could drive a deal. The traders and storeowners quickly learned they couldn't pull the wool over this precocious youngster's eyes. At every turn there were pedlars and shysters trying to part gullible country folk from their hard-earned money, but there were good shopkeepers, too, in amongst all the allure and the numerous grog shops, and Nell and Pap had been reliably informed by the Haddons who and who not to trust. Whenever she and Pap passed by a grogshop, Nell tensed, but Nathan showed not the slightest interest in patronising any of them, and Nell began to relax. He truly was a changed man.

Intrigued as she was by all the merchandise on offer, by the plethora of breeds, creeds, accents, and fashions displayed by the town's hubbub of humanity, Nell confirmed her personal love of and nostalgia for rural existence, and she knew Pap felt the same. She gritted her teeth every time she was taken for a boy, but she was especially outraged when one painted lady, clearly a soiled dove if her over-rouged cheeks were anything to go by, gave her a big wink and crooked a come hither finger at her. Nell almost tumbled off the boardwalk glaring back at the brazen coquette.

The farm wagon Nell and her father had arrived in had taken on a completely different appearance. They'd added the hickory bows, six in all, and the waterproofed osnaburg canvas cover had been duly stretched over them. It could be closed back and front with drawstrings. The front wheels were smaller than the rear wheels to allow for sharp turns and all the wheels were rimmed with iron. Pap finished his 'belly box' under the wagon bed and they packed most of the smaller farm implements they'd brought along inside it. Nathan invited Nell to inspect his handiwork, and she ran a critical eye over his carpentry, walking around and, at her father's request, crawling under the wagon to provide a thorough evaluation. He'd added a padlock to the end that opened out and drilled a triangle of holes in the opposite sealed end.

"What's them holes for, Pap?"

"Let's the air circulate. Don't want the tools rusting now, do we? An' look here, we can balance a water barrel on top of either end. I just have to cut out a curved piece from the bed on each side so's they'll fit snug."

Nell nodded. "You did a good job, Pap."

Nathan looked pleased at this seal of approval. He'd done a quick calculation when Nell had crawled under the wagon, and had filed it away carefully for future reference.

"Frees up the jockey box, Nell, so you can store victuals in there and have them ready to hand."

"Makes good sense, Pap."

Nell had been judicious to a fault in organising their food supplies and had arranged and rearranged the contents of the wagon at least four times to ensure a low centre of gravity and the placement of goods needed every day, like cooking implements and food, where it was easy to access them. Lucinda and Sabrina showed her how to maximise space by hanging utensils and other items from the hickory bows and sewing storage pockets for lighter items into the canvas covers. Having successfully sold the horses, Nathan had selected three fine yolks of oxen and the milch cow Nell had asked for. If they ended up with extra milk and butter, she could sell it to fellow travellers, he reasoned, earning a little money on the way. They hadn't bought heavy furniture with them like some overlanders, so they had space for a spare axle and spare tongue, which Henry Haddon had strongly recommended, and Pap lashed a spare wheel to the wagon's side. Nell had been very sad to leave all their lovely furniture behind, since her grandfather, a skilled carpenter, had made most of it himself, but she saw the sense of including it in the price of the farm. Pap had ruthlessly winnowed their other possessions, too, discarding everything he deemed unnecessary for their quest. "We'll outfit ourselves somethin' flash once we get our new home, Nell. I promise."

In the end, following some futile tearful pleading, Nell had felt pretty indifferent about this shedding of what were, after all, just things. She'd managed to squirrel away some personal little treasures though, including her mother's tiny cache of jewellery and her rosemaled scutching knife, a gift from Nell's Swedish grandmother, as well as some of Priscilla's precious inherited china, and her hand mirror. Other vital keepsakes included her mother's pattern box, medicine chest, and collection of favourite receipts. The Washburn family Bible, with its neatly written records of marriages, births and deaths, and her mother's spinning wheel were also precious cargo.

Those hurts were all fading into irrelevance, now. Nell had not seen her beloved father so motivated for a very long time, and it gladdened her heart. The Haddons insisted they have supper with them every night, and it was plain that the burgeoning affection between their daughter and Nathan was pleasing to them, indeed, encouraged by them. At twenty-one, their beautiful daughter had already spurned several offers of marriage, and they were beginning to despair of ever seeing some grandchildren. Defying the settlers' pervading pragmatism, Sabrina was an unwavering romantic who believed firmly in eventually finding her soulmate, and now it seemed she had, in this good-looking young man twelve years her senior at thirty-three. There was no doubt, either, that the attraction was mutual.

Nell shared in her father's newfound happiness. Social convention decreed that a man needed a wife by his side, and many marriages were arrangements of sheer convenience to achieve this end, any mutual affection eventuating considered a bonus. Some men even married mail order brides, the couple meeting for the first time before the preacher on their wedding day. Pap had enjoyed a deep love match with Priscilla, and now life had generously given him another chance of the same. Nell secretly hoped that they would have a wedding on the trail. That would be a wonderful omen for a future to look forward to. She was suddenly glad she'd packed her best dress. Sabrina was so kind and caring towards her, already motherly, and Nell lapped up the elder female attention she'd missed for so long. To be part of a family again, perhaps with stepsiblings…she hardly dared to hope for fear of jinxing the dream.

As the day for departure drew near, Nell took the time to write a letter to Jimmy telling him all her news and ending with the express hope that one day he'd be able to follow her so they could make a new life together in Oregon. After she'd posted the letter, she felt a kind of euphoria, buoyed by a firm belief that from now on life would be better for the Washburns. She realised that somewhere recently she'd lost that raw, battered feeling she'd had for so long, had shaken off the sensation of being isolated and of not belonging; always on the outside looking in. Everything around her felt lit by the glow of a new beginning, of new promise.

****

Nell was experiencing the same mixture of eagerness and trepidation as the other emigrants while they waited in queues at the landing for their turn to be ferried across the Missouri River. Any river crossing was dangerous and there would be several to face during their odyssey to Oregon. This was just the first and most important, since this crossing marked the start of their incredible journey, the prospect of which Nell still found quite overwhelming. Earlier that very morning a wagon and all its occupants had been lost when their oxen panicked and tipped the entire load into the river. The period of mourning had been brief. These were hardy, resilient people who accepted sudden, tragic death as a routine fact of life.

Nell prayed silently to her mother to watch over her and Pap. The Haddons had already successfully crossed and Nell could see Sabrina standing on the far bank, watching them anxiously, one hand shading her eyes. A comforting thought was that the Mormons who had left in the hundreds for Utah from Council Bluffs had bequeathed excellent ferries for the emigrants that followed. Then the call came, and it was their turn to lumber on to the crude barge that would launch them on their great adventure. Nell was on the seat, holding the reins and running a nervous hand over the brake, which her father would rope for increased safety once they were aboard. Pap, who was a good stockman, was standing between their oxen, talking to them in a soothing voice and trying to project a calm that would be palpable to the great beasts on which so much rested. Nell gripped the reins tightly as they started to move forwards, lips moving wordlessly as she repeated her prayer over and over. Then, gathering momentum, they were lurching on to the ferry, which, while open at back and front, had fence-like barriers either side and was long enough to accommodate both wagon and oxen, moving out across the river that swirled and eddied beneath them. A skiff trailed, tethered to the left side, and was presumably used to rescue those who got a dunking. Nell refused to look at it. It had already failed once in its assigned role that very morning. Pap roped the brake with a slipknot, patted her thigh as he sidled past, instructions to cast off rang through the air, the winch rumbled, and they began to move out into the river.

Heart beating ninety to the dozen, Nell kept her eyes fixed on Pap's back, saw the taut muscles in his forearms as he gripped the oxen's halters, saw his back muscles straining against his shirt, and then looked over to the bank where Sabrina was practically dancing from one foot to the other, equally tense family members ranged behind her, watching the man she loved draw steadily closer. In spite of her fear, Nell smiled spontaneously, which she seemed to do a lot these days, working facial muscles that had not been exercised for so long. Pap's newfound happiness had completely transformed him from self-pitying drunkard to self-assured, unflinchingly focussed and deeply responsible father and sweetheart, the protector of all he loved, just as he'd been in the old days, before Priscilla and the baby died.

There was a heart-stopping moment when the ferry swung sideways in the strong current, but Nell reminded herself that this was the common practice used to harness that very current's power to assist in actually pushing the ferry across the river. They reached the opposite bank safely, the prow extension sliding neatly on to the landing, and Pap leaped off, shouting for Nell to untie the brake, then straining on the harnesses and urging the oxen up the planks and across the increasingly chewed-up mud beyond to safety. Nell held her breath, praying her father wouldn't lose his footing and slip under the animals' spurning hooves, urging them on herself with encouraging hollers and slapping of the reins, but they were good, biddable beasts and they hauled the wagon safely up and over the gentle slope on to the grassland beyond, rolling their eyes and lowing their pleasure at being back on terra firma, bovinely receptive to Pap's vigorous patting and rubbing interspersed with exclamations of praise.

Once Nathan was satisfied that the rig was safe, he turned and flung himself into his hovering sweetheart's open arms, and everyone clapped and whistled until the couple finally broke apart, grinning around at their audience, eyes shining and faces flushed with delight. Nell sighed deeply as she manoeuvred their wagon over to the waiting group. They had just left the United States and were now in Indian Territory. A visibly invigorated Pap swung up beside her, gave her a quick kiss on the cheek, took the reins, and they rolled out after the others in their party, towards the distant horizon. Their great adventure of a lifetime had begun.

CHAPTER SIX

Nell gazed around her, taking in the beauty of the seemingly endless stretch of prairie that flowed away to the horizon. Everywhere she looked there were brightly coloured wild flowers, like purple poppy mallow and buttery yellow primrose, nodding their heads in the soft breeze as far as the eye could see, while the warm sun poured down like honey over fresh bread, and the sky, the sky was so big, a vast canopy of infinite blue. The sense of space and freedom was quite breathtaking. Truly, they must be headed for paradise. She glanced over at Pap who was walking on the other side of the wagon, clucking his tongue encouragingly while he waved his long handled quirt over the oxen's backs. The beasts plodded stolidly on, making about two miles an hour, perhaps totting up fifteen miles in all on a good day, twenty on an excellent one. Like the other emigrants, Nell and Pap did not ride in the wagon, but rather walked alongside, both to ease the animals' burden and to tend them, since the beasts had no reins. Oxen were generally placid, and good doers, happy to eat the tougher sedges the horses and mules disdained. Just the same, Nell had included several bushels of grain in their supplies to feed to the animals when grass was scarce.

Once their party was all assembled after the river crossing, they'd covered about six miles before nooning, and spirits had been high, despite the tragedy of the drowned family being fresh in everyone's memory. They'd watered their oxen and let them graze still wearing their yokes to save time when they moved on again. Cooking fires were normally not lit at this time of the day, time being of the essence, so Nell and Pap shared cold fried breakfast bacon wrapped in a split biscuit, washed down with water from one of the barrels fastened to the sides of the wagon, and Nell passed her father some supplementary dried fruit to nibble on for sweet. Once they'd eaten, Nell cleaned up, while Nathan spent some time discreetly 'sparking' with Sabrina before the call went out to move on.

Nell's acquaintance with Sabrina's young brother, Noah, had grown into a comfortable friendship, and that's all it was as far as Nell was concerned. There was room in her heart for only one true love, and that would always be Jimmy. The rest of the people in the Haddon's group were easy enough to get along with, save for one big, bombastic Irishman, Declan O'Farrell, to whom Nell had taken an instant dislike, along with his sniggering, pimply-faced son, Cormac. The mother, a thin-lipped, beak nosed little woman had a downtrodden air and little to say. Not so O'Farrell senior, who was a self-appointed authority on everything and had teased Nell rudely about her boyish appearance, not even offering an apology when Pap had quietly but coldly pointed out that she had lost her hair grieving for her dead mother and baby brother. Nell had made a silent vow to avoid the hateful blowhard.

She felt very differently, however, towards a sweet little girl named Emily, a slightly built, pretty child with luminous dark eyes and black hair that hung down her back in a thick braid. The youngest of three children, she claimed to be eight years old, but she was very tiny, Nell considered. They had been drawn to one another right off, forming a sisterly bond. Nell loved the sweet child and enjoyed her company, often letting her eat with her and Pap, and plying her with treats to stimulate her bird-like appetite. Pap described the child as 'frail', and Nell couldn't help worrying about the little girl she nicknamed 'Chickabiddy'. The tiniest child in their close-knit party, however, was a newborn baby boy, Ernest Peat, the infant son of a young couple from Indiana, Joanna and Clarrie. Remembering her lost little brother, Nell was drawn to the infant and enjoyed taking him on to her lap whenever she could, petting him and cooing to him, giving the tired young mother a much-needed break. Ernest was a fussy baby.

"I declare he likes you more than he likes me, Nell," said Joanna despondently.

ERIN ELDRIDGE

Nell regarded her thoughtfully. "No criticism intended, Miz Peat, but maybe if you just relaxed a bit more with him he'd fuss less. My mam was good with babies an' she said they soak up their ma's worrisome nature, 'specially firstborns when their ma's tryin' so hard to do her best."

Joanna smiled. "You're very wise for your tender years, Nell. I will try, I promise. Thank you."

Nell glowed. "S'nothin'." She turned to Emily, who was sitting so close she was practically in Nell's lap with the baby. Her small, sweet face was lost at the back of the enormous sunbonnet with neck flap that her mother always insisted she wear. "You wanna hold him, Em?" Then to the anxious mother, "Don't fret none, Miz Peat, I'll mind her. Whyn't you go take a little rest?"

As Joanna hastened off to maximise this reprieve, Nell carefully handed Ernest to Emily, and the little girl cradled the baby in her own small arms, chuckling with delight.

"He's so little, Nell."

"Yep, but in no time he'll he just another growed up, pain in the ass, biggity male. You can count on it."

Emily hunched her small shoulders and placed a hand over her mouth, giggling guiltily. "Nell! You shouldn't oughta say 'ass'! My pa'd whup me if I said that."

Nell patted her head. "Well, you can say it round me, an' it'll be our secret."

78

Emily glanced around slyly, and then whispered. "Ass! Ass, ass, ass!"

Their hoots of laughter made several heads turn curiously, and, sadly, caused baby Ernest to burst into tears.

The first couple of days on the trail did not go smoothly. There were one or two fights, some vigorous jockeying for position, lots of swearing, tearaway animals, animals tangled in their traces, shouting, arguments, women sobbing and children bawling. Livestock whinnied, brayed, and bellowed, while chickens cackled in alarm from their small crates that piggybacked on the wagons' tailgates. Many of the emigrants were greenhorns when it came to handling stock and wagons, so there were some trying, not to mention dangerous, mishaps that frayed everyone's tempers. Eventually, things settled down, and the wagons fanned out across the flat plains, proceeding at their own individual pace but also part of a now-unified train consisting of twenty-five wagons in all, meandering alongside the Platte River, the northern side of which had a better reputation for avoiding cholera. They had elected a captain and guide, a big burly man named Joshua Lambert who'd travelled the Oregon route before and who commanded respect, galloping about on a huge roan horse with a bugle hanging around his neck, an instrument he used to excellent disciplinary effect, especially at dawn when its raucous trumpeting roused the whole camp to startled wakefulness and the beginning of a new day. Whenever Joshua misplaced his bugle, he fired his gun into the air, which was equally effective. He'd also appointed a number of trustworthy subordinates, young men on horseback mostly, who carried out such tasks as scouting, hunting, and herding along the unfettered livestock. Nell kept her little milch cow, which she'd named Hilary, tethered behind the wagon.

Nell quickly settled into the routine of the trail, "schooled in", as the overlanders called it, and she and Pap worked harmoniously together as they always had done…well, mostly. They still had some heated differences of opinion, their mutual rancour often defused by Sabrina's gentle touch. She was an adept peacemaker, and to Nell it felt as if the three of them were already a family. With Nell's approval, Pap had bought Sabrina a ring in Council Bluffs and they had become officially betrothed. Fort Kearney had been mooted as a likely venue for the wedding. In the meantime, life went on, and Nell discovered that once the initial excitement of beginning the epic journey had worn off, the main difficulty she had to contend with was not all the hard work and physical duress – she was used to that – but the grinding boredom. Every day was a mirror image of the preceding one. At dawn, the bugle (or gunshot) sounded and everybody was immediately wakened and ready for the new day. Pap always sat bolt upright and said, "Goddamnit!" which made Nell giggle every time. While the women lit fires to prepare breakfast, the men rounded up the stock. Once everyone had eaten, the women rinsed plates, cups and utensils and stowed away bedding; the men dismantled the tents and loaded them aboard the wagons. Then it was time to gather the teams and hitch them to the traces. At seven, Joshua blew his bugle with enough force to bring down the walls of Jericho, shouted "Wagons ho!" and everybody rolled out to commence the day's journey. The scouts rode up and down the length of the wagon train, making sure everybody had got safely underway. Nell always enjoyed watching them: hardy young men of few words, they wore fringed buckskin pants and jackets, their deep-brimmed hats pulled low over their faces, and they rode with an easy grace, reins held in left hand, long Mississippi rifles in the right. They inspired confidence, and a sense of security, Nell thought. Her favourite was Nathaniel, not just because he cut such a romantic figure, but he always had a nod and a smile for her. To her chagrin, he spent a lot of time with a coquettish beauty called Briar Rose Mallory, seemingly undaunted by the competition he faced from every eligible male in the wagon train.

Everybody except the very old, very young or the incapacitated walked, both to avoid tiring the oxen and because the wagons, lacking springs or suspension, provided such a bone-jarring ride as they swayed and jolted over the rough ground. The women tied on their deep-brimmed poke bonnets with neck flaps to provide protection from the hot sun, but Nell preferred her old felt slouch hat.

As she walked alongside the wagon, Nell amused herself by singing songs under her breath, or reciting poems she'd learned at school. If little Emily joined her for a while, before she got too tired, Nell adapted some of her old school songs to keep the child amused. Along with "Jim Along Josie", Emily's other favourite was "What Shall We Do When We All Go Out?" the lyrics of which Nell altered to match the circumstances.

What shall we do when we all go out,
We all go out, we all go out?
What shall we do when we all go out,
When we all go out to play?
We'll walk, walk, walk 'til our boots wear out,
Our boots wear out, our boots wear out.
We'll walk, walk, walk 'til our boots wear out
When we all go out to play.

This became a favourite pastime and they were often joined by a happy gaggle of kids, all singing lustily. Pap said Nell was a regular pied piper.

One morning, their singing died in their throats as they became aware of a commotion up ahead. Nathaniel, who'd been riding point, came flying along the column at a full gallop, upright as a fencepost in the saddle, hollering for the wagons to halt. Nell and the children froze as he thundered past, the younger ones like Emily all clinging to her fearfully as Nell tried to soothe them. She glanced around for Pap, but couldn't spot their wagon, which was some distance back. Already the men were racing back to the rear to help secure the cow column. Nell knew she had to watch over the frightened little ones so she gathered them in tightly, trying to remain calm. Was it an Indian attack? Her heart picked up a beat.

Satisfied that all the wagons had pulled up, Nathaniel cantered back and dismounted alongside Nell and her chicks, his presence instantly a comfort to the jittery little ones. He flashed them his endearing grin as he dropped on to his haunches next to them, reaching out to stroke Emily's cheek.

"It's all right, don't be scared." He pointed ahead. "Look! Something to tell your children and grandchildren. Ain't that a sight?" He hoisted Emily up in his arms as he rose to his feet, so she had a better view.

They followed his line of direction and gasped, at the same time as the ground began to tremble under their feet.

"Oh my!" breathed Nell.

A seemingly endless stream of buffalo poured out of a vast dust cloud and stampeded past the stationary line of wagons in a heaving black mass of animals: adults, juveniles and calves, all blindly pounding after their massive, snorting leaders.

"What makes them run like that?"

"Somethin' spooked 'em, I guess. Wolves, maybe. After a young calf."

Above the din, they heard two gunshots. Nell looked questioningly at Nathaniel.

"Just the scouts turning them," he reassured her. "The herds are getting smaller. One time, we'd have been unable to stop them. They'd have swept us away."

Nell shuddered at the thought. She and the children watched mesmerised as the seething tide of bison raced onwards, receding away into the distance until they were no more than a dull rumble, and stillness descended once more. The danger over, the wagons moved on, and Nell soon had the children singing again. She knew she'd witnessed something very special, something that would soon be just another legend of the Old West.

The scouts hadn't been shooting solely to keep the charging animals wheeling away from the wagon train, as it turned out, and that evening Pap, Sabrina and Nell enjoyed buffalo steak for dinner.

Nell carried a burlap bag on a strap slung across her body and as she walked she filled this with sweet grasses to supplement the oxen's feed. At midday, they would relish their treats and perform well in the afternoon. Many of the emigrants did the same, most women stuffing the grass into folded aprons. In some stretches, the growth was so tall that, when she glanced over at the wagons with their white bonnets, they really did look as if they were ships sailing on a verdant sea – 'prairie schooners'. The dust stirred up by the wagons was not so welcome, choking throats and reddening eyes, forcing Nell and others to pull bandannas up over mouths and noses to mitigate the effects. Sometimes the wagons were able to fan out across the immense plains, and Nell enjoyed seeing the dust billowing away behind them instead. She was wiry and fit and felt as if she could walk to the ends of the Earth. Not in one pair of boots, though, she thought wryly. They were good for about three hundred miles before they fell apart so she was glad she'd packed spare footwear for both her and Pap – not knee-high boots like those some of the men wore; rather, sturdy ankle length brogans. The long days of walking were thirsty work, and Nell had quickly learned to keep a canteen of water hanging on the side of the wagon for her and Nathan to slake their thirst. Every day she seemed to learn something new, either through her own ingenuity or from listening to others, to ease the trials of the Trail.

At midday, the wagons stopped, and while the animals grazed, drank, and rested, the people did likewise, eating, re-hydrating, and taking a rest. Nell followed the other women in normally having some pre-cooked food on hand, since no fires were lit during the 'nooning'. She and Pap enjoyed bread, cheese, hardboiled eggs, and, sometimes, cold cooked bacon or other meat, if someone had shared game like antelope, rabbit, or prairie dog. Everybody had ravenous appetites and not a spare ounce of body weight.

After cleaning up, Nell liked to stretch out in the shade cast by the wagon, arms folded behind her head, hat plonked over her face, while Pap visited with Sabrina. Often, she was joined by little Emily, and the rule was you had to just lie quietly and 'snoozle' as Nell described it. After their nap, Nell would make the delighted child a grass dolly, or do cat's cradle with her, and then, all too soon, it was time to rouse themselves and get back on the trail. One foot in front of the other, Nell thought, as she fixed her gaze on the shimmering horizon, and soon we'll be in Oregon.

Nell's favourite part of the day came with the captain's announcement that it was time to make camp, after outriders he'd despatched reported back to him that they had found a suitable place to rest for the night. Despite their weariness, everybody got a second wind as the wagons were formed into a circle, stock freed to graze and find water under the auspices of the menfolk, while children dashed off to gather fuel and the women lit cooking fires to make supper. Nell had always aimed to feed Pap well, just as her mother had, and, while choices on the trail were limited, she tried to cook his favourites. This was also a good opportunity to bake bread. Nell had convinced Pap to buy a 'tin kitchen', a small reflector oven, to bring along, and she found it wonderful for baking the bread near the fire while she used the camp oven to make bacon and beans or a hearty stew. Meat and fish could be roasted in the tin kitchen as well. From trial and error she worked out how best to use the device, especially making sure she turned the food regularly to ensure even cooking. The trick was to avoid serving food that was nicely seared or crusty on the outside, but raw in the middle. When supper was ready, she and Pap always ate together, catching up with each other, before he adjourned to the Haddons' campsite to see his fiancée.

After she'd washed up, Nell was free to visit with whomever she chose. Children played games, there was often fiddle music or a squeezebox for a sing along or to dance to, and Nell enjoyed watching the couples, mostly young folk, who partook of this recreation, though she never danced herself. All the girls and women were in dresses, and she would have felt conspicuous in her dungarees. Maybe she'd dance at Pap's wedding, though. Emily joined her in whatever she was doing after supper, until her mama called her for bedtime. Sometimes they chose not to socialise and enjoyed just sitting together in silence, resting up against a wagon wheel, gazing up at the glittering constellations that studded the night sky, pondering the immensity of the heavens and counting shooting stars. Noah often joined them. Around nine o'clock, after all the animals had been rounded up and herded inside the circle of wagons, everyone drifted off to bed and Captain Lambert set the night watch. Another day on the trail had drawn to a close.

Sunday, the official day of rest, was not Nell's favourite, though, since, while the men may have been able to relax some, or potter about doing routine maintenance, Sundays just meant more hard work for all the women. After a religious service, usually comprising some Bible readings and hymns, it was time to catch up on chores like washing, mending, and baking. Nell considered herself fortunate that she had only herself and Pap to take care of. She felt for the women who had large families and were continually exhausted from the work involved in looking after them all. There was one family of eight children in the wagon train, and their mother, heavily pregnant with her ninth child, looked far older than her thirty years. Nell frequently helped where she could, relieving their grateful mother of a few of the younger children and taking them off for games and play. One little boy, Zachary, jumped feet first on to the carcass of a dead ox they found before Nell could stop him, and sank up to his thighs in the oozing, putrescent morass that was its rotting insides. Nell felt really bad as she returned the howling, stinking child to his exasperated mama.

Every party of settlers heading for a new life in Oregon prayed that they would arrive safely at their destination, putting their fervent trust in God to deliver them to their new homes with all their loved ones, having survived the many hardships they were aware they had to face. They were dreamers, all right, but also hardened realists and they knew the odds of that happening were fair to middling at best. Nell herself conceded that their particular journey west was not likely to be an exception from the many that had gone before, and would not be especially favoured by God in any way. The guidebook she thumbed through so often listed quite pragmatically all the ways that death stalked the emigrants along the trail: snakebite, wagon mishaps, children straying, livestock misadventures, buffalo stampedes, fevers, shooting accidents, drowning. The list was long and grim. Everyone noted, as they trudged along, the graves beside the trail marking the tragedies that had beset emigrants preceding them, grim reminders of the fragility of human life, of dreams cut brutally short.

One afternoon, just as the halt for 'nooning' had been called, Emily confided shyly to Nell that she needed 'pee-pees'. Relieving oneself on the Trail was irksome at the best of times, especially so for the women, who always had to squat. Several women would form a protective barrier around a sister who had expressed the need, but Nell never liked the idea and would sneak off on her own to avoid the 'skirt cordon'. Blessed with a strong young bladder, she could hold on before choosing her time and place. Not so a child. After reassuring Emily of her help, Nell quickly sought out her parents in case they became concerned for their little daughter's whereabouts. Emily's mother, preoccupied with setting out lunch for the rest of the family, expressed gratitude for Nell's help. Small children could easily become lost if they strayed off on their own.

Nell led Emily a discreet distance away to some shrubbery, and while the child squatted, she wandered off a little way to give her some privacy. Her attention was snared by a cluster of scattered rocks, and closer attention revealed what were clearly human bones in amongst the destroyed cairn. It was a grave that wild animals had been able to desecrate. Perhaps the burial had been hurried by necessity, the grave too shallow, the piled rocks inadequate to prevent wolves digging up the remains. As Nell tentatively ventured closer, she was horrified to see a human skull amongst the detritus, clearly that of a young woman since long, chestnut tresses, with no hint of grey, still trailed from the grinning death's head, a gilt-edged comb still fastened amongst the hair. Nell backed stumblingly away from the grisly sight, pivoted and hurried back to Emily, plucking up tufts of grass as she went to offer the child for wiping herself. Emily glanced up at her enquiringly as Nell propelled her back to the wagons at what felt like an unnecessarily brisk pace, and in grim silence.

"Are you mad with me, Nell?"

"What? No, course not, Chickabiddy. I – I just seen somethin' bad, that's all."

"What was it?"

"I ain't gonna tell you, so don't ask. Let's go get dinner."

It took Nell days to get the image of that gruesome memento mori out of her head.

As it turned out, they were not far into their journey when they endured their first loss – the second, if you counted the family that had drowned back at Council Bluffs. The casualty was a little boy, a nine-year-old, who slipped under the wheels of his family's wagon when he jumped down while it was moving. He had died instantly when the iron-rimmed wheel ran over his head. The train halted for the burial and Nell was brutally recalled to the day she had stood by the grave of her mother and newborn brother, the flimsy graft lapse of time had laid over the wound of her grief torn asunder once again. Pap held her firmly, arm around her shoulders, as she sobbed bitterly along with the dead child's distraught parents and siblings. Sabrina stood close on her other side, holding her hand and squeezing it repeatedly during the swift and simple obsequies. Then, once the tiny grave had been surmounted by rocks to frustrate wild animals from digging up the corpse, like a metaphor in motion for the relentless obduracy of life itself, everyone returned to their immediate purpose, and the wagons rolled onwards.

CHAPTER SEVEN

Nell pressed her face against the milch cow's warm, rough hide as she rhythmically worked the soft teats of the animal's udder, singing softly while the creamy milk splashed into the bucket. She would skim off some cream into the churn and hang it on the wagon. By the end of a day spent jolting over uneven ground, the cream would be converted to delicious butter, sparing Nell some elbow grease. All she had to do was wash the resulting butter and press it into the butter box, while the buttermilk was conserved to be used in biscuit making.

The wagon train was expected to make it to Fort Kearney today, and Nell was excited about the fact because she knew preparations had been made ever since they'd left Council Bluffs for Pap and Sabrina to be married there. Lucinda had told her lifetime events went in threes: birth (the woman with eight children had produced her ninth, a tiny girl), death (the tragically killed little boy), and a wedding... Nathan and Sabrina! Nell approved of this neat symmetry of fate. She was very happy for her father, and she genuinely adored Sabrina, so she was fairly fizzing with excitement, like a bee in a bottle. Sabrina would be wearing a precious dress she'd made herself in anticipation of just such an occasion, and Nell, suitably transformed for the day, was to be maid of honour. She'd fairly swelled up with pride when the young woman had asked her, but then the smile had abruptly vanished.

"Nell? What's wrong, sweetheart?"

"My hair," whispered Nell. "It looks so tatty."

Sabrina tut-tutted. "It does no such thing. We'll make you a little coronet of flowers, and you'll look just beautiful." She thrust out her bottom lip. "I ain't weddin' your pa without you there by my side. Besides, I read where short hair is somethin' of a fashion statement, now. Women back east are favourin' the style."

The smile returned, albeit a little shakily. "I'll do it, course I will. I'll be your maid of honour."

"Thank you." Sabrina drew Nell in, hugging her tightly and smoothing her wayward tufts of hair. "I know I can never replace your dear, sweet mama, but I aim to be a real good step-mama to you; you can count on that."

Nell picked up the milk bucket, smiling at the memory of that moment. Time to go feed Pap. He was jittery as a long-tailed cat in a room full of rocking chairs at the moment, pre-wedding nerves, she guessed, and she was trying hard to keep him calm and focussed. Nothing could be allowed to spoil their happiness now.

****

Fort Kearney, Nebraska – 'gateway to the great plains'

Fort Kearney was not at all what Nell was expecting. As the wagons approached, she felt something akin to disappointment when the shabby nature of the place was revealed. There were no towering stockades, no watchtowers or impregnable double gates, rather it was a ramshackle collection of dwellings built on a small elevation. A few houses were made of unpainted wood and the rest seemed to be made of adobe, swaybacked structures that looked as if they had been cobbled together in a hurry. Only the presence of soldiers, who rode out to greet the emigrants, and the American flag fluttering above a tree-lined parade ground gave any indication that this was a military establishment.

"It don't look like much, Pap."

"Heartenin', Nell, that's what it is, heartenin'. They clearly ain't concerned about Indian attacks."

Nell nodded slowly. She'd heard a lot of talk amongst the settlers expressing concern about the chances of Indian attacks on the trail, and she'd dismissed them as scaremongering, drawing Emily away from these discussions to ensure she was not alarmed by them. They all knew about past attacks, especially the dreadful tragedy of the Whitmans and the Clark massacre, but Nell was not overly concerned about anything similar befalling their party. The Clark party had been a small group and therefore vulnerable. Their own train was twenty-five strong with plenty of well-armed men. She considered herself a pretty good shot, too, having honed her skills in Iowa using Pap's shotgun, bowling squirrels, rabbits, and the occasional deer. She'd done a lot of hunting when Pap was in his doldrums. He had a superb Ferguson rifle, too, a gift from his pappy. Further on stood Fort Laramie, providing additional protection for the overlanders, and beyond that Fort Hall and Fort Boise. The important thing now was to see her father properly wed, and this was what occupied her thoughts.

A soon as they had established their camp near the fort, in the Platte River Valley, Nell, Nathan, and the Haddon family paid a visit to the commanding officer to make arrangements for the wedding. Colonel George Brabant was a bluff, jovial fellow, short and stocky, with an impressive set of mutton chops whiskers. His wife, Ephigenia, was, in contrast, tall, slim and much more commanding than her husband as she peered down her long nose at the visitors. She offered them all tea and cake, enthused over the prospect of a wedding on site – "so few social occasions, you know" – and once she'd got over the initial surprise of learning that Nell was, in fact, a girl as well as designated maid of honour, she assured the glowering youngster that she was only too willing to assist in bringing about a Cinderella-like transformation.

"I don't know what we can do with that hair, though, child," she said, patting Nell's head. "I'll have to apply my mind to it and go through my bits n' pieces chest. Just as well I enjoy a challenge." She gave a high-pitched laugh, sounding a lot like a braying donkey. Sabrina managed to defuse the situation before it got out of hand and a fuming Nell threw a punch at the well-meaning woman with one of her tightly furled, poised-and-at-the-ready fists.

Having left Pap and Sabrina to discuss the finer points of their marriage service with the chaplain, Reverend Samuel Deschamps, Nell was still breathing like a dragon when they got back to their camp, where Lucinda soothed her ruffled feathers with a cup of cool milk and some candy she'd stowed away. But there was no time for brooding; the wedding was to be held the next day and there was much to prepare. The first thing Nell needed to do was to find and air her best dress, petticoat, stockings, and shoes.

Restrictions on time, space, and provisions meant that only the Haddons' party of family and friends could be invited to attend the nuptials, to be held in the colonel's parlour. The women worked late into the night cooking food for the occasion, and the colonel's wife had put the fort's cooks to work making a wedding cake. Nell made a large potato pudding, a favourite dish of Pap's, and set aside fresh cream to serve it with. Everyone finally got to bed rather late but satisfied that all was more or less in readiness for the happy event on the morrow, scheduled for 11.30 a.m.

Nell was up early, cooking Pap a hearty breakfast, although he ate little. He sat very still, sipping his coffee and gazing into the cooking fire with an abstracted expression on his face. Nell watched him intently.

"You okay, Pap? Not having second thoughts about getting hitched again, are you?"

Nathan stirred, shifted his weight on the camp stool, came back slowly from wherever he'd been, and smiled at her. "No, Nellie, just thinking back to my first wedding day. Never dreamed I'd be doin' it again."

Nell picked up the coffee pot, leaning over to top up her father's cup. "Life's given you a second chance, Pap. You jus' relax now and enjoy every minute." She chuckled. "Probably won't be a third time. Not too many women gonna take on your brat kid."

Nathan chuckled. Then his face became serious. "I love you so much, honey. Don't you ever forget that. You'll always be my number one girl."

Nell took a while to respond, and when she did she tried hard to keep the tremor out of her voice. "Don't you be goin' all mushy on me now, Nathan Washburn." She pointed to the half eaten breakfast he'd placed on the ground beside him. "An' eat up that food I took the trouble to cook for you. I used up three precious eggs. You're gonna need your strength for tonight, an' I hope you remember what it's for, an' that ain't stirrin' your coffee, by the way."

Nathan made a muffled choking noise. "Nell!"

****

Out of the chaos that preceded it, by the time the hour for the wedding arrived, a contrasting calm appeared to settle over everyone and everything involved as the last of the preparations fell seamlessly into place. The guests sat fidgeting quietly on rows of chairs scavenged from all over the fort and set out in the colonel's parlour that had been rearranged and decorated with spring flowers from Ephigenia's garden for the occasion. Nathan sat on the aisle seat of the front row, facing the chaplain, Noah, acting as best man, beside him. Nathan wore his best duck pants, grey shirt, yellow necktie, and a dark vest, his thick blond hair brushed back on to his collar. Out in the hallway, Nell, taking her duties seriously, smoothed and primped Sabrina's dress for the umpteenth time, the young bride, her face radiant with joyful anticipation, looking very attractive in her Sunday-best gown of pink and white checked gingham, clutching a bouquet of prairie wildflowers. Across its narrow brim, her matching calash bonnet was decorated with a crescent of wax-flower orange blossom, an heirloom worn by her mother on her own wedding day and which fitted the bill as 'something old'. Around her neck she wore a string of blue glass beads loaned by Ina O'Farrell, who famously wore them every day, to provide 'something borrowed, something blue'. Her pristine white gloves were 'something new'.

Feeling odd out of her dungarees, Nell wore her best blue calico dress with white cuffs and collar, her wispy hair adorned with a coronet of the same prairie flowers, expertly woven through a pliable wire frame by Mrs. Brabant, and plenty big enough to disguise her lack of tresses. She carried a small woven basket filled with petals to strew before the bride as she walked towards her groom. Sabrina's father, Henry, himself impeccably attired, beamed down at the two women. Leaning over, he whispered in Nell's ear.

"Losing a daughter, but gaining a son and a granddaughter. Pretty fair exchange, I reckon."

Nell chuckled her delight. As always, the prospect of being part of an extended family again made her heart sing.

"Shall I call you Grandpop?"

"I'll be hurt if you don't."

A sudden burst of music from the Brabants' pianoforte caused all three to jump.

"That's the Wedding March," announced Henry, reaching for Sabrina's arm. "I think we're on! Nell, front and centre!"

****

Under the auspices of the well-versed chaplain, the wedding ceremony went off without a hitch, and a few tears were shed as the young couple made their vows, promising to love, honour and cherish each other 'til death parted them. It was very obvious to the congregation that this was no marriage of convenience, but a genuine love match. Nathan slipped her late grandmother's wedding ring on to Sabrina's finger and the service concluded with a rousing rendition of 'All Creatures Of Our God and King'. Nell felt certain she could feel her mother's approving presence, and she beamed with pride as she watched her father, his face shining with joy, gazing into his delighted bride's eyes. Following the service, the newlyweds completed the required paperwork before everyone enjoyed a slice of wedding cake washed down with a glass of wine, generously provided for the occasion by the colonel himself and distributed by impeccably uniformed young soldiers, who were in turn rigorously supervised by Ephigenia.

Formalities over, everyone wound their way back to the encampment where waiting well wishers dressed in their best finery showered the newlyweds with handfuls of rice, and the party really began in earnest. Emily ran forward to seize Nell's hand, looking up at her with adoration.

"You're like a queen. Can I touch your flowers, Nell?"

Nell removed her floral coronet and placed it gently on the ecstatic child's head.

"Oh, see how beautiful you look."

"Can I show Mama, Nell?"

"You sure can. Ask her for the mirror."

Nell grinned as the little girl marched off with regal poise towards her smiling mother.

Alcohol was forbidden on the trail, but Henry Haddon had purchased two kegs of beer from the fort's stores for this most special of occasions, his only daughter's wedding, and some bottles of 'medicinal' whiskey and brandy also suddenly made the light of day. The musicians tuned up their fiddles, flexed their squeezeboxes, a Jew's harp and some harmonicas joined the band, and the dancing and feasting was quickly in full swing. All the women had prepared food for the occasion, and Lucinda had made a maple stack cake, the traditional trail wedding treat, for the bride and groom. The food was arranged on trestle tables borrowed from the fort, and the guests included the colonel, the chaplain, and their wives. Two of the wagon train's men had bagged a deer, and its roasting flesh filled the air with delicious meaty fragrance as it turned on a spit over the cooking pit.

Their fellow emigrants cheered lustily as the newlyweds entered the circle for the first dance, and then it was time for everyone to join in as men seized their partners to usher them into the colourful, whirling company, the women's skirts billowing out as they twirled. Normally awkward in company, Nell felt herself drawn into the spirit of the occasion, laughing and clapping in time to the music, and when Noah asked her to dance, she happily obliged; the first dance of many, as it turned out.

"You look right pretty today, Nell."

"Why, thank you, Noah. You look mighty swanky yourself."

"Kind of you to say so, Nell." Noah executed a curt bow.

They burst out laughing simultaneously at this formulaic exchange of polite compliments, and Noah swung Nell out into the throng of merrymakers with a flourish. As he spun Nell past her father, Nathan called out, "Nell! Save a dance for me!"

"You better count on it, Pap!"

Nell glanced over at Cormac O'Farrell, who was watching her with a simpering grin on his pimply face. *You I won't be dancing with!* She searched out Nathaniel and quickly spotted him, handsome in white shirt, best pants and shiny boots, dancing with Briar Rose, the pair gazing into each other's eyes. Nell sighed. There would be another wedding at Fort Laramie; nothing was more certain.

The day wore on. As the sun slid lower down the sky, there was a respectful hiatus for speeches and toasts, and then many of the travellers approached the bride and groom, who were seated on chairs side by side, to present small gifts. These were mostly of a humble, utilitarian nature: pots, pans, cups, a jug, perhaps a pretty sampler, anything people could spare that didn't add unwanted weight to a wagon. After that, there was more dancing, singing and carousing, and then it was time for the 'shivaree', marching the tired newlyweds around the encampment to the clamour of improvised drums – seconded cookware, mostly – bawdy songs, and much teasing, hooting, and hollering until it was time to deliver them to their wedding night venue, which the women, including Nell, had made cosy and welcoming in their absence, converting Nathan's single bedroll into a suitable double sleeping space complete with beautiful new quilt, courtesy of Lucinda, who had hidden it in the Haddon wagon before leaving Council Bluffs. As the established hour for bedding down, nine o'clock, came around, the newlyweds were finally left in peace and everyone retired for the night, a feel-good atmosphere pervading the camp after such a joyous day. Nell had burrowed out a niche for herself in the wagon, and she was asleep before her head hit the pillow, still smiling.

****

Nell woke refreshed to the sound of Joshua's bugle braying – she giggled when she thought of Pap saying "Goddamnit!" and then having to apologise when he remembered who he was with – and had breakfast cooked by the time her father and Sabrina emerged from their tent, avoiding eye contact with her, and smiling shyly at each other.

"Good timin'," announced Nell cheerfully. "Bet you're both real hungry, so I've fixed plenty: beans, biscuits and bacon, sausage gravy, too. I bought some fresh sausage at the fort so I could make you a special treat. Take a seat."

She set down their laden plates and cutlery on an upturned washtub, picked up her own meal, and tucked in, smiling sweetly at the newlyweds and enjoying their self-conscious blushing. Pap snatched up his plate and handed Sabrina hers, shooting a challenging look Nell's way as he did so. She continued to smile sweetly at him, head tilted, as she chewed. Raised on a farm, Nell knew what transpired between a man and a woman, so she hoped Pap had done his duty well. Maybe there'd be a baby brother or sister on the way before they reached Oregon. The idea delighted her. As usual, Sabrina defused any potential conflict.

"This looks wonderful, Nell. It's so kind of you to make breakfast for us."

"Oh, it's no never mind," replied Nell airily. "I figured you'd both be pretty, um, played out this mornin', after all the, um, excitement."

As Pap made a choking noise, Sabrina said hastily, "I'll pour the coffee, shall I?"

After breakfast, Sabrina paid a visit to her folks, and as soon as he'd stowed the tent and bedding in the wagon, Nathan marched over to Nell who was rinsing the breakfast dishes.

"I oughta whup your backside for that cheek, girl," he hissed, glancing around.

Nell looked up at him, grinning broadly. "Pap, you ain't never whupped me, and if you tried it we both know you'd end up bleeding. Never corner something meaner than you are." She wiped her hands on her thighs, cocking her head to one side. "Sooo, did you have a good time? I hope you upheld the family honour."

Nathan waggled a stern finger at her, opening his mouth to deliver a withering riposte, and then dissolved into giggles instead. "I swear, Ellen Washburn, you'll be the death of me. Quit teasin' your poor old man."

Nell stood up and crossed to him, throwing her arms around him. "I'm so happy for you, Pap." She kissed him soundly on the cheek.

Nathan delivered a crushing hug in return. "Thank you, Nellie. I'm a lucky man. I got me two great women."

As he released her and headed off to get the oxen, he called over his shoulder, "An' the answer's yes!"

Nell chuckled as she tipped her washing up water over the dying remains of the fire, looking after him, the early morning sun reflecting off his blond hair, his broad shoulders held high, gait jaunty. For the first time since her mother and little brother had died, she felt truly, deeply happy.

CHAPTER EIGHT

After the two-day respite at Fort Kearney, during which the overlanders did some vigorous trading and re-stocking, it was time to get back to the reality of life on the trail, and the wagons rolled out through a fragile morning mist to resume their epic journey. Not all, though. Nell felt sad as she watched a small group of 'turn-backs', as the overlanders called them, the wagons heading back east towards Missouri, among them the family of the little boy who had died.

After a nerve-wracking descent down steep Windlass Hill, with, praise the Lord, no casualties, they reached Ash Hollow, the entry to the North Platte River Valley, lush with good grass, fresh water and ample wood, an ideal camping area. Looking back many years later, Nell clung to the memory of those days following the wedding as one of the happiest periods of her life. It was as if Nathan and Sabrina's love for each other gilded everyone and everything around them with a lustrous glow that was totally infectious. The two women often walked alongside the wagon together, chatting away about anything and everything, while Nathan tossed teasing remarks at them from the other side of the team, and little Emily, never far away from Nell, straddled the back of one of the oxen, listening avidly to the conversation and banter as she rode along, securely roped in place. She was safer there than on the seat of the bucking, jolting wagon. The miles, the days, just seemed to float by in a pleasant haze.

Nell loved the evenings when the wagons stopped to cook supper and camp for the night even more than she had before. Sabrina had taken over as chief cook with Nell relegated to assistant, and she enjoyed her new role because it felt like a return to something comforting and familiar, recalling happy times when she had helped her mother with the preparation of family meals. Sitting with her stepmother and father as the trio dined and chatted was heart-warming, too, and Nell enjoyed a sense of wellbeing she'd not known in a long time. Gazing into her little hand mirror by the light of a candle before she retired to bed, she even imagined her hair was beginning to thicken up, a sure sign that her battered spirit was healing.

In the morning Nell woke to find sticky blood clinging to the insides of her thighs. She knew what it was, what it meant, so didn't panic but had herself washed and padded up with clean rag well before Joshua's bugle sounded reveille. She felt a secret thrill over this milestone that inducted her into the company of womanhood and couldn't wait to tell Sabrina, whom by now she quite comfortably called "Ma". By the time Nathan and Sabrina emerged from their tent, Nell was frying bacon in the spider to go with freshly baked biscuits and Mormon gravy.

In keeping with her new sense of renewed joy in life, Nell found herself overwhelmed by the famed landmarks of the Oregon Trail that appeared as the wagons lumbered on westwards. She knew about them from the guidebook and from stories she'd heard back in Council Bluffs, but she was still unprepared for the sheer scale and wonder of them. Becoming visible from days' travel away were Courthouse Rock and Jail Rock, great sandstone monoliths soaring four hundred feet above the Plains. Chimney Rock, the feature Nell was most excited about seeing, was the next natural wonder. Visible for forty miles, it reared up close to four hundred feet high, its sloping base and slender towering pinnacle confirming it was aptly named. Nell stood squinting at it, hands on hips, Emily leaning into her thigh as she sucked on a thumb.

"Lookit, Chickabiddy. Somebody got real careless an' the house burned down around the chiminy!"

Emily removed her thumb with a squeak of amusement. "You're so funny, Nell."

Then they arrived at Scotts Bluff, named by the Indians as 'the hill that is hard to go around', a natural obstacle that blocked the emigrants' path and had to be navigated by way of Mitchell's Pass. Nell read the story behind the Bluff's anglicised name to Pap and Sabrina over supper that evening.

"It's named for a fur trapper, Hiram Scott, who died there in 1828. He an' his fellow trappers were suffering from starvation, so when Scott became ill an' could go no further, they abandoned him. When they found his skel - skelington the followin' summer, it was sixty miles from where they left him. The poor unfortunate man had crawled all that distance before death overcame him."

Nell closed the guidebook. "That is a sad story,"

Pap shook his head. "How could they just leave him there? Why didn't they go back for him?"

Sabrina sighed. "Nobody knows what they'll do until they're faced with a terrible situation, what choices they might make."

Pap smiled at her, his eyes lingering on her lovely face. "You're right, sweetheart. We mustn't judge." He straightened up, gazing around at the darkening landscape. "This country can force hard decisions on any man."

Nell felt the sombre mood needed lightening. She jumped up. "Well, what it means is we covered 596 miles now, one third of our journey. Oh, an' I almost forgot. There's fruit pie for dessert, so let's celebrate."

When they reached Register Cliff, Nell carved her name and the date of her epic journey into the soft sandstone, alongside the names of her father and stepmother. She was intrigued to read the personal details of so many who had passed this way before. The next big milestone was Fort Laramie, where they could rest and resupply, giving their animals a breather, too.

Storm. Nell could taste the metallic tang of it as it approached, the heavens gradually darkening to resemble dusk, even though it was only mid morning. Tiers of lowering grey clouds with massive, dark underbellies rolled menacingly around the basin of the sky before tearing themselves asunder to send down sheets of blinding rain interspersed with jagged flashes of lightning that alternated in turn with ferocious rumblings of thunder. The guidebook had warned about storms on the plains, and Nell had experienced storms in Iowa, but she'd never seen anything like this. This was nature flexing its muscles on a grand stage in a pitiless display of elemental strength. The train stopped and everyone hunkered down to ride it out, the men dashing about in oilskins to calm and restrain terrified animals, the women and children finding shelter where they could, either in tents which soon became sodden, or clambering into wagons on top of the contents, huddled together for comfort and trying to calm sobbing, frightened children.

Nell and Sabrina shot into the wagon, pulling the canopy drawstrings tight and squatting miserably on the chest holding the family's dry goods. A drenched Nathan soon joined them, getting a thorough scolding for flicking water drops on the incumbents as he shed his slicker, and then they laughed as they cuddled up together, all three shivering with wet and cold and doing their best to comfort each other.

"She'll soon blow over," said Pap optimistically. "I hope we can find the stock when it does. They're mostly scattered all over."

"I got lots of containers down," said Nell. "Leastways we'll get some fresh rainwater."

"Good girl." Pap nodded his approval.

They sat in convivial silence, tensing when the lightning flashes cast a brief, eerie light into their gloomy sanctuary, and then counting down together for the roll of thunder that would follow during this ancient symmetry of the storm.

By the time the storm had abated, still grumbling and spitting tongues of fire as it receded over the horizon, a whole day's travel had been lost, and there was nothing for it but to try to restore some kind of order before settling in for the night. Pap went to check on their stock while Sabrina and Nell, always ahead of herself with dry firewood collection, got a fire going and supper cooking, laughing as they sloshed about in the mud. Nell was glad she wore dungarees;

at least she could roll the cuffs up. The hems of the women's long homespun dresses, on the other hand, became steadily dirtier and more shredded as miles were covered, until they were fringes rather than fabric. While Sabrina supervised supper, Nell gathered up her receptacles and emptied the rainwater into the barrels attached to the sides of the wagon, raising the level of the contents considerably.

Nell had covered the milch cow when the storm broke and now she untethered the little animal so it could graze. She didn't have names for the oxen, but she'd christened the milch cow Hilary, much to her father's amusement – "Don't name a cow you're goin' to eat, Nell". She was a good milker, and Nell had already made a nice little pile of money selling butter and cream to the other emigrants. She stowed it all in Nathan's money belt, which he locked in the belly box for safekeeping. The extra money would be helpful in setting up their new life in Oregon. Now that Pap was married again, he could legally claim three hundred and twenty acres. Nell knew the bad times were over. Pap had quit drinking entirely and with Sabrina by his side he was going to build a marvellous life for them all. She grinned. For all she knew a baby sister or brother was already on the way, to be born in the spring. So fitting; the season of rebirth and fresh hope.

The morning dawned bright and clear, and Nell closed her eyes, inhaling deeply as she jumped down from the wagon. The world around her felt thoroughly rinsed, wrung, and altogether refreshed, the overwhelming smell of it earthily fragrant. It was the kind of day that made you feel good to be alive. She retrieved her pail from the wagon and set it down beside the wagon wheel while she went to fetch Hilary, waving to Pap as he emerged sleepily from the tent, adjusting his suspenders. Nell hoped they would have a good day's travel, recouping some of those miles they'd lost to yesterday's storm. By the time she returned with Hilary, Pap was dismantling the tent and Sabrina was preparing a breakfast of bread, bacon and beans.

Despite the positive mood fostered by the beautiful weather and smooth start, they weren't long on the trail when disaster struck. The right front wheel on the O'Farrell's wagon suddenly broke, causing it to lurch on to a sickening angle, hurling Ina from the bench seat, where she rode most days, on to the ground. Fortunately, the little woman was only winded on the rain-softened ground and clambered back on to her feet quickly, if a little shakily, pale with shock. Cormac, who always rode his nice little skewbald alongside, dismounted and rushed to her side to assist her, while her husband wrestled their startled oxen to a stop. The entire Haddon party relayed calls to each other to rein in, and, once all the wagons were halted, the men gathered around to assess the damage, while the women fussed over Ina, who repeatedly insisted she was unharmed, brushing at her skirts and smoothing her hair. Nell observed wryly how her husband did not express a single enquiry regarding her wellbeing, standing with his hands on his hips as he surveyed the damage to his wagon, meaty face reddened with annoyance.

"Damn! The bastard's broken three spokes and the fecking rim!"

"Hey!" Nathan stepped forwards. "There's ladies present, man. Watch your mouth."

O'Farrell spun around, face darkening. "Don't lecture me like no schoolmarm, ye spalpeen. I call it as I see it." He squared his shoulders, taking a menacing step towards Nathan.

Nathan drew himself up, raising a hand palm up and flicking his finger tips in a 'bring it on' gesture, his eyes hard and cold. "Maybe if you hadn't been racing your wagon like a loon day 'fore yesterday your wheel would still be sound, and your poor missus wouldn't have gone ass over tea-kettle, nearly breaking her neck."

O'Farrell spluttered with rage and began rolling up his shirtsleeves. "Why, you impertinent pup! I was trying to get away from all the dust, for Ina's sake!"

"Instead you damn near killed her," sneered Nathan, rolling up his own shirtsleeves, "an' you ain't showin' much concern for her right at this moment."

Nell looked around desperately for intervention, and it came in the form of Henry Haddon, who stepped neatly in between the two belligerents. "Easy, boys, easy. Arguing 'bout who's to blame for this will get us nowhere. We have to get the wheel fixed as quickly as possible, an' we're gonna need to work as a team. Cormac," he turned to call over one shoulder, "ride up to Mr. Lambert and tell him what happened, an' that we'll catch him up soon as we can, probably round supper time. We'll noon here."

"Yessir!" Cormac vaulted into the saddle and galloped off after the other wagons, which had doggedly maintained their course.

Henry watched the boy go before he turned to his father. "I guess you know what happens now, Declan. We have to unload your wagon entirely. I hope you gotta spare wheel, or we're gonna have to find one somewhere. You have? Fine." He wiped his mouth with the back of one hand and looked around the huddle of men. "Who's got the wagon jack?" A hand shot up. "Fine, Gabe, let's be having it, then." He rubbed his hands together. "Time to go to work, gentlemen!"

Nell gave silent thanks for such splendid leadership in a moment of crisis. Her father and O'Farrell deftly sidestepped each other as they put aside their differences to focus on the task ahead. Draught animals were released in their yokes to graze, and Nell freed her milch cow to do the same. A relay team quickly formed and the contents of the wagon were efficiently passed hand-to-hand or hefted off before being neatly stacked by the tail-end recipients on tarps spread beside the wagon. Fully recovered from her harrowing fall, little Ina darted about fussing over the family possessions and

116

supplies. Cormac returned to tell them Captain Lambert had been informed and wished them all good luck and a speedy reunion with the rest of the train.

By noon, they had the wagon unloaded and jacked up, and Henry called a break for food and drink. The repair was going smoothly, and everyone was in high spirits. The women spread out cold fare saved from breakfast and they sat around in the brilliant warm sunshine, talking about the storm and enjoying sips of the fresh water it had provided to wash down their victuals.

It was Nell who spotted him first, a dark silhouette of man and horse standing on a small knoll maybe half a mile away, his outline blurred by the shimmering haze that trembled over the midday plains. There was no mistaking, though, the feathered Indian lance he held in one hand as he sat motionless astride his pony. Whether or not he had seen the small party of emigrants was impossible to tell, but Nell guessed he had. She felt a little tremor of fear ripple along her spine, making her gulp as she swallowed her mouthful of sweet rainwater.

"Pap. Look yonder. Ain't that an Indian?"

"Mm?" Pap turned his head to squint in the direction Nell indicated. Then he stiffened, put down his plate and stood up very slowly, shading his eyes. Sabrina stood up and moved close to him, taking hold of an arm. "Yep, I believe it is. Nell, fetch me the

Ferguson rifle." He reached over to touch her as she leaped to her feet. "Don't be scared none," he said evenly. "Just bein' careful. I've got your back, always."

Nell swallowed with difficulty. "Yes, Pap." She raced for their wagon.

By the time Nell returned with her father's rifle, there was not one but a cluster of figures silhouetted on the skyline, and Pap had alerted the others in their party. All the men stood in a huddle peering towards the motionless group of Indians. The women, presided over by Lucinda, hung back in a tight little group, holding children close, silent and watchful, trusting in their men to protect them. Henry sucked on his bottom lip.

"They may come in, they may not. We better be ready, show them we're well armed and make sure they understand the rest of our train's just along the trail. Every man fetch his gun, keep it handy. They probably just want to trade, so have some goods ready for the purpose."

As the men dispersed, Nell handed her father the Ferguson rifle. "We got trade things in the wagon, Pap. I know where they are."

Nathan nodded. "Good, Nell." He stiffened. "Here they come." He turned and repeated these words in a shout to the other men. "They're comin' in!"

Nell swallowed hard. Sabrina made a little gasping sound. As the Indians drew closer, it became clear that it was a group of considerable size. Nell counted under her breath. "Eight, twelve, fifteen! Pap there's fifteen of them!" Their own combined manpower was seven. They were outnumbered roughly two-to-one, although some of the women would be good shots like her.

Nathan gripped her arm hard with his free hand. "Steady, Nell, steady." He leaned over so that his blue eyes were very close to hers. "Look at me. Don't be afraid. I always got your back, you know that. Go and fetch the trade goods from the wagon."

Nell nodded dumbly, heart going like a trip-hammer. Nathan straightened up and turned to his trembling wife. "Go with her, darlin'. Nellie, bring back the shotgun."

As the two women hurried away, the rest of the men, including Noah and Cormac, both fielding scatter guns, ranged up on either side of Nathan, holding their weapons at port arms as they watched their unexpected visitors drawing ever closer.

****

The group of Indians rode in at a leisurely pace, trotting their pinto ponies towards the stranded emigrants. By the time they reached the cluster of wagons, Nell had joined the men, clutching the shotgun. She'd seen Indians before, of course, both in Iowa and in Council Bluffs, where they'd been wearing European clothing, even top hats. These were nothing like she'd seen before, and she felt a chill when Henry Haddon muttered under his breath, "Cheyenne. Dog soldiers."

One of the children began to wail loudly.

The Indians sat their ponies, halted before the settler reception committee, faces expressionless. They were well armed: guns, feathered lances, bows and arrows, tomahawks tucked into brightly coloured sashes, knives in fringed sheathes at their waists. They wore moccasins, fringed deerskin leggings, shirts and breechclouts. But it was their headgear that struck Nell most forcefully. Their long black hair was topped by strange bonnets consisting of large upright clusters of bird feathers. They had about them an air of coiled menace, something powerful and almost other-worldly. Nell tried to appear calm, shifting her weight casually from one leg to the other, but she found their presence terrifying. Henry broke the nerve-wracking silence.

"I don't suppose any of you speak Algonquin?" he asked out of the corner of his mouth. No response. "Well, it was a long shot." He drew himself up to full height, smiling broadly and raising a hand in greeting. "Howdy, welcome to our camp." He pointed over his shoulder to the O'Farrells' stricken wagon. "We're jus' fixin' a broke wheel and then we'll be heading on after the rest of our train." He pointed down the trail. "Lots more of us further ahead."

The Indians stared at him impassively. Then everyone jumped nervously, guns swinging level in front of them as one of the warriors abruptly dismounted and came forward, stopping in front of Henry. He held Henry's unflinching gaze for a moment and then cut his eyes to the tableau of women, gesturing towards Sabrina who was standing a little apart from the other women, holding the trade goods Nell had given her from their wagon: shirts, tobacco, and blankets. Henry visibly relaxed as he turned to see what had caught the Indian's interest.

"They want to trade. I think you can stand down, men."

The remainder of the party dismounted and joined their leader.

The Cheyenne stayed for about an hour, which got Henry agitated although he tried to hide it. They were burning precious daylight with this diversion. The braves examined everything in the camp with childlike curiosity, accepting offers of food and drink, and trading some of the overlanders' goods for pemmican, two freshly killed rabbits, some buckskin, and a knife in a beautifully bead-worked sheath. Nell began to relax, as did everyone else, although she felt an undeniable sense of relief when their exotic visitors made preparations to leave, seemingly pleased with their new acquisitions. That was when it happened. One young brave suddenly veered away from his fellow tribesmen and advanced on Ina O'Farrell. He stopped in front of the startled little woman and reached for her throat, his attention caught by her string of blue glass beads. As his hand closed around and lifted the beads for a closer look, Ina screamed, and before anyone really grasped what was happening, O'Farrell came charging over to his wife, bellowing with rage, seized the Indian by one shoulder, spun him around, and delivered a bruising uppercut to his left jaw with such force that the young man was lifted clean off the ground before landing forcefully sprawled on his back some feet away. Everybody froze, and then the two groups split quickly into factions again, the Indians grouped around their leader, the settlers grabbing weapons and forming up to face them in a tense standoff.

Nathan and Henry seized Declan, who was advancing on the stunned Indian, fists furled and at the ready, keen to dole out more punishment as his victim struggled to his feet, rubbing his jaw, initial expression of shock changing to one of fury. Seeing his tormentor shouting threats at him, face contorted with rage and struggling to break free from his companions' restraining grips, he whipped a knife from the sheath at his waist and took up a fighting stance to defend himself. The women looked on in horror. The inter-ethnic encounter that had seemed to go so well had turned into something ugly and potentially dangerous for all.

"Calm down, man!" hissed Henry, wrestling with the big Irishman, whose eyes bulged with rage. "You'll get us all killed! He meant no harm. He just wanted to see the beads!"

Ina broke out of her stupor at this point and flung herself on her husband, begging him to stop his rampage, assuring him over and over that she was unharmed, sobbing and pleading, until finally he sagged into submission, wrapping his arms around her and repeating over and over, "I thought he was hurting you! I thought he was hurting you!" Cormac joined his parents, and all three stood with their arms around each other for comfort, while their rattled fellow travellers watched in silence. The disgruntled young warrior, still smarting from the humiliation of Declan's vicious assault, sheathed his knife and stalked off to join his fellows, muttering his outrage. Henry did his best to apologise, but the damage was done, and the Indians mounted their ponies before galloping away without a word, gesture, or backwards glance. Henry stood looking after them, brow furrowed. Nathan sidled up to him and together they watched the departing visitors.

"You think we've seen the last of them?" asked Nathan.

"I hope so." Henry sighed. "Cheyenne, an' dog soldiers in particular, don't take kindly to bein' insulted, that I do know, an' if they're a renegade band, they could be trouble. But they don't like fighting at night, that I also know." Henry looked along the road. "The army runs regular patrols out of Laramie. If they meet up with the others, Lambert might send them back to check on us." He shook his head. "Damn fiery Irishman! Anyways, let's get that wheel fixed an' hightail it outa here! I'll feel a lot better when we catch up to the others."

****

An air of anxiety hung over the wagoners as they returned to the task of repairing the O'Farrell's wheel. There was some heat in the sun now, too, making physical labour more trying. Everybody had been shaken by the events of the last few hours: the shattered wheel, Ina's fall, and the ugly incident with the Cheyenne brave. While, the men worked, the women tried to allay each other's fears with unrelated chatter, discussing recipes, what they might cook up for supper when they rejoined the train, consulting their guidebooks to refresh their memories as to what lay ahead on the trail. A couple even got out their mending. One or two wrote in the journals they were keeping. The children ran about playing games with each other, providing cheer for the adults watching their carefree antics. Guns, however, remained to hand, and everyone cast surreptitious worried looks at the sun as it dipped lower and lower in the sky, their unexpressed dread building as it seemed more and more likely that they would have to spend the night out here alone, cut off from the security of their main party.

The men were having trouble with the wheel, and Declan was becoming increasingly frustrated and irascible. Henry did his best to keep everyone calm, but they were all to a man becoming fed up with O'Farrell and his hair-trigger temper. No one amongst them was a wheelwright by trade, but they all knew the rudiments involved well enough, and Emily's young father, Stephen, had a scruffy manual that proved useful. Once they'd removed the shattered wheel, they needed to knock the boxing out of the hub in order to refit it on the replacement wheel, but this proved difficult with the tools available. By the time they succeeded and had the new wheel on, they still faced the formidable task of loading everything back on the wagon, and Henry stood for a moment to stretch his aching back, pushing his hat back on his head as he surveyed the unmistakeable signs of gathering dusk. Everyone gathered, watching him in silence as they awaited a decision. Emily slipped under Nell's arm, circling her waist with one small arm. Nell looked down at her and smiled.

"Everything's gonna be fine, Em."

"Well folks," said Henry at last, keeping his voice even, "it looks like we'll have to spend the night here. We'll post sentries throughout the night and be off again at first light." He smiled, conveying a sense of ease he didn't really feel. "Time to get the fire going and supper on. As soon as the wagon's reloaded, we'll circle 'em all."

As everyone scattered to his or her appointed tasks, Sabrina slid an arm around Nell's shoulders and squeezed gently as she whispered in her ear, "Please don't fret, Nellie dear. Papa and I would never let anything bad happen to you."

Nell smiled up at her, always struck by how beautiful she was. "I ain't afraid, Ma. But I'll be sleeping with the old side by side, jus' the same."

Sabrina chuckled. "That's my girl."

****

At nine or thereabouts, everyone retired for the night, as was their custom. The O'Farrell's wagon was fully restored, and the women had pre-prepared items for breakfast so that they could all make a quick getaway in the morning. The stock were secured, one fire kept burning, and night guards posted. Nathan was one of them, and Nell went over to bid him goodnight before she settled down in the wagon. Sabrina was standing beside him in the darkness, leaning her head on his shoulder, and as Nell approached them her blood ran cold when she overheard what her father was saying to his bride.

"You'll not be taken alive, darling. I'd see to it."

"Oh, Nathan! It won't come to that, will it? Oh god, we've had no time together."

Nell gave a warning cough as she emerged from the darkness, and Nathan straightened up, smiling at her and adopting a nonchalant air. "Nellie! Thought you were well abed."

"Jus' goin' Pap, Ma. Came to say g'night."

The trio hugged and wished each other goodnight. Nell lingered a little until Nathan told her firmly to go and sleep. "We'll be makin' an early start. You need to go to bed, too, sweetheart," he addressed himself to Sabrina.

The two women embraced him again before drifting away to tent and wagon. As Nell removed her boots and dropped them over the tailgate, they made an unfamiliar clunking noise. She investigated and found Pap's tools laid in a neat pile.

Funny, he keeps those in the belly box. Musta got them out to work on the wheel. Yawning, Nell clambered in and folded up bonelessly on to her bedroll. She thought she would never sleep a wink, especially after what she'd overheard, but all the trauma of the past day caught up with her and she went out like a light, shotgun resting on the coverlet beside her.

****

Nell cried out in terror when violent shaking roused her from a deep sleep, and a hand clamped over her mouth before her father's voice, sharp with anguish, broke through her semi-conscious state.

"Nellie! Wake up!"

"Pap? What's wrong?" She raised herself up on an elbow, sleepily rubbing her eyes.

"Get up! Come with me! Quick as you can, Nellie! Please!"

"Why? What's happened? Tell me what's wrong!"

"No time! Goddamnit, for once in your life just do as I say!"

Someone ran past the wagon, and Nell heard men's voices shouting. She recognised O' Farrell's voice, and Henry Haddon's. A woman screamed. Nell scrambled down from the wagon. She was fully dressed, fortunately, but without her boots. She reached into the wagon scrabbling for them, but Pap tore her roughly away.

"The shotgun! Lemme get the shotgun, leastways!"

127

"No time!"

Nathan dragged her around the back of the wagon and pinned her up against the left side, his face so close to hers that his eyes were only about an inch from her own, bulging and desperate. Nell felt herself gagging with fear.

"Pap!"

She cried out as her father swung her off her feet and lifted her so that she was horizontal. Then her head shot into a darkened space and she felt the rest of her body being forcibly pushed further into the enclosure to follow it. Finally her feet were thrust in, making her knees buckle and slam against a hard surface. She was too shocked to cry out, lying prone where her father had placed her. She knew where she was: in the belly box. Her father spoke to her one last time as he shoved something between her feet.

"I'm lockin' you in, an' you jus' stay and don't move, not an inch, an don't make a sound. 'Bye, Nellie. I love you."

Nell lay rigid, too stunned to move. She hadn't even answered him. His words hung over her like something precious, lost and missed forever: ''Bye, Nellie'.

She heard a single shot, and a shocking image reared up behind her eyes: Sabrina's head exploding in a red mist, blood and brains spattering her beautiful hair; Pap with tears streaming down his face as he turned to face his own death. Then it sounded like hell itself had belched up a tumult of frenzied demons, as bloodcurdling screams, shouts, shots and unidentifiable noises all blended into one cacophony of horror. Indian attack. No one would be spared. Nell squeezed her eyes shut. *Make it stop! Please, please make it stop*!

She began to drift away, disembodied from herself, her only awareness of her physical self the violent shaking she couldn't control.

She returned to herself when the silence fell. A silence that was even more terrible than what had preceded it.

CHAPTER NINE

Nell had no idea how long she'd been in the belly box. She'd lost all track of time. Through the holes Pap had drilled at her end she could see daylight and had air to breathe. She dozed for a while, and when she woke it was dark again. She felt desperately thirsty, but oddly not hungry. She decided she had to try and break out of her stifling, narrow prison so she tried to kick out the padlocked end with her stockinged feet. The attempt was a failure because she couldn't draw her knees up far enough, confined as she was, to get sufficient purchase for a forceful kick, and her socks kept slipping on the smooth wooden surface, anyway. Moreover, her feet were tangled in something she couldn't shed, and which was impeding her freedom of movement. Typically, Pap had made the belly box solidly strong. She felt despair overtake her. Then she had the terrifying thought: what if they come back? They could return to loot the wagons and burn them, and then she'd roast in her little wooden oven like a pig on a spit. She fought and struggled desperately against her prison, cursing Pap for locking her in such a place…what had he been thinking? Why hadn't he put a canteen of water in there with her? Her rational mind chastised her. There had been no time. He had tried to save her life. That had always been his purpose for the belly box, she realised that, now.

Finally, exhaustion saw her lying weak and limp, resigned to whatever happened. She knew a human could only survive three days without water, so death was not far off. It would be a blessed relief, she decided, and then she would be reunited with all her loved ones. She closed her eyes and their faces floated up one by one out of the quivering darkness, smiling lovingly at her, beckoning her to join them. Then their faces suddenly changed to those of hideous ghouls with burning eyes, ghastly leers, and blood-smeared features. She screamed, fearful that she must be going mad, writhing, moaning, contorting her trapped body as the delirium gripped her until she mercifully lost consciousness.

Nell forced her eyes open, groaning softly and with no idea of how long she had been senseless. Her tongue felt grotesquely swollen in her mouth, dry as a cornhusk, while the rest of her body was drenched in sweat and burning up, except for her feet, which felt cold as ice. The best she could muster to indicate any remnant of life were intermittent feeble movements that were more like spasms of pain. She became suddenly still. Despite her fever, she had clearly heard something; even in her delirium, that stubborn auditory faculty was prevailing to the last. There was no mistaking the sound of approaching riders. Friend or foe? She had no way of knowing. The sound grew closer and closer until it stopped in a jumble of stamping hooves, snorting, and whinnying, the unmistakeable protests of animals that had been ridden long and hard. Nell strained to hear anything that might indicate the makeup of these new arrivals, trying to focus her blurred vision to identify something, anything through the ventilation holes. And then the little she could see was blotted out and a voice, a male voice, so close it made her startle, stated with a tone of authority, "Lieutenant, we must gather the dead and organise a burial party. See to it immediately."

And then another voice, one that made her heart leap because it was familiar.

"Oh, my sweet Lord. How could this happen? Oh, my dear sweet souls. All gone, all gone. The children! Oh, Heaven, turn thy face away!"

Joshua Lambert! Nell tried to call out, but no sound came. With a tearless sob, she mustered every remaining vestige of her fighting spirit, straining to work her dry tongue around her mouth and over cracked lips, to cry out with one last agonising effort. She balled her fist and rapped her knuckles against the inside of the belly box, drew in her breath 'til she was fit to burst, released it and cried out with all her might.

"Joshua! It's Nell! I'm in here! I'm in here! Help me!" Her rasping croak was a surprise to her. Her fist seemed to have no more strength than a newborn's. She waited, breath held. At first she thought no one had heard, but then –

"I hear you, Nell! I hear you! We'll soon have you out! Oh, blessed Lord! One saved! Over here! Over here! One is alive!"

Nell laid her cheek on the back of her hand with a sigh.

The rescue got underway quickly, and Nell lay prone, heart thudding, listening to all the activity. Men called urgently to each other; there were sounds of people running; orders were shouted back and forth. Nell became aware of a rustle and commotion at her feet, a few oaths and curses, hefty blows with a solid object, sharp tremors that shook her prison before a gunshot made her jump despite her leaden inertia. The lock was shot away, the sealed door wrenched aside after it, and she felt strong hands grip her shins, then her thighs, waist, shoulders, tenderly cup her head. She slid out of her coffin into bright sunlight, arms flailing weakly, to be laid gently on the ground, blinking up at her saviours like a stunned little Lazarus. Joshua dropped to his knees beside her.

"Oh, my child, my poor dear child. It's all right, Nell, you're safe now." He straightened up and bellowed, "Someone, bring me water!"

A young soldier dressed in a blue jacket sporting vivid green trim, his head surmounted by a shako topped with an emerald pompom, fell on to his knees alongside her, lifted her head, and held the rim of his water canteen to her lips. Her eyes beginning to adjust to the light, Nell stared at this startling apparition as she drank greedily. Soldiers. Why hadn't they come sooner? Joshua handed the young man an object as he recapped his bottle.

"You better take charge of this, Lieutenant Clayton. It's Nell's."

Nell felt a stab of recognition. So that's what had been entangled in her feet – Pap's money belt.

****

Fort Laramie, Wyoming

Nell had no recollection afterwards of the journey following her rescue, just the occasional flashback of being lifted into and out of a buckboard wagon, blurred images of strange women attending to her, soothing voices, immersion in soft cool sheets on a feather mattress, and then oblivion. Now, she struggled to open her eyes, turning her head from side to side and straining to make sense of the soft words someone was addressing to her.

"Wake up, now, Nell. Open your eyes. That's it. Open your eyes. You're going to be fine, Nell."

With what felt like superhuman effort, Nell prised her eyelids apart and blinked hard a few times, striving to discern the person who was speaking to her, seemingly a young woman with a pleasant, soothing voice. Slowly the blurred image coalesced into focus and Nell stared dumbly into the face of the stranger hovering over her own.

"That's my girl! Welcome back. Your fever has broken, and the doctor says you're on the mend. How do you feel?"

Nell rolled her tongue around her mouth, opened and closed her lips, and continued to stare at the woman who sat straight backed on a chair pulled up to her bedside, hands folded in her lap and her expression anxious.

"Oh, here, take a few sips of this water." A cup was held to Nell's lips and her head gently raised to enable her to sip. She drank eagerly before turning away to splutter a little, and the woman lowered her back on to her pillows, dabbing her lips with a sweet-smelling handkerchief.

"That's good; a little bit at a time." She cocked her head to the side smiling sweetly. She was very pretty, her dark hair pinned up with ornate combs, her large sloe eyes bright and kindly. Around her slender neck, she wore a striking gold locket and as she leaned in to smooth the sheets she exuded an aura of scented soap and lavender. "You rest now, while I go tell Mattie to prepare some broth." She stood up and swept out in a rustle of silk, leaving Nell to gaze semi-stupefied around her new surroundings. She was in a room with adobe walls, light provided by a single window to her right, framed by white muslin curtains with a matching ruffle across the head. Beside her bed was a nightstand holding an oil lamp, water carafe, and cup, and against the wall facing her bed and next to the door was a dresser-cum-washstand with a porcelain jug and basin. A few feet away from the dresser, close to the corner, was a free standing wardrobe fronted by a bevelled mirror. Apart from the chair on which the young woman had sat beside her bed, there were no other furnishings, save for a fabric dressing screen and a patterned rug near the door. Lifting the bedclothes, Nell saw that she was wearing a white cotton long sleeved night rail. She reached up to feel her head. The short-cropped hair that had taken so long to recover to its present length was still there. Often, when people had fever, their hair was shaved off, so at least she'd been spared that indignity.

By now fully awake, Nell startled slightly as the woman returned, crossing the room and slipping on to the chair to resume her bedside vigil, smiling sweetly all the while.

"Lunch is coming, Nell." She extended a slender hand. "I'm Marianne, Captain Beaumont's wife. He is the senior officer in charge here. I have been nursing you since you were brought to our home after your fearful ordeal."

Nell squeezed her hand. "Pleased to meet you, ma'am. Um, where am I exactly?"

"Of course, silly of me. You're at Fort Laramie, where they brought you after the – after the attack." Her face grew serious.

"You're safe here, Nell. The captain is away with the riflemen tracking those renegade savages who murdered so many good people. He is a capable soldier and will catch them, too, have no fear, and then they will feel the full weight of our wrath. You and your loved ones will be avenged. The Cheyenne signed the treaty here at this fort, and they despise the defiant warriors who committed the atrocity as much as we do." She smoothed Nell's covers with her delicate fingers. "Do you have any other questions?"

"Where's my father's money belt?"

Marianne blinked at such directness. "Why, it is in the company safe. I can assure you that it is quite secure. The contents have been carefully counted and recorded and you have only to ask the captain if you wish to make a withdrawal." She lifted her small chin. "Is there anything else you want to ask me?"

Before Nell could respond, there was a soft rap at the door, and a young serving girl came in bearing a tray with raised sides and a wooden foot at each corner. The girl, who wore a mob cap atop her light brown hair, had rosy cheeks that gave colour to her plump, homely face. Marianne introduced her as Grace, and the girl bobbed shyly in Nell's direction, in polite acknowledgement of her greeting. Then she and Marianne lifted Nell up with her back bolstered by the pillows, arranged the tray across her thighs, tucked a napkin into the collar of her nightgown, and left her to enjoy her lunch.

"You must eat, Nell," advised Marianne, pausing at the door. "You have much strength to regain. We'll start with easily digested nourishment and plenty of fluids."

Left alone, Nell adjusted the napkin and stared at the food on the tray: a rich broth with little greasy puddles floating on the surface, two thick slices of bread, a baked potato on a side dish, oozing butter. She picked up the spoon, poised it over the bowl, then plunged it into the fragrant contents, dredging up fragments of vegetable with the unctuous liquid. It felt like a very long time since she'd eaten. After the first delicious mouthful had gone hesitantly down, she attacked the remainder like a starved wolf, and when all the food was gone she lifted the tray aside, settled back in the bed, and promptly fell asleep.

When Nell woke again, it was dark. The curtains had been closed, the tray removed, and the lamp, now placed on the dresser, cast a soft glow from a low flame. Nell badly needed to relieve herself, so she fumbled her way out from under the covers and dropped to her knees to grope under the bed, hoping to find a chamber pot. Sure enough, her hand closed around a cold porcelain rim, and she drew out a large ornate pot, squatting over it with a deep sigh. When she'd finished, she pushed the pot and its pungent contents carefully back under the bed and settled down again between the cool sheets, amazed by how weak she felt.

For a long time Nell lay very still, staring at the window, its flimsy muslin curtains filtering soft moonlight into the room. Her head felt very clear now that the fever had gone, and she began a thorough review of her life up to this point, with a cool detachment that enabled her to form a precise analysis of its overall theme. She had lost her mother and baby brother. She had been obliged to take over the running of the farm and the care of her father as he wallowed in his grief while she was still a child. She had been uprooted from everything she held dear and set on a course into the dangerous unknown by her father's quest for redemption. She had then lost that father along with his new wife, her stepmother, and any prospect of recovering the happy family life she craved. What a naïve fool she had been to believe her life had turned for the better! So be it. As it stood, she was all alone in the world at the age of fifteen, and she would have to look after herself from now on, since she no longer had any soul she could call kin on whom she could rely for succour and support. She tried to quell the bitterness she felt, but it crept steadily up and consumed her so that she turned her face into her pillow and gave way to wracking sobs, until exhaustion quieted her. Before she went back to sleep, she made herself a promise that she would never again shed a tear over anyone or anything that came her way in her benighted life.

When Grace entered Nell's room in the morning, pulled the curtains, and arranged her breakfast tray on the quilt, she smiled warmly at her, assuming she was looking at the same girl she'd met yesterday, albeit a little red and puffy around the eyes, which was to be expected given her illness. But, unbeknown to Grace, this was an entirely different girl, and the old Nell was gone, never to return.

When Marianne breezed in after breakfast with a bundle of fresh clothes and a pair of shoes, she thought she detected an almost imperceptible alteration in Nell's demeanour, something hard and steely, almost unpleasant, but she quickly dismissed it as pure fancy. The child had been through a lot, after all.

****

Marianne frowned as Nell twitched, tugged at, and readjusted her dress for the umpteenth time.

"Lord above, have you some wretched insect in there with you that you must jerk about so? Do try to sit still, Nell."

"I got outta the habit of wearin' dresses," said Nell testily. "I'd likely feel more comfortable in my dungarees."

"Those disgusting things! They were filthy. I had them thrown out."

"Nell bristled. "Thrown out! You had no right."

Marianne lowered her sewing slowly, fixing Nell with a cool look. "No right, you say? Well, you were handed to me in such a state that I had no choice but to strip you and have you thoroughly scrubbed from head to toe and put in clean attire. Anyway," her tone softened a little, "They're hereabouts somewhere, so don't fret."

"You just said you threw them out!"

Marianne made an impatient 'tsk' sound. "I want you to try and accustom yourself to a more ladylike mode of dress, dear. The dungarees are washed and put away. That was the sense in which I meant 'thrown out'. Now, stop vexing yourself and eat up your bread and butter. You are grievously thin."

Nell plucked up the slice of bread she'd just buttered and crammed it into her mouth in the most unladylike way possible so that her cheeks bulged like those of a hoarding chipmunk, followed this with noisy, open-mouthed chewing and then painstakingly licked every finger. She looked over at Marianne, eyes gleaming triumphantly, as she drew the last finger slowly out of her mouth with a prolonged sucking sound.

Marianne shook her head slowly, keeping her eyes on her sewing. "I see that you are not in the mood for polite and pleasant company today, Nell. A pity, as I had planned to take you on a tour of the fort, before sharing some conversation that may help you to unburden yourself. Instead, you may choose a book from the bookcase, then retire to your room for a rest and to read in solitude until you feel like being sociable."

Nell opened her mouth to say something along the lines that she would please herself what she did and when she did it, but she thought better of it, pushed her chair back from the table with unnecessary force and strode towards the door with her nose in the air, making the point that she declined to read any of Marianne's fashionably frivolous novels, whose fanciful titles she had already reviewed. As she wrenched the door open, Marianne called to her, "I have received word that I can expect the captain back tonight, so we will discuss your future prospects over dinner. Use this time to consider how you will respond."

Nell made no reply, but flung herself out, closing the door with some force behind her. There was a woman, she thought scornfully, with all her society airs and graces, who knew nothing of suffering, but had lived a charmed life, pampered and waited upon and accustomed to having her every whim catered for by others she considered her inferiors.

As she slouched back to her room, tripping more than once over the hem of the dress on the stairs, she met Grace carrying an armful of linen.

"Grace! Can you bring me my dungarees and my shirt? Mistress says they are stored hereabouts."

Grace hesitated, biting her lip, but then nodded, albeit without much conviction. "Yes, miss."

"Thank you." Nell swept past her and on to her room.

CHAPTER TEN

By the time Nell was called downstairs to dinner, a good long nap had restored her equilibrium and she felt a little foolish when she recalled her peevish behaviour of the morning. Grace had returned her dungarees and shirt, not only washed and ironed, but also mended where they needed to be. Nell was mollified. She brushed her hair, washed her face, and took a deep breath.

Captain Beaumont and his wife were already seated at the dining table when Nell was shown in, and she felt awkward when the nice-looking young man with smooth black hair and an elegant moustache rose to his feet as she entered.

"Good evening, Nell. I hope you're feeling better." He thrust out his hand. "Sholto Beaumont at your service."

The sound of his words sent a chill down her spine, for she recognised immediately the disembodied voice that had spoken alongside the belly box, giving the order to organise a burial detail. She wanted to ask him outright if he had caught the marauding

Indians, but conceded that the evening dinner table was neither the time nor place.

"Pleased to make your acquaintance, sir."

Nell squeezed his hand and slid on to the chair he drew out for her, murmuring a greeting to Marianne as she sat down. The table was formally set, with silver candlesticks, gleaming cutlery, crystal wine glasses, and a pretty floral centrepiece. Nell took it all in, feeling more than a little self-conscious and out of her social depth. As the most senior officer and his wife at Fort Laramie, the Beaumonts lived well, as befit their status, with their own personal cook and servants. Marianne interrupted her musing.

"How are you feeling, Nell?" she enquired, adjusting her napkin across her lap. "Did you have a good rest?"

"Yes, ma'am, thank you." Nell copied her hostess's disposal of the napkin.

"And are you happier in the dress, now? You seem a trifle more relaxed."

"Yes, ma'am. The dress suits me jus' fine. I'm obliged to you."

Marianne gave a little cough, and Nell glanced at her sideways. Her exemplary politeness seemed to be unnerving the woman, who smiled helplessly at her bemused husband. Nell guessed he'd been told what a handful she was and grinned inwardly. Grace came in with the soup course and the awkward moment passed, thankfully. Nell blew a held-in breath softly across her lips and picked up her spoon, hoping she'd chosen the correct utensil; there was such an array of these as she'd never seen before. The captain poured her a little wine, making Nell feel very grown up, even when he subsequently diluted it with water.

Dinner proceeded quite pleasantly. The captain carved the fragrant roast chicken himself, handing Nell a generous portion, to which she added gravy, potatoes, carrots and greens from the bowls passed to her in what felt like endless succession, before devouring it all with as much decorum as she could manage in the face of her raging hunger. Marianne complimented her on her appetite, and the captain insisted she have seconds. Nell had avoided looking into the tall mirror in her bedroom, and so had no real idea just how thin she had become, although she was well aware that her ribs were all painfully exposed, as were her sharp little pelvic bones. Her legs and arms had always been wiry thin.

After a fine dessert of apple pie and cream, the trio withdrew to the parlour where a fire had been laid, and Grace brought them coffee and a bottle of port for the captain. Nell felt contentedly replete after the fine meal, her little belly stretched like a drum, and sat staring mesmerically into the flickering fire, sipping her coffee in silence – and waiting. She knew the time had arrived to discuss her situation, and she had some hard questions for the captain, things she had to know, even if she didn't want to. She had to know the bitter truth in order to pay respect to her loved ones. She waited for one of the adults to broach the as yet unspoken topic of her fate.

The captain refilled his port glass, sat back in his chair, and said softly, "Nell…"

Nell had her cue, and he got no further. "Tell me what happened. I want to know everything." Her interruption was stated in a tone that made him look up sharply. He realised he would not get away with any glossing over of the terrible truths she wanted him to reveal. She appeared fragile, but he had already detected a toughness and resilience far beyond her years. Her shockingly frayed hair was testament alone to a hard wrung life.

As the captain opened his mouth to reply, Marianne said quickly, "Nell, are you sure you wish to pursue this – this painful, em, post mortem?"

Nell shot her a look that made her sit back stiffly. "Yes. I'm sure."

Marianne rose from her chair and picked up the coffee pot. "Then I shall go and request more coffee, and bring the brandy, too. Pray, do proceed, Sholto dear. Do not hold off for my return." She swept out, leaving Nell alone with the captain. Nell fixed him with an unflinching gaze.

"You can be open and honest with me, sir. I am not of a squeamish nature. I seen plenty of unpleasant things, so open up and tell me the truth of what happened to my poor, dear family and fellows."

"I will, Nell, but promise me that, if my revelations become too overwhelming, you will call a stop."

Nell nodded. "I promise."

By the time Marianne returned, Nell had most of her answers. She and the captain were sitting in silence, the captain smoking his pipe, while Nell sat very still, hands motionless in her lap, staring into the fire. But she was not done. Not yet.

"The small children. Did you happen to notice a little girl? Her name was Emily Ryder. An' there was a baby, no more'n a few weeks old."

The captain removed his pipe, clearing his throat. "We have identified all the dead, Nell. Emily Ryder was not among them. We assume she has been taken captive, and we will continue to seek her. She was not with the dog soldiers, though, when we caught up with them. Her whereabouts is currently unknown."

My beautiful wee Em! "An' the baby?"

"He perished with his parents."

Silence followed during which the fire crackled and Marianne refreshed the coffee cups. She added a drop of brandy to each cup and passed Nell's to her. Nell replaced it on the side table. The captain broke the silence, his voice gentle. "They were interred with great respect Nell, and our chaplain read a moving Christian service, which, sadly, you were too ill to attend. Our smith is making a

147

commemorative plaque to adorn their final resting place. I can take you there when it is done, if you'd like."

Nell nodded. "Thank you, I would like that."

"Good." Her sangfroid, her impregnable self-control astonished him. He caught his wife's eye and she raised an eyebrow.

Nell had just one more question. "Have you killed them all?"

The captain leaned over and knocked out his pipe on the hob. He straightened up, regarding her directly. "Yes. Our Indian trackers are exemplary. Rest assured, Nell, your family and friends have all been avenged."

Nell nodded. "What has become of our – my – wagon, do you know?"

"Yes. It was brought to the fort and is secured in the commissary. We will go there tomorrow so that you may inspect it."

Marianne clasped her hands together. "We will do that tour I promised you, Nell."

Her attempt to lighten the atmosphere in the room was ignored by Nell, who rose abruptly to her feet. "Thank you for a fine supper, sir, ma'am. I will go to bed now. Goodnight."

When she reached her bedroom she fairly sprinted to her bed, flung herself on her knees and only just yanked the chamber pot out in time before she regurgitated her fine supper into it.

****

The following morning, after breakfast, Nell accompanied the captain and Marianne on a tour of Fort Laramie. Marianne watched her anxiously. She looked pale and tired, had only picked at her food, and was even more monosyllabic than ever. Marianne had offered her a bonnet, shawl and parasol, all of which items she made use of herself, but Nell had answered curtly that she did not need them. Marianne could not understand Nell's willingness to flaunt her tatty hair in public – or in private, for that matter.

Marianne had not sought out from her husband the details of the overlanders' deaths in the massacre, but she could well imagine what horrors had been inflicted on them, and poor Nell, at her own insistence, now had those doubtless ghastly images fixed in her head forever. Sholto, in his soldier's way, claimed he had not spared her, since she had a right to know all the facts, and, although still young, was of a background and hardiness that made her capable of dealing with the truth, however unpleasant. 'Better to know than torment herself with wild imaginings' was how he'd put it. Marianne remained unsure, especially after seeing the unmistakeable signs of the girl's distress this morning. When Grace had whispered to her before breakfast that Nell's supper had reappeared in her chamber pot, she was not surprised. Perhaps the exercise in the morning sunshine would revive her spirits. She linked her free arm through her husband's and said briskly, "Come along, Nell."

****

The captain, straight-backed and broad shouldered, set a cracking pace and Nell, glad to be out in the fresh air, felt her spirits lift as she followed him and his wife around the environs of the fort. It was a beautiful day, calm and sunny, and she felt some strength returning to her limbs as her wasted muscles gradually loosened up.

Like Fort Kearney, Fort Laramie was not stockaded but quite open, with many new or restored buildings, both wooden and adobe. From the verandah in front of the Captain's quarters, they walked along beside the parade ground towards a cluster of solid stone houses, where the captain paused, waiting 'til Nell was alongside.

"Officers' row, Nell."

Nell studied the row of identical buildings. They made a marked contrast with the captain's mostly timber house. Then she looked around, shading her eyes. "Where does the stone come from?"

The captain chuckled. "They are not built of stone, Nell. They are built of adobe bricks that are smoothed over while still wet. We had to make our own mix, following, believe it or not, an ancient Roman recipe for concrete and using lime from the nearby bluffs mixed with sand, gravel, and water. The Romans strengthened theirs with seawater, but we had to make do. Consequently, these buildings do not weather well, so we must carry out regular maintenance. We are very short on timber here." He set off again, turning left. "Come along, now. I will take you to the sutler's."

When she stepped into the sutler's trading store, Nell baulked at the sensory overload, trying to take it all in: blankets, tools, cooking utensils, kettles, cloth, clothing, weapons, tobacco, candy, buffalo hides, ammunition, airtights, preserves, furniture, and even fruit and vegetables, surplus from the fort's own garden – altogether a staggering array of commodities.

"Apart from supplying the soldiers' wants, this is where the emigrants who take rest here at the fort from their journey come to buy replenishments or to barter goods. It is a very important service provided by the fort."

Nell nodded as she scanned the overflowing shelves and displays. After completing one third of their arduous journey, this colourful store would seem like a treasure trove to the Oregon Trail travellers.

Next, they visited the bakery, and Marianne selected a still-warm loaf to be delivered to the house kitchen. Nell enjoyed watching the men working and her nostrils flared, savouring the homely smell of freshly baked bread. None of them was a trained baker, the captain informed her. The soldiers all had to take a turn. Then they moved on to the commissary, where the captain had said her family's wagon was stored. As soon as she saw it, Nell felt her chest clench and tears start to her eyes, momentarily overwhelmed by so many memories, good and bad, that came flooding back. Marianne saw her falter and, thrusting her parasol on to her surprised husband, moved swiftly to her side, hands fluttering uncertainly. Nell recovered quickly, however, and clambered up to inspect the contents. Everything was just as she remembered. Her boots, felt hat, and jacket were there, but not the shotgun. She clambered down, addressing the captain.

"Was the gun there? A shotgun? Did you find a Ferguson rifle? It belonged to…" her voice trailed off.

The captain shook his head. "No. We don't have those items. You may find some things missing, Nell, but the war party did not, in fact, carry out much looting. They knew about our regular patrols and doubtless made their escape fairly quickly. We removed the perishable foods like bacon, of course, for the fort's consumption, and I have added their estimated value to your funds. You are welcome to scrutinise our bookkeeping."

"What about – the other wagons?"

"The rest of the train took them onwards, under Mr. Lambert's supervision. It seemed like the best solution. They had spare draught animals for them, and we would have had a hard job finding relatives and arranging collection. The unconsumed food, especially, was useful to the other emigrants. Nothing will be wasted, Nell."

Nell nodded her agreement. That made sense. Personally, she wouldn't want anything to do with murdered people's belongings, but overlanders were a hardy, practical breed who couldn't afford to be fastidious.

The captain placed a hand on the wagon, patting it as if it were animated. "You know, Nell, your friends have moved on now, but you could join the next wagon train that comes through, if you want to. We would have to find you a guide-cum-wagon hand, but I'm sure they'd have someone willing to fill the role, if you're prepared to pay them, and we'd supply oxen for you. You could continue on to Oregon."

Nell responded with fierce indignation. "Oregon? I never wanted to go to Oregon in the first place. It was my father's idea and now it's got him killed. I hate the very word 'Oregon'!" She stomped off and stood framed in the doorway with her back to the bewildered Beaumonts, arms folded, snorting like a rankled little dragon. "Oregon!" she continued to mutter. "I'll never go there, 's long as I live!"

Marianne came and stood beside her. "Do you want to go back home where you came from, Nell?"

Nell's head swivelled to eye her coldly. "Iowa? What fer? There's no one left there for me, neither. I shoulda been killed with the others, 'cept Pap had to stuff me in that darn belly box. He shouldn't have done that."

Marianne said nothing for a moment, following this vehemently expressed death wish, then she placed a tentative hand on Nell's shoulder. "The good Lord has spared you for a reason, Nell, and with His help you will discover it. There is no rush for you to make any hasty decisions about what course you choose to follow, now. You are still healing, after all, and we are more than happy to have you stay with us as long as you want. I hope you know that."

Nell looked into Marianne's sweet, earnest face and felt her antagonism dissolve. She had no excuse for taking out her bitterness on these good people who had saved her life and shown her exemplary kindness. She sighed, visibly sagging as she let go of her anger. The captain had moved to his wife's side, and both watched her anxiously.

"I'm obliged to you both." Then she added, with a typical assertion of independence. "Soon's I'm up to it, I'll be earning my keep, though."

The captain touched his hat brim by way of a pleased gesture. "Then that's settled. Come on, Nell, and I'll show you the barracks and the stables, where I'm afraid I'll have to leave you both to carry on without me. Duty calls." He took his wife's arm. "Nell will be nice company for you, my dear."

As Marianne voiced her agreement, Nell thought, *Well, I don't know about that. God forgive me, but the woman irritates the hell outta me!*

****

In the days that followed, Nell quickly regained her strength and vitality, as the young are wont to do, although the illness had left her painfully thin. She enjoyed good food, gentle exercise, clean clothes (though she still smarted in a dress), regular hot baths, and hours of unconscious sleep from which she had to be shaken awake for breakfast despite the dreaded nightmares that plagued her, mesmerising and repelling her simultaneously. Always possessed of a sturdy work ethic, she insisted on making herself useful, running errands, delivering treats to the captain whose office was adjacent to his and his wife's living quarters, helping out in the kitchen, where Mattie, the cook, found it hard to conceal her fondness for the little waif foundling. Grace, closest to Nell in age, also became a friend.

As she settled into her environs, Nell roamed further afield, enjoying spending time with the women who did the soldiers' laundry and maintained the fort's vegetable garden. During the warmer months, they lived in tents near their garden patch and outdoor washtubs, only moving indoors in the winter months. Then it was on to the bakery, the hospital, where her presence cheered the patients, to the sutler's, to the cavalry barracks and everywhere else Nell considered to be under her purview. She especially loved the stables, and Old Mac, in charge of livery, allowed her to ride about the fort on a pretty little grey mare named Misty that she'd taken a fancy to. Sometimes Marianne joined her on her own splendid roan, riding sidesaddle, while Nell rode astride, each shooting disapproving glances at the other.

Nell quickly became a familiar sight around the fort and made many new friends, including the other officers' families. Lieutenant

Lafayette Crayshaw, who'd given her the water when she'd been rescued, and his wife, Deirdre, had a sweet little boy of two years named Kelvin, and Nell visited them often. She was always included when the officers' wives came for cake and tea with Marianne, or were invited to dinner with their husbands. The soldiers, who all knew of her tragic circumstances, treated her with kindness, spoiled her, in fact, regarding her as something of their own little fort mascot. The fort's chaplain, who visited her often, had organised a school for the soldiers' children, with his daughter as the schoolmarm, and Nell frequently dropped in to help out. She kept very busy – which also kept her out of Marianne's clutches.

Almost every day, Nell did her rounds, visiting everybody from the humblest workers to the highest ranked officers, while Marianne fretted over this vagabond behaviour. Sholto reassured her that Nell's rambles were perfectly fine and that no harm could come to her as she had so many good people watching over her. He was just a little alarmed when he found her dining with the soldiers in their mess, swigging small beer with her meal, but she was clearly having such a good time that he didn't want to spoil it. She was subsequently delivered home, cheeks glowing, by her own personal armed escort.

This was how she filled her days, trying to keep a step ahead of the demons that now stalked her dreams and disrupted her sleep so that she would wake and sit bolt upright, gasping and sweat-soaked, heart pounding, the last fearful image in a seemingly endless procession, the one that finally forced her to claw her way back to wakefulness, still dancing before her eyes: a blood soaked lance with scalps streaming from the shaft, the two she dreaded most to see throbbing with garish light, one auburn, the one above it blond. Then, when she remembered where she was, she'd collapse on to her pillows again: *Pap? Sabrina? Chickabiddy? Where are you? I have to find you.* Dark circles formed under her eyes.

It was spending time in Marianne's company that Nell found most trying, prompting much of her meandering. She also found it difficult to explain to herself why, but the woman just purely grated on her. Every day after lunch, Marianne liked to brush her hair, her reasoning being that regular gentle brushing would stimulate both the scalp and the hair's natural oils, resulting in renewed growth. Nell gritted her teeth and tolerated this ritual, as it seemed to please her hostess. On one particular afternoon, though, she became quickly goaded into irascibility by a comment Marianne made as she brushed diligently.

"The hair is not regenerating as I'd hoped, Nell. Tsk. Good Lord, there are other ways to control head lice besides shaving your entire scalp bare."

"I never had no head lice!" responded Nell indignantly, swivelling her head around to give Marianne a baleful look.

Marianne rolled her eyes. "I never had any head lice. I can see we're going to have to work on your grammar, too."

"My granma's daid, both of 'em."

Marianne suppressed a shrill giggle with her fingertips. "Oh, you're really precious. Did you know that? I said g-r-a-m-m-a-r, meaning correct use of the English language."

Nell jumped up and stood fists clenched, glowering at her groomer, uncertain whether 'precious' was good or bad, and infuriated by the aspersion cast upon her speech. "Never you mind fussing over me like some sort of dolly," she spat. "You ain't my mam. Whyn't you got a babby of your own to pet? How long you been married? Mebbe you need me to give you some tips on getting' in the family way, missus know-it-all."

The colour drained from Marianne's cheeks, and she opened and closed her mouth several times before she finally got the words out. "You are a vulgar, ill-spoken, ill-mannered little stripling, missy, and if it were in my power I would give you a good spanking." She dropped the hairbrush on to the table with a clatter and pointed towards the door. "Go to your room this instant and reflect on your lack of manners and – and – your ingratitude!"

Nell placed her hands on her hips and leaned forwards slightly, her tone sneering. "First of all, it ain't my room. An' I don't remember asking either you or your poncy husband to take care of me, so why should I feel any gratitude. If your soldier boy had been doin' his job proper, he might have got there in time to stop those savages murdering so many good folk an' takin' their hair for ornaments!" As Marianne's jaw slackened with shock, Nell pointed to the ceiling. "I'll go to my room sure 'nough so I can change outta this goddam dress and into my dungarees, an' then I'm goin' to find me some decent company that don't nag and don't act the queen with ordinary folk!"

As Marianne burst into tears, Nell spun on her heel and stormed out, thumping loudly up the stairs and slamming the bedroom door hard enough to make the whole house shake. She felt a savage rush of glee that she'd made the woman cry.

****

Upstairs in her room, Nell furiously unbuttoned her dress, wrenched it off, and tossed it into a corner of the room. The shoes Marianne had given her followed the same trajectory. Then, she got into her old flannel shirt and dungarees, laced up her boots, which she'd retrieved from the wagon, and stood in front of the dress mirror to appraise the result.

"That's better!" She gave a little snort of satisfaction, ran her fingers through her brush-tamed hair to tousle it, and headed off downstairs. She'd reached the front door and was about to grasp the handle when she stopped, hesitated, did an abrupt about-face and retraced her footsteps along the hallway towards the kitchen, Mattie's and, a lot of the time, Grace's domain.

Mattie, the household's cook and a large-bosomed, maternal woman in her fifties who'd grown fond of Nell, greeted her warmly as she stepped into the kitchen. She was seated at the big scrubbed wooden table peeling vegetables for dinner, sleeves rolled up and meaty arms wielding the knife with a skill honed by years of practice, peelings fairly flying into the bowl.

"Nell! Come sit down and I'll fetch you some cool buttermilk." She hoisted herself up and waddled over to the pie safe, removing an earthenware jug and stopping by the sideboard to uplift a pottery mug.

"Thanks." Nell slid on to the bench opposite her. Mattie filled the mug and passed it to her, before returning the jug to the pie safe and resuming her seat with a soft grunt. Nell took a long pull of the buttermilk, made a satisfied. "Ah," and wiped her mouth with the back of her hand. "So good. Where's Grace?"

"I sent her to the sutler's for a bottle of horseradish sauce. It's the captain's favourite."

Mattie picked up her knife along with another sweet potato and asked nonchalantly, "You have another spat with Miz Beaumont?"

Nell placed the mug on the table in front of her, folded her arms, and sighed. "Yep. She just got my dander up again." She straightened up, adopting an air of wounded pride. "She said my hair is the way it is 'cos it needed shaving off after I got cooties in it! I ain't never had no cooties. My mam was extra careful about that, always combed my hair every day, scrubbed it with soap under the pump, an', let me tell you, in the middle of winter that ain't no fun!"

Nell threw back the rest of the buttermilk and thumped the empty mug down on the table. "An' then, she mocked my way of speakin'. I might not be as educated as her, but I know my letters and numbers. I had to give up school when Mam died to look after Pap an' the farm. What'd she know 'bout that? Miss spoiled lady muck."

Mattie chuckled, shaking her head. "You sure are a feisty one, Nell."

Nell buried her face in her hands. "I done made her weep," she said in a muffled voice.

Mattie looked at her aghast as she lowered the knife and the semi-peeled sweet potato. "Miz Beaumont cried?"

"Yep." Nell clasped her hands on the table in front of her. "I mocked her right back fer – fer – not having a babby to torment instead of me."

Mattie gave a shocked little gasp, clasping her hand over her mouth. Upon removing it she said seriously, "Oh, Nell. That was cruel. Not having a baby has caused the young mistress much sorrow." She lowered her voice, adopting a confidential tone as she leaned closer to Nell. "She and the captain went to any number of doctors back east, and nobody could help or throw light on what was the problem. They've taken refuge here because she can't face her family. Her two sisters have three children apiece."

Nell sighed. "Well, I done cooked my goose, I reckon. She's really gonna hate me now." Nell stood up. "Thanks for the buttermilk, Mattie. I'm goin' for a good long ride, clear my head."

"Nell, we know it's your grief makes you lash out. Don't take on so."

Nell didn't answer. She strode off, and when she reached the verandah, she stood for a moment gazing around, deeply inhaling the fresh air. Then she jumped down instead of taking the steps, tilting her head back when she landed and squinting up at the sun. It's high time I was movin' on.

She bypassed the stables and headed for the sutler's. Mr. Johnson looked up from scribbling something in his accounts book, smiling his recognition.

"Nell! What can I do for you?"

Nell fumbled in her dungarees' pocket and drew out some bills, placing them before Mr. Johnson, on the counter. "I want to buy a haversack, and mebbe a few other bits 'n pieces. Don't worry none, it's my money."

CHAPTER ELEVEN

Once she had selected and paid for her haversack and other goods, Nell made her way to the commissary and retrieved a few items from the wagon, including her bedroll and the farm journal. Then, forgoing her ride on Misty, she surreptitiously made her way back to the Beaumonts' quarters, sneaking in by the back stairs. Safely back in her room, she stowed everything under the bed, and rested until dinnertime was announced, when she changed into her dress and made her way downstairs. She addressed the captain and Marianne politely and took her place at table without making eye contact with either. Grace brought in the soup course and eating commenced in silence, the atmosphere taut.

The captain was, by this time, well used to an almost daily atmosphere of tension at his dinner table, and it was beginning to make him dyspeptic. His hopes that the two women would derive mutual enjoyment as companions to each other had been dashed, and, clearly, they had once again had a falling out earlier in the day: Nell had her fixed 'What? Me?' expression on, and his wife was pale, red-eyed, and tight-lipped. Neither entered into any convivial table talk and silence reigned. The captain loved his wife dearly and felt her pain over their childless state keenly, a lacuna in their domestic life he'd hoped Nell might fill. He, at least, had his army career to distract him, but Marianne had little to fill her days. To make matters worse, the Crayshaws had just confirmed that they had a second child on the way, and he knew that, beneath her bravery and her sincere avowals of delight for the couple, his wife was suffering anew.

When Nell had spurned the idea of continuing on to Oregon, the captain had entertained the idea of having her stay on at the fort in some capacity, of perhaps making her his ward. Now, he was just weary of the palpable antagonism that blighted his home and hearth, of seeing his wife upset, and of tolerating Nell's free-spirited, high-handed ways. For the life of him, he could not understand how Nell could not love his sweet, kind, gentle wife, but there it was; they were apparently chalk and cheese. At any rate, he felt he could no longer cut Nell the slack he had been doing because of her personal tragedy. Better for all concerned that she move on.

The captain's scouts had reported the imminent arrival of a large wagon train at the fort, and he had resolved to attach Nell to it. There were bound to be young, single, able-bodied men amongst the emigrants. Nell was almost sixteen and had a commendable dowry in the form of her father's remaining capital as well as the wagon and its contents. There was a considerable shortage of women on the frontier, and she would be able to pick and choose for her future spouse. Disastrous coiffure aside, she was a pretty girl with a lithe figure and excellent domestic and practical skills. God help any poor future husband, the captain thought wryly, but he had no doubts, either, that Nell, whose tiny stature belied her formidable strength, would make a superlative pioneer wife. Anyway, she would need a husband to acquire land. That was the law. As he finished his soup and Grace removed the empty bowl, he smiled at Nell, who, having no inkling of his train of thought, was regarding him darkly for staring at her with a vacant expression that masked his calculated plotting. Emerging from his trance, he flashed his wife a happy smile also and she managed a tentative response; he would talk to Marianne about his decision as soon as they were alone. Then, he would speak firmly with Nell. For now, he could at least do his bit to dispel the cloud that hung over his table.

"Burrows brought in a fine elk today. I have reserved a haunch for us to enjoy, once the meat has hung for a while."

Of course, the captain had no idea that he was not the only one hatching plots.

****

When dinner was over, and the Beaumonts adjourned to the parlour, Nell did not join them, instead excusing herself in preference of an early night. The captain was secretly pleased. Now, he could talk freely with his wife. As soon as Grace had fetched the coffee and port and withdrawn, he broached the subject of their fiery little houseguest.

"Marianne, tell me what has happened. I can see you are upset."

His wife replaced her bone china coffee cup on the side table with a deep sigh. "I will spare you the unpleasant details, Sholto. Suffice it to say that I have come to accept that Nell and I are a bad match. She despises me, and I am fully to blame, since I am who I am, but to her I am like tinder to a flame. I am also become a poor sort of wife to you, gloomy, quiet and hardly good company, which you do not deserve." She looked her husband in the eye. "I cannot handle her, and she deserves to be with someone she respects and loves. I trust you to make – other arrangements for Nell."

The captain sat forward, reaching for his wife's hand, and she clasped his own firmly, her eyes brimming with tears. "I do not accept that you are to blame for the impasse, my dear, as no sweeter nor more accommodating nature than yours could be found. Nell was bound to be a bad bet after all she has been through. I blame myself for giving you responsibility for one so broken by her circumstances. I should have known better. That onus ends now. I will summon her to my office tomorrow morning and tell her she will be moving on with the wagon train my scouts have reported will be here within a day or so. She is bound to find some kindred spirits among the farming folk and someone will take her in, a large family, perhaps, where the mother needs help with the children." He stood up, lifting Marianne to her feet also. "Now, let us go to bed. A good night's sleep will restore you."

Nell lay in bed listening for the familiar sounds that meant the Beaumonts were retiring for the night: stairs creaking, candle-light bleeding briefly through the gaps around her door marking their passage to their room, door closing – silence. She allowed extra time for Grace and Mattie to go to their beds, and then she slid out from under the covers, tiptoed downstairs and into the parlour, where she very carefully removed the captain's crystal decanter of whiskey from the liquor cabinet. Removing the stopper, she filled the flask she'd bought from the sutler's, assuring a bemused Mr. Johnson it was a gift for the captain. Before she returned to bed she took a sheet of paper from Marianne's desk.

****

At breakfast the following morning, attended by Nell and Marianne alone, since the captain was already gone to his work, Marianne told Nell that her husband wished to talk to her immediately she had finished her meal. Nell accepted this instruction with a curt nod, and breakfast continued in silence.

When it was over, Nell rose without a word and headed off to the administration rooms alongside the dwelling. She was immediately ushered into the captain's office by his adjutant, as per his express orders, and once Nell was comfortably seated, Captain Beaumont told her of his decision, made in conjunction with his wife's agreement, and assured her that there would be no appeal against it; she would leave Fort Laramie with the next wagon train, once the emigrants were rested and resupplied. Then he sat back in his leather-padded captain's chair, hands folded across his abdomen, and waited for her response. If he had anticipated protestations of outraged betrayal, or tearful pleading, or passionate avowals of a personality change forthwith, he was disappointed. Nell stared him down for a moment before she answered.

"I thank you and your good lady for your many kindnesses to me, Cap'n. Now, can I have the rest of my pappy's money so I can commence to plan for my departure?"

The captain blinked, recovered, and stood up, looking a little abashed as he wrested the keys to the safe from his jacket pocket. "Of course, Nell, and you must tell me if there is anything else you'll need that I can provide."

Nell took the money belt from him, wrapping it around her left forearm. "Thanks, but I don't need no handouts. I always paid my way." She stood up. "Can I trouble you for an envelope?"

"Yes, of course." The captain opened the top drawer on one side of his desk, removed an envelope, and handed it to her.

"Thank you." Nell tucked it into the pocket of her dungarees. She shifted awkwardly, watching the captain, her face expressionless. "Are we done?"

Captain Beaumont sighed as he resumed his seat. "Almost, Nell." He pushed two documents lying on his desk towards her. "Army paperwork, I'm afraid. They're sticklers for records. In the absence of a will, I have drawn up an affidavit confirming that you are the sole beneficiary of all your father's worldly goods. I have already signed. Could you please also sign both copies? One is for you."

Nell read the documents carefully before taking the pen the captain offered and signing her name as he'd asked. The captain blotted the signatures before he carefully folded one document and handed it to her.

"Thank you, Nell. You may go now."

Nell turned on her heel and left. The captain sat for a long time just staring out the window, overwhelmed by a sadness he could not put into words.

Nell implemented the final elements in the plan her sharp mind had worked out with military precision, and then spent the rest of the day doing the rounds of her familiar haunts and passing the time with the many friends she'd made at the fort. Before returning home, she dropped off the flask of whiskey to Old Mac at the stables, by way of expressing her thanks for his kindness in allowing her to ride Misty whenever she wished. She made him promise to enjoy it as a nightcap, which, she insisted, would alleviate the symptoms of rheumatism he frequently complained about, giving him a sound night's sleep. She felt a momentary pang of guilt for callously manipulating the weakness for alcohol, which he'd confided had seen him busted back to private so many times in the profession he was dedicated to, and finally relegated to hostler. However, that soon passed, and she skipped back to the house feeling confident that things were falling into place nicely, but at the same time aware that she could not let her guard down for an instant. Then she did something very unusual for her: she went to her room and had a nap.

****

When Nell joined the Beaumonts for dinner that night, inwardly smiling at their obvious apprehension, she gave no indication that she held any resentment towards them for her abrupt dismissal, was instead serene in her manner, conversed politely, passed compliments about the food and excused herself from parlour time again. The by now quite relaxed Beaumonts were relieved to see this absence of rancour, and congratulated themselves over coffee and port, with Marianne even taking a small glass, which delighted her husband, that they had done the right thing by Nell and themselves. They would soon learn what the words 'pre-emptive strike' meant.

****

Nell waited, lying quietly, wide awake, until she was certain the household were all asleep before she rose from the bed where she'd been resting in her clothes – boots and all. Her cat-like eyes were by this time fully adjusted to the darkness. Now, she put on her jacket and, moving with the stealth of a panther, gathered the few belongings she'd hidden creatively about the room. Finally, she slung the haversack across her body, put on her hat, placed the letter she'd written after dinner on her pillow, and glided to the door. She felt no fear or anxiety, only elation. Her next adventure was about to begin.

Nell had spent the last few days working out which of the staircase slats creaked when trodden on and now she moved smoothly down the steps, silently counting and using the banister for leverage to hop over the noisy ones. Safely at the bottom, she made a detour through the kitchen and relieved the pie safe of a cold cooked chicken and some cakes, which she wrapped in a clean cloth and stowed in her bag. Then, she unlocked the kitchen door with painstaking care, tongue clamped between her teeth, before slipping out into the night. She paused to glance up at the sky, where a gibbous moon was all but concealed behind cloud. Perfect. Just as she'd hoped for. There would be sentries, but she was confident she could get past them without being detected. Avoiding the cluster of Sioux teepees that abutted the fort would be easy. Weeks of familiarisation with every aspect of Laramie's layout meant she had a perfect map in her head and knew exactly where she was going. Taking a deep breath, she headed with the stealth of a phantom for the stables, where she knew Old Mac would be dead to the world.

****

By the time the captain and Marianne had almost finished their breakfast and Nell had still not put in an appearance, Marianne rang the bell to summon Grace. When she appeared, Marianne asked her to take a tray up to Nell.

"Otherwise cook will be in a bad mood if breakfast drags on too long."

Grace made a compliant little bob, smiling her understanding. "Yes, Ma'am. I'll see to it directly."

Marianne was enjoying her third cup of tea, her favourite beverage, when Grace rapped sharply on the door and re-entered, white-faced, eyes bulging and wringing her hands. The captain rose slowly to his feet, alarmed by the girl's agitation.

Marianne lowered her cup. "Grace? What is it?"

"Ma'am, Sir, she's gone. Nell's gone."

"Gone? Are you sure?" Marianne had also risen to her feet, cup clattering on to its saucer.

"Yes'm, all her things are gone." She fumbled in the pocket of her pinafore and drew out Nell's letter. "I found this on her pillow."

The captain reached over and took it from her trembling fingers. He recognised the envelope as being the one he'd given Nell. On the front of it was the single word: 'Bomonts'.

"Thank you, Grace. It's all right, you may go now."

"Yes, sir." The tearful girl almost ran from the room.

Marianne sat down heavily. "Gone?"

The captain picked up the fruit paring knife, and resumed his seat. He slit open the letter and removed a single folded page of paper, along with a sum of money, which he counted before laying the notes on the tablecloth. "Eighty dollars." He frowned. Then he shook open the letter and began to read.

Dear Captin and Mrs Bomont

By the time you are reeding this I will be gone. I am sory it had to be this way but I cant joyn no wagon train. I have put in $80 to pay for the horse and saddle I have taken. I hope I can return for my wagon sometime and visit my familys grave. Thank you for all the kindness you shewed me and for looking after me. Thank Mattie and Grace for me to and tell them I took the chiken and cakes. I am sory if I gave you any hartake, specialy Mrs Bomont.

Nell

Marianne sobbed into her handkerchief. "Oh, Sholto, she's just a child. I can't bear to think of her out there, all alone, surrounded by danger. Wild animals, bad people. Will you go after her?"

Her husband folded the letter and replaced it in the envelope along with the money. Crossing to the sideboard, he propped the poignant little missive against the base of an ornate oil lamp. Then he went to his wife's side, dropping on to his knees beside her and sliding an arm about her small shoulders. "I cannot, dear heart. I have despatched the men to escort the approaching train into the fort. Only a small but essential guard force remains for the moment." He kissed her cheek tenderly. "She will be well away by now. God speed her safely to some haven, but there is nothing more we can do. The best we can hope for is that she joins another train headed west."

Marianne's blue eyes brimmed with tears as she looked into her husband's. "I hope we will see her again, Sholto."

The captain stood up. "Well, my dear, I am not sure I share that sentiment. Please do not distress yourself further." He straightened his jacket. "Now, for my first duty, I am off to see Private MacDonald, to find out how the little scallywag was able to make off from under his nose with a horse and saddle. Then, I'll be questioning whomever was on sentry duty last night."

The captain strode out with a purposeful air, in his full military persona. As he whipped his hat off the cloak stand in the hallway, he called out, "Grace! Tend to your mistress!" To himself he muttered, "I do pity any wild beast or varmint who has the foolhardiness to tangle with young Nell Washburn!"

CHAPTER TWELVE

Nell hadn't actually travelled very far that first night. Everything had gone smoothly during her nocturnal flight from the fort; Old Mac had been sound asleep, snoring sonorously as anticipated; sweet-tempered Misty had remained calm and cooperative during saddling, bridling and securing of the bedroll, and while being led out of her warm stall into the cool enveloping darkness. Once Nell deemed them to be well out of earshot, she'd mounted and urged the little horse onwards at a leisurely pace, which would not endanger either of them when it was hard to see terrain ahead. As soon as they'd covered a mile or two, she dismounted, unbridled and unsaddled the horse, hobbled her for the night, and then wrapped herself in her bedroll intending to sleep until first light. Rising with the first flush of dawn, she ate one of her cakes for breakfast, washed it down with some water, saddled up, and resumed her journey. She knew her absence would be discovered in a few hours and she wanted to be well away by then. In daylight, finding her direction was easy; she simply followed the wagon tracks headed west. Even if there had been no tracks, all she had to do was follow the trail of discarded items that marked the emigrants' progress, all manner of personal effects and household items that had been abandoned to lighten wagons and ease the strain on the tired oxen – stoves, trunks, oak bureaus, tables, rocking chairs, a child's cradle, cooking utensils. Nell shook her head as she passed by these forlorn items that had once been people's treasured possessions and then smiled as she recalled the emigrants' name for the abandoned chattels: 'leverites', as in "Leave 'er right there." Switching her gaze to study the terrain ahead once more, she pondered her journey. She had already toyed with the idea that she may go to California. She'd make a decision before she reached the cut-off, or 'parting of the ways' as it was known. Before her, stretched seemingly endless red-tinted, bone-dry prairie bejewelled with wildflowers. She could see that the feed was sparse and of poor quality. Nell knew this stage of the trek west would be a tough trial for man and beast.

Now, on the evening of the first full day's travel, she sat quietly, staring into the fire and gnawing on a chicken leg, while Misty, tethered on a long rope, grazed contentedly nearby. Nell watched the horse as she chewed, certain that the animal, too, was enjoying the freedom. She wished she had some coffee, but she'd been fairly limited in what she, as one small girl on her own, had been able to bring with her. She had her bedroll, but no saddlebags. She also had no weapon, either for protection or hunting, only her knife, and some cord she could use to snare rabbits and other small game. She had her small amount of requisitioned food and a cloth bag of beef jerky, a water canteen, and some matches to simplify fire making. The latter had been pinched from the sutler's while Mr. Johnson was distracted stretching up to find some item on an elevated shelf that she'd feigned interest in examining more closely. She didn't like the idea of being a thief, especially not stealing from good people, but needs must on occasion, she told herself. She'd taken great pains not to arouse anyone's suspicions. Apart from these few items, she had the guidebook, a good rope retrieved from the wagon, a small hatchet, an extra blanket that she wrapped up in the bedroll along with her slicker, a spare flannel shirt, spare pants, a small frying pan, a tin plate, and a tin cup. She'd also retrieved her mother's housewife and a block of lye soap. You never knew when you might have to do some mending or sew back a button, and her mother had raised her to be a stickler for cleanliness. The money belt was secured tightly about her waist, next to her body. As she turned in for the night after damping down the fire, her dramatically altered circumstances and aloneness in this sprawling wilderness suddenly hit her hard, but, with typical resilience, she dismissed these negative thoughts and focused on being the arbiter of her own fate, without anyone ever telling her what to do again, and having no one to look out for but herself, a freedom in itself. *Mam, Pap, Sabrina, watch over me. Don't let no more bad stuff happen.*

In the days that followed, Nell travelled steadily west, following the Platte River and confident by now that no one was coming after her. She saw wagon trains, but she did not join them, instead riding parallel to them at a considerable distance, careful not to disclose her presence, and avoiding any scouts or outriders. If the route narrowed, she waited until the wagons had passed through the defile before she followed on. Seeing people, hearing their distant voices, raised her spirits and dispelled the sense of her isolation for a while. By now her food was running low and she was constantly hungry, fearful that the need to eat might finally propel her back into human company. Then she caught a rabbit and a prairie hen in quick succession, staving off the spectre of starvation and restoring her strength. She knew she'd need more than just meat though, if she were to maintain the good health she'd acquired under the Beaumont's care. The river provided ample water for drinking and washing; the weather remained clement, only one storm interrupting her journey with the need to seek shelter until it blew through. Nell felt that her odyssey was going well, but she remained sharply alert and cautious, shunning any slide into complacency. Wolves and hostiles were her two greatest fears. The thought of perishing alone and unmourned in the wilderness, like the poor trapper at Scotts Bluff, was terrifying, but she ruthlessly pushed it to the back of her mind. By now, she had made up her mind that she would go to

California, fabled land of gold and opportunity, bordered by the ocean.

As a rosy dawn dissolved the darkness beneath her eyelids, Nell stretched luxuriously in her bedroll and reluctantly let go of her languidly sleepy state. The moment she opened her eyes, she froze, heart surging into her mouth. There appeared to be a man wearing a jacket, with one torn shoulder peeled away, and a floppy brimmed black hat crouched over her fire with his back to her, feeding buffalo chips into the embers to revive it to flaring, crackling life. Beyond him, she could see a big bay horse, tethered near her own mount, a rifle butt protruding from a Horn Loop at the front of the saddle. Nell always slept with her knife, and now she stealthily slid it from the sheath, gripping it hard as she slithered silently out of her bedroll and got to her feet, heart thudding steadily.

"Who the hell are you, mister?"

Her uninvited guest whirled around on his haunches and then stood up slowly, eyes flicking from her face to the knife in her hand and back again. He wiped his hands on his jacket before holding them up, palms forward. "It's okay, sonny, easy now. I don't mean you no harm. I'm not armed. Well, I got a rifle over there." He gestured in the direction of his horse. "I spotted you here with the fire all ready like, just the cracklings needin' a stir up, and thought maybe we could share some breakfast." He pushed his hat back and placed his hands on his hips. "I got bacon and coffee; flour, too."

Nell cocked her head, eyes narrowing as she lowered the knife. How the hell did he know she had a craving for coffee? "Okay." She sheathed her knife, blade left protruding slightly, at the same time deciding she would not disabuse him of his assumption regarding her gender. He was young, probably no more than eighteen or nineteen, tall and lean, with shoulder length brown hair, dark eyes, and a pleasant face. "But don't get no ideas. I travel alone." She sat down and began to pull on her boots, not taking her eyes off him.

The young man grinned. "So do I. I welcome company from time to time, though." He extended a hand as she approached warily. "Name's Nick. Nick Hardy."

Nell gave his hand a perfunctory shake. "Nathan. Nathan Washburn. I gotta pee." She shot out of sight around the nearest outcrop.

Nick had well-stocked saddlebags containing all manner of treasures, including a much bigger frying pan and a battered old coffee pot. Soon, they had bacon sizzling, coffee brewing, and Nell made fresh biscuits with the flour, drizzling bacon fat over them to make them bake crisp and golden. They sat in blissful silence, chewing, swallowing, sipping. Nell sighed with happiness. This was the kind of breakfast she'd enjoyed with Pap and Sabrina, before…she ruthlessly wrenched herself away from that train of thought.

"More coffee?"

"Thanks." Nell held out her cup and Nick filled it. He returned the pot to the hearth and studied her.

"No offence, sonny, but aren't you a little young to be travelling out here all alone?"

Nell bristled. "Why? What age d'ya have to be?"

Nick shrugged. "I dunno, but maybe a bit older than you. You look somewheres between hay and grass." He saw her eyes flash and added quickly. "I ain't makin' no judgement, mind. You got spirit, that's clear. Chances are you're more'n capable of fending for yourself, whatever your age."

"I am," snapped Nell.

Nick looked unconvinced. "Was you with a wagon train?"

"I was. I can cover ground faster by myself."

"That's my thinkin', too."

Nell stood up, tossing aside the dregs from her cup. "I'd best get on my way. I got time to make up. Thanks for the victuals."

Nick stood up, too. "Where you headed?"

Nell thrust her small chin forwards. "None of your business, but since you been nice, California."

"California?" Nick's face broke into an attractive grin. "Why, I'm headed there myself." He looked away, squinting into the distance. "We could travel together. Two's better 'n one, I say." He turned his head to look squarely into her eyes, and Nell felt something flip over in the pit of her stomach.

"How'd I know I can trust you? Why, you could bushwhack me an' cut my throat while I'm sleepin' an' take all my worldly goods, though I ain't got much," she added hastily, conscious of the money belt plastered to her body under her shirt.

Nick drew himself up to full height, looking decidedly indignant. "Why, if you recall, you was in the land of nod when I got here, an' I coulda bushwhacked you then, but I didn't, did I?"

"Maybe you're just bidin' your time."

"How'd I know you won't bushwhack me?"

"You're three times my size." Nell folded her arms, head cocked to one side, implying 'your move'.

The young man regarded her seriously for a moment, chewing his lip, and then glanced around as if he were looking for something or someone to vouch for him. Then, drawing himself up to full height, he pointed to his dozing mount. "Ask my horse," he instructed loftily. "He'll tell you I'm a fine, Christian man, as honest as they come. His name's Beauregarde, Beau for short."

Nell looked over at the large, obviously well cared for animal, head drooping sleepily in the early morning sunshine. Then she burst out laughing, really laughed, for the first time in a long while. The young man had made his point. Sometimes you just had to trust.

And this young man had a firearm. And coffee. Truth be told, she felt deeply relieved to have some company on her journey.

Nell took a deep breath. "Good enough. I'll ride with you, but" – she thrust a small forefinger at him – "I'll be watchin' you like a hawk. I hope you know where we're goin', 'cos I got no idea, 'ceptin' it's west of here."

Nick grinned. "Well, south-west, anyways. I'll get you there safe an' sound. You can count on it. 'Sides, I got me a map. Well, more of a chart. Kind of a drawin'." He grinned sheepishly, rubbing his jaw.

Nell kicked dirt on to the dying fire. "Best we get movin' then." She chuckled. "Looks like we'll be lost out here together, like the Israelites I learned about in Sunday school."

Nick pushed back his hat and scratched his head. "Well, not for forty years, I hope."

****

In the days that followed, Nell and Nick settled into a comfortable routine, feeling increasingly at ease in each other's company. When Nell didn't feel like talking, Nick was quiet. When she felt the urgency to distract herself from black thoughts, he chatted away amiably and, best of all, could make her laugh, which was like pouring a healing balm into her soul. Even when he called her 'Nathan' it felt good rather than jarring with her, as if Pap was somehow still around. What pleased Nell more than anything was

183

that Nick didn't probe her about her life before they'd met on the trail. She reciprocated, respecting his reticence about his own background. It was as if they had started out afresh together from the moment they'd clapped eyes on each other, and that seemed to suit them both fine. Sometimes, when he appeared lost in a reverie that was almost trance-like, unaware she was watching him closely, Nell caught glimpses in Nick's far away eyes of the kind of hurt only life's random cruelty can inflict. She wondered if he detected the same in her, and thought they must both be like wounded birds: the rest of the flock, whole in body and spirit, had moved on, leaving the broken-winged ones, unable to put their pain into words, to provide unexpressed comfort for each other and survive as best they could.

After they left the North Platte, there was a stretch of twenty miles or so of dry, stunted sage and little water, apart from alkaline ponds that the guidebook warned were poisonous for man and beast alike. The stinking carcases and scattered bones of dead draught animals in the vicinity bore witness to the truth of that caution. They nursed the horses along with a water skin Nick had filled, rationing themselves from their own canteens. Nick had a small sack of grain as well and always included Misty at feed time, for which Nell expressed her thanks. When they reached Willow Spring they were finally able to water the horses properly, allow them some grazing time, and take much-needed refreshment themselves before travelling on.

One hot day, near noon, after Nick had glanced over at a drooping Nell more than once, he suggested they take a break to rest themselves and the horses at a shady spot they came across beside an attractive spring some distance from the trail, to which suggestion a woozy Nell agreed willingly, sliding sweaty and tired from the saddle. She felt decidedly off colour and didn't really know why – until Nick spoke softly..

"Nathan? Did you hurt yourself?"

Nell turned around, puzzled at the way Nick had chosen to express concern for her obvious malaise. "No, not hurtin'. I just feel…"

"Nathan, you have blood on your britches."

Nell froze, sliding a hand behind her back to feel the giveaway sticky patch on the seat of her dungarees. A quick inspection of her reddened fingertips confirmed Nick's observation. They stood motionless, staring at each other, and then Nell began to back away a little. "Don't you get no ideas, mister!" she hissed.

Nick raised his arms and then let them drop, the corners of his mouth curling up in a little smile. "I ain't dumb, missie. I got four sisters. Hell, I know'd you was a girl straight off. I just humoured you, is all, since I could see you were tryin' to pass for a boy an' I didn't want to scare you none." He chuckled. "Little hellcat waving an ole apple peeler at me." As Nell glared at him, Nick put his hands on his hips, leaning forwards. "Gonna tell me your real name?"

****

Clad in her shirt, the lower half of her body girded in a blanket, Nell sat sipping a cup of cold spring water while her partially laundered dungarees dried in the sun on a nearby rock. Nick had insisted on spot-washing out the stain himself in a nearby stream, and Nell had only put up a feeble protest. What was one more humiliation, after all? She'd become blasé about her periods because they seemed to have disappeared after the massacre and her subsequent illness. That they'd returned, she assumed, was a positive sign that her body, at least, was healing. Nick dropped down beside her, handing her one of two cold split biscuits filled with bacon, which Nell accepted with murmured thanks, and they ate in silence.

Eventually Nell cleared her throat. "Most folks take me for a boy 'cos of my hair, an' havin' no femy-nine figure to speak of."

Nick swallowed a mouthful and wiped his mouth with the back of a hand. "Well, those folks must be a bit dim. You have pretty hair, beautiful eyes, and no wisp of fuzz on your cheeks. As for your figure, it's just buddin' nicely. I hope I ain't bein' too personal here."

This was stated with such matter-of-factness that Nell stared at Nick for a long moment before she spoke again. "My name's Nell.

186

Ma and Pap called me Ellen, but I go by Nell. I'm fifteen, comin' up sixteen."

"That's a pretty name. I'm Nicholas, but I go by Nick. I'm nineteen, just turned."

"Well, how do you do, Nick?"

"Fine and dandy. How do you do, Nell?"

They both laughed as they pumped each other's hand with exaggerated formality.

"I guess we're both fully acquainted now," said Nell.

"Yup. And I want you to know one thing, Nell. I'm gonna take care of you, as long as we're together."

"No more'n I'll take care of you. I ain't no delicate flower."

Nick grinned. "I already know that."

Nell felt the familiar little squirm in her tummy as she looked into Nick's soft brown eyes. He abruptly jumped up, pulling his hat down firmly by the front brim, manner businesslike.

"Those pants oughta be dry. Time we was movin' on." He stretched an arm towards Nell, she gripped it without hesitation, and Nick pulled her to her feet.

"You go and sort yourself out while I see to the horses."

As they headed off on different tangents, Nell called, "Tonight, after supper, you gimme that jacket an' I'll mend it for you."

Nick turned, smiled, and touched the brim of his hat.

****

Now that the question of Nell's gender had been satisfactorily resolved, the time seemed right to reveal other truths to each other. It was Nell who probed first. While Nick set up camp, Nell mended his coat. Then they had enjoyed a fine meal of flatbread, bacon, and beans, cooked by Nick, since he considered Nell poorly, and were sitting contentedly gazing into the crackling fire while they sipped their coffee. Nell was impressed by Nick's coffee making skills, not to mention his culinary expertise. She studied him thoughtfully.

"You said you had four sisters."

Nick tossed some buffalo chips on to the fire. "Yes, all older than me, and two brothers younger. We grew up on a farm in Missouri, near Springfield. I never really took to farming, and my father was pretty hard on his sons. The girls all married and moved away, so it was just us boys left behind to do the work. He was hard on Ma, too, and she went downhill after the girls left, so I took over most of the household chores, too, like cookin' our meals, but Pa made no allowance for that. Nothin' ever pleased him; he picked fault with everything and worked us to death, never gave us anything an' you sure felt the lashes from his hickory stick, or the blows from his fists, if you came up short. I felt sorry for little Joey; he was but ten years old, an' skinny as all hell." He grinned. "You kinda reminded me of him first time I saw you." The grin vanished under Nell's flinty gaze, and he quickly resumed his story. "Even in the winter, Pa was always on to us – 'coat up and go an' do this, coat up and go an' do that.' " Nick sighed. "I stuck it out 'til ma died of the wasting, and then I left. I crossed at St Jo and here I am. I don't never want to be a farmer." He straightened up, breaking into his attractive grin. "I want to be a drover. That's how I aim to get to California, earning me some money on the way. Have me an adventure afore I settle down somewheres."

Nell absorbed all this without comment. Then Nick said, "What's your story, Nell? How'd you end up out here all alone, and you just a slip of a girl?"

"I ain't no slip of anything. I'm comin' up sixteen, like I said," snapped Nell defensively. Then her face softened. She thrust her coffee cup towards him. "Top me up an' I'll tell you the whole sorry tale."

"Actually," said Nick, rising stiffly to his feet, stretching limbs, "I can do better 'n that." He gestured towards his saddlebags. "I got some whiskey in there."

As he was on his knees rootling about amongst his possessions, Nell said, "What else you got stowed away in those bags? You keep fetchin' things out like you got your own little treasure trove squirreled away. I 'spect to see you pull out an ole armchair for dozin' by the fire." She chuckled. Nick swung around holding up the flat bottle with a triumphant whoop.

"Here she is! Got her at Fort Kearney."

Nell pursed her lips. Whiskey revived memories of her father she'd prefer to forget, but Nick's enthusiasm was contagious.

"You okay with it?" Nick was typically sensitive to her hesitation.

Nell grinned, waving a hand. "Sure, why not. Keep out the chill if nothin' else."

When they each had a fresh cup of coffee fortified with a generous dollop of whiskey, Nick settled himself comfortably beside the fire and looked at Nell expectantly. Following a brief splutter as the cheap raw whiskey set fire to her alcoholically virginal throat, and once Nick's responding chuckles had died away, Nell commenced her story. She spoke softly, evenly, her control never once lapsing. She told it as if it were someone else's story and her role was merely that of detached raconteur. When she finished, she held out her cup. "Gimme another splash of that whiskey, if you can spare it. The feelin' it makes is better than the taste, that's for sure."

Nick filled her cup by about a third. "Better go a bit easy, seein' as how you ain't used to it." Then he sat down beside her. Didn't say anything. Didn't touch her. Just sat with her as they watched the fire die down together, until it was just a small nest of glowing embers, like a pulsing open wound in the blackness of the night.

That night, Nell enjoyed a leaden, dream free sleep such as she'd not experienced in a long while. The addictive demons stood off, watching her sulkily before they drifted away.

CHAPTER THIRTEEN

In the days that followed, Nick and Nell travelled steadily west, passing Independence Rock, Split Rock with its distinctive gun-sight cleft, traversing broad South Pass, crossing the continental divide into Oregon country, and entering the Pacific watershed. By the time they neared the turn south for Fort Bridger, about eighteen miles on from South Pass they were seasoned travelling companions who had established a firm bond. Sometimes food had been scarce, but they'd managed to keep themselves adequately fed. Nick, who was something of an erratic shot, still managed to bowl some small game with his rifle, and they'd even caught trout in the Sweetwater. Increasingly, they came across the carcasses of Oregon emigrants' dead livestock which had succumbed to the rigours of the long journey, or the remnants of a buffalo or antelope that hunters had shot, and, if they got there before the wolves, there was always good pickings to be had if the meat wasn't rotten. Their cooking utensils were limited and Nell missed her camp oven and tin kitchen badly, but either she or Nick always managed to cook up something tasty to fill their hungry bellies, often foraging native plants like prairie turnips, wild onions, or lambs' quarters to supplement the meal and provide some vegetable content. Their supplies of basics were low or had run out altogether, so they were counting on being able to re-stock at the fort. Nell had no idea whether Nick had any money, and she hadn't told him about her own stash of dollars, not because she didn't trust him by now. It just hadn't ever come up. As frequently happened, it turned out they'd both been thinking the same thing.

After supper, Nell sat close to the fire reading her dog-eared little guidebook in the flickering light it cast, frowning with concentration.

"Nick, I reckon we'll reach the fort tomorrow, noon, mebbe. We gotta take the ferry over the Green River first. That'll cost us a couple of dollars, I guess."

Nick stirred, clearing his throat. "All righty. Do we have a plan?"

Nell looked up sharply. "A plan?" With those two words, Nick had just brutally yanked out a memory from her past, from those long ago days, or so it seemed, when she had tried to get Pap motivated every morning to deal with the chores waiting to be seen to on the farm. C'mon, Pap, we'll make a plan.

Nick cleared his throat again. "Well, remember I said that's when we turn south west, leave the Oregon Trail an' head to California. If you still want to, that is." The soft brown eyes regarded her seriously.

"Course I still want to. I told you, I ain't never goin' to Oregon."

"Just checkin'. I ain't goin' to railroad you into anything, is all."

Nell raised one eyebrow and surveyed him from under lowered lids, her faint smile sardonic. "Nick Hardy, ain't no one on this Earth can railroad Nell Washburn, and that's God's own truth."

Nick lay down, wiggled his shoulders into a comfortable position, crossed his boots at the ankles, and placed his hat over his face. "Hell, I already know that, little wildcat," he muttered. "Hey!"

Nell had bounced the guidebook off his precious hat. As she retrieved it, Nick raised himself on an elbow and said, "Soon's we reach the fort, you're a boy again, okay?"

"Okay." His protectiveness made her feel warm all over.

****

Fort Bridger was a bit of a letdown, as it turned out, nothing more than a crude collection of rough-hewn log buildings, although the Mormons who were currently in charge of both the fort, having chased off Jim Bridger, and the Green River ferries, had built a stone palisade around it and added a few stone buildings by way of improvement. Nell and Nick were pleased to be given a place indoors to bed down and livery for their horses, but, just the same, they decided they would replenish their supplies and not dally. This was their point of parting from the Oregon Trail to head south into

Utah territory and on to California. It turned out that Nick did have some money after all and he insisted on using it to buy what they needed. He explained to Nell that he'd earned it over months of hiring himself out to farming neighbours who were short on manpower, and had squirreled the money away carefully for his escape, letting his father have just enough to satisfy him.

"Lord, it was backbreaking," he explained to Nell, "rushing through my own chores and then startin' in on the work others gave me; hardly any sleep, up at dawn an' workin' 'til after dark most days so's I didn't know where I was half the time, but I had a goal an' I stuck to it."

"No wonder you're so danged skinny," said Nell, unable to keep the note of admiration out of her voice. "Not so much as a shiver of spare on you."

The prices the Mormons were asking for goods were high, but Nell stood up to them and haggled fiercely 'til she obtained the bargain she wanted. Nick watched her in action with a new respect. She was a good partner, all right. No alcohol of course, he surmised ruefully, not with the Mormons in charge. One thing of interest he did learn was that a very unusual man had passed through the fort recently, creating quite a sensation. Everybody was still talking about him, it seemed. He was an Italian aristocrat and he was driving a herd of three thousand cattle from St Louis to San Francisco.

"The oddest little dandy you ever saw," said the wizened old fur trapper yarning with Nick and Nell in the dingy little dining room where they'd treated themselves to a bought supper, "all decked out in fancy clothes and a silk waistcoat, big, twirly moustaches with waxed tips, and the funniest way of talkin', always wavin' his arms around." He shook his head, chuckling, as he sucked his pipe tobacco to a ruby intensity. "Antonio somebody, an Eyetalian count, I believe. Even had his own valetty."

"How long ago did they pass through?" asked Nick, his excitement obvious.

The trapper scratched his head. "Mebbe two, three days ago? They aimed to follow the Mormon Trail to Salt Lake, so you could mebbe catch them thar. The Eyetalian fella wants to meet Brigham Young. Seems he's real keen to know more about their havin' lotsa wives." The old man grimaced. "Can't think why any man would want more 'n one wife."

Nick turned to Nell, eyes aglow. "We could try and catch them up, join the drive. What do you think?"

Nell grinned. "I'm up fer it, if you are."

Nick grinned back. "We'll leave early tomorrow morning."

The old fur trapper removed his pipe, eyes crinkling up with mirth. "Young 'n loco," he said.

Before they left Fort Bridger, Nell bought herself some good saddlebags as well as a buffalo hide blanket for each of them to supplement their bedrolls. Nick was so insistently and repeatedly grateful that an exasperated Nell eventually told him to please shut-up.

****

The sun was barely up when Nick and Nell rode out of Fort Bridger the following morning, heading southwest into Utah territory. The cattle drive had a two-day start on them, but they would also be moving slowly to ensure the cattle didn't lose precious condition, covering no more than ten miles a day, and if Nell and Nick made good progress they were confident they could easily catch up to them. It was roughly one hundred miles to Salt Lake. Now they had finally left the westward trail at 'the parting of the ways' to follow the Mormon Trail instead, and Nell felt a sense of relief that she was at last steered away from the hated Oregon, that she no longer faced the prospect of scrabbling a living from the land again. She and Nick were definitely united on that score.

"Is the lake really salty?" Nell asked out of the blue.

Nick shrugged. "I dunno. I guess it must be if they call it that." He grinned. "We'll have to take us a taste."

The trail was well defined and the scenery, on a clear summer's morning, breathtaking. They could see unmistakeable signs of men and cattle having recently passed this way so knew they were bound to overtake them before long. The only niggling doubt for both of them was eventually expressed by Nell.

"What will we do if this Eyetalian count fellow won't hire us on? I don't know nothin' 'bout cattle driving. Do you?"

Nick pursed his lips. "Not really, 'cept for some stuff I read. But I figure this Eyetalian didn't know a whole lot either, so he might cut us some slack if we promise to work hard. We're both good riders, that has to count for somethin'."

Nell nodded. "It's best they don't know I'm a girl. I'll be Nathan again."

Nick reined in his horse, Nell followed, and they sat their mounts eyeballing each other. "I was goin' to talk to you 'bout that. I reckon it's best if we pass you off as a boy again. You okay with that?"

Nell rolled her eyes. Nick could be a bit slow on the uptake at times. "I just said, didn't I?" She frowned. "I better start practisin'. You had me figured out, didn't you?"

"Not all men got four older sisters. Besides, you kinda handed me a giveaway."

Nell reined in, scowling at him. "Don't go bringin' that up. I got that under control." She sniffed. "Anyways, you can gimme some mas-coo-line pointers, startin' after supper. I gotta swagger about like I own the place, right? Break wind, spit, an' generally be ornery."

Nick grinned. "Okay. An' I'll trim a little bit of your hair so's I can make a few whiskers to stick on your face, so's you look like you're verging on manhood. You okay with that?"

"Sure. Good thinking."

They urged their horses onwards.

After a bit, Nell said, "What's our plan if the Eyetalian won't hire us?"

Nick, whom she was following through a narrow defile with deep wagon ruts at this point, half turned in the saddle. "I guess we'll carry on to California." He chuckled. "Mebbe we'll find us some gold."

Nell snorted. "If that means grubbin' about in the dirt you can forget it. I ain't never doin' that again!"

Nick laughed. "Me neither."

They were quiet as the horses picked their way through the last of the rough terrain before emerging on to flat, grassy land, enabling them to ride alongside each other again.

"I fancy openin' a little business," said Nell, "dry goods, mebbe. Household stuff on the side."

Nick looked at her, digesting this disclosure. "Well, that sounds right promising. I could help with the hard work, humpin' the heavy stuff an' the likes. That's if you want…" his voice trailed off and he looked away.

Nell looked at him sideways, taken by surprise at the sudden rush of warmth and affection she felt towards the young man who'd become her comfortable, trusted travelling companion. "Why, that's right nice of you. There you go; we got us a plan."

Nick flashed her a dazzling smile. Nell made a clucking noise with her tongue and the horses stretched out across the flat, Nell in the lead.

****

That night as they sat contentedly by the campfire after supper, sipping hot coffee, Nell told a riveted Nick the story of the ill-fated Donner Party of 1846 who had made a bad decision to break with their wagon train after Fort Bridger and take what was known as the Hastings cut-off as a means of reaching California sooner. In fact, not only was the shortcut longer, but they'd also ended up trapped in the Sierra Nevada Mountains over winter and had to resort to cannibalism to stay alive. Almost half the party had perished by the time they were rescued.

When Nell finished the gruesome tale, Nick shook his head slowly. "That's the saddest thing I ever heard. I don't think I could eat another human, no matter how hungry I was."

"Nobody knows what they'll do until they're pushed hard enough. Hunger's a terrible thing."

Nick nodded. "I guess." He sat up stiffly. "Did…did they eat their own kin?"

"S'far as I know they labelled the chunks of flesh so's you could skip your kin."

Nick grimaced. "Good lord, Nell, where'd you get this story from?"

"I heard the folks in my train talking 'bout it one night when I joined them after supper. That's the first I knew of it."

"Do you think it's true?"

"Oh, it's true, sure 'nuff. One of the fellas had a newspaper cutting telling all 'bout it. He let me read it."

As they settled down to sleep in their bedrolls, Nick's plaintive little whine made Nell laugh.

"I ain't never goin' to sleep, now. I'm jus' goin' to have the worst bad dreams 'bout eatin' folks."

Nell yawned unrestrainedly, squirming down into her blanket. "In the morning you can tell me how they tasted."

"Arghhhh!"

"They even ate the brains, apparently, an' the, er, personal bits n' pieces."

"Arghhhh!"

****

They caught up to the cattle drive the following day, around noon. The men were taking their break, seated around the supply wagon, hungrily devouring their victuals, the smell of which made both Nick and Nell salivate. Not far away, they could see a heaving mass of cattle and horses grazing quietly, enjoying their own noon browsing. The drovers regarded the new arrivals with indifference, squinting at them impassively as they chewed, but the cook came forward, a huge, barrel-chested man sporting a long grubby apron tied at the front across a vast expanse of belly. He had a head of wild, curly red hair, a lush moustache to match, and looked quite intimidating as he stood feet apart, eyeing Nick and Nell, a ladle clutched in one meaty hand, the other resting on his hip.

"Good day to ye. What can ah do for ye?" His accent was broad Scots.

Nick and Nell dismounted, leading their horses forwards, but Nell hung back a little, leaving the introductions to Nick, who respectfully removed his hat.

"Howdy, sir. I'm Nick Hardy and this is my friend, Nathan Washburn. We've a mind to sign on for the drive."

The cook nodded. "Well, that's no up tae me, laddie, vital as ah am tae this insane enterprise." He jerked his head to his left. "The count and the trail boss are doon by yon crick. Ye'd best make yer way over there and parley with them."

The drovers continued eating in silence. The cook turned back to his wagon. Nick thanked him, glanced over at Nell, who shrugged helplessly, and then they led their horses down a gentle slope in the direction the Scotsman had indicated. After tethering the horses, they pushed their way through some brush to emerge on to a green sward that bordered a small stream, where a strange sight confronted them. Under an awning, apparently erected for shade, a man lay on his back close to the stream, trouser legs of a deep blue shade rolled up to his knees, and his feet immersed in the gently flowing water. Beside him on the ground lay a white hat sporting a large brown feather and, standing erect, a pair of crimson leather boots with grey stockings draped across their tops. The awning was decorated with stripes of brilliant green, white, and red – the colours of Italian nationalism. A man squatted on his haunches alongside the supine gentleman, and Nick and Nell could hear the murmur of their conversation. The Eyetalian and his trail boss. Standing to one side of the awning was a neatly dressed man with a towel draped over one arm. The 'valetty' – valet.

Nick leaned over and whispered to Nell, "I think that's what you call a colourful character."

Nell's responding burst of spontaneous laughter that escaped before she could clap a hand over her mouth saw the Italian abruptly sit up, looking curiously over his shoulder, while the other man unfolded himself and rose slowly to his feet to confront their visitors.

"And who the hell might you be?" he growled, eyes narrowing.

Nick cleared his throat, while Nell tried hard to look serious after her gaffe. "Beggin' your pardons for the interruption, sirs. The cook sent us this way to ask about joinin' the cattle drive. I'm Nick Hardy and this here's my friend, Nathan Washburn."

The tall, unfriendly looking man opened his mouth to reply, but his companion beat him to it, clambering to his feet and advancing on Nell and Nick with a warm smile and outstretched hand. He was slim, of medium height with rippling black shoulder length hair brushed back from his forehead, dark eyes, and neatly trimmed beard and moustache, waxed and curling at the ends, just as the old codger at Fort Bridger had described him. He was indeed wearing a beautiful pale blue silk waistcoat over his white shirt. "Neek and Nathan, I am pleased to make your acquaintance," he said in fluent English made all the more charming by his Italian accent. "I am Count Stefano Cremonisi and thees ees my trail boss, Meester Wrenn Cheney." He shook hands vigorously with them both before turning to Cheney, who made no move to greet them but was still glaring. "Thees ees most fortuitous, ees eet not?"

"Possibly," conceded Cheney, crossing his arms, and relaxing his frown a little. He took a step forwards. "Either of you had experience droving?"

"No, not really, but we're both used to handlin' stock and we both ride well." Nick fingered the brim of his hat nervously. "We're real keen to learn."

Cheney snorted. "We don't need shavetails and sappy children. We need experienced men." He cast a disapproving eye over them both, his hostile gaze lingering on Nell. "Don't look like you even got any rig."

"Wrenn, Wrenn, that ees not too important for what I have een mind." The count smiled kindly at the two youngsters, who were looking rather crestfallen at this stage. "One of our wranglers, Weelliam, just died of pneumonia, a good boy so a very sad loss. Neek, if you are good weeth horses you could do thees job. We have many horses, seence the riders must change their mounts three times a day. Henry has been doing thees job since Weeliam died, and he will help you learn." He turned his soft brown eyes on Nell. "You are very young, but I can use you. Can you cook?"

Nell nodded. "Been cookin' all my life."

"*Va bene*! Angus, our cookie, needs an assistant. He was, how you say, exhausted caring for our seek amico and trying to feed everyone as well. I theenk you weel do very well. Twenty-five dollars a month each." He clasped his hands in front of him, beaming benevolently. "What do you say?"

Nick looked at Nell. She shrugged. Nick addressed the count. "Can we jus' have a moment to chew this over?"

"Of course!" The count threw his arms into the air in a conciliatory gesture. "Talk eet over and tell me what you decide." Sweeping a hand through his luxuriant hair, he flounced off back to the stream, where his valet handed him the towel. The count sat down and began to dry his feet and lower legs vigorously. Cheney remained scowling at his prospective employees.

"Don't take all day about it," he rumbled. "We're moving out." He strode past them, managing to clip Nick's shoulder as he did so, and disappeared into the brush.

"What do you think?" asked Nick softly, eyeing Nell earnestly. "Twenty-five dollars! I ain't never earned twenty-five dollars! I can do the wranglin', takin' care of the spare horses, no sweat, an' we can get us some proper rig in Salt Lake."

Seeing that Nick had his heart set on this venture, viewing it as an essential step towards becoming a fully fledged drover, Nell nodded, despite her misgivings. "Truth to tell, I'm kinda relieved to be cook's assistant. Less chance of my bein' found out, an' I'll be better at that than drivin' cows, I reckon – or wranglin' horses."

Nick grinned. "Yep, you'll be fine. The cook seemed okay, s'far as I can tell. This way we go to Californy with money in our pockets." He glanced towards the brush. "Think we both need to stay clear of that trail boss, though. Hated us on sight, for some reason."

"Why'd you 'spose that is?"

Nick looked thoughtful. "Some folks just take agin you, is all. Ain't no rhyme nor reason to it."

Nell nodded. "Yessiree. Well, let's go tell the count."

CHAPTER FOURTEEN

"Mustard plaster, laddie. Ah thought that would set the puir wee gomeril tae rights, but it did nae guid in the end." Angus shook his head sadly. "Looking after puir wee Willy and trying tae keep yon wolves fed, it was hard."

Nell nodded. "Woulda been."

They were perched on campstools near the fire, busily peeling potatoes for the drovers' supper, Angus grunting his approval when 'Nathan' produced wafer thin peelings that did not waste any flesh. They had been together for a week now, the big Scotsman and the disguised girl, and if Angus had suspected anything, he had certainly not let on. They had instantly gelled, in fact, and Angus had frequently expressed his appreciation for Nell's willingness to work hard as well as her skills in the culinary department, which he had been sceptical about to begin with, especially since he considered her puny – the word he used, 'peelie-wally', was unknown to Nell, but she'd grasped his meaning as he ran a dubious eye over her. Her initiation test had been to make an apple pie, and Angus had waxed euphoric over the result, moustache working rhythmically as he chewed.

"Mam's recipe," Nell explained proudly. "She liked to use fresh apples in autumn, but she kept strings of dried apple rings by the stove to make the pie during winter." She closed her eyes. "I can see those apples hangin' there, like big necklets. She always looped them round n' round." She shook her head, smiling at the memory.

Angus swallowed another mouthful of the pie and smacked his lips. "The pastry is verra, verra guid, and ah do like the way ye made the wee leaves tae garnish the top, curling over so coddy like. Himself will be verra happy with such goodly fare. Well done, laddie. Guid gear comes in sma' bulk, mo charaid. Ye and me will rub along grand."

Nell had also proved a fast learner of the trail routine, just getting on with the job and ignoring the taunts and teasing from the men, both as the youngest hand and newcomer. (They referred to her as 'the Mary,' a derogatory term for a trail cook's assistant, akin to the cabin boy jokes in the Navy.) Those jibes were growing more infrequent, too, as big Angus made it clear he disapproved, ('Haud yer wheesht, numpties, or ye'll go hungry!') and nobody wanted to run foul of cookie, thus jeopardising their victuals. Angus was a gifted cook, considered worth his weight in gold, and he was shown the appropriate respect as a result. Not only was he skilled in the kitchen, but for a trail cook he was also remarkably even tempered, despite his forbidding appearance, reinforced by his fierce blue eyes and fiery red hair.

At first, Nell had found it really difficult to understand Angus, both his accent as well as some of his more obscure Caledonian expressions, or if he lapsed into dialect under duress, but she was becoming attuned to him by this time and there wasn't much she missed any longer. She'd given him a brief, selective version of her background, only because he'd asked, and had been taken aback to see him wipe away a tear when she revealed her orphan status. Big and burly the man was, but a softie at heart, Nell sensed. For his part, Angus, whose full name was Angus Duncan Macpherson, revealed that he had emigrated to America five years previously, working his passage as a ship's cook, and had been roaming ever since. A chance encounter with the count in Illinois, where he'd been cooking in a hotel, saw him accept the Italian's offer to join him on his already legendary cattle drive, a decision he had not regretted: the cook's salary was second only to the trail boss's. He held the count in high esteem, both as a friend and as an employer. "Oh, aye, they all laughed at him, said he'd come tae grief, but he's got us this far, laddie. He's one o' the best. This'll give me a wee stake, ye ken? Ah always wanted tae go tae California. Ah might even pan fer a wee bit o' gold tae add t' the pot."

Nell had quickly picked up on the men's affection for the count (or 'Himself', as Angus called him) and she shared it. Although a foreigner, as well as a wealthy and educated aristocrat, he was no pampered, supercilious fop. His English was excellent and he was relaxed and informal with the men without over-fraternising, concerned with their welfare and surprisingly tough when he needed to be, never shy of mucking in and doing his share of the work, incongruous though he may look in his glamorous clothes. His valet, Sandro, also Italian, attended to his comforts, for example washing his clothes, seeing to his personal grooming, and erecting his private tent every night, but Stefano always ate supper with the men and genuinely enjoyed their company. A superb horseman, he seemed to revel in his role as fellow drover, respectfully leaving the practicalities of the marathon trip he had embarked on to his foreman, and listening carefully to advice. For these reasons, the drive hummed along with minimal problems or friction. The fact that Angus provided great grub certainly helped. The count had chosen him wisely.

Nick had also taken his share of teasing from the drovers, but his easygoing nature and affability ensured his acceptance and he was truly enjoying the experience. He had promised Nell he'd keep an eye on Misty for her, as she'd joined the remuda, Nell's transport now being the supply wagon. Nell visited with the little horse when she could, thankful for Nick's vigilance. He and Nell mainly caught up in the evenings and always looked forward to sharing recounts of their day with each other, talking about their plans for a shared future, or more often than not just sitting in companionable silence. One of the drovers, a wiry little man called Huck, was a wonderful guitarist and harmonica player with a fine singing voice as well, and Nell never tired of listening to him as everyone rested around the campfire at night, the men smoking, relaxing, reflecting on the lyrics of songs about love, loss, homesickness and dreams, under a sky lit with a feverish jostle of stars. Sometimes the count was persuaded to sing an Italian song or two, or tell stories about his life growing up in Sardinia, which everyone enjoyed. Nell decided she had to learn Italian, which the count frequently lapsed into, this beautiful language so suited to emotion and romance. At moments like that, letting her soul float free with the music, or listening to the various shared tales, she felt most at peace.

The only fly in the ointment – wasn't there always one – Nell reflected wryly, remembering cantankerous O'Farrell in the wagon train, was the flinty-eyed trail boss, Cheney. He remained cold and unfriendly and she'd often catch him looking at her, something about him, about the expression in his eyes, making her flesh crawl. She was glad she had Nick and Angus – and the count, who made clear his fondness for her, calling her "piccolo chef", as opposed to "grande chef" (Angus).

Nell made a conscious effort to keep out of Cheney's way. Actually, she kept out of everybody's way except for Nick and her immediate boss. She and Angus were always so busy in their own little ménage a deux that this was relatively easy. Nell kept her hat pulled down over her face, deepened her voice when she spoke, and through her surreptitious observations of the other men, made a conscious effort to emulate male mannerisms and body language. Think like a boy, act like a boy became her internal mantra as she went about her chores. With some variations, life on the trail followed the same pattern every day.

Nell and Angus were always the first to go to bed and the first to rise, Angus about an hour before Nell, around 3 a.m., moving about with silent stealth for such a big man. First, he stoked up the fire before he ground coffee beans in the grinder mounted on the pantry box and got the coffee brewing with water from the barrel attached to one side of the wagon. The coffee had to be thick and 'strong enough tae float a horseshoe' to earn the hands' approval. This first precious cup of the day was what got them sharply awake and energised every morning. Angus added eggshell to the pot to help with 'settling' the grounds.

Once the coffee was brewing, Angus would gently shake Nell awake and she got to work on the sourdough biscuits while he sliced sowbelly from a flitch and fried it up with sliced potatoes. Angus liked to sleep with the crock containing his sourdough starter to keep it 'warm 'n raddy', which amused Nell no end. She pinched off a sticky glob to add to the flour and ensure the biscuits rose well. She knew that being trusted to make biscuits was a huge compliment, since the drovers were very particular about this item of their daily fare. They praised her flapjacks as well, but Angus always insisted on making the bread himself. He favoured sourdough because it was traditional and the drovers preferred the texture, but Nell considered 'quick bread' using saleratus a much easier option in terms of work.

A hinged platform with foldout legs attached to the rear of the supply wagon (Angus called it 'the mess wagon') provided their shared work surface. One of Nell's jobs was to keep it scrubbed clean. She worked on one side while Angus worked on the other. They spoke little as they went about their respective tasks, moving around each other with practiced ease, their routine by now thoroughly rehearsed.

Then it was time to rouse the young men as the sun came up, and Angus liked to do this by banging a large metal spoon on a pot lid while chanting, "The bacon is fryin', the coffee is hot. Do ye want it or do ye not?" This familiar ditty saw the men crawling silently and sleepily out of their blankets and by the time they'd performed their toilet and packed away bedrolls, breakfast was ready to serve. The hands queued in an orderly fashion as Angus and Nell dispensed the food, then found a comfortable spot to squat while they devoured their breakfast and drank their coffee. Using any part of the supply wagon as a table to rest food on was a strict taboo. Once, they'd eaten, they dropped their plates, cups and utensils into the 'wrecker', the prepared wash tub full of hot water, saddled their horses picketed nearby, and headed off to the herd. Sandro collected the count's breakfast at some point in this schedule and delivered it to him in his tent. Nell and Angus ate their own breakfasts in the company of whichever two men had done last nightwatch duty with the cattle before washing up all the pots and pans, packing everything away, hitching up the mules, and heading out on the trail to beat the herd and the drovers to the noon stop. A smaller 'hoodlum' single axle wagon, in which were stowed the drover's packs containing personal belongings, bedrolls, tools, ropes etc, along with the count's tent and accessories, was attached as a trailer to the larger supply wagon. Angus had given Nell and Nick spare gunnysacks for their own personal items, and Nell's saddle and bridle were stored in the wagon, too. As they travelled, Nell would leap down from time to time and gather wood or chips they spotted, tossing them into the possum belly, a rawhide pocket fastened to the wagon's belly. Then it was off again, racing to their next stop. Since they were always well out in front of the herd and riders, Angus carried a rifle slung inside the wagon as protection against any 'marauders', as he called them. Nell assumed he meant hostiles or rustlers.

Nell seldom found time for more than a few words with Nick during the morning ritual, but they always managed to wish each other well for the day, even so. Whenever Cheney appeared, Nell felt herself tense, and she studiously avoided eye contact with him. She told herself she was afraid of nothing. But for some reason that she couldn't put into words she was afraid of this man.

Life became pretty miserable when it rained. Hats pulled well down, wearing their slickers, Nell and Angus battled their way to the next campsite to prepare hot food for the equally soaked and famished hands. The supply wagon was fitted with a large waterproofed tarpaulin that could be rolled out and propped overhead to cover the preparation bench, providing some shelter for the cooks, while getting the fire going in driving rain was quite a challenge. Angus's word for this sort of weather was 'dreich'. The drovers had their own concerns, fearing a dreaded stampede if the storm brought lightning and thunder as well. The cattle were easily spooked and if they did stampede, riding them down to head them off and turn the leaders into a circle that broke their charge was a dangerous business. Everyone relaxed once the storm had passed, while the generous-spirited Angus helped the men dry wet gear once they stopped for the evening. Angus was much more than just the cook, Nell realised early on. He was medic, vet, barber, banker, letter writer for the unschooled, and confidant/mentor to the predominantly youthful hands, all of which added to his personal cachet.

****

Great Salt Lake City

Ten days after joining the drive, Nell, Nick, and the rest of the drovers rode into Great Salt Lake City with the herd lowing their pleasure as they sensed rest and respite from their odyssey. Likewise, the drovers were in good spirits, anticipating the welcome layover. Once the cattle and horses were safely corralled, the twelve hands, along with Cheney and Angus, dispersed into one or another of the few boarding houses available to clean up and rest, while the count set off to his pre-arranged sojourn with Brigham Young. Salt Lake did not really live up to its name as a 'city', but it was a pleasant enough settlement with some amenities. This was no wild frontier town. It was a conservatively religious Mormon enclave, the refuge they had trekked to in order to escape persecution in the east. There were no saloons, and no alcohol, no soiled doves to provide horizontal refreshment, but the weary drovers didn't mind. They had been paid and they looked forward to hot baths, clean clothes, and a soft bed for a change. The Mormons were happy to accommodate travellers going to or coming from California.

Nick and Nell checked into a boarding house on the perimeter of the town, taking separate rooms. There was a communal bathroom accommodating several men at once, but Nell asked if she could bathe in her room, so a tin tub was duly delivered and filled with hot

216

water by the kitchen maid, who obligingly traipsed up and down the stairs with steaming kettles. There was even a bar of soap, to Nell's delight. She carefully locked the door before she shed her clothes and stepped into the tub, closing her eyes and squeaking with bliss as she lowered herself into the hot water. She washed her hair first before the water became too scummy, her fingertips confirming its increasing thickness and length. It was still short enough to enable her passing herself off as a boy, though.

Feeling like a new woman, she dressed in clean clothes – pants and a flannel shirt – and went downstairs to join Nick in the dining room for dinner. Before she put on the shirt, she bound her burgeoning breasts tightly with a strip of linen, as she couldn't wear her jacket in the dining room, or hide her face under her hat, for that matter. The fresh air, satisfying work, and the easy friendship she enjoyed with Nick and Angus were all having a beneficial effect on her growth and wellbeing. How much longer, she wondered, would she be able to hide her womanhood?

Nick was waiting for her on a seat in the hallway, and Nell did a double take when she saw him, scrubbed clean and shiny, in fresh clothes like herself, shaved and with his dark hair neatly combed and slicked down. It struck her again forcefully how nice looking he was. In the dining room, Nell was pleased when Angus joined them at their end of the table, seated opposite her, and looking similarly refurbished. Once all the drovers were seated, the staff brought out bowls and tureens of food to furnish the table from end to end, and everyone bent to the task of enjoying the hearty fare. Glancing along the table, Nell noted to her relief that Cheney was not with their group.

"Food tastes verra guid when ye dinnae have tae cook it yerself, aye, Nathan laddie?" Flushed with enjoyment, Angus swept another laden spoonful of beef stew and dumpling past his walrus-like moustaches.

Nell nodded her agreement. "An' even better is not having to wash up the plates after!" She bit off a chunk of buttered bread, chewed, and swallowed, emulating the masculine voracity of the other young men at the table who were wolfing down the delicious homemade fare.

Angus slapped the table, eyes creased with mirth and nodding vigorously. "Nae truer word, laddie. Nae truer word."

After supper, Nell and Nick went for a stroll on what was a beautiful summer's evening. Nell thrust her hands into her pockets and moseyed along in the style of an insouciant young man. They sat down on a public bench and Nick began fossicking in his pockets, eventually drawing out a tobacco pouch, book of papers – 'prayer book' in drover slang – and matches. Nell made a 'tsk' sound as he placed them on the bench between them with an air of importance.

218

"What? Nick Hardy, are you givin' in to the smokin' vice?"

Nick tried hard to look nonchalant, and a little haughty. "The other hands all smoke."

"So you gotta be a big sheep and follow them? Waste a money is smokin'."

"Didn't cost much. Anyways, I got the makin's now so better get on with it."

Nell watched in amusement as he fumbled his way through rolling and lighting his first cigarette, striking the match off his boot sole the way he saw the drovers do it, giving a shriek and waving her arms wildly when little fragments of blazing paper flew about their heads.

"Lord almighty, are you tryin' to burn us alive here?"

"I guess I need some practice," said Nick, blushing and swatting away the last of the fiery wisps. He settled himself comfortably, placed the severely shortened cigarette between his lips, drew tentatively on it, and then went into a paroxysm of coughing and spluttering, eyes watering furiously. Nell pounded his back, laughing so hard she nearly fell off the bench. When Nick finally stopped gasping, he looked decidedly green around the gills. Nell shook her head sadly.

"Nick, I don't think you're cut out for smokin'. Try a pipe, mebbe?"

Nick ground out the remains of his cigarette with noticeable vehemence and returned the makin's to his pocket with a wounded air. "Doesn't help you mockin' me," he muttered.

Nell studied him seriously for a moment. The long days in the saddle had toughened him, making him even more stripped down and stringy, but he still looked so young and boyish, touchingly vulnerable. "Sorry, Nick. If you wanna try agin, we could share puffs 'til you get the hang of it."

Nick smiled. "You sure?"

"Yeah, I'm sure. Here give me the makin's and I'll roll it for you. I roll 'em for Angus when he's driving. Watch careful now."

By the time Nell and Nick returned to the boarding house, Nick was reasonably proficient in the art of rolling a cigarette, smoking it without choking to death, and clearly very pleased with himself.

"Course, you gotta be able to roll your quirley with one hand while holdin' the reins with the other to really be one of the boys."

"Oh jeez."

****

The following day, Nell worked with Angus to replenish their supplies since they were scheduled to leave Salt Lake early the following morning. At a loose end, Nick offered to help and Angus expressed his appreciation.

"Yon Nate's a verra willing laddie, but he's nae too spry and some of these sacks are well heavy."

Nell didn't mind being dismissed as a bit of a weakling. She made up for her physical deficiencies in other ways that Angus valued, like her seemingly uncanny ability to pre-empt a chore he had mentally listed as needing attention, only to find it already done and entirely to his satisfaction. He had become very fond of his "wee laddie".

By noon they had finished, washed up at a communal pump and trough, and returned to the boarding house in good spirits for a well-earned break and some lunch. As they approached, Nell saw to her dismay that Cheney was lounging in one of the wicker chairs on the verandah, smoking a pipe, lower right leg resting across his left thigh and looking typically arrogant.

"All squared away, cookie?" He smiled, but he never looked pleasant when he smiled. Nell loitered behind Angus, not wanting his eyes on her. They were remote and dead, like those of an ancient tortoise, although he was only about twenty-seven, Nell reckoned.

"Aye." Angus made an encompassing gesture with one arm. "Thanks tae mah braw helpers."

Cheney unfolded himself from the chair with languid ease and walked to the edge of the verandah, where he tapped out his pipe on a support post. "Good. Going in to dinner? I'll join you."

Nell's heart sank, but she knew she must do nothing to draw attention to herself or arouse suspicion. She thrust her hands into her pockets and sauntered up the steps, gaze fixed firmly to the front. Nick stayed close to her as they entered the dining room, and when she sat in the end chair he sat down on her left. To her horror, Angus had stopped to talk to one of the hands as he entered, and Cheney drew out the chair directly opposite her instead. Nell swallowed hard, keeping her eyes lowered. Angus arrived and took the seat to Cheney's right. He was in a cheerful mood after such a smooth run morning, and waxed talkative as a result. Nell was pleased to see that Cheney was barely able to get a word in. She ate quickly and then pushed back her chair, dabbing her lips with her napkin.

"Well, I'm off to write some letters an' get them posted afore we move on." She fairly bolted for the door of the dining room and raced up the stairs. Safely in her room, she closed and locked the door before leaning back against it, eyes shut tight, making a conscious effort to slow her breathing. Being in close proximity to Cheney was like being within striking distance of a rattlesnake.

Once she'd calmed down, she seated herself at the small table by the window and began to write – not a letter; she had no one to write to besides Jimmy, although she thought rather guiltily that she should write to the Beaumonts at some point. Instead, she wrote in her tattered old farm journal, no longer needed for its original purpose, using her shrinking pencil stub to continue with what had become her diary, and which had been sorely neglected lately. She enjoyed the writing process and liked to think that some day it might be of interest to her children or even grandchildren. Nell made a mental note to purchase a new pencil – or even two – before they left town.

When she finished writing, she went to find Nick and explain her hasty exit from the dining room. She knew he'd understand.

CHAPTER FIFTEEN

On a brilliant summer's morning the drovers herded their restless herd of cattle out on to the empty plains beyond Salt Lake, watched by the city's inhabitants who had turned out with their children to witness this rare event – an unprecedented and ambitious cattle drive under the aegis of a bona fide Italian aristocrat. The count played up to all the attention, hallooing from the back of his prancing mount, crimson waistcoat shimmering in the sun's rays, sweeping his white hat with its large feather through the air above his head in acknowledgement of the assembled crowd, who clapped, cheered, and waved in return, delighted by his flamboyance.

Angus chuckled as he watched their boss's high-stepping antics. "Yer one's a real showman, nae doot aboot that."

Nell grinned. She felt rested and refreshed, eager to be on the move again. The drive would link up with the Central Overland Trail beyond Salt Lake, and then it was on to California and, hopefully, a fresh start for herself and Nick. Nell patted the money belt under her dungarees, reflecting that Pap would be proud of the way she'd husbanded their stake. She'd only had a small spend in Salt Lake, mostly personal items that she'd stashed in her gunnysack: socks, soap, and another shirt. She'd also bought some flannel cloth, ostensibly for patching shirts, but actually to cut up and use for her periods. She'd only had one on the drive so far, and had been able to sneak off and wash out her strips in a nearby creek, hiding them in the brush to dry, and retrieving them in the morning.

Nick had been similarly frugal, and apart from his smoking paraphernalia had only purchased ammunition for his rifle and another pair of pants. They'd agreed that they'd pool all their money to finance their joint venture in California, whatever that might turn out to be. Nell said they'd be equal partners in whatever they decided to do, and have everything drawn up proper and legal. They both felt quietly confident about the future. Nell hadn't given much thought as to whether they'd end up as a couple, man and wife, but she had to be honest and admit that the idea appealed to her somewhat. She and Nick had simply just clicked with each other, like bacon and beans, and she felt completely comfortable with him, sensing that he felt the same way about her. Being wed though? That was way in the future. And though she was fond of Nick, Jimmy still remained her only love.

Angus's voice, urging the mules to pick up the pace as they headed out for the noon stopping place, snapped her out of her reverie. "Ready for a quirley?"

"Aye, laddie. Thank ye."

Nell reached behind her for Angus's tobacco tin, smiling as she recalled Nick's loss of smoking virginity. *Hope he don't make an ass of hisself front of the hands.*

****

The days ran into each other and everyone was talking about soon arriving at Washoe, later Carson City, Nell and Nick looking forward to this as much as anyone else. There was a trading post and stopover there for travellers at the Eagle Ranch.

One evening, with supper pretty well prepared, Nell excused herself to answer nature's call at a nearby creek, assuring Angus she'd be quick. Angus nodded happily as he stirred the beans. "Dinnae fash yerself, laddie."

As Nell made her way to the creek, she noticed a rider approaching camp, but the setting sun was behind him and she couldn't make out who it was. There were unwritten rules about entering camp when food was being prepared, the principal one being to go gently and not stir up any dust. The rider seemed to be obeying the rule, ambling along. Thinking no more about it, Nell found some shrubbery near the stream, unfastened her dungarees, drew them down, and squatted with a sigh, eyes closed. When she'd finished, she dabbed herself with a clump of dry grass and stood, pulling her clothing up as she did so. Soft laughter saw her whirl around and freeze as she registered the menacing figure of the trail boss, Cheney, who'd been standing a few feet behind her, his manner casual, one boot propped on a fallen log, thumbs hooked in the waistband of his pants. Nell took a step backwards, keeping her eyes fixed on him, every muscle tensed and ready for flight. She hadn't had time to refasten her dungarees so she held them up with one hand, the other arm hanging loose.

Cheney ran his eyes over her slowly, and then smiled, although the smile did not reach his cold, reptilian eyes. "Hey, little girl, am I interrupting something? Saw you slippin' in here an' thought maybe you'd like company." He cocked his head to one side. "You sure as hell ain't no boy, are you?"

Nell swallowed hard, trying not to show her fear. "I dunno what you're talkin' about. I'm Nathan Washburn. I gotta get back."

She turned to run, but he sprang on her like a wolf, one arm circling her waist, holding tight, his other hand clamped over her mouth. One finger slid under her chin and stroked her throat. "No Adam's apple. That tipped me off. Other thing was that nice, rounded little ass when you climbed on the wagon. Ain't no boy got an ass like that, jus' baggy saggy britches. An' then I catch you squatting so I'm guessing you ain't got no pecker." He chuckled. "Let's have a look, shall we? Anyways, arsehole or quim, it don't matter none. I'll have you either way." His hand slid up under her shirt to grope her breasts and he paused when he felt the money belt. "What's this, eh? You carryin' cash?" He snickered. "Oh, well, pleasure before business."

Nell struggled furiously, clawing at him with one hand in a futile attempt to break his grip, trying desperately to hold up her dungarees with the other, but he was too strong for her. He dragged her across a small clearing to where a fallen tree lay, higher at one end than the other, and threw her across it at just the right height to level his crotch with her behind, winding her as he did so. Then he yanked her dungarees down over her hips until she knew her bare behind must be exposed to him. She heard him grunt as he roughly fondled her privates, and she screamed into his hand still so tight across her mouth that no sound emerged. She tried to bite him, but she couldn't get any purchase on his hard, calloused palm with her teeth. Squeezing her eyes shut, she braced herself mentally for the coming assault she knew she could not prevent. He kicked each of her inside ankles in turn, sweeping her feet outwards to spread her legs apart and she heard him say, "Quim it is, sweetheart."

And then his grip loosened, he seemed to lose all strength, slowly releasing her and making a horrible gurgling noise as she felt him fall away. Nell spun around and saw Nick standing motionless, looking down at Cheney's crumpled form, a bloodied knife clutched in his hand. It was obvious that Cheney was dead, the cold eyes staring lifelessly up at nothing.

"Oh, Jesus, Nell. Oh, Jesus. I had to stop him. I stuck him twice. I done killed him."

"You sure did. Got him in the kidneys fair and square. Dropped the snake like a stone." Nell drew up her dungarees with trembling hands and refastened the straps. Then she crossed to Nick and flung herself on him with a strangled sob, shaking uncontrollably. He dropped the bloodied knife and wrapped his arms around her, holding her tight.

"Are you okay? Jesus, if I hadn't a got here when I did." He shook his head violently as if trying to rid it of a fearful image. "Angus said you went to the crick, an' then I seen this one's horse, his favourite dun. I kinda knew…"

Nell looked up at him, pale with shock and trying to control the trembling that shook her limbs. "I'm fine. You saved me from the varmint; 't ain't your fault, Nick. He was lyin' in wait for me, jus'a matter of time. Snake know'd I'm a girl, don't know how."

Nick nodded. "Some men got a sense for it, I reckon, the way cows smell water."

Nell looked down at Cheney's corpse. "I guess. But you picked I was a girl, too. How many more of them drovers know it? Maybe even Angus knows. They all seen how he stared at me, tried to get close to me."

"I never heard a one of them refer to it. You was always duckin' about with your head down an' all they wanted to do was eat. I reckon it was just Cheney, Nell." He bent down and retrieved his knife, then looked into her frightened blue eyes, his expression earnest. "You're changin', Nell. You can't stop nature."

Nell seized his arm. "We gotta get outta here, Nick."

While Nick nodded dumbly, Nell indicated towards camp. "Angus is gonna come lookin' for me if I don't get back. Criminy, but we gotta work out one helluva plan this time, an' quick!"

****

By the time Nell returned to the campsite, she had herself more or less under control, setting about her chores with her usual energy, and Angus suspected nothing, offering only one flippant comment about the length of time she'd taken to relieve herself – "I was aboot tae come an' look fer ye, laddie." – to which Nell had replied with an apology as the hands began to drift in for supper.

"Sorry, Angus." She patted her abdomen. "My guts got the squitters."

"No from mah cooking, ah hope! Nae man, nor laddie fer that matter, has ever accused me of givin' them a bad wame."

"No, no. Prob'ly put too much molasses on my flapjacks this mornin'."

"There now, that'll larn ye." Angus chuckled.

Nell managed a shaky smile. She took the spoon off him. "Here, I'll do that."

She and Nick had dragged Cheney's body into thick undergrowth before they led his horse to a small clearing beside the creek, where they unsaddled and unbridled it before slapping its rump to send it, under cover of dusk, to join the rest of the remuda, already browsing a short distance away. They carefully concealed the saddle, blanket, and bridle under some brush and, while Nell returned to camp the way she'd come, Nick took a different route after washing his knife thoroughly in the stream before returning it to its sheath. As they'd carried out their subterfuge, they'd settled on a hasty plan for making their escape.

When everyone was happily devouring their supper, Nell and Nick catching each other's eye as they tried to force their food down into fluttering stomachs, the count suddenly sat upright, looked around, and asked, "Where ees Signor Cheney? He does not meess hees supper as a rule."

A young hand, who went by the name Ned Crowther, craned his neck around, scanning the diners, and shrugged, "He ain't here. Mebbe he's mindin' the herd and comin' in later. The cows were spooked some earlier on so he's prob'ly jus' helpin' to bed them down. I'll go take a look when I'm done here. I pulled first watch anyway."

Nell cut her eyes to him. She wasn't surprised he'd volunteered since she'd long since noticed he and Cheney were thick as thieves. In fact, he seemed to be the only hand Cheney had any time for. She recalled his words when he was attacking her: 'arsehole or quim, it don't matter none.' Could he be...? She arrested the thought with a shudder.

"Grazie, Ned. Meester Cheney ees most diligent, eesn't it?" the count accepted an offer of seconds from Angus, and supper continued without comment.

Angus had excelled himself, producing a superb supper on this particular evening: a big, tender chunk of fatback with red pepper sauce, fried potatoes, and fresh bread. Nell and Nick were so agitated they were unable to appreciate it, both watching Ned like hawks, braced for the moment he would finish his meal and set off to search for Cheney, the moment that would signal time had come for them to make their move and hightail it out of camp to god knew where. However, Ned seemed to be in no particular hurry. He enjoyed seconds, like most of the hands, and then lingered contentedly over a pipe and a third cup of coffee. Nell thought she was going to burst with fearful anticipation, while, seated across from her, Nick looked strained and tense.

Finally, Ned tossed his coffee dregs aside, knocked out his pipe on the sole of his boot, and clambered to his feet, arcing his replete belly forwards, hands on hips, to ease his back. "Okay, I'll head off to find Cheney now."

As Ned placed his dishes in the wrecker, giving Angus an appreciative nod, Nick shot to his feet. "I'll come with you."

Nell looked at him aghast, but even as his eyes said 'stay calm' she realised what he was doing. It was the perfect opportunity to saddle his horse without arousing suspicion, and to fetch up Misty for her.

Ned nodded his thanks, and he and Nick made off towards the picketed horses, carrying their saddles. Nell began the after supper clean up with her usual briskness. Angus was still eating. By the time he'd finished, Nell had everything in order, and once more excused herself to answer the call of nature, patting her stomach and wincing for emphasis. By this time it was pitch dark. As Nell headed for the hoodlum wagon, parked away from the illumination of the fire, she glanced back over a shoulder to look at Angus one last time and sorrow gripped her. He'd been a wonderful boss and a good friend, and she'd become very fond of him. Swallowing her emotion, she crept around to the far side of the wagon and located her saddle and both her and Nick's gunnysacks, bedrolls and saddlebags, which she'd placed within easy reach earlier while making out she was fetching some personal item. She knew Angus suspected nothing.

Weaving somewhat under the weight of her burdens, Nell crept into the trees where she knew Nick was waiting, having told Ned he was having trouble with his cinch, advising him to go on ahead and he'd catch him up. Nell stifled a shriek as he loomed up out of the darkness and she walked right into him, dropping her load. "Nick! Scared the daylights outta me!" she hissed.

Nick gripped her arm. "Shhh! Gimme your saddle!" His own horse was ready and standing quietly, eyelids drooping.

"Wait, Nick, I been thinkin'. We should take one of Cheney's horses, too."

"Horse stealin's a serious crime, Nell. You can hang."

"I know that, but it won't look like stealin', don't you see? They'll mebbe think he's run off with me, an' you're followin' us. They won't even look for him if they figure he's alive, jus' went plumb loco and took off."

The puzzlement in Nick's voice was clear. "Why would they think he's run off with you? They believe you're a boy, don't they?"

"Probably, but I don't think girls are his only fancy, and they – some of them anyways – maybe think that, too. I'll explain why later."

Nick stood still and silent for a moment, processing this information. "Okay. By jiminy, Nell, that's real smart. I'll fetch his dun." He paused. "What about all his stuff. Won't it look strange that he left it behind?"

Nell groaned. "We ain't got time to worry about that, nor finding his stuff in the pitch dark. It was hard enough finding ours. Now, go get his horse!"

By the time Nick returned with Cheney's horse on a lead rope – as the wrangler, he knew all the men's mounts well – Nell had saddled Misty herself and secured their few possessions. Cheney's horse would prove useful as a pack animal. Nick gave her a leg up, and they turned their respective mounts away from camp, Nick leading the third horse, away from the hopes and dreams the cattle drive had represented for them both, once more adrift in an indifferent and savage world. They knew that their disappearance coinciding with Cheney's would arouse suspicion, especially if his body was found, or even his saddle, but they had no other choice. If they stayed they risked Nick being found out. Someone could remember something; someone might recall Cheney's fascination with the 'laddie' and put two and two together. They'd made their plan and they had to stick to it. Nell had expressed the hope that wolves would eat Cheney, destroying the evidence. Nick had drily responded that eating that sonofabitch would give any wolf a bellyache, and in spite of everything, Nell had laughed.

****

They rode all night, maintaining a steady pace that did not exhaust the horses. As dawn broke, Nell thought about Angus, picturing his bafflement as he went to rouse her for the breakfast preparation and found no sign of her. Once more the sadness of loss gripped her and she fought back tears.

Riding up ahead, Nick called back to her. "We gotta stop, Nell, rest the horses. There's a cabin up ahead. You stay here an' I'll go scout."

"Okay, Nick." Nell drooped wearily in the saddle, beyond any kind of care or concern, indifferent to everything. All she wanted to do was sleep. She wasn't even aware of her fall until she came to with a shock, lying flat on her back on the ground, an anxious Nick bending over her.

"Nell? You okay? There's no one hereabouts. The cabin's been left some time ago, I'd say. We can rest here an' it's close to a stream." He helped her to her feet and then swung her up in his arms to carry her to their shelter. Once inside the dilapidated cabin, he laid her gently on the stamped earth floor and removed her boots. "You rest now. I'll get your stuff."

"I can help." Nell attempted to rise, but Nick gently pushed her back down. "No. Stay put an' I'll fetch your bedroll, see to the horses and such."

Nell didn't argue.

Later, when Nell stirred, she realised she was securely wrapped in her bedroll, her jacket scrunched under her head as a makeshift pillow. Nick lay a few feet away, his soft regular breathing confirming that he was in a deep sleep. Nell laid her head back down and promptly fell asleep again.

****

They slept until mid-afternoon. When Nell woke, Nick had a fire going in the crumbling hearth and had cooked some pre-soaked beans with slivers of dried beef to accompany the chunk of bread Nell had snatched from the supply wagon as she'd left. She hated the idea of stealing from Angus, but she knew he'd understand. Food was an issue they'd have to solve as they travelled. Fortunately, they'd restocked with some non-perishables at Fort Bridger, and there were still remnants left in their saddlebags: pinto beans, rice, coffee, flour, dried meat, and dried fruit. They were both good foragers, too. Nick hoped to shoot some game, but they had to be careful not to expose themselves, and the sound of gunfire carried a long way. As soon as the food was cooked, Nick smothered the fire and they ate hungrily.

Once they'd eaten, they cleaned up, packed up, and made sure there was no trace of their fleeting presence left behind. Then they saddled up and were on their way, still headed west, but unsure of their final destination. It was another beautiful summer's day, and

Nell's spirits lifted after the refreshing sleep and welcome food. The horses, likewise rested and fresh, stepped out willingly. It felt good to be riding Misty again. Nick looked over at her and smiled, and she smiled back, mindful once more of the terrible ordeal he had spared her. Having linked her destiny to that of this young man, she had no regrets. They'd be all right. They'd be all right.

CHAPTER SIXTEEN

They rode steadily northwest, each lost in their own thoughts. They could no longer risk going to San Francisco, the ultimate destination of the count's cattle drive, but they still intended to go to California – some part of California. It was big country, and they could easily lose themselves in it, change their names if they had to. It was plain to both of them, though, that Nell could no longer pose as a guileless youth. The trusted companionship that being with Nick had brought into her life, the settled nature of working with Angus on the trail, his fatherly appreciation, and the stimulus of adventure with a goal to aim for, had affected her wellbeing dramatically. Her hair was getting thicker and longer every day, and she was developing the curves and contours of a young woman that only a blind man would fail to see, even in her dungarees. Her features were settling into a feminine loveliness, too, especially her mouth, which was generously proportioned with the lips a deep rose colour that required no rouging or artifice to accentuate. In short, nature had been more than kind, and she was maturing into a beautiful young woman. Now away from the male world of the cattle drive, she stopped binding her breasts and wore her hat further to the back of her head instead of pulling it down to cover most of her face. If any posse were looking for two youths, she and Nick would not fit that description.

As the sun sank lower towards the horizon, and while Nell waited below, Nick rode up to the summit of a hillock, where he scanned the territory they'd traversed thus far. He lingered, shading his eyes as he looked for any indication of dust trails or riders, listened for any sound, but he could not see any sign of pursuit, and reported the fact to a relieved Nell. They decided to camp for the night in a small grassy basin near a stream, where they could risk a fire, and while Nick saw to the horses Nell got a fire going and started preparations for supper. They didn't have much, but Nell cooked rice, adding wild greens, and some shavings of dried beef to give it flavour, and she used some of their dried fruit and flour to mix a simple pudding of sorts to enjoy with coffee. She and Nick hadn't really had a chance to talk about or process the terrible events that had precipitated their flight, and once they'd eaten and cleaned up, they hunkered down by the fire, sitting side by side, to do just that. Nick rolled a quirley, drew on it, then spoke first.

"Nell, was you brought up to know the Bible, an' go to church?"

"Course. Mam was real strong on it. Pap, not so much. He humoured her."

"I broke the Sixth Commandment, Nell. I killed a man. I guess I'll go to Hell now."

Nell put her hand on his arm and squeezed. "Nick, you saved my life. He woulda killed me fer sure once he'd had his evil way, to shut me up. I reckon that cancels out what you did. You ain't no killer."

Nick sighed, shifting his weight. "Well, I spose I coulda whacked him on the head or somethin' but I was jus' blind mad when I saw what... what he was goin' to do. Next thing the knife was in my hand an' I jus'..." His voice trailed off.

"You stuck 'im like the pig he is... was," Nell finished matter-of-factly. "Hell, we ain't gonna shed no tears over him."

She shifted closer. "Now, let's talk about stuff that matters, like what we're gonna do, an' come up with a plan. You still got that ole map?"

"Yup." Nick drew the folded map from his jacket pocket, spread it across his knees, and they huddled up, peering at it in the firelight. Nell stabbed a finger at a scrawled place name. "That sounds like a good place for folk on the run." She chuckled. "What kinda name is that?"

****

Nick and Nell rode into Yreka (Why-reek-ah) on a cloudless, hot summer's day, walking their horses slowly along Miner Street, the main thoroughfare, and gazing around in fascination at the bustling little gold mining boom town that had mushroomed on the valley flats, presided over by the towering majesty of snow capped Shasta Mountain. In 1851, a mule train driver named Abraham Thompson had discovered gold near Black Gulch. His mules had actually unearthed tiny nuggets as they champed grass during a rest break, causing great consternation for the muleteer, who'd stared with rising excitement at the unmistakeable golden fragments glittering in the trailing roots of the weeds his grazing animals tore up. Thus, the California gold rush migrated from south to north and Yreka was born. By August of that year, it had a population of 5,000 and had continued to grow from a cobbled-together, hardscrabble settlement into something of an established township featuring new buildings as well as shacks and canvas dwellings.

Nell gawked as two Chinamen walked past wearing dress-like robes, black mandarin hats, single dark pigtails hanging down their backs and what looked like black slippers on their white-stockinged feet. Wagons, carts, riders, pedestrians raised dust as they passed by on the dirt street, typically wide enough to allow for turning oxcarts, its surface crisscrossed with deep ruts cut during winter's mud season and now baked hard by the summer sun. Nell's nostrils twitched as she processed individual odours from the all-pervasive stink: manure, rubbish, blood and butchery, human waste, woodsmoke. A small dog ran across in front of the horses, spooking

242

them, and was hotly pursued by a small boy shrieking, "Max! Max!"
The street was lined with stores and service providers, their hastily
erected clapboard facades announcing their purviews – bakery,
butchery, miners' hardware, stoves, drugstore, general merchandise,
a bank, saloons, and an assay office. Then her gaze fell on a narrow
two-storey brick building across to her right which had a fancy red
and gold sign hanging above the front entrance: Pride of Erin Hotel
Kitty Callahan Proprietor. A woman stood outside on the
boardwalk, looking up and down the street, her pose relaxed as she
surveyed the hustle and bustle of the township between intermittent
sips from the china cup she held in one hand, the other resting on a
hip. She wore a blue silk dress with a white lace collar, her dark hair
piled up in a knot on top of her head. Turning her head, she met
Nell's eyes and smiled. Nell thought she looked thirty-something.
She also thought she had a pleasant face.

"Nick, that could be a likely place to stay over there, at least for
a night or two."

Nick followed her gaze. "Sure. Good idea."

They walked the tired horses over to the hotel frontage and
halted, nodding to the woman, who looked them over with a keen
gaze that hinted at an equally keen mind.

Nell removed her hat and ran her fingers through her damp hair.
"Mornin', ma'am. I'm Nell Washburn, and this here's my friend,
Nick Hardy."

Nick whipped off his hat. "Mornin', ma'am. Pleased to make your acquaintance."

The woman smiled, her striking green eyes alight with shrewd interest. "Kitty. Kitty Callahan, proprietor of this hotel." She tossed dregs from her cup on to the street. "What can I do for ye?" Her accent was broad Irish.

"Would you have some rooms going vacant for two weary travellers?"

"I would indeed, provided ye have the means. Payment's up front." She jerked her head towards the end of the street. "Livery's down there. See to yer horses and come back to register. I'll be waiting for ye."

****

Once they'd made arrangements for the horses, Nell and Nick strolled back to the hotel, saddlebags over a shoulder, carrying their gunnysacks.

"This looks a right lively place," observed Nell.

Nick nodded. "We could do a lot worse, I reckon."

"Well, we'll see, anyways."

Kitty was sitting on a stool behind a small desk in the foyer as they entered the hotel, an oil lamp with a striking red, green, and amber stained glass shade casting a pool of light over the open register in front of her, quill pen and ink pot at the ready. The place

244

was simply furnished: a plush red velvet settee against the wall opposite the desk, a dining room with coat rack alongside its entrance off to one side, a saloon to the other. The bar's patrons could be seen through the ornate glass panels in the doors. A narrow staircase with banister flowed up the wall ahead, presumably to rooms above. A sign hanging behind the desk read "Rules For This Establishment," next to a plaque with two rows of keys dangling from metal hooks.

Kitty stood up, smoothing her skirt, her manner businesslike. "Welcome. Two single rooms, was it?"

Nell looked around her room, which was next door to Nick's, and felt a sense of approval. While it was small and sparsely furnished, it was clean and tidy, the single bed draped in a pretty patchwork quilt, giving a homely touch. There was one oil lamp attached by a bracket to the wall, a washstand with jug and basin, a single chair, and a chamber pot visible beneath the bed. Nell drew down the bed covers and saw that the linen looked fresh and clean. This was clearly a respectable establishment. She leaned her saddlebags against the wall, dropping the gunnysack beside them, and sat down on the chair to ease off her boots. Her priorities now were a bath and a change of clothes, and she imagined Nick's would be the same. Kitty had given them directions to a bathhouse and laundry she recommended that were operated by Chinese immigrants. They were good people, she'd assured them, who would not try to cheat them. Nell crossed to the bed and flopped on to it, stretching out on her back and folding her arms behind her head. She closed her eyes and promptly fell asleep.

Soft tapping on the door roused Nell from her slumber. She raised herself on an elbow, rubbing her eyes sleepily as she looked around, taking a moment to remember where she was.

"Come in."

Nick stuck his head around the door, a big grin on his face. "Are you awake at last, sleepyhead?"

Nell sat up, swinging her legs off the bed and stretching luxuriantly. "How long I been out?"

Nick stepped into the room. "'Bout five hours."

"Good lord." Nell ran a critical eye over him. He was wearing clean clothes, still damp hair washed and combed, boots shined. "My, don't you look the spiv?"

Nick chuckled. "You wanna freshen up? Bathhouse's good. They do laundry there as well."

Nell stood up. "Nah, bit late. I washed in the crick this morning while you were fixin' breakfast. I'll do." She raised an eyebrow. "I'd like to change my clothes, though, if you'd kindly step out for a moment."

Nick backed up to the door, blushing. "Supper's ready. I'll meet you in the dining room."

"Be there in a jiffy."

****

Supper was a choice between chicken and dumplings or venison stew, and both Nell and Nick chose chicken and dumplings. It was delicious, the chicken tender and flavourful, the rich, unctuous gravy thickened with rice. The young girl who waited on them was unobtrusive and efficient. Following a generous dessert of apple pie and cream, Nell and Nick lingered over fresh, hot coffee, and Nick rolled a quirley, Nell noting with a smile that his technique showed great improvement. She gazed around the room full of diners, thinking that the hotel must be full, or nearly so, and that she and Nick had been lucky to get rooms. Most of the diners were men. Nell could only see two other women, who looked as if they were with husbands.

They both turned their heads as Kitty entered the packed dining room, pausing for a moment inside the doorway for full theatrical impact. She looked like a queen in a grey silk dress, beautifully draped in the front with a bustle behind. Ropes of creamy pearls adorned her neckline, lustrous pearl drops swung from her ears, rings, which included a wedding band, glittered on her fingers, and her immaculate coiffure reflected the soft lamplight. She looked every inch the successful hotelier as she went from table to table, chatting with guests, dipping her head gracefully when they praised their meals before gliding on to the next table, placing a languid hand on a chair back or patting a shoulder as she leaned in to greet patrons. Nell thought her a consummate businesswoman, almost certainly ahead of her time. The clientele, all well turned out, clearly respectable people, seemingly warmed to her caring approach, smiling and joshing with her, their manner respectful. Kitty stopped before their table last, and to their surprise, drew out a chair and sat down with them, no mean feat considering the size of her bustle.

"Good evenin', Mr. Hardy, Miss Washburn."

"Good evenin', Miz Callahan."

"Was supper to yer likin'?" she purred in her lilting Irish brogue.

"It was very fine, ma'am," answered Nick. "Best chicken and dumplin's I ever tasted."

"For me as well, ma'am" Nell agreed. "The pie, too."

Kitty inclined her head in appreciation. "That's grand. I have a new cook, so I need the feedback from guests to make sure he's doing his job properly." She gave a rueful smile. "My previous cook got the gold fever."

"Well, I don't think you have any cause for concern there, ma'am." Nick patted his abdomen appreciatively.

Kitty chuckled. Then her face became serious as she leaned forwards, placing her elbows on the table and clasping her hands under her chin. "So, what brings ye two youngsters to Yreka? Just passing through, or planning to stay? Gold fever, perhaps?"

Nick lowered his eyes, tapping ash off the end of his cigarette and shifting awkwardly in his chair, lips firmly compressed. Nell realised it was up to her to answer Kitty's questions since Nick had obviously closed up like a clam, and what did she say? 'Well we're on the run after murdering a man.' The wheels of her mind swung into gear quickly, and she lifted her coffee cup with a nonchalant air, boldly eyeballing Kitty as she replied.

"We're interested in settin' up a business here. After all, it's the merchants and suppliers who make the money in a gold rush, isn't it?" To emphasise her point, she cast her eyes casually around Kitty's busy dining room.

Kitty nodded, tugging down the corners of her mouth to indicate her thoughtful consensus to this piece of commercial wisdom. She smiled, eyes alight with interest. "What manner of enterprise did ye have in mind?"

"We are considerin' dry goods," replied Nell loftily. "Mebbe other merchandise on the side. I guess we need to look around, try and figure out what the town might need."

"That would be prudent. I could help ye out there, too. I know this town well." She stood, pushed the chair in under the table, and smoothed her dress. "Why don't we move next door to the saloon?

I'd like to buy ye both a drink." Seeing Nell's hesitation, she added, "I'm the owner so ye're my guests."

Nick noticeably perked up at this invitation, stubbing out his cigarette and rising to his feet. "Why, that's right neighbourly of you, ma'am. Thank you."

"My pleasure."

Kitty swept out of the dining room, calling "Good evenin', to all of ye" over her shoulder as she did so, prompting a chorus of replies, and Nick and Nell followed her across the hallway towards the decoratively etched glass panelled doors that led into the saloon. Nick darted ahead to open them for the two women, which gentlemanly gesture earned an appreciative nod and smile from Kitty.

Like the dining room, the saloon was busy, the noise of conversation and music assaulting the ears as they entered, and it crossed Nell's mind that Kitty must be doing very well for herself. No reason, she thought, why Nick and I can't do the same. As with the chorus of farewells from the diners, Kitty was hailed with a raucous welcome from the congregation of drinkers when the trio entered the bar, a salute of raised glasses accompanying their cheery greetings. She dipped her head with her customary grace, acknowledging the men's exuberance with a flutter of one bejewelled hand and a dazzling smile.

"Thank ye, gentlemen! Enjoy yerselves! Lily, give everyone a drink on the house!"

This generous gesture resulted in an even more deafening cacophony of cheers, whistles, hoots, hollers and expressions of appreciation.

Kitty was certainly pleasant and friendly, and clearly popular, but Nell wasn't feeling altogether comfortable as she and Nick followed her to a relatively private table in a corner opposite the bar. She couldn't possibly know they were fugitives, could she? As Kitty paused, gesturing with a lace-cuffed hand for them to be seated, her green eyes met Nell's, and as Nell looked beyond the contrived warmth into their shrewd, calculating depths, she thought with terrifying clarity, "Yes. She does."

CHAPTER SEVENTEEN

Kitty left Nick and Nell seated at the table while she sashayed up to the bar. There were two young women moving skilfully up and down behind the counter, serving the men crowded there, laughing and chatting flirtatiously, and expertly dodging any groping hands as they poured the drinks without missing a beat. At one end of the bar a huge burly man with a thick head of oily black hair and an impressive beard stood back discreetly, arms folded across his massive chest, serenely surveying the mêlée but still managing to project a powerful air of coiled menace. Nell concluded he was the muscle, there to deal with any problems that erupted as the patrons got liquored up. Those patrons ranged in age from boyishly young to the quite elderly, with long white hair and snowy beards. They were all dressed much the same, as if mining required some kind of uniform: faded flannel shirts, sturdy pants held up by cord or suspenders, rugged work boots, felt hats with the front brim folded back. They all appeared to have made an effort to tidy up a bit for their night on the town. Beards and hair had been combed into something resembling neatness, and, though worn, their clothes looked clean. Many of them, Nell noted, carried side arms.

Neither Nell nor Nick had ever been in a saloon before so they were rather daunted by all the noise and jollity, neither speaking as they took it all in. In the far corner, a man squeezed tunes out of an accordion, and there were tables where groups of men played cards, faces intense with concentration. Some of the men had linked arms and were shuffling round in a circle in time to the music, a rather poignant means of enjoying a dance when there were no ladies to partner with, swaying to the rhythm, their boots clattering in unison on the wooden floor. A miasma of tobacco smoke hung over the room. On the wall behind the bar, an enormous gilt framed mirror reflected all the activity, the saloon's interior illuminated by bracketed oil lamps on the wall behind the bar, and one large wagon wheel supporting four more lamps with ruby red frilled glass shades suspended from the central ceiling. Nell noticed that the big man sprang forwards to serve Kitty himself, greeting her with a smile, his manner deferential. Kitty leaned on the bar, surveying her boisterous patrons with a satisfied smile. She was the queen of her domain, all right.

When Kitty returned, she placed a bottle and three glasses on the table and Nick sprang to his feet to draw out her chair, for which gentlemanly gesture she thanked him as she wiggled her cumbersome bustle into a comfortable position. "So nice to meet a young man with manners," she said silkily. Then she poured a generous measure of whiskey into each glass, placing her guests' in front of them before she raised her own brimful tumbler.

"Welcome to Yreka. Here's to a grand stay for both of ye. Yer very good health."

Apart from the raw hooch Nick had given her that one time when she'd unburdened herself, Nell was a whiskey novice, and she took only a small sip before replacing her glass on the table, hoping she didn't make a fool of herself by spluttering as the fiery liquid burned her throat. Kitty, however, drained her shot class in one smooth toss, licked her lips, and then immediately refilled it. As she raised her glass, she used it to gesture towards the packed premises and asked, "Well, what do ye think of my saloon, Pot O' Gold?"

"Looks like it's doing well," said Nell. "Is it like this most nights?"

"Well, 'tis a Friday, and that's always a good night, along with Saturday. The miners need to let off steam, enjoy a bit o' craic and a drink or two, eye up a pretty girl. There's a fierce shortage of women all over the diggings." She sipped her whiskey, her smile coy. "I run a respectable establishment here, mind ye. Don't let the red lampshades fool ye!" She gave a shrill little giggle. "They can go elsewhere for that. Many of the men who come in have wives and sweethearts waiting at home for them to make their fortune. They just want to relax, look at a nicely turned out girl, chat to her, flirt a bit, buy her a drink perhaps. They know they'll get a fair deal here and if they're too drunk to make it back to the diggings we'll look after them, tuck them up somewhere and mind their purse for them." She sipped her whiskey. "That's what I provide, a quality hotel, too, but not so fancy as to put ordinary folks off. Many miners here are forty-niners, come north to try their luck with a new strike. The Chinese came here in 1853, just a few hundred, but they stick with their own kind. Most of them work in mining, or as cooks and washers, but they have shops as well. Mostly, they sell Chinese goods to their own people."

Nick and Nell listened to all this local history with interest, and Nick thanked Kitty as she refilled his glass. She poised the bottle over Nell's glass, too, raising an eyebrow, but Nell slid a hand across the rim. "I'm fine."

Kitty sighed. "Looks like it's just ye and me drinking tonight, Mr. Hardy."

"Nell's not used to hard drink. She'd probably prefer a sarsaparilly."

"Would ye?"

Nell nodded, shooting Nick, ever the protective one, a grateful look. She had no desire to be a wet blanket. Kitty pivoted in her chair to address the giant with the black hair.

"Billy, fetch over a sarsaparilla, will ye?" She turned back to Nell. "Thoughtless of me. Ye're just a young girl, after all. I need to remember this stuff is not mother's milk to everyone."

Once Billy had delivered Nell's drink, Kitty got down to business. "So, ye're keen to set up here in Yreka?" she asked casually. "Dry goods, ye mentioned. That takes capital, of course."

"We have the means," said Nell, wishing she hadn't answered quite so quickly, almost snappishly.

"Oh, to be sure ye have," replied Kitty, "otherwise ye wouldn't have considered it, now, would ye?"

Nell and Nick said nothing. Kitty heaved a sigh, swirling her drink in its glass, her expression serious, lips pursed as if she had bad news to deliver. "Ye know there are any number of stores in Yreka selling any amount of goods and foodstuffs. It's three years since the strike, after all, but the miners keep pouring in because everyone believes there's a second mother lode yet to be struck. The town has need of other things, now." She refilled Nick's and her own glass, took a swig, and then leaned in with a conspiratorial air. "What do ye think might bring even more customers in here, for instance?"

Nick and Nell looked blank. She'd already said she didn't accommodate horizontal recreation.

"Food! Victuals!" announced Kitty, slapping a hand down on the table for emphasis. "Good, plain grub that reminds them of home."

"Do you mean like a restaurant?" asked Nell.

"Yes! That's exactly what I mean. I've been mulling over the idea for a while." She pointed to the ceiling and both Nick and Nell reflexively looked up. "There's wasted space above the saloon, so I could either add more hotel rooms or set up a fine restaurant." She swivelled her hand to point to the opposite wall. "Put a staircase in there. The men work up an appetite, with the drink making them hungry as it always does, and then they go on upstairs to eat." She flashed a triumphant smile. "What d' ye think? I'd grubstake ye as well, if ye need me to, but it would be yer business in the main. Ye 'd have a free hand. I wouldn't interfere."

As Nell sat dumbly processing this unexpected offer, Nick cleared his throat and spoke up. "That's an, um, interesting offer. I guess we'd need to talk about it some before we decided. What do you think, Nell?"

"Hmm? Oh, for sure." Nell gathered her wits. They'd only been in town a matter of hours, and already they were being offered a stake in a business. "It's a big decision, Miz Callahan. But we'll definitely give it some consideration."

Kitty rested back in her chair. "Of course. All business propositions must be carefully considered. I can arrange for ye to talk to someone with the right commercial savvy, if ye want. Take yer time to think it over properly."

"We're obliged, ma'am," said Nell. "It's a big step for us and we ain't high rollers by any means. We need to get it right."

Kitty nodded. "I understand." She leaned in again. "Just two more things," she said.

Nick and Nell found themselves leaning in also, faces expectant.

"First, please call me Kitty, and, second, it's probably a good idea, in the circumstances, if ye get wed, the sooner the better." She gave a long, slow wink. Nick made a choking sound that then became a prolonged coughing fit, prompting Kitty to deliver several hearty thumps to his back.

"Jasus, lad, does the prospect of marriage frighten ye that much? Ye're probably wise to be afeard!" She threw back her head and roared with laughter.

****

Nell and Nick felt too awkward to even contemplate talking about either of Kitty's remarkable proposals after they left her, and retired to their respective rooms with a mumbled 'Good night' to each other. Nell undressed, shoved the money belt under the mattress, blew out the lamp, and got into bed, where she lay, covers pulled up to her chin, staring into the darkness. The offer of the restaurant was certainly worth considering, since, clearly, Kitty was a shrewd businesswoman who had made some sound choices that were paying off nicely. She sighed. Cooking for others seemed to be the one connecting thread in her changeable life thus far. The suggestion that she should marry Nick, though, required some analysis. Was it for her protection? Kitty had said there were few eligible women in Yreka and that might possibly make a young single woman like herself vulnerable to unwanted attention. The incident with Cheney had left no illusions about men's lust, or their physical strength that enabled them to take a girl by force.

Or was it just good business for Kitty to have a husband and wife team who were committed to each other and by association with any commercial enterprise as well? It certainly guaranteed cheap labour. But marriage to Nick? Nell couldn't deny that the thought had crossed her mind, and was not without attraction, but mostly, if she were honest, she considered him as no more than a close companion, someone she liked and trusted and who was kind and protective towards her; he'd saved her from a horrible attack that still gave her nightmares, and had almost certainly saved her life into the bargain. He was someone she felt totally comfortable around, arriving in her life like an unexpected gift and rescuing her from the awful loneliness, both physical and spiritual, which had followed the death of her family. Her being disguised as a boy when they'd stumbled upon each other had set a pattern of mateship rather than any male-female attraction. But when her true gender had been irrefutably revealed he had been decent and respectful; not for one second had he tried to take advantage of her. She'd got accustomed to having Nick alongside her, but she saw marriage as something she might do in the future, not right now. God, she was still a month off sixteen! Then her thoughts turned to Jimmy, whom she did love and always would, even though thousands of miles now separated them. She definitely did not have that same strong depth of feeling towards Nick. He was a dear friend, nothing more, and any love she felt for him was within that context. But the chances of her ever seeing Jimmy again were remote, and she had to concede that she could do a lot worse than Nick. If she couldn't marry for love, then she could marry for affection and friendship. A lot of women had to settle for a lot less. With this final, pragmatic sentiment, she fell asleep.

Two doors down, Nick lay on his back, eyes wide open, his thoughts following the same train as Nell's. He'd become deeply fond of her and she sure was blossoming into a beauty, no doubt about that. She'd matured, too, from the feisty little she-cat he'd first encountered on the trail, could hold her own with any man for sheer guts and boldness, and he liked her kind, caring side that often shone through. She always mended his clothes, although he never imposed on her, and she'd make a point of cooking things she knew he liked. Likewise, her honesty and her willingness to work hard had always impressed him, and he readily acknowledged that she'd make any man a wife to be proud of. His wife? Well, yes. He had to admit the idea was very appealing. Very.

****

At breakfast the next morning, neither Nell nor Nick made mention of any impending nuptials, nor did they discuss the offer of the restaurant. Nick was feeling a little queasy as a result of all the whiskey Kitty had plied him with, and he picked indifferently at his food before pushing his plate away. Nell, on the other hand, did swift justice to Kitty's famous full Irish, smiling smugly across the table at Nick, who scowled back. Just as they finished eating, Kitty came into the dining room, looking resplendent in a green silk dress, her thick auburn hair piled up and lanced with several ornate pins. Her face lit up when she saw them, and she made a beeline for their table.

"Top o' the mornin' to ye! How are ye both this fine mornin'?"

Nick leaped to his feet to draw out a chair for her, and Kitty settled herself at their table, looking as fresh as a daisy, even though she'd done most of the drinking the night before. No hangover there, thought Nell. Right on cue, the young girl who waited table arrived with a cup of coffee and set it in front of her mistress.

"Bring me some fried eggs, please Delilah, with buttered toast. Oh," she added, running an appraising eye over Nick, "bring a pot of strong coffee, too, there's a good girl."

"Yes, ma'am."

Delilah gave a curt bob before scooping up empty plates and hurrying off to the kitchen. She was quickly back to deliver Kitty's breakfast and a tall pot of coffee with steam wisping from the spout. On Kitty's instructions, she replenished Nell and Nick's cups before filling her mistress's to the brim and withdrawing just as quickly as she'd arrived.

As she tackled her breakfast, wielding her cutlery with precise and ladylike finesse, Kitty asked what plans Nick and Nell had for the day ahead. Since Nick, slumped over his coffee cup, looked as if he wanted nothing so much as to return to bed, Nell took charge of the conversation.

"Reckon we'll have us a good look around, get the feel of the place, an' then take some time to talk about your generous offer, Miz Callahan."

Kitty waved her knife airily. "Kitty, remember, and from now on ye're Nick and Nell. I hate formality. As I said to ye, take yer time. Ask around about me, too, so ye know who it is ye're dealing with. Folks in this town like me and speak well of me. I have good standing here." Kitty placed her knife and fork side by side on her plate and dabbed at her lips with her napkin. She looked from Nell to Nick, squaring her small shoulders. "I consider myself a good judge of character, and I took strongly to ye both right away. Maybe some day ye'll trust me enough to tell me yer stories."

She stood up, smiling at the startled expressions on the two youngsters' faces. "Have dinner with me tonight so we can get better acquainted. I'll see ye then." She paused, placing both hands on the back of the chair, nibbling her lip before she spoke. "This is a good town, but it is a mining town, just the same, so we have our – " she stared over their heads momentarily, apparently searching for the right word, and then smiled at them both. "Challenges. But we handle them in our own way."

Nell looked after her as she swept out, absorbing this enigmatic statement. When she was sure the coast was clear, she leaned across the table. "To be honest, that woman makes me feel like she knows everything about me, down to the colour of my drawers," she whispered to Nick. "I can't figure whether I like her or she gives me the heebie-jeebies. She wears a wedding ring but I don't see no husband."

Nick rubbed his temples with his fingertips. "You're imaginin' things, Nell. She's jus' a nice lady, with an eye for the main chance. Nobody asks questions 'bout you out here. They jus' take you at face value an' don't pry. Lotsa folks got secrets, I guess, maybe runnin' away from somethin', like us." He sighed. "Anyway, first thing we need to do is sell Cheney's horse. It's kinda unusual, so we need to get rid."

"You look like hell."

"Thanks."

****

By noon, Nick had perked up, hangover a bad memory, and was, he claimed, starving hungry into the bargain. They'd sold Cheney's distinctive horse to the livery owner himself for a good price, and Nick felt they both deserved a slap-up lunch. The hotel served only breakfast and supper, so they had to look elsewhere. Besides, they were keen to find out what passed for good catering in Yreka, apart from Kitty's establishment, of course. Everyone they'd mentioned her name to over the course of their sortie about town had spoken of her in glowing terms, although nobody seemed to know many details about her except that she was widowed. No issue there, then. Nell queried the owner of a goods emporium where Nick stopped to purchase tobacco and he recommended The Pick and Shovel on the corner of Gold Street, saying it was popular and served simple but good quality food. Nell and Nick followed the man's directions and quickly found the place. They needed to take some time, they agreed, to assimilate and talk over all the surprising things that had happened.

****

The Pick and Shovel was an unpretentious place with a simple clapboard sign above the entrance proclaiming its name. The single window that fronted the street was framed by red and white gingham curtains that featured a matching frill across the top. The overall effect was one of homely welcome. Nick opened the door, triggering a vibrant peal from a small brass bell swinging from the jamb, and they stepped inside to be warmly embraced by savoury cooking smells that set taste buds tingling. A large jolly-faced woman, cheeks flushed red and perspiration glistening on her forehead, emerged from what must have been the kitchen, welcomed them and

264

conducted them to one of about eight round tables, all with seating for four. With the arrival of Nick and Nell, three of the tables held occupants, the other two circled by groups of comparatively well-dressed men of varying ages. They eyed the newcomers briefly before resuming their conversation. The woman took their hats and jackets and hung them on pegs on the wall-mounted coat rack beside other patrons' attire.

After their hostess disappeared back into the kitchen, a young boy, who looked about twelve, brought them a pitcher of water and two tumblers, placing them carefully on the table before stepping back to intone the menu of the day with rehearsed solemnity. A little white towel draped over his left arm sealed the impression of a well-practiced if somewhat juvenile steward. He had a sweet, round face, carroty red hair, and lots of freckles, with an extra generous dusting across his nose.

"Today we got three choices. Venison pie, rabbit pie, or chicken pie. All meals are served with seasonal vegetables and buttered bread, and coffee is com-pal-i-men-tary. Cost per plate is four bits."

Nick rubbed his jaw thoughtfully, playing up fully to the youngster's serious approach. "Well, let me think, now. I had me a glut of chicken lately and I'm right partial to game. I'm going to settle for the venison pie."

The child nodded. "Yes, sir. Excellent choice." He turned expectantly towards Nell, big blue eyes drinking in her loveliness.

"Make that two. I hope the meat is tender."

The youngster bobbed his head emphatically. "Oh yes, ma'am. My mam's the best cook in the whole state."

"Really? What's your name?"

"Toby, ma'am. Toby Entwhistle. My mam's name is Addy Entwhistle. My pappy, Jed, shot the deer." Without much enthusiasm, he added, "I got a younger sister, too."

"I'm Nell and this is Nick."

"Pleased to meet you, I'm sure." He marched off back to the kitchen with great dignity.

Nell chuckled. "Must be a family concern. He's a sweetheart. Got it all down pat."

"Saves on waiters' wages, I guess," said Nick, as he poured their water.

Toby brought their meals out on a tray, along with cutlery, napkins, coffee, and condiments. He placed everything with great care and wished them enjoyment before he withdrew, gaze lingering on Nell long enough to be registered, but not quite long enough to be interpreted as precocity.

The food was very good, and there was precious little conversation to be had as the young couple devoured their generous servings. The pastry on the pies was feather light and buttery, the meaty content tender and delicious, oozing rich gravy, while carrots, potatoes and greens made up the vegetable element, all cooked perfectly.

When Toby came to collect their barely blemished plates, Nell said, "Tell your mam that's the best meal we've eaten in a long time. If I coulda ate the plate, too, I would've."

Toby beamed. "I will, ma'am. Thank you." He replenished their coffee and left them, having declined the desserts on offer, to postprandial contentment.

Nell gazed around the restaurant, which was now full, buzzing with good cheer, and a big man she took to be Toby's dad assisting him with the busy service. She sighed. "I don't see how we can compete with this, Nick."

Nick lit the quirley he'd rolled and drew on it. "We wouldn't be aiming to, would we? They cater to the hoi polloi here. We'd be feeding hungry miners, most of 'em too drunk to realise what they're eatin'."

Nell snorted. "You're right, I guess. Which brings us to the hub of it, eh? What did you think of Kitty's offer?"

Nick frowned, looking past her and clearly taking time to consider his answer. "It was sudden, an' we really don't know much about her. On the other hand, she's plainly good at what she does an' I reckon we could do well here, too. I know you were set on a store, but she was right about that. There's a glut of them." He shifted awkwardly. "We ain't talked about it, but I know you got more money than me, so, whatever we decide, you have the final say. I think that's fair."

Nell smiled. "I don't care about that. I owe you, Nick Hardy, an' 's far as I'm concerned we're equal partners, straight down the middle. All right?"

"That's mighty generous of you. An' you owe me nothin'."

"We'll jus' have to disagree' bout that, then." Nell paused. "Nick?"

"Yes?" Nick's furrowed brow revealed his concern over what might be coming.

"When I first met you, you were hankerin' after adventure. I seen how happy you was on the cattle drive – until things went belly up. I don't want you to feel you have to give up what you really want in your heart to – to be with me. What I'm tryin' to say is, I don't wanna spoil your dreams." Nell had suddenly become very interested in her fingernails, which were a bit grubby. She jumped a little when Nick reached across the table and folded her little hand inside his big one.

"Nell, you're the best adventure I could ever have. I mean it. I'm with you because I want to be."

Nell gave him a wobbly smile, fiercely swiping away a tear. "You mean that?"

"Of course I mean it. Fate brought us together." He applied gentle pressure to her hand. "Which kinda brings us to Kitty's other proposal, doesn't it? I guess she figures a husband and wife team is, uh, more steady. Have you given it any thought?"

An attractive rosy flush crept up Nell's cheeks and she looked directly into his warm brown eyes, his innate kindness always evident there. "I have."

"And?"

"I like it."

"So do I."

"I want to wait a month, 'til I'm sixteen. My mam made me promise I'd wait 'til I was sixteen to marry."

"Done." He frowned. "Promised your ma. Why? Did you have someone in mind?"

Nell bit her lip. Dang. She hadn't intended to bring up the subject of Jimmy. She waved a hand airily. "No, not really. There was this one boy at school, like a childhood sweetheart kinda thing, but nothin' serious. Didn't you have a girl at school you were sweet on?" She felt like a traitor, being so dismissive of her beloved Jimmy.

"I wasn't at school much. But yeah, I guess I had one crush. Her name was Harriet Jarman. She's prob'ly wed by now. All the boys liked her."

Nell nodded. "Anyways, is that it? You ain't gonna make a nice romantic proposal, on your knees an' all?"

"When the moment's ripe, I will." Nick looked around. "Definitely not in here. They're our competition now."

Nell laughed. "Let's pay the bill and go find Kitty." As she rose from the table, she added. "Nick, do you think we're safe here?"

Nick pushed in his chair as he gave her a reassuring smile. "Yes," he said firmly. "I do."

CHAPTER EIGHTEEN

Kitty was delighted by Nell and Nick's decision to invest in the restaurant above Pot O' Gold saloon and, after a brief discussion, they decided to name the new venture The Shamrock, which Kitty assured them would bring them lots of good luck while preserving her Irish theme. Everything was drawn up legally, with Kitty opting to be a silent partner while investing twenty percent of the estimated cost to establish the modest venture. Since they now planned to wed, further adding to Kitty's overall joy, Nick and Nell pooled their money and thus had more than enough to set up a business while banking the remainder, which they hoped they could build on together. Kitty seemed to be able to find reliable, hardworking tradesmen with consummate ease, and in an impressively short time the little eatery was completed and set to officially open with suitable fanfare, all organised by Kitty of course. She had colourful bunting and billboards all over the place in case anyone missed the advertised opening date. The miners who faithfully frequented the saloon were looking forward to this grand occasion more than anyone. The idea of enjoying a good home-cooked meal along with their alcohol consumption was very appealing to them, as was the knowledge that they only had to climb a few steps to reach this delight. Kitty wisely knew that the delicious odours of cooking that drifted downstairs into the bar would bring them up in droves, salivating, well-oiled, and ready to spend large.

"The poor craturs have no woman to cook for them and they miss that so."

About two weeks before opening, Kitty sat down with Nick and Nell to work out a menu. They'd already bandied about some ideas, but now they had to finalise things, and Kitty was adamant that the food should have an Irish theme. Nell was familiar with soda or 'quick' bread, so that posed no problem, and most of Kitty's other suggestions, like boxty, colcannon, shepherd's pie, and Irish stew, were the kind of simple fare she espoused as a cook, anyway. Since he was the only male in their culinary crew, they picked Nick's brains for his favourite fare, and his face took on a dreamy expression as he listed his late mam's specialties. Without too much haggling, they settled on a menu they were all happy with and Kitty offered to treat everyone to a round of drinks to celebrate.

"As long as it's not bacon and beans, they'll be happy," Kitty assured them as Billy fetched the bottle and glasses, "Catsup! Don't forget catsup. Sourdough! The miners love their sourdough bread.

And we'll listen to requests as well. The men come from all over and miss the dishes from their home countries. If we can tap into that nostalgia, we'll be winning." As they raised their glasses in a toast to their new enterprise, Kitty promised to take them on a tour of the hotel's kitchen garden after lunch. "Ye're welcome to source yer vegetables from there. I have a Chinese gardener, and he's wonderful."

In between sharing the cooking Nick and Nell would take turns waiting table, while Kitty insisted she would often pop up to help out when things got busy. For his part, Kitty's factotum, Billy, would divide his time between bar and restaurant to handle any trouble that might arise. "Not that I anticipate any shenanigans," Kitty added with a smile. "With all that good food in their bellies those boys will be docile as lambs. Just the same, I'll be keepin' the shillelagh and scatter gun handy!"

Everything was settling nicely into place, but then, just two days before Shamrock's official opening, an unexpected visitor turned up in the restaurant where Nell happened to be alone doing some last minute tidying up while Nick and Kitty were out organising supplies of comestibles.

"Mornin', Miz Washburn."

Nell hadn't been aware of anyone entering as she concentrated on blacking the big wood range to ebony perfection, and she whirled around in surprise.

"Toby!" She put down her brush and flicked back a strand of hair. "What can I do for you? We're not open yet."

Toby blushed, chewing his lip. "Yes, ma'am, I know. I'm sorry to bother you. I've come about a job." He held his tattered wee felt hat in front of him with both hands fidgeting nervously, his manner mendicant, his soulful blue eyes regarding her hopefully. "I want to wait table for you."

"But you wait table for your folks. I cain't headhunt you an' mebbe rile up yer folks."

Toby shook his head. "My mam sent me. But I was willing to come," he added hastily. "She said it's time I earned my keep. My sister, Hattie, is gonna take over the waiting at our place. She's near eleven now." He frowned. "You would pay me, wouldn't you?"

Nell grinned. "Of course. I don't hold with child slave labour."

Toby's face was wreathed in a seraphic smile. "Does that mean you'll hire me?"

Nell pursed her lips. "Oh, hell, why not? I seen what you do an' you're right good at it."

Toby wrung his hat into a shapeless mass, his face aglow. "Oh, thank you, Miz, thank you!"

"How old are you, Toby?"

"Almost thirteen, Miz."

"Okay. An' if you're gonna be working here, you can call me Nell."

Toby blushed, merging his complexion with his thatch of red hair. "Thank you, Nell."

"The men gonna be comin' in here won't be like the well-heeled polite folks you're used to at your mam's. You'll likely get a hard time from some of them, bein' so young an' all."

Toby grimaced. "I got red hair and more freckles than a trout, Nell. Blame, I'm well used to teasing."

Nell smiled. "Okay. I gotta clear this with Nick, but I'm sure he'll be just fine with it. Come back tomorrow mornin' and we'll talk wages and such. Scram now, I'm busy."

"Yes, Nell, right away, Nell." Toby clattered off downstairs and Nell chuckled as she reclaimed her blacking brush. He was such a sweetheart. Their little team was shaping up nicely.

****

"A dress?" Nell's eyes narrowed as she regarded Kitty with frank suspicion. "Why do I need a dress?"

"Sure now, ye look grand in yer pants an' all," said Kitty, hastily backtracking under Nell's glare, "Ye've a slim waist, shapely bottom, and legs like a young colt. But a dress would altogether show off yer comely figure in a womanly manner." For emphasis she sketched a curvy outline through the air with her hands.

"Humph. Show it off to whom? The stove I'll be toiling over? It'll be hidden by my apron, anyways."

"But ye'll be serving sometimes as well." Kitty gave an insouciant shrug, raising her cup of coffee to her lips. They were in her private parlour at the hotel, going over lists of comestibles. Nick was at the restaurant organising the storeroom.

"Hah! Now we've come to it!" said Nell. "You want me to be a pull for the men to come eat there, don't you, like them bar girls."

Kitty lowered her cup making a 'tsk' sound. "Barmaids, Nell. Barmaids. And what's wrong with that, anyway? Having a pretty girl to look at while they eat will aid their digestion. They're not just starved for victuals, ye know."

Nell laughed, shaking her head. "An' make them spend more." She levelled a thoughtful look at Kitty. "All right. I'll get me a dress. Better be somethin' simple and hardwearin' though."

"Splendid! I'll send for Ursula, my dressmaker, right away." She smiled, cutting half closed eyes towards Nell with a sly look. "She can measure ye up for yer wedding dress at the same time."

Nell sighed. "An' I guess you'll be in charge of that, too."

Kitty's smile assumed dazzling proportions. "Of course, cushla macree. Of course."

****

Nell smoothed her skirts and flexed her shoulders as she settled into her chair at the dining table she shared with Kitty and Nick. It was the night before the official opening of The Shamrock, and Kitty had insisted they dine together at the hotel before launching the venture, an opportunity to discuss any last minute details, and, more importantly she insisted, just to celebrate all the hard work they'd put into setting up the restaurant. She'd had a flower arrangement and candles placed on the table to emphasise the special significance of their get-together. Nell was wearing a dress for the occasion: a simple calico print that she'd insisted should be nothing fancy. Her steadily lengthening hair was pinned up after a fashion with two tortoiseshell combs, and Kitty had lent her a pair of green glass earbobs that twinkled prettily in the lamplight. Nick couldn't take his eyes off her as the candlelight highlighted her beauty. She looked nothing like the surly little androgynous waif he'd picked up on the prairie – well, there was still the odd strike that lanced you straight in the jugular. Flashes of spirit aside, there was little doubt, however, that Nell was maturing into a beautiful young woman whom any red-blooded man would covet for his wife.

"Ye look lovely," purred Kitty. "Nick, doesn't she look a picture tonight?"

"She sure does. I'm gonna have to watch her like a hawk 'mongst all those men."

"I can take care of myself," snapped Nell, and then felt bad when she saw the hurt in Nick's eyes. Being back in dresses didn't suit her at all. She'd grown accustomed to the comfort of shirt and trousers and felt annoyingly constrained. It hadn't escaped her attention, though, the way the male customers' heads had all turned appreciatively towards her when she'd entered the hotel's dining room, their obvious admiration giving her a heady sense of her own female power. She tilted her head demurely to one side. "I'm glad you'll be with me, Nick, just the same. I'll feel safer." She hated the idea of hurting him. She owed him her life.

Nick's chest visibly swelled as he smiled at her, the slight forgotten.

"Excuse me a moment." Kitty, resplendent herself in purple silk, rose from her chair and glided across the dining room to greet a tall, imposing man who had just entered and stood looking about him as if he were searching for someone. He broke into a broad smile of recognition as she touched his arm and he swung around to face her. He was well groomed and impeccably dressed, projecting a prosperous air. After a brief chat, he obeyed Kitty's bidding to follow her.

"Who's that?" whispered Nick.

"Dunno. Looks important. Kitty is sure preenin' up to him."

They both looked on curiously as the pair paused before their table while Kitty made introductions.

"Nell, Nick, this is Mr. Hank Humble. Hank, meet Mr. Nick Hardy, and Miss Nell Washburn, the new proprietors of The Shamrock restaurant."

Nick leaped to his feet, thrusting out a hand. "Pleased to meet you, sir."

"Likewise, young man." The stranger shook his hand warmly and then turned his attention to Nell, his interest apparent. She lifted a hand and he squeezed it gently. "How do you do, Miss Washburn?" Nell dipped her head as she slid her fingers from his clasp, which she felt had lasted a little longer than a mere introduction warranted.

Kitty clapped her hands. "Have a seat, Hank. I'll go and organise our dinner. We have a special menu, just the four of us."

Hmmm, thought Nell. So his presence here is no accident.

As Kitty swept off, her guest drew out a chair and sat down, adjusting his cuffs and smiling serenely at the young couple, his gaze lingering on Nell. He had slick, black hair, ice-blue eyes, a generous mouth, and an attractively dark complexion. There was no denying that he was a handsome man. The suit he wore was well tailored and had an expensive look about it. His manner was refined and he thanked Nick graciously as the young man poured him a tumbler of water and pushed it over. As he raised the glass he said, "I'm sure we can run to something better than Adam's ale tonight, hopefully some good wine. No doubt Kitty has it all in hand. This is a celebration, is it not?" He flashed a smile, which highlighted his white teeth against his tanned complexion. A heavy gold ring gleamed on the little finger of his left hand, its central stone a cabochon ruby of impressive size.

Nell lifted her own glass and took a sip. Her gut was telling her to be wary of this man. She already disliked him. He was a flasher version of Cheney. A snake. Her thoughts were interrupted by a returning Kitty, dispensing orders over her shoulder to the two serving girls trailing in her wake with food-laden trays. Close behind them was a young sommelier armed with bottles of wine and crystal glasses. Hank leaped up to slide out Kitty's chair and once the table was furnished to her satisfaction, she dismissed her waiting staff and beamed around her guests, hands clasped under her chin.

"A spatchcocked quail each," she announced, clearly delighted with the crispy golden birds that rested on the gleaming white plates set before her diners, "and do help yerselves to gravy and vegetables. Nick, ye can start with the potatoes."

Dinner progressed pleasantly enough. The food was excellent, the birds deliciously tender, and Nell found herself really enjoying the accompanying wine. She felt like a real lady as she sipped the sweetish ruby liquid from its exquisite cut crystal glass, enjoying the sensation of its warm flow over palate and down her throat before blooming in her head. Kitty had made a real effort tonight for sure, and Nell noticed the sparkle in her eye as she conversed easily with Humble, who kept topping up everyone's glass with assiduous vigilance. He was a bit of an enigma, Nell thought. Why was he here? Was he Kitty's paramour? All was soon revealed as they relaxed contentedly over coffee, the two men smoking absently, reclining back in their chairs. Kitty asked for a bottle of port and one of brandy to be fetched, and after everyone had a glass of one or the other, she cleared her throat and turned to Humble.

"Hank, I think it's time to explain yer reason for joining us tonight. Do, please, enlighten Nick and Nell."

As the intrigued young couple watched the big man, he straightened in his chair, placed his pipe in the ashtray, and leaned his elbows on the table, his expression serious.

"Thank you, Kitty." He looked from Nell to Nick and back to Nell again. "What do you think of Yreka?"

"What do we think of it?" It was Nick who answered.

Humble gave him an indulgent smile as his question was repeated. "Yes, what are your impressions of the town? You must have formed some thoughts about it. You've been here some weeks now, according to Kitty."

Kitty nodded vigorously by way of encouraging them to answer. It was Nell who did so, choosing her words as carefully as a slightly floaty post-vinous feeling allowed.

"We like it well enough. We've been lucky to meet Kitty right off, I guess, an' now we got us a stake in the place. The people all seem nice an' friendly, made us feel welcome. We aim to do well here, don't we, Nick? If others can, no reason why we shouldn't."

Humble leaned across the table to refill her port glass, but Nell swiftly placed a hand over it, and he shrugged, topping up his own glass instead. "You're right, Nell, you should do well here and I'm sure you will. In a gold rush, it's the mercantile people who frequently come out wealthy, not the miners. Kitty here is a prime example." He placed his hand over hers and gave it a brief squeeze, while Kitty rewarded him with a radiant smile.

"If I may be so bold as to ask, Mr. Humble, what business are you in?" Nell's large, soft blue eyes looked boldly into the ice-blue ones opposite.

Humble retrieved his pipe and methodically sucked it to glowing incandescence. "I'm in haulage. Freight."

"You done well at that?"

The indulgent smile again. "Yes, I would have to say that I have indeed done well."

"Fine. So I'm thinkin' you're buildin' up to some point here. What exactly is it?" Out of the corner of her eye she saw Kitty stiffen, and Humble's fixed smile slid off his face like butter off a hot plate.

"Yes, I will get to the point," he replied with a noticeable edge in his voice. It was dawning on Humble that he was not dealing with any shrinking violet here. The ice-blue eyes were now glacial.

"Perhaps you've noticed that there is no law in this town. We have filled that vacuum with a committee of responsible and respectable citizens who ensure the safety of all. Of course, we need funds to operate effectively for the protection of the good people, business and otherwise, of Yreka." The smile, though thin, returned. "Everybody contributes. You would be expected to also. In return, we will provide all the security you require to keep your business running smoothly, making a nice profit, while we take care of any threats or dangers." He gestured towards his hostess. "Kitty here is well aware of the benefits of belonging to the scheme, as are all our clients. Is that not right, Kitty?"

"Oh, yes. Ye can't put a price on safety." Kitty's smile was frozen as she nodded vigorously, her eyes silently entreating Nell to comply.

Nell's own eyes narrowed. The growing tension between her and Humble was palpable. "So you head a bunch of vigilantes. Hell, any of our boys get out of hand, we'll kick 'em back down the stairs into the bar, but we ain't payin' no protection money an' that's final." Her lip curled. "Bet you make more of a 'nice profit' from your 'clients' than from your haulage business."

Humble stared at her coldly for a few moments and then turned to Nick. "What do you have to say, Nick? You're a partner, aren't you?"

Nick glanced at Nell before he cleared his throat. "Nell put in the biggest pot. What she says goes, 's far as I'm concerned."

Humble abruptly pushed back his chair and stood up. "You're both making a mistake," he said softly. "I'll leave you to talk this over with Kitty, and hopefully she can drum some sense into you." He bestowed a brittle smile on the anxious looking Kitty. "Thank you for a wonderful dinner, my dear. We will speak soon." His gaze swivelled back to Nell, the smile vanishing. "I hope your opening is a success," he added ominously, subtle emphasis on the last word. "Good night."

Kitty looked after him as he strode out of her dining room, pausing in the doorway as Delilah fetched his coat and hat before casting one final, dark glance their way. She had visibly paled, the habitual cockiness and swagger all gone. Then she rounded on Nell. "What d'ye think ye're playin'at?" she hissed when he'd departed. "Ye just pissed off the town's most powerful man, and no good will come of it."

Nick looked down, Nell snorted. "Takin' hard workin' folks' money and more of a threat to them than any local hooligans or liquored up miners, I'll bet. He don't frighten me none, jus' a cheap bully boy." She paused, eyeballing an aghast Kitty. "'Sides, you got Billy, don't you? An' you said he'll take care of us, too."

"Ye foolish girl! Billy works for Humble!" Kitty stood up. "This is how things are done out West an' if ye don't understand that ye'll make life hard for yerselves. Ye'd both better sleep on this, an' I'll discuss it further with ye in the mornin'. Ye can't sidestep Humble and the committee. Ye just can't. They won't tolerate it." She swept out.

Nell looked across the table at Nick, eyebrows raised. "Life is sure gettin' interestin', ain't it?"

Nick sighed. "That's the girl I know and love. She's back. Nell, it's time I got myself a gun. A good sidearm."

****

They didn't see Kitty at breakfast the following morning, and Nell felt a mixture of relief and regret. Apart from all her other kindnesses, the little Irishwoman had given them a very fair fixed rate to stay on at the hotel for as long as they liked, and Nell hated the idea of falling out with her or creating ill feeling. However, this was opening day for the restaurant and she didn't want anything distracting her from that fact, especially not a confrontation with their benefactor.

Nick was quiet, too, and he excused himself as soon as he'd finished eating to go off on some errands, assuring Nell he'd meet her back at the restaurant in an hour or so. Nell looked after him as he strode off, shoulders noticeably slumped. She bit her lip as she toyed with a last piece of bacon. She still wasn't convinced that he was happy with his new life, was doing what he really wanted to. Well, she told herself, squaring her small shoulders, it didn't have to be forever. They could give it a trial period, hopefully make some money, and then review their options. She made a mental note to talk with Nick later and probe him thoroughly. His happiness was important to her. He was her man, after all.

After breakfast, Nell set off for the General Store to purchase one or two last minute items, then returned to the hotel and climbed the stairs to the restaurant. As she stood, hands on hips, surveying her pristine little domain, she thought of her dead family. *Pap, Mam, baby Jesse, Sabrina, please watch over me and Nick and help us do this right.*

CHAPTER NINETEEN

The day passed smoothly, and Nell found that being busy was a good way to keep her mind off the previous night's ugly altercation with Humble and Kitty, who still hadn't put in an appearance. Someone who did put in an appearance, though, was Toby's mam. Addy Entwhistle thanked Nell sincerely for giving her boy a job, and they agreed on a time for him to arrive for this most important of nights as well as confirming his terms and conditions. It was all very affable and the women felt a friendship had taken root. Before she left, Addy helped Nell mount a sign on the wall, which proclaimed: 'No Spitting on the Floor'.

As they stepped back to gauge the accuracy of its placement, Nell pronounced, arms folded, "If there's one male habit I detest more 'n anything it's their blamed spitting. Nick never spits, thank god, but I'd cure him fast if he did."

Addy nodded her agreement. "It ain't so bad on dirt floors, but you got puncheon floors here." She pointed. "If I were you, I'd place a spittoon at the top of the stairs. Get 'em 'fore they come to table."

Nell had just slid the last of three meat and potato pies into the stove and was having a break for a cup of coffee with Nick when their little waiter arrived right on time, just as dusk was deepening…'candle time', they called it.

"Evenin', Nell, Nick," Toby said breathlessly as he removed his hat. "I'm ready for work."

Nell slowly lowered her coffee cup on to its saucer, falling back in her chair as she made a big show of taking him in, eyes widened, lips parted. She raised her arms and let them drop to her sides.

"Well look at you. Ain't you just the most handsome thing I ever did see?"

Toby blushed and squirmed self-consciously under this approbation, his delight obvious. "Thank you, Nell." The already long-suffering felt hat got another tortuous wringing.

The youngster had clearly made a great effort to impress. His thick red hair was neatly parted on one side and slicked down with grease. His face was scrubbed to a rosy glow and he exuded a faint aroma of fancy soap. He wore a boiled white shirt buttoned up to the neck and his neatly pressed trousers were held up by what looked like a brand new pair of deep blue suspenders. To complete this aura of professionalism, his flawlessly laced short black work boots were polished to a dazzling ebony shine.

"Wait there," ordered Nell, rising from her chair and disappearing into the storeroom. She emerged holding a folded piece of dark cloth, which she handed to the curious Toby. "I made this for you. I hope you like it."

Toby shook out the cloth and held it up, his face breaking into a radiant smile. "It's an apron." He turned it around, his finger tracing a neatly embroidered strip sewn to the bib. "You put my name on it!"

"Sure did. You're our waiter, with a real important job so it's fittin' you should have a title." She chuckled. "I thought a dark colour was best 'stead of white; hides stains and splashes better. Protects your clothes, too. Your mam wouldn't thank me for sending you home with them all splattered, 'specially that flash shirt." She grinned. "Not sayin' you're gonna be clumsy or anything like that, but we're gonna be victualling rough men with likely few table manners to speak of."

Toby seemed unimpressed by this practical reasoning or caveat. He stood like one in thrall, staring at his name that Nell had so painstakingly stitched on to the fabric with bright red thread, close to the colour of his hair. It was clearly the most important facet of the apron, as far as he was concerned.

Nell clapped her hands to bring him back to the moment, and then pointed to the storeroom. "There's hooks in there, so go stow your hat an' put your apron on. I have a couple chores lined up for you before I give you some tucker to keep your strength up 'til your proper dinner."

"Yes, ma'am." Clutching the apron reverently to his breast, Toby did as bid.

Nell crossed to the stove to check her pies and Nick followed her. He shook his head and rolled his eyes. "You know what you done, don't you?"

Nell straightened up, frowning. "What?"

Nick leaned forwards, speaking with deliberate slowness, eyes half closed. "That ain't no apron to that kid. That's a lurrrrv token."

He skipped away with a high-pitched giggle as Nell came after him brandishing a wooden spoon.

****

Despite Nell and Nick's apprehension, opening night at The Shamrock went off without a hitch. The miners ascended the stairs in a steady stream, ate quickly, paid up in gold dust, dollars, or other coins in circulation, and vacated the tables for impatiently hovering new customers. For three bits each man received two courses, either soup and mains or mains and pudding. Anything on top of that cost extra. Their menu was simple, the choices limited, but they hoped the good, wholesome quality and generous portions of the food they served would compensate for any deficiencies. Kitty appeared once or twice, looked around briefly each time, and disappeared back downstairs as abruptly as she'd arrived without speaking to anyone. There was only one small incident, and Nell personally defused things before they got out of hand by belting the aggressor over the head with her ladle, which attention he seemed to find flattering rather than irritating. One miner, so drunk that he fell face down on to his dinner plate, was quickly and efficiently removed by his companions without undue fuss. His place at table was promptly taken by another.

The evening flew by, and finally silence descended on the dining room as the last customers left, voicing their appreciation, and promising to return. Nell served up three plates of leftover food for the hungry, sweaty team and they sank, weary but ebullient, on to chairs at one of the tables to enjoy their late supper. Nick and Nell watched intrigued as Toby shovelled massive spoonfuls of pie into his mouth with relentless rhythm.

"Steady on, Tobe," Nick admonished the boy. "You'll give yourself a bellyache."

As Toby looked up with a shy smile, Nell said, "You've earned it. Never got a single order wrong, an' worked like a little Trojan. Well done, Toby. We'll be keeping you on."

Toby beamed. "Thank you, Nell."

"Soon's you've finished that you get on home 'fore your folks get in a pucker."

"Yes'm." Toby belched and grinned, took a long swig from the tall glass of milk Nell had given him, and, a milky moustache cresting his top lip, resumed his assault on the pie. As soon as his plate was scraped clean, he removed his apron, swapped it for his hat and jacket, wished his employers goodnight and then paused at the head of the stairs. "When will I get paid, Nell?"

"Once a week, so next Saturday."

Toby touched the brim of his hat and skipped off down the stairs. Nell chuckled. "He'll do well for himself, that wee tyke."

Nick fetched cups of coffee, and they sat quietly, Nick rolling a smoke. He swept a hand through his damp hair and rested his elbows on the table, one hand wrapped around the other holding the cigarette. Nell glanced at him sideways. His face was a mask. Good time to draw him out now he'd had a taste of being a restaurateur.

"A penny for 'em." She pushed the ashtray towards him.

"Hmm?" Nick blew a leisurely stream of smoke into the air and then smiled at his business partner. "I'm jus' thinkin' 'bout how lucky I am."

"Lucky?"

"Yeah. I never ever dreamed I'd have my own business, however humble, an' I never dreamed I'd be doin' it with a girl I loved."

He stubbed out the cigarette and got to his feet, extending a hand towards her in a self-assured way that said he wouldn't take no for an answer. With her eyes fastened on his, Nell clasped his hand and he pulled her up and towards him, drawing her in close so that her body was pressed hard against his and his arms enfolded her, holding her tight. Nell's arms were quickly around him, and it felt like the most natural thing in the world when he kissed her, their first real kiss. Nell kissed him back and it was some moments before they broke apart, both breathing hard and looking at each other in wonder.

"I love you. Marry me, Nell."

"I love you, too. I want to marry you." She cocked her head to one side. "Ain't you forgettin' somethin?"

"What?"

Nick looked puzzled. His face cleared when Nell pointed to his knees. "Oh, that!"

Nick dropped on to one knee and clasped his hands in front of his chest as he cleared his throat. "Nell Washburn, will you do me the honour of marryin' me? Sooner the better."

"I will!" Nell flung herself at him with such enthusiasm that Nick toppled over sideways with her sprawled on top of him. He looked up into her beautiful eyes as they laughed like loons, and then their lips came together, drawing the breath out of each other again.

Behind them a laconic female voice drawled, "Jasus, rolling about on the floor, is it? Musta been a grand night, so it must."

****

Nick and Nell scrambled to their feet, adjusting clothes and smoothing hair as they grinned sheepishly at Kitty, whose eyes sparkled with amusement.

"We'd better get the pair of ye wed quick." She chuckled. Then her face became serious as she glanced around the little restaurant before returning her straightforward gaze to the still blushing pair. "Feedback from the boys down in the saloon was all good. Ye did well. Very well."

"Thanks, Kitty." Nick and Nell gave each other pleased looks. They also felt relieved that she appeared to harbour no ill feelings about the previous evening's encounter. They knew they owed her a great deal, and falling out with her was the last thing they wanted. Ever one to clear the air, Nell blurted out, "What about Humble? Will he make trouble for us?"

Kitty shook her head. "I've negotiated a reprieve for ye, asked him to let ye get on yer feet first. Anyway, we'll talk about that later. Ye finish up here, now, and get yerselves to bed. Ye'll be all in."

With that advice, she disappeared down the stairs, leaving the youngsters smiling happily at each other. Nell slid her arms around Nick and they held each other tight, his head resting on top of hers.

"She's a smart woman."

"Yes, I wish I know'd more about her background, how she ended up here makin' a name for herself. She's a mystery, really."

"She probably thinks the same about us. Anyways, I wasn't talkin' about her business savvy when I said she was smart."

"Oh? What was you talkin' about, then?" Nell looked up into Nick's face.

"I was mindin' what she said about us getting married quick."

"I'm sixteen in two weeks. We can set a date."

"Yes! Let's get married on your birthday!"

"Well, one thing at a time!"

****

Nell and Nick's wedding was a quiet but nevertheless joyous affair, the marriage taking place two days after Nell's sixteenth birthday in the town's recently built little church and the wedding breakfast held in the dining room of Kitty's hotel, where the small number of guests gathered to toast the bride and groom. Those in attendance included, the Entwhistle family, Billy, and the Humbles, which Nell was not thrilled about, but which Kitty had insisted on. Nell was coming around to conceding that, with the arrogance of youth, she had probably got that one badly wrong and was willing to learn from the mistake. As Kitty had pointed out, she needed to understand the ways of the West.

Nell, looking ethereally beautiful in white muslin and floating veil secured by a circlet of apple blossom, was escorted down the aisle by a delighted Toby. He'd been personally requested for this role by Nell, to stand in for her father by giving the bride away to the nervous but ecstatic groom, and he carried it off with great aplomb. Kitty, resplendent herself in rose coloured silk, served as matron of honour.

The newlyweds now occupied just one room at the hotel as Mr. and Mrs Hardy. Kitty had a bottle of champagne delivered to their room, and then the young couple was left in peace to enjoy their wedding night.

Nell, wearing only her shift, accepted a glass of wine from her still fully clad husband, watching him closely.

"Nick, you okay?"

"Yes." Said tersely.

"You're acting like a cat on hot coals. Hell, we're both nervous, both bein' virgins an' all." She giggled. "I got no more idea than you, but we'll work it out. It's just nature, after all." Stepping closer, she placed a hand on his arm. "We don't gotta do anything if you ain't ready."

Nick squeezed his eyes shut and made a groaning sound. "That shoulda been my line. Oh, what the heck. Nell, I'm scared I'm gonna hurt you."

"Well, yeah, prob'ly the first time. That's normal. But we'll get better at it," she added brightly.

"No, I don't mean that. Oh hell, I gotta tell you."

Nell's eyes widened. "Tell me what?" She gave him a sly, sideways look. "Nick Hardy, you got somethin' amiss south of the border?"

Nick squirmed with embarrassment. "Not 'amiss', exactly." He took a deep breath. "When I was at school, a group of us boys went skinny-dipping on the way home one afternoon, in the river. Boys is boys, an' we got around to comparing the size of our peckers, an', well, mine was the biggest, by some measure." He covered his face with his hands.

"So? Better 'n having a tiny todger." Nell chuckled.

Nick whipped his hands away. "Yeah," he said with anguish, "but you're a small girl, and I'm just afeart, well, you know, afeart I'm gonna hurt you too much." He seized his glass and took a long gulp of champagne.

They studied each other in silence for a few moments, and then Nell took Nick's glass and returned it to the tray. She then took him by the hand and led him over to the bed, a massive brass structure with a vibrant patchwork quilt, one of their wedding presents. She turned to face him.

"Nick, you're my husband an' I'm your wife. I love you. Let's just climb in here and see what happens."

Nick nodded, managing a tremulous smile. "If you're sure."

"I'm sure. Prob'ly best if you start by takin' off your clothes."

Nell drew her shift over her head and tossed it aside, standing fully naked before her young husband for the first time, the interplay of light and shadow in the room sculpting the delicate curves of her slender body. She shook out her hair to tumble in golden waves about her shoulders, its sheen enhanced in the glow cast by the cluster of candles Kitty had insisted should grace their room for their wedding night. Cocking her head invitingly to one side, she coiled a golden tress slowly around a finger before letting it spring back into place. Nick stared at her like one thunderstruck, and then began to remove his own clothes, quickly and with no sign of fumbling.

****

Nell lay with her head in the hollow of Nick's shoulder, the only sound the soft sputtering of the candles as they guttered out. Nick lay with one arm folded behind his head, the other curled around his wife. His eyes were closed, and he was smiling.

"Nick, you okay?" Nell whispered.

"Hmmm? Oh yes. I'm okay." He opened his eyes, turning his head to look at her. "How 'bout you?"

"I'm okay, too." Nell squirmed closer. "You were wonderful."

"I was? Sure you're not just sayin' that?"

"No," murmured Nell sleepily. "Once you hit your stride you were fine, jus' fine. What about me?"

Nick's response was a gentle snore.

"Well, I guess that's a mutual."

Nell had felt keenly the absence of family at her wedding, and she knew Nick felt it, too, although neither of them had mentioned it, not wishing to blight the happiness of the occasion. Their homes were so far away and so much had happened to them both that they had, by necessity, to focus on their future, and they at least had one another now. They were an official couple, signed and sealed. That thought gave Nell a warm sense of security she'd not felt in a long time, not since Pap and Sabrina's own wedding.

Nick had told her that he'd like to bring his younger brothers out West one day, and if they made a success of things in Yreka, then hopefully they could do that. And of course they would have their own family, though not too soon, she hoped. Nell snuggled into her husband's hard young body, determined to milk this rare moment of true happiness for all its worth.

CHAPTER TWENTY

The Shamrock had become the big success story of Yreka, no doubt about that, and Nick and Nell were kept frantically busy by the demand for their wholesome style of home cooked meals. The savoury smells drifting down to the saloon below drew men up the stairs in a steady stream, reeling them in like beings in thrall. Toby raced about as if he had wheels on his boots, his face sheened with perspiration, his manner always cheerful and unflappable. They'd had to purchase a second stove to cope with all the cooking required and Nell found herself rushed off her feet as she strove to fill the list of orders without too much delay. However busy she may be, she still made time to greet patrons, learning their names and something about their circumstances, which she carefully filed away for future reference. It was enough of a reward to see a miner's work and weather ravaged face light up when a beautiful young woman enquired about his personal wellbeing, or news of his kin.

Nick was everywhere, taking care of this or that, filling in as extra waiter or back-up cook, sorting out myriad problems as they came up, and generally providing Nell with masterly support. He was her rock, solid and dependable, and she appreciated him more with each passing day. By the time fall approached, the little restaurant ran like a well-oiled machine and its youthful owners were delighted with its success. Their bank account was mushrooming nicely and Kitty was more than happy with her cut. Nell had seen to it that Humble's committee was paid the designated fee and cordial relations were restored.

In the mornings, Nell did the banking and took care of the books, while Nick tended to practicalities like inventories and ensuring their larder was well stocked. They found they didn't have a lot of spare time to spend together, just the two of them, and they'd been unable to enjoy any sort of a honeymoon, but once in a while they got away for a pleasant ride through the beautiful countryside surrounding Yreka. Nick mused that they should think about buying up land for when the gold ran out. They could farm and raise cattle he suggested, but Nell remained antipathetic towards the idea of becoming farmers again. She promised to think about it, though, guessing her husband had it in the back of his mind that it was the best way to accommodate his two little brothers, and she didn't want to stand in the way of that. For the time being, anyway, the young couple both felt happily settled in this picturesque area of Northern California.

With Nell's approval, Nick bought the handgun he'd been hankering for, a Colt Navy 51, a handsome revolver with walnut grip and octagonal barrel. It used cap and ball ammunition, which made it tedious to reload, but Nick was besotted with it in spite of this drawback. The gun was comparatively light, weighing only two pounds, so he patiently taught Nell how to use it, including breaking it down, cleaning it, and carefully reloading to avoid chain fire. Nell smiled secretly at the touching earnestness with which her husband approached his wife's tuition.

"Now, remember, Nell, you only ever load five chambers and you make sure the hammer is on the empty chamber, otherwise when you tuck it in your belt or holster you're likely to blow your foot off."

"Criminy, I'd hate that! An' you'd have a gimpy wife!"

Firearms accidents were common, but Nell felt reasonably confident with guns because Pap had taught her respect for them from a young age. Never having used a handgun before, she was keen to try it out.

They found a spot by the river where they could practise their target shooting by popping away at some old tin cans. Nick was impressed by Nell's accuracy and the way she handled the recoil.

"You're a natural, Nell; you got a real good eye, better 'n me any day."

Nell smiled. This kind of statement was so typical of her husband. He was the least self-aggrandising male she'd come across. She set out to soothe any bruised ego. "My daddy was a good shot, so I mebbe take after him. I can't match you with a rifle, though, Nick. You're the best shot I ever seen with a rifle." That wasn't strictly true, but she had to give him something. One of the first things Nell had noticed about Nick was that he had a tiny black wedge of pupil seeping into the iris of his right eye. She'd never drawn attention to it, but she wondered if the little defect impacted on his vision.

Nick put his arm around her shoulders, visibly pleased. "Guess we're a good team then, if it comes to fightin' off hostiles."

Nell chuckled. "You an' me against the world." She smiled up at him and Nick drew her in for a long, lingering kiss. Their love grew deeper daily, it seemed to Nell, strengthened by what it fed on, physically and emotionally. She pulled away reluctantly. "We better head back."

Nick nodded. "Saturday night. They'll be tearin' up those stairs like ravenous wolves."

****

As they got deeper into fall, the temperatures dropped, making working in a hot kitchen less burdensome, and the rains came as well, further cooling things down after a very hot summer. Kitty

303

branched out on a new venture, too, at this time, that of supplying breakfast to miners who patronised the saloon and became so drunk they couldn't make it back to camp at closing time. She allowed them, never more than a few men, to doss down in the bar for the night and then charged them for a hot cooked breakfast in the morning when they'd slept off their excess and sobered up. She employed a Chinese cook for the breakfast shift so as not to overburden Nell and Nick, who'd been a bit apprehensive at first, and to their relief he always left the kitchen spotlessly clean for the evening dinner shift, meaning they suffered no inconvenience. Kitty, who organised her own supplies, was pleased with this additional little earner, and Nick and Nell didn't mind since she'd been so kind to them. Their days conformed to a predictable but, nonetheless, enjoyable pattern, and they looked forward to a good life together, reaping the benefits of their hard work, consolidating their circle of friends, and savouring the feeling of being a respected part of a flourishing community. They attended the newly built church and were frequently invited to Sunday dinners and other social events that didn't clash with business hours. They began to talk about building their own real home.

Nell did not drop her guard, though. She knew only too well how unpredictable and dangerous life could be on the frontier, especially in times of such exceptional flux, lawlessness, and misadventure.

****

"Nick Hardy, as I live and breathe. Fancy meeting you here."

The man greeting him was standing with his back to the sun, and Nick squinted, shading his eyes, while somewhere inside him a panicked voice was saying he knew only too well who this person was, and he felt a chill ripple up and down his spine.

The young man thrust out a hand. "Ned. Ned Crowther," he drawled. "We both worked for the Count, I think, until you lit out with your friend, Nathan." He rubbed his chin. "Wrenn Cheney went missing at the same time. Had us puzzled to all hell, that did, the three of you disappearin' like that an' all at once, specially as Wrenn up and left all his belongings; war bag, bed roll, valuables." He snapped his fingers, then cocked his head to one side. "Well, here you are."

Nick recovered his wits sufficiently to manage a limp handshake. "Howdy, Ned. I remember you. What brings you to Yreka?" *Hell! What are the chances?* Nick's brain raced. One slip could give him away. He'd ignored Ned's insinuations and was desperately trying to think what his next move might be. Cheney missing, he'd said. Did that mean they hadn't found his body? His heart was thumping rhythmically.

Ned casually shifted his weight on to one leg and hooked his thumbs into his waistband. He turned his head to spit a stream of tobacco juice into the street, before returning his cool gaze on to Nick.

"Well, we delivered that herd to San Francisco, an' I stayed on for a while, spendin' too much money. I never liked bein' in one place too long, so I thought I'd come up here an' try my luck. The gold in southern Californy is pretty well played out, but there's still pickin's up here, so they claim." His blue eyes narrowed. "How'd you end up here? One minute you were ridin' out to the cows with me to look for Wrenn an' then you were gone. You still ridin' with that Nathan lad?"

Nick took a step back and lifted his hands in a helpless gesture. "Look, I gotta go. I'm on an errand and I'm already late. You can find me at The Shamrock restaurant. Ask anyone; they'll point you in the right direction." Feeling sick inside, he hurried across the street and away. Glancing back, he saw Crowther still standing there, looking after him. He had to find Nell fast and forewarn her about this totally unexpected development.

****

The spoon Nell had been using to stir the batter dropped from her fingers into the bowl with a soft plop. "Ned Crowther! Here? Has he tracked us?"

Nick shook his head. "No. I reckon it's no more 'n happenstance that he ended up here. He looked pretty surprised to see me."

306

Nell retrieved her spoon with a trembling hand. "Oh, Nick, I never thought a one of 'em would ever turn up here, let alone that one." She looked at her husband, her expression anguished. "What are we gonna do?"

Nick chewed his lip. Then he reached over, took the spoon from her hand, and dropped it back in the batter. It was some hours before the restaurant opened. They had a window to organise their thoughts.

"Go sit down an' I'll fetch us some coffee. I'll tell you exactly what was said, and then we need to figure out how to deal with this. Jus' stay calm."

Seated at one of the dining tables, Nell cradled her cup in both hands as she listened intently to Nick's careful word-by-word recount of his conversation with Ned. Nick's eyes were closed and he tapped the fingers of one hand on the tabletop as he concentrated on remembering every word and nuance of his recent conversation in the street. When he finished, he took a deep breath and looked at his wife, whose eyebrows were solidly knit in a deep frown.

"You told him where to find us?"

Nick spread his hands. "Me, not us. Hell, it's a small town, Nell. He'd find out about us easy enough."

Nell's face cleared. "Course." She took a sip of coffee, then lowered the cup and stared into it. "So, it sure sounds like they never found Cheney. Was that your take on it?"

"Yeah. He's curious about why all three of us left the drive at the same time, but I'm pretty sure he has no way to link us to Cheney. It's jus' all a mystery to him."

"Specially since he and Cheney was prob'ly more to each other 'n jus' fellow hands." Nell gave a wry smile.

"You really think so?"

"I'm sure of it." Nell repeated Cheney's words to her as he was about to commit rape, and Nick's lip curled in disgust. "I think the other men knew it, too, 'cos they never teased Ned 'bout his baby face like most young'uns would do. They knew he was protected by Cheney, an' they were scared of that rotten man."

"So we killed his lover," said Nick bluntly. "That complicates things a bit. He surely believes Cheney musta had a good reason for deserting him."

"He did," said Nell with equal bluntness. "He was dead. But Ned ain't goin' to say anything 'bout Cheney not bein' likely to leave him. That would raise eyebrows." She pushed her cup away and took a deep breath. "Okay, let's go through this step by step an' make a plan. We both gotta get our story straight if he asks questions, and it has to sound like the truth. Fetch me paper an' pencil, Nick. I need to make notes. We ain't got much time."

****

The dinner service at The Shamrock that night was extremely busy, so busy, in fact, that Nell actually forgot for a while the fact of Ned Crowther's presence in Yreka…until, as she cleared a table, she saw him appear at the head of the stairs, and her heart lurched. She hurried back to the kitchen and whispered to Nick, who was busy cooking steaks, that Crowther had arrived. He whispered back, without turning his head, to say they must both stay calm and act natural, just carry on with what they were doing. "Let him make the first move," he concluded. "Toby can take his order."

Crowther ordered a steak, and when he'd finished he lounged back in his chair, picking his teeth and asking Toby for a refill of coffee. With the crowd thinning out, Nick, unable to avoid him any longer without making it obvious, strolled over to take a seat opposite him, offering him a quirley as he sat down.

"Thanks." Ned occupied himself rolling the smoke, and neither spoke for a few moments until he had lit up and enjoyed his first draw, blowing the smoke out of the corner of his mouth and spitting stray bits of tobacco off the tip of his tongue. Finally, he lounged back in his chair again and, glancing around the emptying restaurant, stated, "You done well. Must be rakin' it in. It is your place, right?"

Nick nodded as he rolled his own quirley. "Mine and Nell's, an' Kitty Callahan, who owns the hotel and saloon, has a stake in it as well."

Ned nodded slowly, pulling down the corners of his mouth, face serious, to convey how impressed he was. He took another draw on his cigarette. "Who's Nell?"

"Nell's my wife. You knew her as Nathan, Angus's helper."

Crowther swung bolt upright, planting his elbows on the table, eyes widening. "Nathan's a girl?"

Nick kept his voice steady. "Yeah, she is. We made her up as a boy so she'd be safe – safe from the wrong kind of attention."

"Well, knock me into a cocked hat! I had no notion. A girl!"

"That's why we left," Nick continued, his voice even. "She was startin' to fill out an' we got worried someone might catch on. Girl among a bunch of men – you know what I mean. It was a spur of the moment decision. Felt right at the time." He swivelled in his chair. "Nell, come over here."

Nell, who'd been acutely attuned all along to what was happening behind her, nevertheless strolled over to the table with an insouciant air, wiping her hands on her apron. She'd sent Toby home earlier with his dinner in a pail, not wanting him to witness any unpleasantness that may occur. Now, she sat down next to her husband and smiled sweetly at Ned. "Hello, it's a surprise to see you here, Ned. Did you enjoy your meal?"

Ned gaped at the lovely young woman opposite him for a moment before he remembered his manners and shot to his feet, extending a hand. "How do, Nell." He leaned forwards slightly.

"Oh, yeah, I see it now. You are a woman. Indeed you are. Sorry for starin'." He ran his fingers through his hair, shaking his head in disbelief. "I guess I was always too busy eatin' to take a proper look at you, an' you always so shy an' all."

Nell squeezed his hand, smile still in place, before he sat down again with a thump, adding, as he recalled her enquiry, "Oh, the meal? The steak was very good. Best food I had in some time. Better 'n a fancy eatery I went to in San Francisco." He was practically stuttering as he gushed.

Nell said, "I'm glad. Tell me about Angus. Is he all right?"

Before their guest could answer, Nick pushed his chair back. "I'll fetch us some drinks. Then you can tell me an' Nell all 'bout San Francisco, an' your plans in Yreka."

Having, he hoped, set up a neutral topic for any further conversation, Nick headed off to the saloon downstairs to get a bottle of whiskey. It was a relief that Ned seemed to have accepted without question his explanation as to why he and Nell had left the cattle drive so suddenly, and her feminine transformation had clearly beguiled him, hopefully distracting him for the time being. But Cheney's disappearance was going to crop up sooner or later, and that was the really dangerous territory they had to manoeuvre their way through.

When Nick returned with the bottle and three glasses, Ned was holding forth about San Francisco, while Nell was listening attentively.

"No, I ain't joshin'. Built hisself one of them pree-fab-ree-cated houses. Had all the panels shipped in from Italy and set up on a patch of land he bought by the waterfront. Had marble statues an' all. He was a rare man all right, the count. A real one off."

****

"He said Angus was deeply upset when I left and acted like a bear with a sore head. I felt so bad, since I didn't even say goodbye or leave a note. He was a good, kind man."

They were lying side by side in bed, talking over the encounter with Ned. Nick squeezed her gently. "Don't be hard on yourself, Nell. Neither of us had a chance to really think much about things. We did what we had to do an' hightailed it outta there."

"I guess. Anyways, Ned said the last time he seen Angus he was plannin' to stay in California, look around and settle down some place, work hard 'til he had enough to start his own business, jus' like he told me."

"That's good. He'll do it, too. He's a great cook and everyone likes him." Nick held her close. "Did he mention Cheney to you at all?"

"Nope. Doesn't seem to connect him with us at all, an' sure didn't question our reasons for leavin'." She raised herself on an elbow, peering into her husband's face. "Will we be okay, Nick?"

"Sure we will." Nick sounded more confident than he felt. "He'll be headin' outta town to the diggings an' we won't see much of him, then. Prob'ly move on sooner rather than later. Strikes me as a bit shiftless." He drew Nell in for a lingering kiss. "You sleep now. Been a long day."

****

In fact, Ned returned to The Shamrock on the following day, as Nell and Nick were taking a break before the dinner service commenced, and he had Hank Humble with him. Nick and Nell rose slowly to their feet, exchanging a quick look of alarm while trying to appear outwardly calm. For his part Ned appeared singularly agitated as he removed his hat and took a seat, mumbling a greeting. Humble seated himself last, looking hard at Nell as he did so, his features inscrutable.

"What can we do for you?" asked Nick evenly. "We're not open yet, but I can offer you a cup of coffee."

Humble removed his hat and placed it on the table. "Thank you, but no. I'll get straight to the point of our visit. This young man," – he indicated Ned – "has sought me out because he is deeply disturbed by something he has discovered. He has given me a brief summary of certain events, which involve the both of you, and he is

313

hoping you can throw some light on this discovery he has made. Ned, can you tell Mr. and Mrs. Hardy what you told me?"

Ned nodded, taking a deep breath. "Well, I told Mr. Humble here how we was all on the cattle drive and how you two up and vamoosed, at the same time as the trail boss and my compadre, Wrenn Cheney, went missing. Now, you done told me your reasons for goin' so sudden like, an' I can 'preciate the truth of that after seein' Miz Hardy here is no boy, as we all thought. We cleared all that up yesterday." He took another deep breath. "I didn't put you two together with anything that might have befallen Wrenn – that is until I went to the livery stables to board my horse for a few days while I acquired me some tools. That was when I seen Cheney's horse, large as life, the big dun he called Otis."

Nell groped for Nick's hand and squeezed it hard.

Humble shifted his weight, raising a finger. "Pause there, Ned. Explain how you knew beyond doubt that the horse in question is – or was – Mr. Cheney's."

"Well, sir, I wasn't full sure at first, but then I know'd because he had his initials tattooed inside its left ear: WHC – Wrenn Harlan Cheney, his full name. I checked an' there were those three letters, clear as daylight. Wrenn showed me those letters himself and said he did that to help him claim ownership if it was ever stolen. A lotta folks admired that horse."

"That's understandable, Ned. I've seen it myself and it's a fine animal. I actually offered Les a handsome sum for it, but he turned me down. Now, you naturally enquired of Mr. Lester Durrant, the proprietor of the stables, how he came by this horse." Humble's lips twisted in a wry little smirk. He was clearly enjoying himself. "Tell us what Mr. Durrant said, will you?"

Ned turned solemn baby blue eyes on Nick and Nell, who were sitting deathly still, staring back at him.

"Mr. Durrant said he bought it off the couple who run The Shamrock: Nick and Nell Hardy. So I asked him who made up the law in this town an' he sent me to Mr. Humble." He thrust his face forward. "How the blue blazes did you two end up with Wrenn's horse?"

No time to make a plan, so she had to get them some. Nell's mind was spinning like syncopated clockwork as she stared at Ned. When she opened her mouth to answer, Humble held up an arresting hand again.

"I must warn you to think very carefully now before either of you answer Ned's question. Your response is crucial to whatever might happen next."

Nell's eyebrows clashed together atop the bridge of her nose. The man's pomposity was unbearable. She released Nick's hand and soared to her feet, eyes ablaze. "How dare the pair of you come into our business premises makin' wild accusations concernin' somethin' you think you know all about when you know nothin'! Get outta here afore I have you both done for trespass! Me n' Nick is saying nothin' until we get us a proper attorney-at-law. Must be one somewhere in this neck of the woods."

She thrust out an arm, fist clenched, forefinger pointing stiffly, with such ferocity that the two men flinched. Nick gazed up at her, mouth slightly agape. Ned's expression was similar. She was magnificent.

"Now get outta here before I tell my man to fetch his pistol!"

Nick rose menacingly, standing squarely alongside her, head erect, jaw thrust forward. "You heard my wife."

Humble placed a firm hand on the mesmerised Ned's shoulder. "Come, Mr. Crowther. We'll go to my office and discuss this further." He addressed Nick and Nell as he stood up and donned his hat. "You haven't heard the last of this. You clearly have something to answer for, and I will pursue it. Good day to you both."

"You ain't the law! We ain't afraid of no vigilantes!" Nell called after him.

Humble turned at the top of the stairs, a tight smile on his face. "You should be."

****

As soon as she was sure the two men had gone, Nell gripped Nick's arm. "Nick, I gotta stay here an' watch my pies. You go find Kitty. Quick."

As Nick headed for the stairs, Nell called, "Where's the Colt?"

"Top drawer of the dresser, in the storeroom."

Kitty, who had responded to the summons immediately, sipped her whiskey as she listened to Nell's recount of her past before she arrived in Yreka. When she reached the part where she met Nick, he took over the story at her invitation. Again Kitty sipped and listened intently, occasionally smiling, occasionally nodding her head. Nell knew she must have been curious about the young couple's background, but, as Nick had pointed out to her, nobody asked questions about your history in a mining town on the frontier. Now the little Irishwoman had it all. When Nick came to describing the attack on Nell, he faltered, so she took over, concluding with their arrival in Yreka and the unfortunate encounter with Ned Crowther. Finally, she gave Kitty a blow-by-blow account of the confrontation with Ned and Humble before silence descended. Downstairs, however, the noise from the saloon was building in volume. The men would soon be up for their suppers.

Nick slid an arm around Nell, and she rested her head on his shoulder; she was feeling completely drained, and not really in any condition to face the night of hard work ahead. She'd been feeling like that a lot lately.

Kitty chewed her lip, drumming the fingers of one hand on the tabletop. Finally, she lifted her head, face serious, and said softly, "I need to take some time to consider this carefully. I believe ye have told me the truth, since I know ye as good, honest folk." She jerked her head towards the growing tumult downstairs. "Ye're goin' to be very busy any minute, so now is no good for makin' any decisions. We have to do that tomorrow, with clear heads." She stood up. "Try not to fret. We'll sort this out, I promise ye. Ye've done nothin' wrong, so ye haven't."

As Kitty descended the staircase, the first diners ascended, greeting her cheerfully as they made way for her to slip past, and Nick and Nell headed for the kitchen. Toby had the night off because he'd been poorly, so they were going to be run off their feet. Better to be busy, Nell thought. Keeps your mind off other things. Apron fastened, she breezed back into the dining room, smile firmly in place, calling welcomes to the men who were always so eager for her attention, whose faces lit up the moment they saw her.

CHAPTER TWENTY-ONE

In the morning, Kitty joined Nick and Nell for breakfast in a secluded corner of the dining room. Neither of them looked as if they had slept very well, Kitty noted, especially Nick. She did her best to make light of the situation, sounding as confident as possible while she disclosed her plan of action and the options available. Nick and Nell listened in silence as she ran her ideas past them.

"Now, the way I see it, there is no evidence of Cheney's death. They have no body and they're not going to find one now. It's too late. Wolves and bears will have eaten the lot. So all ye have to do is explain how ye came by the horse. Ye either took it the night ye left the drive, which ye did, and which is horse stealing, or ye found it. Now, I don't think owning up to horse stealing is a good idea. Humble would come down hard on that. I believe ye should say ye found it, wandering out on the trail all alone, and ye naturally brought it along with ye for its own safety as much as anything and used it for a light pack animal in the meantime. Cheney, we can

319

conclude, was bushwhacked, the horse stripped of saddle and bridle, and either released or escaped, we don't know. Ye might have decided it looked like Cheney's horse, but ye couldn't possibly know that for sure and it had probably lost some condition. There's more than a few dun horses around, so there is. Ye sold it because ye felt ye were not its rightful owners. Think about it. The committee will ask themselves: if they'd killed Cheney they'd hardly have kept his horse as evidence. Humble will search, but he'll find nothing." She paused. "Will he?"

Nick shook his head. "We wanted no souvenirs of that man." He sighed. "Ned probably won't believe I didn't recognise Cheney's horse, though, even if I didn't know about the tattoo in its ear, because I was the wrangler. I knew every horse in the remuda like the back of my hand. Had to."

Kitty looked away, clearly thinking this through. "Were there other duns in the herd?"

"Yes. Three altogether. Otis, Cheney's horse, was the biggest."

"So, ye knew him by his size?"

"Yep. That's how I picked him out."

"So, away from the herd ye didn't have that reference?"

"I guess not."

"Well, there ye are then. Ye don't see what ye're not looking for, and s'far as ye and Nell were concerned, Cheney was still on the cattle drive. I got a matched pair of greys myself; can't tell one from the other, and with duns, why, their stripes an' markings can differ by a real tiny degree."

"That could make sense all right. Ned admitted he wasn't sure about the horse at first. He had to check for the tattoo."

"Did he say that in front of Humble?"

"Yes, he did."

Kitty topped up her coffee cup and sat back with a nod. "Well then, we brazen it out because they can't prove a thing." She sipped, eyes darting from Nell to Nick. "What do ye think?"

"I think it's a good plan," said Nell. "It doesn't explain why Cheney disappeared the same night as us, though."

"Yes, it does," replied Nick. "We tell Humble we left suddenly because we knew he was closing in on you, Nell. He musta followed us and come to grief somehow."

Nell frowned. "But Ned knows he was already missin' at supper time that night."

Nick shook his head. "No. He doesn't. He said himself Cheney was prob'ly out with the herd. That's where he went to look for him."

"An' he wouldn't have found him, would he? So, what I'm sayin' is, if Cheney came after us, how come he went missin' first?" Nell buried her head in her hands. "This is one big mess."

Kitty reached across and patted Nell's arm. "That's good, Nell. That's smart. If we plug those loopholes, we'll be all right." She placed a finger on her chin, eyes squinting in thought. "They could simply have missed each other in the dark. Or Cheney could have had men after him for some bad thing he'd done, enemies wanting to kill him. Maybe he spotted them in Great Salt Lake and knew he had to find a chance to make a run for it. No one knows what's in a man's heart."

Nell eyed the little Irishwoman dubiously, but with a flicker of hope lighting her eyes. "I suppose."

Nick sighed. "Maybe we should just leave town. We don't want to cause any trouble for you, Kitty."

Kitty's response was fierce. "No! If ye run away that's as good as sayin' ye're guilty! Humble will come after ye with a posse and his lynching rope! Don't even think 'bout that! We fight!" She glanced around and then lowered her voice. "We fight. An' we win!"

Nick nudged her foot with the toe of his boot, and she followed his gaze. Humble was striding towards them, and he had Ned with him.

Nell abruptly stood up and said, "I'm goin' to be sick!"

Humble and Ned both pulled up in surprise as she brushed past them, one hand over her mouth.

****

Nick strolled along the new boardwalk, heading back to the hotel. Fall had brought some heavy rain, churning the roads of Yreka to a dark, stinking mass of mud, waste, and horse manure, so the boardwalk was a welcome addition that helped you avoid having your boots caked in mud. You still had to cross the open spaces at the ends of the alleys before mounting the boardwalk again on the other side, but the mud wasn't so deep there, anyway, because the storefront awnings provided some shelter. Nightfall came earlier now as well, and the lamps in the saloons and bawdy houses cast yellow pools of light on to the street from their windows. Somewhere, a honky tonk piano started up. Nick was in an ebullient mood; he'd spent an enjoyable couple of hours with Joe Cooney who ran the gun shop, learning how to make paper cartridges for the Navy Colt, and he couldn't wait to try out the handful of finished bullets Joe had kindly given him. He wore the Colt low on his hip, relishing the feel of it against his body and the sense of manhood it aroused in him. The gun wasn't the only thing giving him a sense of manhood at the moment, though: Nell was having a baby! He broke into a spontaneous grin every time he thought about it. The tiredness, the sickness in the mornings, the mercurial shifts of mood, were all explained now. Thankfully, Nell was now beyond that early phase and burgeoning beautifully into the glowing, placid stage of settled pregnancy. The child would be born next summer and Kitty had already agreed to be godmother. He was going to bring his own child up very differently from the way he'd been raised, he decided, with love and kindness rather than blows and ridicule. Nell, he knew beyond doubt, would make a marvellous mother. A warm glow suffused him, making him shiver a little. He loved her so much, more than ever, in fact, if that were possible.

As he walked, he reflected also on the outcome of the inquiry into Wrenn Cheney's possible murder. He and Nell had been summoned to appear before the Yreka Committee, and thanks to Kitty's shrewd and incisive preparation, not to mention her brilliance as their ad hoc attorney cum character witness, the decision had gone in their favour. There was, the Committee decided, insufficient evidence, the most significant omission being Cheney's actual body, to implicate Nick and Nell in his disappearance, which remained unsolved. All they could be sure of was that he'd disappeared around the same time as Nick and Nell left the drive. Ned himself admitted he knew little of Cheney's past, having only befriended him since joining the cattle drive. Humble, as expected, had given them the worst grilling, but Kitty's coaching won the day and he'd been unable to find a chink in their armour. There had been an unpleasant scene with Ned afterwards, during which he'd flung around a lot of wild recriminations and threatened all manner of vengeance, but then he'd disappeared himself, back to the diggings, and the dust had well and truly settled over the whole dreadful affair. Nick no longer felt guilty for killing Cheney, and the only person who knew the truth besides him and Nell was Kitty, whom they trusted implicitly. She'd known they were fugitives, all right, the first moment she'd met them. She was fey Irish. She'd also known instinctively that they were good people, and the townsfolk and miners backed her in that.

As Nick drew near to the hotel, hoping Nell wouldn't be mad at him for taking longer than he'd said he would, he savoured the thought that he was the luckiest man alive, with everything to live for, so much to look forward to, and he murmured a quick prayer of thanks to the Lord under his breath.

As he stepped off the end of the boardwalk and into the gloomy rectangle at the end of the alley, Nick didn't hear the rifle shot until after the bullet hit him between the shoulder blades, and it was the last thing he did hear in this world. He stayed on his feet for a moment, swaying, eyes bulging with shock, before the second bullet hit him and he toppled slowly forwards to sprawl face down in the yielding mud. *Oh Nell, oh my love. I'm so sorry.*

****

Nell stared dumbly into the brutal gouge in the earth that was her husband's grave, the pale pine of his coffin gleaming forlornly far away at the bottom of his deep, muddy resting place. Kitty stood alongside her weeping softly, one arm firmly encircling Nell's waist. The graveside part of the service completed, the reverend and the sorrowing townsfolk stood in silence under a brooding sky, a misty rain beading droplets of water on hats, shawls and coats, adding to the profound sense of desolation that hung over the scene.

Finally, the undertaker made a move, scooping up a trowel of soil from the mound of fill and walking across to hand it to Nell. She accepted it with a murmured 'thank you', and walked unsteadily to the edge of the grave, still supported by Kitty, to toss the wet earth on to Nick's coffin. As she completed the ritual, a sharp little cry was torn from her and she staggered sideways as if someone had struck her. Grasping her now with both arms, Kitty turned to signal Billy who stepped forward, swept Nell up in his massive arms and carried her with giant strides back to the hotel, where the wake was to be held.

In the dining room, Delilah had everything prepared and a fire blazing in the hearth. Kitty manoeuvred a chair to one side of the fireplace, and Billy gently lowered Nell on to it before spreading a blanket across her lap. On Kitty's instruction, Delilah poured a large brandy and thrust the glass into the bereaved young woman's chilled hand.

The other mourners filed in after shedding wet coats, cloaks, and hats in the hallway. Many miners had attended the church service and then drifted tactfully away. Determined to farewell her husband from this world without giving way to public grief, Nell quickly revived and received each person who approached to pay his or her respects with calm dignity. Throughout, Kitty remained standing by her side, thanking those in attendance on Nell's behalf and ensuring they were partaking of her famous hospitality by directing them to the splendid array of food and drink laid out on the tables.

Toby was the last one to approach Nell, and as she looked up to smile at him, he burst into tears, flinging himself on to her and holding her tight as tears streamed down his freckled cheeks. "Sorry, sorry, sorry, Nell," he blurted out between sobs. Addy hurried across, but as she reached to pull Toby away, Nell held up a hand in an arresting gesture, and Addy stepped back, biting her lip. Nell held Toby for a long time, making soothing noises, patting his twitching back, and rocking him gently, her eyes closed. She knew he'd loved Nick and looked up to him like a protective elder brother.

Eventually, Toby's sobbing diminished and he released her. He hung his head, swiping at his eyes. "Sorry, I didn't mean…"

"No" Nell seized his hand. "Don't be sorry for showin' how much you loved him, too. Will you come to his grave with me tomorrow to place some flowers? I'd really 'preciate it if you would. An' maybe you can help me with choosin' some fine words for his headstone, too."

Toby managed a wobbly smile through his tears. "Oh, may I? I'd like that very much, Nell."

"Thank you, Toby."

Nell slumped back in her chair as Addy led her tearful son away. She felt utterly exhausted and knew from past experience that she was still processing the shock of Nick's death, that the grief wouldn't hit her properly for some time yet. When it did, it would bowl her over like a runaway horse. That grief was twofold. She placed a hand on her abdomen. Everyone knew she was pregnant and now facing the prospect of raising a child on her own, even though she was not yet seventeen. In an instant her life had plummeted from looking rosy to looking bleak, indeed. Cheney's brutal attack on her had culminated in the loss of three lives.

Nell decided she didn't want to think about any of that now. She stood up, swaying a little, aware that the brandy had made her feel languid and sleepy. She'd barely slept since Humble had sought her out to tell her Nick had been murdered. He wasn't at the funeral. He was heading a posse to go after Ned Crowther, who'd fled Yreka following the shooting and after stealing some fellow miners' tools...almost a worse crime than murder, in Humble's opinion. Mrs Humble was in attendance, though, and did a sterling job of helping Delilah distribute the refreshments to the guests.

"Kitty, can you help me upstairs? I want to rest now." As Kitty moved in to help her to her feet, she added, "Please thank everyone for comin'. Nick would've been proud."

****

The posse returned three days after Nick's funeral with Crowther's body draped across the saddle of his skittish horse, and Humble stated to the townsfolk who gathered around the tired, travel-stained men that the case was closed, justice done. The stolen mining tools were returned to their rightful owners and Nell was invited to view the body before it was buried. She declined this rather crude attempt at closure of a sort, and informed Kitty that she was going back to work.

"No, acushla, it's too soon! Give it more time."

"So, when is the right time? I'd rather be doing something than sittin' around mopin'. I'm not made that way. Nick worked hard to help build up our business, and I won't let him down by allowin' it to stall, now. I'll have Toby to help me."

Kitty rolled her eyes. No point arguing with her when she was like this. "All right," she said, her manner conciliatory, "but I insist ye have Dingbang, my breakfast cook, to help ye. He's wonderful. I'll find someone else to cover his morning shift."

Nell stifled a giggle. "Is that his name? Dingbang? I don't think I'll be able to say that with a poker face."

"It's a common enough Chinese name," retorted Kitty, "an' ye better say it without smirkin' or he'll take it sorely. Losing face is a fierce insult in Chinese culture."

Nell assumed a serious air, lifting her chin. "I will indeed do nothin' to upset Dingbang's personal pride. Thank you. I'm sure we'll get along just fine." Then she exploded into an eye-watering attack of the giggles, and Kitty offered no reprimand, because it was just so good to hear her laugh again.

****

That night, Kitty put a sign up in Pot O' Gold to the effect that The Shamrock was open again for business, and the delighted miners soon began to trickle up the stairs. At first, things were a little awkward as they approached Nell, who awaited them at the head of the staircase, to murmur their condolences. She was so composed, smiling, and sincerely welcoming that any strain soon evaporated and it was quickly back to business as usual.

Dingbang was everything Kitty said he was and his English was good, too, so there were few misunderstandings. Toby worked harder than ever to make sure things ran smoothly, and when the last customer left Nell swept back her hair from her damp forehead and broke into spontaneous applause. Toby beamed, Dingbang bowed and then set about the washing up, until Nell stopped him.

"Please," she said earnestly, "leave those and come share some dinner with me an' Toby. You've earned it."

As they sat around the table, tucking into their chosen meals from what was on hand, Nell said, "Dingbang, tell me about some Chinese recipes we could offer the men. I'm sure they'd like that, somethin' a bit exotic for a change."

The young Chinaman looked bemused. "You want to serve some Chinese food, Miz Nell?"

"Yes, I had some noodles one day when I was in Hoptown lookin' for spices, and they were delicious."

"Well, chop suey would be good to try, and chow mein. I can make them for you and then you can decide. I can get you good pork, Miz Nell."

"It's a done deal," said Nell. "Now finish up that stew an' have a slab of apple pie. Put lotsa cream. I'll have some, too." She patted her abdomen. "By the time this baby's born I'm gonna be big as a house."

Toby blushed and giggled. Dingbang looked inscrutable.

CHAPTER TWENTY-TWO

Nell peered curiously at the small swaddled infant cradled against her breast. His red puckered face seemed to be contorting itself in all directions, making the oddest kind of grimaces that caused her to forget how hard his birth had been, how exhausted she was, and made her laugh.

"He sure don't look too happy to be here," she mused. "Is he all right? Check his eyes."

Kitty, who had acted as midwife along with Addy Entwhistle, leaned over the bed to stroke the baby's soft little head with its thatch of dark blond hair. "He's so beautiful, aren't ye, wee man? Gave yer mammy a hard time of it, but ye're here now safe and sound, so ye are. His eyes are perfect, blue like his mam's. Do ye want to try him on the breast, acushla? Start to let yer milk come down."

Nell loosened the ties of her shift to expose a swollen, blue-veined breast, and Addy, who'd been bustling about cleaning up, joined Kitty at the bedside for this precious moment. As soon as it probed his lips, the baby latched on to the nipple with a single-minded ferocity that made Nell wince, and began to suck vigorously.

"Oh, look at that," said Addy, clasping her hands rapturously to her own breast, head tilted with delight. "He's a strong one, a real good doer."

Nell watched her little son, smiling as he snuffled and worried at the nipple, suckling greedily. "His pappy loved his food, too." She smiled up at the watching women. "Oh, I feel all tingly in there."

"That's good," said Addy. "Means your milk is coming in just fine. What will you call him?"

There was no hesitation. "Nicholas. After his daddy. Nicholas Hardy."

"No middle name? His grandfather's perhaps?"

"No. That will come later," said Nell mysteriously, and both Kitty and Addy exchanged a glance, eyebrows raised.

The baby had stopped feeding and was very still, eyes closed in sated bliss. Addy lifted him gently from his mother's arms. "I'll bath him now, while you get some rest."

"And I'll see to supper," said Kitty, before sweeping out.

When both women had left, Nell sank back on to her pillows with a heavy sigh, eyes closed. It had been a very hard winter followed by a beautiful spring and summer. Now she was just happy to have that big belly deflated and the baby born at last, safe and sound. A breeze toyed with the curtains and wafted towards the bed, caressing her nearest cheek. "Nick?" she murmured. "You here, Nick?"

There was no answer, and Nell was quickly asleep.

****

"Ye can't be serious! Jasus Mary and Joseph I never heer'd of such a thing! Did somethin' happen to yer brain there, givin' birth? Mother of god, that's a desperate thing to be telling me!"

Kitty and Nell were having breakfast in the hotel dining room, the baby asleep in his little portable wicker basket alongside their table.

Nell ignored this indignant outburst, calmly lifting another forkful of eggs to her mouth and glancing down at her little son instead of making eye contact with Kitty. "It's all arranged. We leave next week. They're goin' to meet me at Fort Hall and bring my wagon. High time I claimed it." She set her fork down. "Dingbang and Toby will take care of The Shamrock. Dingbang has a cousin here who will help out if they get too busy." Without looking up, she added, "I'm hopin' you'll keep an eye on things."

Kitty pushed her plate aside with a jangle of cutlery and leaned forwards, elbows planted on the table, hands clasped under her chin as if in supplication. Now Nell was looking directly at her, blue eyes cold and challenging. "Please, please reconsider, Nell. If ye do this, ye are going to regret it for the rest of yer life. He's yer own flesh and blood and he's part of Nick, too. What would he think?"

334

"He's dead," snapped Nell, "and he'd approve of what I'm doin'. I know he would. He'd want the best for our son, same as me, an' the best means havin' two parents." Her eyes narrowed. "No money is changin' hands, if that's what you're thinkin'."

"I wasn't, Nell. But the best for yer wee babby is to be with his mother!" hissed Kitty. "Many a babby grows up fine with only one parent." She shook her head, slumping back in her chair, then shot upright again, eyes bright with resolve. "I can take him, bring him up. At least ye'd be near him, then."

Nell made a noise of exasperation. "You're single, same as me. I want him to have two parents. I sure as hell don't want him growin' up around a saloon. No offence intended. Anyway, I've already promised him, an' I'm relieved they want any child I whelped. I was a demon at Laramie when they were carin' for me. I was 'specially ornery to Marianne. She was the one I mostly took things out on. I taunted her for bein' childless an' I feel real bad about the way I behaved now."

Kitty snorted. "I think ye're more than making up for it, acushla."

Nell gave a wry smile.

"Losin' a babby, however it happens, it – it scars ye for life."

"Then I'll add it to all the other scars." Nell regarded her friend coolly.

Kitty was not giving up easily. "Ye can marry again. God knows, there's plenty of men in Yreka eager enough. Ye can pick an' choose."

When Nell responded to this putative solution with a heavy-lidded, pitying look, Kitty sighed and slumped again, conceding defeat. "I can see yer mind is made up. May God forgive ye. I don't know if I can. I will stand by ye, and I'll keep my counsel, but once this gets out – and it will get out – there'll be no place for ye in this town. I know ye'd never trade yer babby for money, but they will think exactly that, and nothing that I say will change their minds."

She shot to her feet and fled, one hand covering her mouth to stifle the sobs. She was halfway to the dining room's exit when she spun on her heel and came marching back, face grim, tears glistening on her cheeks. Nell tensed, bracing for another altercation.

Kitty halted, gripped the back of the nearest chair with both hands as if to steady herself, and said in a quavering voice, "I'll not let ye do this alone. Jesus Mary and Joseph, ye' could be chawed up by a bear or scalped by hostiles. I'm comin' with ye, an' I won't hear any arguments. Billy will come, too, an' that's that."

Nell sighed. "All right. Fine."

Kitty nodded once, turned and stalked away. Nell looked after her sadly. She'd dreaded telling Kitty that she was giving Nicholas to the Beaumonts because she knew it would provoke a scene like the one that had just ensued. Well, at least now it was done and she could get on with her plans. She poured another cup of coffee, took Marianne's letter out of her pocket, and began to read it, as if she needed convincing one more time of the painful reality she had set in motion.

My Dearest Nell

I cannot begin to describe the surprise and joy Sholto and I experienced when we received your letter. We often speak of you, so to receive your news was very welcome although it saddened us deeply when we read that, once more, tragedy affecting your beloved kin has blighted your young life. Please allow me to offer our sincere condolences for the death of your dear departed husband. This is such a cruel blow, and one on which I shall not dwell.

Sholto and I have discussed at length your breathtaking offer along with the reasons you have detailed for coming to such a decision, and I am overjoyed to be able to inform you that we accept it wholeheartedly. The baby, I promise you, will have a wonderful life with us, will be cherished, and given every opportunity to advance himself in this worldly sphere. Your letter is timely, because we are soon to leave Fort Laramie and move back east. The baby will be treasured by our large family and will have more relatives than he may actually desire! However, you may be assured that all of them will wish nothing but the best for him. As his parents, we will provide him with the best education possible and ensure that he mixes with the best society.

Sholto will have the legal requirements drawn up so that everything is done according to what is right and proper for such an adoption. Please let us know how you would prefer to hand the baby over. Sholto thinks it best if we journey to meet you approximately half way, so that the travelling will not be too arduous for either party. How does Fort Hall rate with you as a possible rendezvous? We could meet you there at the end of September, if that suits. We look forward to your response with keen anticipation.

Finally, my dear Nell, I know you do not make this offer lightly, but I beg you to be absolutely sure that it is what you truly desire before we proceed further. If you have second thoughts we will not resent you for it. It is a brave and daring decision and I know in my heart that your little one is deeply blessed to have such a selfless mother who cares solely for his happiness at the expense of her own. You have our word that his Christian name will remain Nicholas, and we have chosen Sholto Charles for his middle names, Charles being the name of his paternal grandfather.

Your devoted friend,

Marianne Beaumont

Nell thrust the letter back into her pocket before sitting quietly with her head in her hands, eyes squeezed shut, the sense of desolation that enveloped her almost overwhelming. Delilah, who'd been approaching the table to clear the dishes, paused, then turned, and tiptoed away.

Nathan. His maternal grandfather is Nathan.

****

The unusual little entourage left Yreka early one morning in early fall, the air already beginning to cool on the cusp of seasonal change. They were travelling in two buckboards with two teams of horses, Kitty driving Nell and the baby in one along with their personal luggage, Billy following in the other with the provisions for the journey, all stored under waterproof canvas. Nell was back in pants and flannel shirt, the Navy Colt buckled in its holster around her waist. This was not any flamboyant gesture but rather a wise precaution. There had been Modoc Indian attacks along the trail they would follow, and not so long ago, either. Billy bristled with armaments, too, his broad chest dramatically criss-crossed by two fully laden bandoleers of ammunition.

Nell wore her old flop hat still, but her worn old ankle boots had been discarded for a brand new pair of calf-length flat-heeled boots that she'd bloused her pants into. She wore her long blonde hair tied back, her old trail kerchief knotted about her neck. The baby hung close to her chest, secured in a shawl slung papoose style about her shoulders, and thoroughly immersed within the soft, protective folds of the fabric. Never one to sacrifice style, by contrast Kitty looked suitably regal in a fine set of dark grey travelling clothes that included a wide-brimmed straw and taffeta bonnet secured under her chin with silk ribbons and featuring a Cambrai lace veil draped over the face. No wonder her travelling trunk was the largest, Nell thought wryly.

A sombre group of townspeople, which included a tight-lipped Addy Entwhistle, came to see them off. Standing beside his mother, Toby tentatively raised his hand to give Nell a little wave goodbye, and she smiled at him in return. Nell had made no secret of the reason for her journey in an attempt to pre-empt gossip, and the townspeople's mood was not a supportive one. She had internalised that she would probably have to move on as Kitty had forewarned. In a period of high infant mortality no one, man or woman, could understand a mother giving away her child. The ever-devoted Toby, of course, did not share in the negativity building against her. She would miss him. And Kitty, of course. And Dingbang.

Billy pulled away first and Kitty swung out to follow him. The townsfolk watched them until they were out of sight, and then drifted away, only the tiny group of women that had peopled the throng loitering, before drawing into a huddle, heads together, talking in low voices.

****

It was day two of the journey, and Kitty had already swapped her flash clothes for pants, flannel shirt, and boots, the same as Nell. Her felt hat was similar, too, and her dark glossy hair had tumbled from its habitual swept up bouffant to be tied back in a simple ponytail. Nell smiled inwardly. Her companion had ensured that she departed Yreka in her accustomed style to impress, and doubtless she would return wearing the same apparel to cement her reputation with the locals as the queen of la mode.

The weather was settled and sunny, the baby, who was placid by nature anyway, coping well, and Nell found herself actually really enjoying being out on the trail again, despite the heartbreaking nature of her mission. The beautiful scenery intensified her bittersweet nostalgia: she and Nick had taken this trail into Yreka.

As they travelled, Nell and Kitty hadn't spoken much, and the latter radiated a disapproval still that was almost palpable. Nell didn't care. Nothing could deter her from her resolve now. In her mind, she pictured an excited Marianne and indulgent Sholto eagerly heading towards their agreed rendezvous at Fort Hall.

The early autumn evenings were noticeably drawing in a little sooner, and Billy called a stop for the night when his vast belly signalled to him that it was time for dinner. The horses were unhitched, grained, watered, and hobbled nearby to graze. Nell fed the baby while Kitty helped Billy set up camp and get a fire going to cook their supper. He'd shot a jackrabbit earlier and now prepared it in a tasty stew, the smells of which set Nell's mouth watering.

They were following the Yreka Trail until it joined the Applegate Trail, a safer, quicker option established by pioneers for reaching Oregon and its Willamette Valley by veering off southwest after Fort Hall. Nell watched Kitty bustling about from the corner of her eye. She'd wondered how the little Irishwoman would cope with a rougher way of life, but so far she'd surprised her. Somewhere, Kitty had mastered the skills required of any overlander woman and slipped back into the role with seeming ease. Her bread was especially delicious. Nell hoped that, with the two of them thus thrown together, she might find out a bit more about Kitty's mysterious background. Meanwhile, Nicholas fed and contentedly slumbering, she set about washing his baby clouts in a nearby stream. As she draped them over brush to dry, Kitty called out that supper was ready.

****

Kitty and Nell sat beside the fire while Nell gave the baby his late feed. The night cloaked them in velvety softness, dark and silent, a canopy of star-studded sky above their heads. Billy had already retired, his sonorous snoring making the two women chuckle. Kitty idly poked at the fire with a stick, watching Nell gently rubbing the baby's back to get his wind up.

"He's such a sweet babby."

"Indeed, he is."

"Nell, I…"

"Don't. Please."

Kitty sighed. She tossed her stick into the fire and held out her arms. "Can I coddle the wee mite a bit?"

Nell passed the baby over, and then stretched her back, sighing deeply. They were quiet for a few moments, and then Nell said softly, "Let's talk about you, for a change."

"Me?" Kitty stopped her soft crooning to the child and looked over at Nell.

"Yes. You know pretty much everything 'bout me, but I know doodly about you, 'cept what I learned in Yreka. High time I heard your story."

Kitty didn't speak for a moment, and then she stood up, handing the sleepy baby back to Nell. "I'll tell ye," she said softly, "but first ye settle him down and I'll fetch us a wee nightcap. I have a bottle of brandy in my trunk."

Kitty poured a generous dollop of brandy into Nell's cup, and chuckled. "That'll make the babby sleep well next time he suckles. *Sláinte*"

She settled herself back on her campstool and sighed. "My story, is it? Ah, well, I suppose it's high time I told ye, as ye said. Truth is, there's not a lot to tell. My experience of comin' west is pretty tame compared to yer own." She took a sip, and leaned forwards, gazing into the fire, resting her forearms on her thighs, the cup of brandy nestled in both hands. "I emigrated to America from a tiny village in County Cork, Ireland, with my husband, Liam. We were both nineteen and had been married nought but three months. Things in Ireland were desperate, with the tater crops failing and the hunger everywhere. It was hard leavin' family, but we wanted a better life for ourselves and any children we hoped to have." She paused to sip again and looked up, smiling at Nell. "We have that in common, Nell, uprootin' ourselves to follow a dream."

"It was never my dream," said Nell shortly. It was Pap's. Go on."

"We came over to New York on one of the 'coffin ships' in 1850. It was a terrible voyage and many died, but Liam and I managed to survive. He had the fever bad, but I nursed him through it. We stayed with relatives who'd come over earlier and, as soon as we were strong enough, made our way westward to California, to join the gold fever."

"So that's how you learned your frontier woman skills."

Kitty regarded her solemnly. "I didn't come from a rich background with servants or such, Nell. We were dirt poor and cooked what little we had over an open hearth, graftin' from dawn to dusk."

"Course. Sorry. I don't know much 'bout other places. It's just you're such a lady an' all."

Kitty hooted with laughter. "Is that how ye see me?"

"Well, yes. You're the most genteel lady I ever met."

"I wasn't always 'genteel', Nell." She topped up their brandy. "Anyway, on with the story. After months of travelling, we arrived in Sacramento and headed on from there to the goldfields at Hangtown. The living was rough, but we were both so happy. Sometimes I helped Liam pan, and other times I made pies for the miners and did their laundry." She chuckled. "I was makin' more than Liam and squirreling it away. There were hardly any women, and the men went mad for my pies. Before I knew it, I had a booming little business. When the Chinese arrived I had to compete with them for the laundry work, so I gave that away and focused on my pies. Liam had some luck o' the Irish and we ended up with a good stake to help us set up a business. I was expecting a babby, so we left the gold fields and returned to Sacramento, where we purchased a modest boarding house." Kitty sighed. "That was such a happy time. I had two girls to help me and we did very well. The house was always full. I got some nice clothes and Liam bought me jewellery. We thought we had it all."

Kitty rose to place more wood on the fire and both women were quiet for a little as they watched the sparks shoot upwards. Kitty resumed her seat.

"Of course, the good times didn't last. They never do. Liam took ill suddenly and within a month he was dead. The doctor said the shipboard fever had weakened his heart. The shock of it left me reelin'. The baby came too early and was stillborn. I lost everything in a matter of weeks. I carried on for a while, but the pain was so great I knew I had to get away. I sold up for a very good price and moved up to Yreka to make a fresh start." She tipped her cup back to drain the dregs. "That's my story. Now ye know."

"I'm sorry, Kitty. No wonder you took on so when I told you I was giving up –"

"Shush now, acushla." The little Irishwoman slapped a knee. "We're women, Nell. We go on. Now, ye get off to bed and I'll take first watch. Billy will take second. Sleep well."

In her tent, Nell lay next to the baby, listening to him snuffling as he slept. She was suddenly aware of the tears spontaneously rolling down her cheeks, but she made neither sound nor movement, remaining perfectly still and just letting them flow. Kitty's words echoed in her head. "We're women. We go on."

What else can we do?

CHAPTER TWENTY-THREE

They met fellow travellers on the Yreka and Applegate Trails, and even more once they joined the California Trail, travelling alongside the Humboldt River. Sometimes they shared camp at night with these wayfarers and enjoyed the company around the fire. Being in a group of any size engendered a sense of security. Kitty usually dealt with any questions regarding the reason for their journey, her stock reply being that they were going to meet relatives at Fort Hall.

The nature of the terrain changed dramatically as they drew closer to their destination, and Nell felt her emotions fluctuating accordingly. She knew she had come too far to turn back, but there were moments when she did not know if she could actually go through with the dire decision she had made. Misery overtook her when she felt the baby's distress at her resolve to keep him at arm's length, her distance from him, and the detached nature of her care, however conscientious. He would cry inconsolably for no apparent reason, staring up at her with his blue eyes brimful of tears and his little lips trembling. At such times she passed him to Kitty and abandoned the buckboard to walk on her own. Poor Kitty was left to both console the child and manage the team. Thus, the days passed and, as all journeys must eventually end, theirs did, too, with their arrival at Fort Hall on the Snake River.

Principally a fur trading enterprise that had also provided support to emigrants heading west, the fort had never been a military outpost, although soldiers had camped nearby for a while. Currently, the army regularly patrolled the trail to ensure the safety of the wagon trains, and had, the weary travellers learned, a contingent of men and officers temporarily camped three miles to the north when Nell and her party arrived. She left Kitty and Billy with the wagons and the baby while she ventured into the fort to make enquiries. It was her guess that, if Marianne and Sholto were already here, they would be billeted in relative comfort within the fort itself. She couldn't believe that Sholto would condone his precious wife living in a tent amongst rough men. The fort, which had a chequered history anyway, had been severely damaged in floods recently, but was patched up and operating still.

Nell stared at a group of Shoshone Indians squatting around a fire in front of their tepee outside the fort's white adobe perimeter near the main gate, and they stared back at her impassively. It was clear she was not interested in trade of any kind. They were 'tame

Indians', waiting for the next wagon train of emigrants to arrive. As the weather grew colder, more and more would arrive to winter over at the fort, living on handouts. The Indians who lived wild called them 'hang-around-the-forts'. Nell had seen them when she was at Fort Laramie, where they were known as 'Laramie loafers'. Just the same, she flicked back her jacket as she passed them, exposing the Navy Colt on her hip, and eyeing the Indians coldly. The sight of them revived painful memories.

No sooner had Nell stepped within the palisade, pausing to gaze around the interior of the fort, when she heard a voice cry out her name and spun around. There was a figure standing in deep shadow beneath the steeply sloped verandah that ran along the front of most of the buildings.

"Nell! Is that you? Oh, Nell!"

Marianne came forward into the sunlight to stand on the uppermost step outside what appeared to be the fort's administrative block, teetering on tiptoe, hands clasped to her chest, face alight with joy. Then, abandoning her usual ladylike restraint, she gathered up her skirts and came flying across the courtyard towards Nell, who gritted her teeth, bracing for the inevitable hugs and kisses. "Shite!" she muttered, and forced a welcoming smile.

****

Sholto had, of course, organised everything. Nell, Kitty, and the baby were billeted in rooms at the fort, while Billy was provided with a bunk in communal quarters. The Factor and his wife, Henry and Catherine Drummond, insisted on everyone joining them for dinner, and a fine spread that included braised beef, onions and potatoes was laid before them in the Company Hall, with wine, beer, and port accompanying the food. Nell had bathed and changed her clothes, but had declined to dress up, while Marianne and Kitty were resplendent, vying with each other for the honour of most fashionable dress, jewellery, and elaborate hairdo, which finery, if her obsequious manner were anything to go by, greatly impressed the Factor's contrastingly drab little wife.

Also at the table, with little to say, was the young woman who was to fill the role of wet nurse. Agnes was the wife of a sergeant at Fort Laramie who had recently lost her own little girl shortly after birth, and had agreed to accompany the Beaumonts. She looked sad and withdrawn, Nell thought, hoping Agnes hadn't been pressured into her surrogate maternal role. According to Marianne, she had two other young children, stated with a matter-of-factness that rather gave Nell the impression she felt this fact precluded any depth of sympathy for her loss of the third one. Nell had ground her teeth and reminded herself to focus on Marianne's good points. Being childless for so long had doubtless blunted her compassion for anyone with above zero children. The baby, meanwhile, dozed in his basket by the fire, and Marianne kept craning her neck in his direction, between flashing radiant smiles at her husband, who, clearly revelling in his wife's happiness, was in a talkative humour, waxing eloquent about life at Fort Laramie in response to the Factor's questions and in turn asking Kitty all about her businesses and life in Yreka. Nell was content to sit quietly, nibble at her food and listen. Sholto eventually got around to her though, as she knew he would.

"Nell, will you drive your wagon back to Yreka yourself?"

"I will, Captain. We'll be leavin' in convoy early tomorrow morning, right after we restock with some provisions." The look of relief that flickered across Marianne's face did not escape her. The sooner she left, the sooner Marianne had sole custody of the baby.

"Well, they're a good team of oxen and I had their shoes replaced by the blacksmith as soon as we arrived."

"Thank you. I'll pay you what I owe you before we leave, if you'll jus' work out the amount."

"I should say not! Wouldn't hear of such a thing!"

"I pay my way," said Nell stiffly, sitting upright and eyeballing Sholto. "I don't need no favours. I have the means."

"Nell, we'd be grateful if you'd accept the oxen." The plea came from Marianne. "It's the least we can do, after all."

Nell stared at her. The very least. *My son is worth a lot more than four oxen. He is beyond price.* She opened her mouth to reply, but just then Nicholas woke and began to fuss, and both she and Marianne rose to their feet simultaneously.

As Marianne opened her mouth, awkwardly twisting her fingers together, Nell said, "I'll give him his last feed, and then you can take him. He'll sleep right through."

Marianne hesitated, but then nodded and sat down. Sholto put a hand on her shoulder and she looked up at him with a tremulous smile. Nell sighed inwardly. *Prob'ly convinced I'm gonna change my mind, 'specially recallin' my ole ornery self.*

Excusing herself, Nell lifted the baby from his bed, thanked the Factor and his wife for their hospitality, and climbed the stairs to her room. Kitty likewise excused herself, thanked her hosts, and followed Nell, carrying the baby's basket.

****

In her room, Nell laid the baby on the quilt while she pulled off her boots. Kitty closed the door behind them and turned up the lamp. Then Nell stretched out on the bed, propping the pillows behind her, undid her shirt and cotton cami, lifted Nicholas, and put him to her breast. The baby instantly fell quiet, suckling greedily and Kitty chuckled as she watched from the end of the bed. Nell watched the rhythmically working chin of her tiny son, smiling as she heard the milk hit his stomach, then looked up at her.

"You could put his things together for me, if you like. That hold-all should take everything." She nodded towards a carpetbag, propped against the far wall, sagging open.

Kitty put the basket down on the bed. "Of course."

By the time Nell had fed the baby, winded him, and changed his clout, Kitty had everything ready. Nell sat down to pull her boots on and stood up. She lifted the baby and turned to Kitty. The two women remained looking at each other in silence, as if waiting for the other to make the first move. Then Kitty held out her arms.

"I – I can take him to her."

"No." Nell stroked the child's head, fingers lingering on the silky smoothness of his baby fluff. "I'll hand him over. That's on my conscience, not yours. You bring his things and the basket."

"Ye can change yer mind, Nell. There's still time. Jasus, it's clear ye don't even like the woman!"

"That's neither here nor there, and more my fault than hers. Besides, I've signed all the papers and the Factor witnessed them. I did it this afternoon when you weren't around. Where were you, anyway?"

"I had an errand. Ye can still change yer mind. Feck the papers."

"Kitty, please don't make me angry. Not now."

Kitty swallowed hard, and bit down on her lip, trying to stop it from trembling. "Very well." She quickly gathered up the baby's meagre belongings.

Nell opened the door, glanced over her shoulder as if to check that Kitty was following her, and they descended the stairs to the room below, where Marianne and Sholto were waiting. Husband and wife stood up as she and Kitty entered. The atmosphere in the room was charged, expectant. Ever the gentleman, Sholto stepped forward to relieve Kitty of her burden and then all eyes were on Nell. Marianne did not move. Nell took a step and then froze. Kitty felt as if her heart would stop. Then Marianne stepped forwards, slowly lifting her hands, and Nell crossed to her without a word, placing the baby into her outstretched arms. As she carefully slid her own arms out from under her child, he looked up into her face, his gaze remarkably intense, and his little face lit up in a sweet smile that exposed his gums. It was the first time he'd smiled. For a moment, Nell froze, unable to tear her eyes away from this precious infancy milestone. Then she turned on her heel and left. This time, Kitty did not follow her. She sank white-faced into a chair beside the hearth, and Sholto poured and handed her a large brandy. Marianne strolled to the window, where she stood with her back to them, swaying gently and crooning softly to the baby, cheek pressed to his little head where it rested on her shoulder.

Back in her room, Nell washed the baby's soiled clout and hung it over the windowsill. Then she undressed, blew out the lamp, and climbed into bed.

****

When Nell and her entourage made their departure the following morning, Marianne and Sholto were in attendance, wisely without the baby, who'd been left in the care of Agnes. Kitty and Billy made their farewells before climbing aboard their respective wagons. After an initial awkwardness, Marianne wished Nell a safe journey and pressed on her the address of Sholto's family in Boston, assuring her that wherever she and her husband may be posted with Nicholas, mail sent to that address would always reach them. She also promised to send Nell news of the little boy from time to time, including small portraits. Nell did not speak a word. She thrust the address into her jacket pocket and stood silently, looking past the woman to whom she'd entrusted her little boy. Then they embraced after a fashion, while Sholto stood back to allow them this moment, after which he escorted Nell to her wagon and assisted her aboard.

"Nell, my offer of a gratuity still stands."

Nell shook her head. "No."

As he stepped back and Nell gathered up the reins, Sholto said softly, "God bless you, Nell. I can never, ever find adequate words to thank you."

Nell responded with an almost imperceptible nod, staring straight ahead; then she released the brake, slapped the reins on the oxen's backs, uttered a cry that could have been an exhortation to the animals, or a curse hurled into the face of God, and the wagon rolled slowly out to follow Billy and Kitty.

CHAPTER TWENTY-FOUR

Nell was relieved to be alone as the oxen plodded stolidly after the two buckboards driven by her travelling companions. That way, she didn't have to talk to anyone, which would have proved burdensome in her present mood. Her head told her she'd done the right thing, that her son would have a marvellous life, rich with opportunity, that her love would have turned out to be a curse for him as it had for every other person who'd been precious to her – Ma, baby Jesse, Pa, Sabrina, Nick. But her heart, of course, would have none of it, treacherous wellspring of emotion that it was. She distracted herself by drinking in the scenery around her as her journey progressed, as if seeing it for the first time, while she sang softly every song she could remember, and when she'd exhausted the repertoire, she started all over again. But images of a sweet little face with big blue eyes, a tender little neck, the feel of fair hair soft as thistledown, tiny hands so perfect they mesmerised you, that unique musky baby smell – all of these memories were just too raw, too fresh to be easily dispelled.

By the time Billy called a stop for the night, Nell felt utterly drained and exhausted, and, although she'd sneaked off to express some milk during the noon break, her breasts, swollen and tender, were hot and aching, as if her body, too, was determined to torment her for her betrayal of motherhood. Expressing the milk, of course, she thought ruefully, only increased the supply.

While Billy was busy feeding and hobbling the stock, Kitty got the fire going before she sidled up to Nell and pressed a small hide drawstring bag into her hands. Nell regarded it curiously. "What's this?"

"Remember when I went missing at the fort and ye asked where I'd been? I got this from an Indian medicine woman. It's a special tea, if ye like, for easing the pain that can come when ye stop feedin' yer babe. Take a draught as soon as I get some water boiling. It will help, I promise ye."

"Thanks, Kitty."

"Are ye all right?"

"I'm fine. Please, don't keep asking. I'll help you with supper."

"Only if ye're up to it."

"I am."

"Fine. We'll make a stew with the piece of beef Henry gifted us."

****

The return journey to Yreka was smooth and uneventful, the autumn weather mellow and settled. The Indian medicine woman's tea proved efficacious and Nell's mastitis quickly cleared. With the shrinkage of her breasts came the feeling that her last link to her baby had been severed, and she tried to focus on other things, like wondering how The Shamrock had fared without her hand on the tiller. She also pondered her future in the town, recalling Kitty's words when she'd first informed her of her decision to adopt out her child – "There'll be no place for ye in this town." Well, only time would tell.

Just as Nell had suspected, Kitty changed back into her smart travelling clothes just before they reached Yreka, ready for the grand entrance, and looking every inch the local queen-bee, returning to reclaim her rightful place in the town's hierarchy. The citizens who stopped to watch the little procession looked suitably impressed as Kitty raised a gloved hand to wave to them. Nell kept her eyes straight ahead, hands firmly on the reins. She heard a voice call out, "Where's your baby, Nell?" but she did not recognise it.

Nell's qualms about the Shamrock proved unfounded. As it turned out, Dingbang, Dingbang's cousin, and Toby had done a sterling job of keeping the restaurant running smoothly and well patronised, while Addy had taken care of the banking. Toby couldn't disguise his joy at seeing Nell again, but she quickly sensed that something was troubling him. The reason for this became clear on the first night of her return to The Shamrock, a couple of days after her return to Yreka, once she'd had a chance to rest and recoup after her long trek. When the last customer had left and Nell set out the usual late supper for her employees, Toby demurred, eyes downcast, shuffling his feet awkwardly and wringing his long-suffering hat once again.

"Sorry, Miz Nell. Mam said I was to come straight home."

"Just 'Nell' will do, an' surely she meant after you'd had your victuals." His sudden formality and obvious distress gave her a cold feeling.

Toby looked up at her, his homely, freckled face contorted into an image of misery. "I cain't work for you no more, Nell." His lips trembled and his eyes filled up. "Mam let me stay on while you was away, but now you're back an' she says I cain't work here no more 'cos..." His voice trailed off, he backed up, turned, and fled down the stairs in a swift clatter.

Seated at the table behind her, Dingbang clicked his tongue, and Nell turned around slowly, taken aback by what had just happened and trying to gather her thoughts. She looked at him in silence for a moment before she pulled out a chair and sat down heavily. Toby? She hadn't expected that. Dingbang was shaking his head.

"Sorry, Miz Nell. I knew that was coming. He was dreading having to tell you."

Nell picked up a plate and served herself a helping from the bowl of chicken chow mein Dingbang had placed on the table. "Well, looks like it's just the two of us now." She picked up her fork with a sigh, and twirled it around in the noodles.

Dingbang poured her a tumbler of water from the jug. "I can get Jiang to help out again. His English is not so good, but he enjoyed the work, and he's a good cook, too."

"Thank you, Dingbang. We'll see what happens. You did well while I was gone, but now I'm back an' the clientele may just fall away a bit. If a town gets a set on someone, it can infect a lot of people."

"We were busy tonight."

"Yes, but many wouldn't have known I'd be here, an' by the time they figured it out they were too plumb hungry to care."

"They were pleased to see you, though."

"Seemed that way. I guess we'll have to wait and see." Nell frowned at her glass as she lifted it. "Can you find us somethin' stronger than this here water?"

"Yes, of course."

****

In the days and weeks that followed, Nell, felt the full force of the township's censure. Kitty remained fiercely loyal, of course, insisting Nell ignore the subtle – and not so subtle – animus directed her way, but many of those Nell had previously considered friends and good neighbours gave her the cold shoulder at every turn, and it hurt, no matter how hard she tried to shrug it off. She knew the ill feeling was being driven by the wives of the business class in the town, women who put the hard word on their husbands to fall into line with their nasty campaign against her, even Addy. The numbers coming to eat at The Shamrock had thinned considerably, too, which surprised Nell, who had thought these hardy, independent men would be less judgmental. But they were also dependent on the goodwill of the town's commercial elite. Dingbang's suggestion of employing Jiang turned out to be superfluous. Some nights, there were barely enough customers to keep the two of them busy. Nell decided that the time had come for her to move on. The little gold mining town held some good memories for her: her wedding to Nick, the stunning success of their business venture, the birth of a son, Kitty becoming a surrogate mother to her. But it held bad memories, too: Crowther turning up to dredge up the past, Nick's murder, her decision to adopt out her baby, which had led to this ostracism. She sighed as she lay in bed, mulling over her prospects, and gradually her resolve firmed. She knew what she must do. Telling Kitty would be the hard part. She felt a deep affection for the feisty little Irishwoman, and would miss her badly.

Nell spent her eighteenth birthday quietly with Kitty over dinner in a secluded corner of the hotel dining room, cheered by the fire, which had been lit for a cold night that saw flurries of snow waft across the windows. Kitty ordered her staff to close the heavy drapes to keep in the warmth.

While they ate – and after one or two draughts of wine – Nell summoned the courage to inform her friend of her decision to leave Yreka. Kitty lowered her glass and looked at her aghast.

"Oh, Nell. Please don't be hasty. I know it's not been easy, but just ride it out an' they'll soon get sick of their holier than thou nonsense. God knows, they all sit in church of a Sunday, but they've forgotten what Jesus said about casting the first stone."

Nell shook her head. "No, Kitty, an' it ain't fair to you, tryin' to shield me all the while an' puttin' up with dirty looks yourself. I've done well here, largely thanks to you, but it's time to move on." *Leaving behind yet another grave.*

Kitty refilled their wine glasses and waited until Delilah had cleared their empty plates. "Well, I know I'm wastin' my breath if I try to get ye to change yer mind once it's made up. Where will ye go?"

Nell smiled. "I fancy heading south. Mebbe see where that takes me. Anywhere but Oregon." She chuckled.

Kitty frowned. "A woman on yer own in this wild country...I fear for ye, acushla." Then she brightened as her businesswoman persona reasserted itself. " I'll buy out yer share of The Shamrock, give ye a good price for it."

Nell grinned. "I'd hoped you'd say that."

Delilah arrived with a prettily decorated birthday cake, which she placed on the table, handing Kitty a bone-handled knife and setting out two plates with cake forks. Nell clasped her hands with delight.

"Oh, that's lovely, Kitty. Thank you!"

"I had it made specially for ye." Kitty carved out a generous slice, manoeuvred it on to a plate, and handed it across to Nell.

As she tucked in Nell said, "I'll be leaving in the spring."

"I'll help ye with whatever ye need."

"I'm obliged."

"I'll miss ye somethin' fierce, acushla."

"I'll miss you, too, dearest Kitty."

Delilah returned with coffee and brandy, and the diners lapsed into a companionable silence, each lost in her own thoughts.

****

Over the next several weeks, Nell sold most of her belongings, including the wagon and oxen, keeping only a few precious items from the goods she and Pap had intended for their new home in Oregon, and storing them safely with Kitty. She signed the documents for the sale of her share in The Shamrock, and Kitty promised to keep Dingbang on, since that had been one of Nell's provisions. Nell still cooked there up until the time for her departure, now working for Kitty's wages. Most of her money would remain in the bank with the understanding that it would be forwarded on to her when she settled, while she set aside funds for her journey, folding the notes and stashing the coins carefully into Pap's old money belt, bringing back many memories.

Finally, having reluctantly sold Misty, she purchased a sturdy pony with good feet and a calm disposition, and made ready to travel as soon as the weather improved with the arrival of spring. Whenever she could, she rode out to the place where Nick had taught her to shoot the Navy Colt, practising her skills until she was satisfied that she was a good shot – a very good shot. With the optimism of youth, she felt ready to put a painful past behind her and move on to her next adventure. *Mam, Pap, baby Jesse, Sabrina, Nick watch over me.*

She smiled as she remembered the words Pap once said to her as a little girl, when she was crying hot, angry tears over something she couldn't even remember now: 'You don't learn anything if your life always goes right.'

****

A very small, somewhat disparate group of people assembled outside Kitty's business establishment to farewell Nell on a bright, sunny spring morning. Kitty was at the forefront, of course, flanked by Billy, Dingbang, Delilah, and Toby, who kept nervously checking over one shoulder for his mother, while trying to use

Billy's impressive bulk to conceal himself, since he'd bunked school to see off his beloved Nell. Humble was there as well, trying to look cheerful for Kitty's sake. Nell, who had made her farewells to a tearful Kitty the night before, now had no intention of getting into a similarly emotional wracking with any of the others in her small band of well wishers. She quickly stroked Toby's cheek, then stepped away and swung up into the saddle to say her piece from there.

"I'm obliged to each and every one of you for your kindness and friendship. God bless you all. I'll write Kitty soon as I'm settled somewhere."

Then she pulled her hat down firmly, dug her heels into the pony's flanks, and trotted out of Yreka without a backward glance.

As the others drifted away, Dingbang consoling a sobbing Toby, Kitty remained looking after Nell. She murmured a traditional Irish farewell blessing under her breath:

"May God hold ye in the palm of His hand. May yer days be many and yer troubles be few, May all God's blessings descend upon ye, May peace be within ye, May yer heart be strong, May ye find what ye're seeking, wherever ye roam."

CHAPTER TWENTY-FIVE

With some distance covered, the pain of her departure from Yreka and her friends there eased, and Nell found herself enjoying being on the trail again, the sun on her face, filling her lungs with the pure, fresh air, taking in the landscape, and just relaxing into the rhythm of the journey. Her little pony seemed to be relishing the adventure, too, as his muscles warmed, snorting, nodding his head, and looking around him as he trotted along with ears pricked forward and eyes bright. Nell had named him Whiskey because his coat was roughly the colour of the beverage, which would always evoke memories of a lot of people she loved, both dead and alive, all of whom enjoyed a wee dram: Pap, Nick, Angus, and Kitty. She sighed deeply. It was good to get away from the negative atmosphere in Yreka, though. Wherever she ended up, nobody would know anything about her, and she could start afresh, with a clean slate. Knowing she had the money now to put into any enterprise she fancied gave her confidence. She glanced down at Nick's rifle in its leather scabbard and her hand went to the revolver on her hip, the ball of her thumb stroking the smooth butt. Whatever came her way, she was sure that she could handle herself well and hold her own with anyone who might threaten her.

The old Siskiyou Trail, which ran from San Francisco up into the Willamette valley of Oregon was easy to follow, worn in by a stream of miners lusting after gold, mule trains, and herds of livestock trekking both north and south. The old foot trail through the western river valleys had been established by local Indians and then become more defined as California was opened up to European settlement. Nell settled comfortably into the saddle, enjoying the deep peace of the forest and the pools of dappled sunlight that broke up the shady stretches of the trail. At length they emerged into a flat stretch of river valley and she gathered in the reins.

"Let's blow away the cobwebs, boy!"

Nell urged Whiskey forwards into a smooth, unhurried canter.

****

That night, squatted by her campfire, sipping coffee, Nell pondered her future as she peered into the flames. Kitty had given her a list of names of people she knew or had dealings with during her time in Sacramento, and Nell thought that might be a good place to hang her hat for a while. It was a mining town, just like Yreka, though a sight older and larger, too, with a nasty tendency to flood,

Kitty had warned her. Anyway, she could have a look around, size the place up. Who knew? Maybe it would suit her well.

Following supper, Nell moved the pony closer and banked the fire, reminding herself to wake at some point in the night to keep it burning well, a deterrent to any wild animals that may be lurking about during the hours of darkness. Her rifle was placed to hand, along with the revolver. As Nell wrapped herself in her bedroll and settled down to sleep, her last waking thoughts were of her little boy. She'd had a long letter from Marianne just before she'd left Yreka and in amongst its folds she'd found a small daguerreotype of her son, which she kept tucked in a pocket over her heart. Marianne's letter had been brimming with happiness and detailed reports of how brilliantly the baby, now on solid food, was thriving. The family was now back east in Boston, and little Nicholas was being fussed over by a throng of doting relatives that included aunts, uncles and grandparents. Nell removed the little portrait from her shirt pocket and took one last look at it in the glimmering light cast by the fire. He was clearly growing well, as Marianne had said, a bonny little lad who bore a strong resemblance to his mother – his real mother, that is. I hope he doesn't turn into a spoiled brat. Maybe she'd see him again one day? Not likely, she told herself, with her habitual brutal realism – him on one side of a vast nation and her on the other. Nell tucked the portrait carefully back into her pocket, making a mental note to get a frame for it in Sacramento. *You may never know me, but I will never, ever forget you.*

****

Nell encountered several mule trains on her journey, hauling their freight both north and south. She often rode in company with the teamsters going south during the day, especially if they had women and children with them, because they provided security, but she always made her own camp alone in the evenings, despite invitations to share supper. When she rode into Sacramento on a sunny spring afternoon, she felt relieved to be done with her journey and back to relative civilisation. After putting up Whiskey at a livery for a well-earned feed and rest and storing her gear, she strolled through the town shouldering her saddlebags and taking in the sights. Nobody much spared her a glance. They were used to all kinds from allover in their town, and a young woman in men's clothes was nothing unusual.

Sacramento was another bustling little metropolis birthed by the gold rushes. The streets teemed with people, wagons, and horses, and there was a pervasive smell of horse manure, river water, and unwashed humanity. Nell thought it very different from Yreka. The town had a stolid, determined look about it, reinforced by buildings with solid iron doors, shutters and thick walls. The raised boardwalks with their canopied overhead sidewalk shelters lent a distinctive air to the place, as did the many balconies on the storeyed

370

buildings. The deep verandahs seemed to offer defiance to a cruel sun, scything winds, and heavy rains, which were such a feature of life here, according to Kitty. Thought of her jogged Nell's memory, and she took Kitty's list out of her pocket to read again the name of a boarding house she'd recommended, Rosie's. A friendly passerby gave her instructions on how to get there and she headed off hopeful of finding accommodation, first priority before getting a bath, a change of clothes, and a hot meal, in that order.

Nell found the boarding house easily enough. The door opening on to the street was open, pinned back by an enormous doorstop in the form of a large cast iron kettlebell, and Nell stepped through the doorway into the cool gloom of the interior, pausing to let her eyes adjust to the change of light. There was a desk to the left of the entrance, but nobody was manning it. There was, however, a brass bell on the desk and just as Nell picked it up to ring it, a skinny youth clad in a long apron and carrying a mop and bucket came out of a room further along the corridor, halting abruptly when he saw her.

Nell touched the brim of her hat. "Howdy, mister, I'm lookin' fer Rosie Jarrow, the lady who runs this establishment."

The boy nodded. "Yes'm. Wait there." He scuttled off, almost tripping over his apron in his haste, slopping a little water from his pail. Nell sighed, looking around. The place looked clean and well appointed so she hoped they had a spare room. She turned to the sound of footsteps as a bulky figure loomed out of the semi-darkness of the hallway and realised quickly that this was no woman approaching her but rather a large hulk of a man, of similar build to Billy. Dressed in a white shirt with open collar, the sleeves rolled up to the elbows, and dark trousers held up by robust suspenders, he did not fit any image of an elegant hotelier. His thick curly hair was jet black, and he sported an impressive handlebar moustache. Halting in front of Nell, he thrust out a giant hand, his dark blue eyes appraising her frankly.

"Good afternoon, ma'am. How can I help you?"

Nell shook his hand and released it to check the paper Kitty had given her. "Er, you ain't no Rosie, I'm guessin'."

The big man gave a deep, throaty chuckle. "No, I am not. Rosie's my mother, but she's in San Francisco at the moment visiting with kinfolk. I'm taking care of things for her 'til she gets back. I'm her son, Elijah Jarrow."

"Pleased to meet you. I'm Nell Hardy. Rosie's place was favourably commended to me by my good friend, Kitty Callahan, also a friend of your mother an' a fellow businesswoman."

Jarrow clasped his hands together, his smile obsequious. "Best boarding house in town," he intoned. "May I offer you a room?"

There was something off-putting about the man, a perceptibly oily insincerity, but Nell cast that thought aside, focusing on her immediate needs instead. Kitty had said this was a worthy establishment, and that was good enough for her. "You may, indeed. I'm a weary traveler seekin' a soft bed, a bath, an' a meal. I'd be right obliged to you if you can fulfill those three cravin's. I can pay in advance."

"Music to my ears! Step over here," boomed Jarrow, indicating the secretaire, "and I'll get your details. Then it will be my pleasure to see to your wants. Your friend was right to send you here. You will be most comfortable."

Nell smiled. Those words at least were music to her ears.

****

Nell was pleased with the room. It was nothing fancy, but it was clean, cool and the window overlooked the street behind, which was quieter. Nell took off her boots and stretched out on the bed, smiling as she sank into its feathery softness. No sleeping on the hard ground tonight. She raised herself to sit on the edge of the mattress, wiggling her freed toes blissfully inside their socks. A knock on the door and the skinny youth entered to place a tin bath on the floor. He was quickly followed by a succession of girls and women who filled it from steaming kettles before withdrawing as quickly as they'd arrived. The last one draped a towel over the back of the only chair in the room and placed a piece of yellow soap on it. Murmuring her thanks, Nell got up and followed her to the door, which she then closed and locked. First, she emptied her pockets, placing her little son's portrait carefully under the pillow, then she peeled off her clothes along with the money belt, stepped into the tub and sank slowly down into the hot water with a long, drawn-out "Ahhhhhhh!"

They'd left her a body brush as well as the soap, but there was no knowing where that had been. Nell wrinkled her nose as she tossed it out of the tub and used her own instead. After a thorough steeping, during which she scrubbed herself to a rosy glow all over and washed her hair, she toweled herself dry, dressed in clean clothes, secured her money belt, and made her way downstairs feeling like a new woman, one that was hungry enough to eat the ass end out of a bear. The view through the open doorway of the boarding house showed the shadows lengthening as dusk closed in.

Seated at the far end of the dining room's communal table, Jarrow pushed to his feet as she entered, raising an arm in greeting. "Miz Hardy, please do join me. I've arranged an early hot supper for you." He sat down, indicating the chair opposite. Nell would have preferred to eat alone, but the man had been very kind and accommodating so she was happy to oblige him. As she sat down she said, "Please, call me Nell. I ain't one to stand on my dignity."

Jarrow inclined his head. "Of course. Nell. But only if you call me Elijah."

Nell grinned. "As you wish. It's a fine name."

Jarrow rolled his eyes. "My mother is devoted to the Good Book. I have a brother, Jacob, and a sister, Sarah."

"Splendid names."

At that point, a serving girl arrived carrying two plates bearing generous slabs of meat and potato pie with rich butter crust, which she set in front of the diners with a little bob, before returning with a pitcher of milk and two cups.

"Thank you, Sally." Jarrow stared intently at the girl, who backed away hurriedly before turning to flee towards the kitchen. "Shy," said Jarrow dismissively, but Nell sensed fear from the girl. Why? She wondered.

Jarrow poured milk into Nell's cup and then his own. "Please, tuck in."

Nell had thought he might want to say a blessing before they commenced eating, since he'd hinted at a biblical upbringing, but now she needed no second bidding. Tucking her napkin into her collar, she seized her cutlery, and attacked the pie with gusto.

"We don't serve liquor here," Elijah added apologetically.

Nell shook her head, forced to answer him around a large mouthful of delicious pie. "That's fine. I don't need no liquor." She closed her eyes, expression dreamy. "Mmmm, this pie, though, is exactly what I do need." The boiled cabbage on the side, although not her favourite vegetable, tasted like nectar as well.

Jarrow chuckled. "Plenty more where this came from. Mother has the most excellent Scottish cook."

Nell's eyes snapped open. "Scottish?"

Jarrow watched slack-jawed as Nell dropped her cutlery with a clatter, tore away the napkin tucked under her chin, erupted on to her feet and raced off towards the kitchen. She burst through the beaded curtain separating the scullery from the dining room and stopped dead. Sally and the other young female kitchen hand froze as she came barreling in, and the cook, a squat, bald man busy manoeuvering something around a hissing frying pan turned from the stove in surprise to stare at the young woman who had invaded his domain so dramatically, the big wooden spoon he'd been wielding poised aloft.

"Something wrong with ma food, lassie? Or have ye come to compliment the chef?" He raised a quizzical eyebrow and grinned. It was not Angus.

Nell slumped. "I'm sorry, I thought you were someone else. I – Mr. Jarrow mentioned he had a Scottish cook an' I thought maybe –"

She drew herself erect, clearing her throat. "The food is very good. I'm sorry I disturbed you." Then she beat a hasty retreat back to the table, avoiding eye contact with Jarrow as she slid on to her chair.

"Everything all right, Nell?"

"Yes. Fine." She clipped her words. "Jus' got the wrong end of the stick, is all." Nell tucked her napkin back into her collar and recommenced eating. She felt foolish. Angus was most likely in San Francisco, running his own establishment as he'd envisaged. The man had been like a father to her for a short time and she had fond memories of him.

Nell felt a sudden deep yearning to see a friendly face, not to be surrounded by strangers. The sharpness of the emotion took her by surprise, making her catch her breath. Sally came to clear the plates and a second girl brought bowls of apple pie and cream, followed by a pot of coffee. The boarding house guests began to troop in for their supper. The moment of desolation passed.

****

Nell spent the next few days resting, writing to Kitty (a letter for Toby included), getting her laundry done and exploring Sacramento. She found a lovely oval silver frame for the daguerreotype of Nicholas that Marianne had sent and carried the precious miniature next to her heart. Using the list Kitty had given her, she visited the contacts she'd recommended and found them all welcoming and hospitable, eager for news of the plucky little Irishwoman and more than happy to talk about the pros and cons of life in Sacramento over the dinners and lunches for which they insisted she join them. By the end of the week, though, Nell found, to her consternation, that she had not formed any solid commitment to settling in their town. There was much she liked about Sacramento, but she missed the small close-knit community atmosphere of Yreka. She pondered this as she climbed the stairs to her room at Rosie's late one afternoon, but was suddenly torn from her reverie as Sally, the young domestic at the establishment, shot past her almost knocking her over, the girl clearly distraught and sobbing noisily, her hair disheveled and her pinafore awry.

"Sally?" a startled Nell called after her once she'd gathered her wits and was upright again after falling back against the banister. "Sally? What's wrong?"

As the weeping girl vanished through the doors to the dining room, a voice from the top of the stairs said, "Don't mind her. She's just having a crying fit because I scolded her for her sloppy work."

As Nell continued slowly up the stairs, Jarrow descended until he was on the step above her, blocking her passage. "Mother's too soft on them." His tone was ingratiating, self-justifying. "I've had to be a hard taskmaster to keep the place running smoothly. Some don't like it much. Had it too slack. It's not easy, running an establishment like this." He smiled, flashing his white teeth that contrasted with his heavy black moustache.

"I'm sure," said Nell, looking past him, and he stepped aside. *She seems awful upset for someone who's only had a bit of a scoldin' from the boss, and her hair and clothes are all mussed up.* Nell continued on up to her room, and Jarrow carried on downstairs. From the landing, Nell saw him veer off into the parlour. Somethin' about him I just ain't sure of. She recalled Sally's palpable fear in the dining room, the way she'd shrunk away from Jarrow. As far as her own dealings with Sally went Nell had warmed to the girl instantly, and they'd struck up something of a rapport since she'd been staying at Rosie's, maybe because they were close in age. Sally always had a big smile and a greeting for her, and Nell always gave her the time of day. She decided to find an opportunity to talk to the girl.

****

The next morning, after breakfast, Nell deliberately lingered in her room, waiting for Sally to arrive and make it up, as was her daily custom. Normally, if she wasn't headed out somewhere, Nell would go down to the guests' parlour and read the paper over coffee to avoid getting under the girl's feet. Now, while she waited, she did something she hadn't done for a long time: she wrote in her journal, recording her thoughts about Sacramento and expressing her desire to move on again, a desire that was rapidly becoming a firm resolve. Just as she closed the journal, Sally arrived, pulling up short when she saw Nell lying on the bed fully clothed.

"Sorry, Miss. I'll come back later." She started to back out the door.

Nell put her journal aside and swung her legs off the bed. " No, please don't go." She patted the coverlet. "Come an' sit down. I want to talk to you." When she saw the girl hesitate, she added, "It won't take more 'n a minute. You ain't in no trouble."

Sally sidled over and sat down on the edge of the bed next to Nell, eyes cast down, twiddling nervously with her fingers.

"You were mighty upset when you passed me on the stairs yesterday. You want to tell me why?" As Sally continued playing with her fingers, Nell added. "You can tell me anythin'. I won't blab to nobody."

Sally inhaled deeply. "It's – it's been hard with Mrs. Rosie away." She turned to look at Nell, face brightening. "We jus' got word. She's on her way back. Should be here by tonight."

Nell squeezed the girl's shoulder. She was barely out of childhood, a slender little wisp of a thing. She'd have no chance standing up to a man like Jarrow. Nell just hoped the worst hadn't happened. "That's good news."

"Oh yes. She's a fine lady, been real kind to me. I'm an orphan, you see. Mrs. Rosie took me in. You'll be able to meet her now, Miss Nell."

"Well, I planned on headin' off today. This is a grand place. Sacramento, I mean, but it ain't for me. I'm sorry I'll miss Mrs. Rosie, but I'll leave her a letter with news of our friend, Kitty. If I'm back this way I'll look her up. I'm glad she treats you well. Meanwhile, keep out of that man's way, much as you can."

Sally shot her a knowing look. "I will, Miss Nell. Jodie, she looks out for me. She ain't scared of him."

"That's the other young girl who works here?" Jodie was a well-built lass with a lantern jaw.

"Yes'm. She's been real good to me, too, like a sister." She sighed. "I been real happy here until…"

"You need to tell Mrs. Rosie what he's like."

Sally twiddled with her fingers again. "I don't want no trouble, Miss Nell."

Nell nodded her understanding. "Well, let's hope he moves on as soon as his mother gets here, and doesn't come back in a hurry. Where'd he come from, anyways?"

Sally frowned. "I ain't sure. He seems to drift around. He was workin' at the gold diggings further east, but I don't think he did any good there. Mrs. Rosie gets angry with him whenever he turns up here, so he never stays long. He's only in charge 'cos she had to go sudden like, to tend a sick relative, and he was on hand."

"He behave himself when she's around?"

"Oh yes'm. She's the only one he shows any respect."

"Good." Nell stood up. "You get on now, an' please leave all my things on the bed after you done made it up, so's I can pack everythin' up later."

"I will, Miss Nell." She dipped her head shyly. "Thank you for – for lookin' out for me. I wish I could be as strong as you."

Nell smiled. "You are, Sally. Believe me. You are."

****

Once she was packed and ready to depart, Nell sought out Jarrow in order to return the key to her room and found him lounging in his private parlour with his feet up on a footstool, smoking and drinking what looked like whiskey as he thumbed through some papers. Obviously the liquor ban didn't apply in his private quarters, and his cheeks were already flushed. He appeared to be quite surprised that she was leaving.

"Mother will be here in a few hours. Seems a shame you'll miss her after all."

Nell handed him the key, and a sealed envelope that held her letter to Rosie. "I've left her this, an' maybe we'll catch up if I'm back this way."

"Where you headed to?"

Nell had no intention of telling him that. She shrugged. "See where the road takes me."

Jarrow thrust out his bottom lip, face serious, nodding slowly. "Well, then, I wish you a safe journey. I'll see that mother gets this."

"Thanks." Nell turned on her heel and left, glad to be free of the man. He made her flesh crawl. *Just like Wrenn Cheney.*

Outside on the boardwalk, saddlebags slung over one shoulder, Nell took a deep breath, letting her gaze wander over the town one last time. A sudden break in the crowd gave her a clear view to the opposite side of the street and as she looked over she gasped, her body tautening and her heart leaping into her mouth. A young man was standing outside one of the stores, leaning nonchalantly against a verandah post, smoking a cigarette as he watched the roil of people, wagons, and animals that passed by in a steady stream. There was something terribly familiar about him. Then the crowd closed again, and Nell lost sight of him. Undeterred, her excitement mounting, she launched herself into the street, nimbly dodging hooves and wheels of the traffic that flowed both ways, ignoring the occasional curse from a driver or rider. As she reached the other side and got a better view of the man, she knew she was right. *It's Jimmy*!

Having safely negotiated the teeming thoroughfare despite a few near misses, Nell stood panting, staring at the young man who hadn't yet noticed her presence; his head was turned away from her as he craned his neck to watch a stoush between two wagoneers further along the street. It was Jimmy! He was very well-dressed in suit and tie, a gold watch chain looped across his vest, black leather shoes polished to a high sheen and the lot topped off with what looked like a new charcoal wool derby hat. Unexpected sartorial splendour aside, it was definitely Jimmy.

"Jimmy? Jimmy Hochstedder?"

His head snapped around. Those kindly eyes she remembered so well lighted on her as an expression of deep shock immobilized his features. Straightening up, he flicked the cigarette from his fingers and took a step forward. "Nell? Nell, is that really you?"

Nell stepped on to the boardwalk and stood facing him. "Yes, Jimmy, it's really me." She dropped her saddlebags and was in his arms at the same time as he reached for her, and they clung to each other, oblivious to the curious looks of passersby. Jimmy whispered 'Nell' over and over, while she laughed and cried at the same time. He was taller, even more good looking, if anything, had filled out some, looked posh, but he was her old Jimmy, her same old Jimmy, the love of her life.

Jimmy lifted her away from him, hands still holding her upper arms firmly, tears standing in his eyes as he ran an appraising gaze over her. "You look wonderful. Older, womanly, but," he gathered her in again, squeezing his eyes shut, "my same sweet, beautiful Nell."

Nell laughed with sheer delight, clinging to him tightly. "You look pretty good yourself. Hell, ain't you the spiv?"

At the sound of a high-pitched 'Ahem!' behind her, Nell swung around and Jimmy quickly released her, subtly pushing her away a little. Nell looked at him bewildered, and then again at the frowning young woman who had emerged from an emporium behind them.

Jimmy whipped off his hat, looking more than a little flustered. "Nell, allow me to introduce my – wife." He gave a sheepish grin. "Sadie, this is Nell Washburn. You must remember her."

Wife? Wife!

The young woman thrust out a kid gloved hand while running a disapproving eye over Nell's manly garb – pants, boots, flannel shirt, new grey slouch hat. She, on the other hand, was dressed in the latest fashion: a lavender coloured silk crinoline, topped off with an impressive green velvet bonnet. As Nell squeezed Sadie's hand politely it dawned on her in a rush who she was, the recognition deepening her shock. The gawky, freckle-faced adolescent had transformed into an attractive young woman with thick waves of glossy brown hair and big dark eyes. "Sadie? Sadie Petttigrew? Sid Newberry's crush? He put a frog down your dress, I recall."

Sadie dropped Nell's hand as if it were the aforementioned frog, stepped lightly over to her husband and slipped her arm through his, pulling him towards her possessively. Jimmy was still smiling sheepishly, the very picture of excruciating discomfiture. His wife stuck her small nose in the air with a marked air of offence. "Well, that was a long time ago. I can't think why you'd bring that up. Sid wed Minnie Priory. I'm Sadie Hochstedder, now. We been wed six months." She smiled adoringly up at her husband, then turned a smug simper on Nell. "He's training to be an attorney, in San Francisco."

Nell looked Jimmy squarely in the eye. "So you did come west. With your folks?"

Jimmy shook his head. "Ma died of pneumonia, and Pa sold the farm. He remarried, to a widow who runs a store in town. Mr. Cosgrove helped me get a law apprenticeship and we, Sadie and I, moved to San Francisco, last year. We're just here a few days having a look around. Sadie wanted to see Sacramento." He smiled down at her. "Did you get your ribbons, sweetling?"

Sweetling? How much more of this can I stand before my heart bursts and comes shooting out of my chest in a bloody pulp, squishing down right here on the sidewalk?

Jimmy fumbled in a pocket. "Here's my card." He thrust the small rectangle of paper towards Nell. Struggling for control, she accepted and read it.

James Francis Hochstedder

Junior partner in the esteemed firm

Bailey & Geddes

Attorneys at Law

San Francisco

Nell turned the card over. The address was on the back.

"Isn't that something?" twittered Sadie.

"It surely is." Nell tucked the card into her top pocket. "I always knew you'd do well for yourself, Jimmy, havin' such a sharp mind an' all. An' heartiest congratulations to the both of you. I hope you'll be very happy." She picked up her saddlebags. "Now, if you'll excuse me, I have to be on my way."

Jimmy dropped his wife's arm and stepped forwards. "But, Nell, we haven't even caught up. You must have lots to tell me – us. Please, join me and Sadie for lunch at our hotel."

Hell no!

Nell knew only that she was desperate to get away. "Sorry, I gotta go." Before she plunged into the mêlée of pedestrians she backed up a few steps, holding up her left hand with its slim gold wedding ring still in place. "I ain't Nell Washburn anymore. I'm Nell Hardy. I got me a husband an' a baby." It sounded desperate and pathetic, especially since she no longer had either husband or child, but she wasn't leaving this distressing encounter as the poor cousin. Jimmy looked floored. The simper vanished from Sadie's face.

Nell shouldered her way into the throng, elbowing people out of her way in her haste to escape. Tears partially blinded her, and her heart felt like a hot coal in her chest. She heard Jimmy call once, "Nell!" but she did not turn around nor slow her pace. As she crossed the street to the livery, she wrenched his card from her pocket and tossed it into the mud.

Who's tending Ma and Jesse's grave now you ain't, Jimmy?

CHAPTER TWENTY-SIX

By the time Nell was clear of the town, riding the trail northeastwards, a happy Whiskey beneath her, snorting his pleasure at being on the move again out in the sunshine and fresh air, she had calmed herself somewhat. The jumble of conflicting emotions that had followed the chance encounter with Jimmy and his bride had sorted themselves into some sort of order as she pursued a rational discourse with herself. Separations never ended well, and her separation from Jimmy had come at a crucial time for both of them. Had she been able to stay at school, stayed in Missouri, she'd almost certainly be in Sadie's place, but her destiny had been with her beloved father, no matter what. She'd promised to write to Jimmy and she'd only sent the one letter. She doubted that would have changed anything. Young men reach marriageable age and that was that, same for girls. The pull of the flesh was a strong one, specially for men. It wasn't meant to be, her and Jimmy. Simple as that. Hell, she'd married herself, quickly enough, hadn't she? Once she'd met Nick, Jimmy had faded into the background. You went with what was in front of you; that was how life was. Anyway, she'd always have her treasured memories of their adolescent love for each other and of his immense kindness to her after her mother's death and her father's breakdown. Jimmy hadn't had it easy in his young life. He deserved to be happy. Sweetling, though? Nell screwed up her face and burst out laughing.

"Anybody called me that I'd punch him!"

Whiskey nickered as if in agreement and Nell urged him into a gentle canter. She was headed for Placerville, also known as 'Hangtown' because of some notorious lynchings that took place there, a boisterous gold mining town she hoped might be more to her taste as well as furnishing an opportunity to advance her way further in the world. It was only a few days' ride away and Placerville was where Kitty had claimed to have been at her happiest with her young husband. Maybe it would be lucky for her, too.

****

Tucked up in her bedroll, saddle for a pillow, Nell lay watching the pulsating red embers of the fire, enjoying the soothing feeling engendered by their cheery glow after the emotional turmoil of the day. She'd also enjoyed a fine supper: two cold pork sausages Sally had pressed on her, with buttered bread and coffee. Now, with Whiskey picketed close and her guns to hand, she was ready for sleep. As she drifted off, she thought, I hope I don't dream about those two.

Nell gagged with terror. This was no nightmare. This was really happening. Some violent force had wrenched her from her sleep and from her blankets, and now she was pinned face down on the ground by what felt like a solid mass pressing hard between her shoulder blades. *A bear? A monster of some kind, like a skinwalker?* She screamed and heard a frightened whinny from Whiskey in response.

"Shut up!" a voice snarled. Human, anyway. A man. Probably much worse to come. Her hands were pulled together hard behind her back, straining her shoulder sockets, and tied so tightly at the wrists that she grunted with pain. Then the crushing weight came off as she was unceremoniously flipped over, enabling her to see her attacker. Nell lay on her side, sucking her breath in sharply as recognition dawned. "Elijah Jarrow! What the hell do you think you're doin', you sonofabitch!"

He stood legs akimbo, arms folded across his broad chest, his distended belly thrust forwards. He sniggered. "That's not a nice way to talk about my sainted mother." He dropped on to his haunches, running his tongue across his lips as he leered at Nell. "Don't worry, I ain't goin' to hurt you none. Not yet, anyways. You'd just put up a fight and I want to keep you unblemished, so to speak." He giggled unpleasantly. "You're going to make me rich."

Nell struggled to sit up. "What're you talkin' about? You let me go right now, or you'll be sorry!" She looked over at her scattered bedding but there was no sign of either rifle or pistol. Glancing down at her hip, she saw that her knife was missing from its sheath. Damn! She must have been sleeping really soundly.

Jarrow stood up, white teeth flashing as he grinned. Then the grin vanished and he leaned towards her, a huge bulk in the darkness, cruel and menacing. "Believe me, lady, you'll be the sorry one if you don't shut up and do exactly what I say when I say it."

Nell gasped as he seized hold of her and dragged her across the hard ground back to her bedroll and blankets. In a horrible parody of a parent tucking up a child, he arranged her in a sleeping posture before he tied her feet together as well and covered her with the blankets. "Nighty–night." He chuckled again, then strode over to the fire and tossed on some of the wood Nell had placed aside. She lay still, watching him organize his own bedding. She would not antagonize him, she decided. He was much too strong. She would bide her time and find a way to escape.

"How'd you know where to find me?" she called.

"You shouldn't have trusted me with that letter telling my mother your plans."

"You read my letter?"

"Soon's you'd gone. I was worrit you'd badmouth me to my mother. I knew you'd talked to that sniveling Sally. The only letter she's getting is one from me telling her I had to leave sudden like. Then I just tailed you. Watched your campfire and waited 'til you fell asleep. Easy." He wriggled himself into his bedroll and blankets, farting like a horse as he subsided into a shapeless dark mound. "Shut up, now."

****

The following two days were terrible for Nell. Jarrow was so vigilant and kept her trussed up so thoroughly that she found no opportunity to escape. He untied her to enable her to perform her ablutions and other personal devoirs, but, while she did, having no choice in the matter, he stood close by with a gun trained on her the whole time, affording her not so much as a modicum of privacy. Nell's face burned with humiliation as she kept her eyes straight ahead, forced to listen to his gross heavy breathing as he leered over her. He took her money belt, itemizing its contents while she was forced to watch, burning with indignation as he gloated over her hard-earned assets. She was defenceless and penniless. He even kept her tied up when they ate, adding to her sense of degradation by feeding her like an infant. Nell swallowed it all down, though, determined to keep her strength up. She kept up her morale by fantasizing about what she was eventually going to do to the bastard.

Jarrow deliberately deviated from the main trail so there was precious little chance of meeting other travelers to whom she could cry out for help. Just as well, Nell decided. She didn't want to get innocents killed. Jarrow was clearly an amoral man capable of casual violence. He forced her to ride with bound hands, looping the reins around the saddle pommel and leading Whiskey on a rope. He'd removed her boots and socks as well, so that if she did try to make a run for it her feet were unprotected in rough terrain. Nell knew that she would almost certainly have to wait for Placerville to make any attempt at escape. Meanwhile, she appeared to lapse into resigned compliance to lull him into a sense of uncontested dominance. But all the time her mind was working, working.

On the last night before they were due to reach Placerville, Nell sat watching her abductor shoveling his supper down after he'd fed her first, praying for the glutton to choke to death. "How are you plannin' for me to make you rich?" she asked, knowing full well what he had in mind. She wanted to hear him say it.

Chewing vigorously, Jarrow looked over at her, one eyebrow raised, his expression mockingly cynical. He swallowed. "Oh, I think you must have a pretty good idea. I was going to snatch that little fool, Sally, but Mother would have objected, and anyway, you're much better. I mean to pimp you out at an establishment I have a partnership in and which caters to men looking for some fun with the totties."

"You're gonna force me to be a soiled dove?"

Jarrow scooped up another spoonful of beans. "I prefer whore. You'll get used to it. You might even enjoy it. Men'll pay top price for a good looker like you. I'll let you keep a portion if you work hard."

"I won't do it. You can't make me."

His expression became cold and pitiless. "Oh yes I can. I'll hold you down first few times, if I have to, and after that you won't care. When you're nice an' broken in, I'll be takin' my turn, too." He belched loudly and patted his ample gut. "Time for bed. Here comes daddy to tuck you in."

****

Just before they rode into Placerville, Jarrow gagged Nell as well. He lashed her already bound hands to the pommel of her saddle, his intent to thwart any ideas she may have of leaping from Whiskey and bolting away into the town to secure rescue. Then he waited for dusk before he guided them cautiously along back streets and alleys to avoid as many prying eyes as possible. Eventually, he reined in outside the back of a two storey building where a small, grubby boy, barefoot and in tattered clothes, was perched on the topmost of a flight of steps leading to a narrow closed doorway, wolfing down a plate of food. He went rigid the moment he recognised Jarrow, then shot to his feet and scarpered across the rickety porch to disappear down a side alley, clutching his supper. Jarrow chuckled.

"Wart never did like me much."

Nell thought of little Sally. *Oh, god. He hurts children.*

He tethered the horses, took a blanket from his roll, and advanced on Nell. He loosed her hands from the pommel, dragged her none too gently from the saddle and having wrapped the blanket around her head and body flung her over his shoulder, while Nell made muffled sounds of protest.

"Just as well I can't make out what you're sayin'. Would probably make a mule skinner blush." He carried her thus swaddled up the steps, pushed open the door, and went inside. Nell heard the door thump shut behind them, and she was aware of light, but she couldn't see anything because the blanket covered her head. She could smell the foul miasma of the place, though, an unpleasant mix of male sweat – in addition to Jarrow's – stale food, cheap perfume, whiskey, and tobacco smoke. Somewhere, a honky-tonk piano played and there was loud men's conversation and laughter. Jarrow was speaking with someone in a low voice, but even though she strained to hear, Nell couldn't make out what he was saying. Then she was swung about sharply and they were ascending a staircase, Jarrow's boots clumping solidly on the treads. Nell squirmed and writhed valiantly, but to no avail. His grip on her was like iron. There was the sound of a door opening and closing and she realized they had entered a room somewhere on the first floor. By this time, Nell had formed a pretty good idea of what this place was. She was in a saloon-cum-brothel. Jarrow dumped her unceremoniously on to a bed and yanked away the blanket she'd been cocooned in.

"Your place of employment," he announced, sweeping an arm around the room, which was lit by one oil lamp, and laughed heartily, making his big belly jounce. "I'll have that gag off you, now, but don't bother about screaming. We get a lot of screaming here so nobody takes any notice." He laughed again, accompanied by the abdominal jiggle. Clearly, he was enjoying himself.

As he loosened the gag in her mouth and pulled it away, Nell watched him coldly. *Underestimating me will be your undoing, you fat bastard.*

****

Nell was perched with one leg tucked under her on the end of the bed, arms stretched straight out in front because Jarrow had tied her wrists to the brass bed knob. She'd given up trying to work her hands loose. The bastard certainly knew his knots. The first night in her new abode had seen her left alone to sleep after her harrowing journey, although still trussed up like a turkey. Come morning, a sallow-faced young woman with a harelip had freed her, seen to her toileting, and helped her to bathe and wash her hair, with Jarrow ceaselessly hovering to prevent any conversation. He'd also taken her clothes and forced her to dress in a pink silk petticoat, a black lace bustier that cinched her slender waist while pushing up her breasts, and a faux pearl choker, after which one of his minions, a dispirited young woman with pinched features, had fastened up her hair with a bejewelled barrette and rouged her lips and cheeks. All

396

the female workers here look similarly miserable, Nell reflected. It did not bode well. She endured all the primping stoically, although she had been angry and upset when Jarrow pocketed the precious miniature of her son and took her wedding ring as well. As he mocked her in crude terms, the overall theme of which was her previous sexual experience as a married woman, Nell subsided into simmering loathing, conserving her energy.

Both items of underwear smelt of previous ownership, making Nell wrinkle her nose, but Jarrow seemed pleased with the end result, rubbing his hands together as he cast an appraising eye over her. Once again, she had to endure the humiliation of being fed by him before he hustled off to, Nell surmised, find her first client. She tolerated the feeding, suppressing the urge to spit it all back in his face, because she was ravenously hungry, and because she needed to keep up her strength. The tattered child Jarrow called Wart had brought the food to her room, taking flight like a nervous little sparrow when he saw his tormentor. Nell had thanked the child, greeting him with a smile, and he'd given her such a piteous look of terror mixed with yearning in return that it broke her heart.

Now alone in the room, the only sounds those of the revelry taking place downstairs and the odd catcall from the street below, Nell cast around desperately for a means of escape. The room was sparsely furnished: the bed, which smelled unpleasantly of past sexual activity and which squeaked ominously whenever she shifted her weight, a shabby bureau featuring a wash basin, jug, and mirror, and a narrow freestanding wardrobe with double doors that had seen better days. A stool topped by a threadbare cushion fronted the bureau. The single oil lamp sat in a sconce to the right of the door. Not a high-class establishment, Nell thought wryly. The only window was pulled down and fastened shut, drab crimson curtains drooping listlessly either side of the panes. Outside was inky darkness. Above the bed hung a painting in a chipped gilt frame depicting a voluptuous naked woman reclining on a chaise longue. The back of the door featured several clothes hooks, where the clients no doubt hung their clothes before setting about their sport. Nell took a deep breath. It had to be the window then, as to try and flee downstairs meant almost inevitable recapture. Even as she mulled the thought, Jarrow burst in, making her jump. Closing the door behind him, he gave her a wolfish grin, and Nell shrank back as he advanced on her, pulling a knife from a sheath at his waist. He smelled of whiskey and tobacco as he loomed over her.

"Time to earn your keep."

He severed her bonds, which brought instant relief, and re-sheathed his knife. Nell watched him warily, rubbing her chafed wrists. In places the skin was red and raw where she'd struggled against her restraints.

"Come in, Gil!" he shouted, addressing these words towards the door, while his eyes never left Nell, perhaps expecting her to try and make a bolt for it. She felt her heart pick up a beat as the door swung open and a skinny man of indeterminate age with weasel-like features entered the room. He was dressed in a shabby suit and scuffed derby, which he removed, revealing a thatch of lank, greasy hair that touched his collar. His eyes went straight to Nell, and the moment she met his cold, reptilian gaze she knew this was a man who hated women; things were not going to go well.

"Come over," Jarrow beckoned the man. "Didn't I say she was a beauty?"

His customer nodded slowly, shrewd eyes revealing his appreciation of the girl before him. "You have not been false, Elijah. I thought you mighta been all gum, but I see you have played me fair. How long do I have for what I paid you?"

Nell felt a flare of white-hot anger hearing herself thus discussed in the third person. The man called Gil laughed unpleasantly. "Look at her eyes flash! I warrant she'll put up a fight."

"I can guarantee it. I'll leave you now, but I'll only be downstairs if you need me."

The man flicked a snake-like tongue across his lips. "I won't need you."

Jarrow leaned over Nell, and whispered with soft menace, "You can make this hard or you can make it easy. Up to you, missie." Nell delivered a look of withering hatred. At the door, Jarrow paused "Not too, uh, enthusiastic, Gil. I don't want her ruined for others, or you'll have to compensate me for lost business. No repeats of Chrissie, please."

Gil tipped his head to one side, his expression one of wounded innocence. "I'll be my usual gentle self, Elijah,"

Jarrow smirked, shot a final warning glance at Nell and left. Nell felt suddenly nauseous, before reminding herself that she must stay calm and focused, must dissemble as cunningly as she could if she were to survive this encounter. She stood up slowly, locking her hands demurely behind her back. "I'm Nell."

Gil took off his coat, hung it up, and commenced to unbutton his vest. "I don't care what your name is, girly. Let your hair down. I want to see it loose."

As Nell removed the barrette and pins from her hair, her eyes were drawn to the pistol in the waistband of his pants. It was smaller than the Navy Colt, the Pocket Pistol variant of the Dragoon revolver, but Nell guessed it was just as deadly. He drew it out, glancing around, before placing it on a corner of the bureau, along with his purse. Having hung his clothes on the hooks attached to the back of the door, he turned towards her now clad only in what looked like infrequently laundered long johns. "Well, get your clothes off, girly. I'll watch." He sat down on the stool, crossing his legs, his pale eyes dull with lust, idly running his fingers through his thick, greasy hair. Nell suppressed a shudder. Not since Cheney, had she felt such revulsion.

Nell's fingers went up to the laces on her bustier, but then paused. "Do you mind if I open the window? It's real stuffy in here. I don't want to come over faint."

"Be quick, then."

Nell darted obediently around the bed to the window, unfastened the clasp, and pushed the sash window right up, jamming it tight with the wooden wedge she spotted on the sill. No breeze entered. The night was as still and dark as heavy black velvet, with a lingering smell of recently fallen rain. She sidled coquettishly towards her impatient client, peripheral vision locked on the pistol, calculating the distance to it, all the while smiling sweetly. Without warning, the man leaped to his feet and delivered a stinging, open-palmed slap to her left cheek.

"I like it rough, sweetie. It gets me going." His voice was hoarse and he was breathing heavily.

Shocked as she was, adrenaline and naked fury kept Nell focused. She clasped a hand to her cheek staggering sideways a little before doubling up over the dresser and moaning pitifully, stifling a sob for extra effect even as her other hand snaked out. A split second later, when she straightened up, sweeping the pistol into her grasp in one fluid movement, she was coiled taut as a lioness pitilessly confronting its prey, her manner so cold and resolute that her tormentor backed up a step, briefly registering surprise in his lust glazed eyes. Then he gave a sneering laugh and thrust out a hand, head back, arrogantly flexing fingers with dirty black nails.

"Gimme me that gun, bitch!"

Nell drew back the hammer, closed her left eye, and fired.

CHAPTER TWENTY-SEVEN

Nell rode hard, wanting to take advantage of the cover of night while knowing it was also dangerous: the horse could stumble, break a leg, or fall and kill them both. He seemed to be a sure-footed little thing, just the same, willing and with a good turn of speed. The night was a dark one with only a sliver of moon to cast any light. That suited her fine.

Eventually, Nell reined in and dismounted, one hand on the pony's muzzle to quiet his snorting, clicking her tongue, and shushing softly to ease his stamping; his blood was up. She listened intently for sounds of pursuit. There were none. Maybe not now, but Nell had little doubt that Jarrow would come after her. Or the law. Or what passed for the law. She remembered how the town had earned its original name – Hangtown – and a cold shudder squirmed along her spine. Nell vaulted back into the saddle and rode on. Some time later, she began to feel desperately sleepy and she could tell the pony was flagging, too. She found a sheltered spot, unsaddled and hobbled the animal with a strip torn from the bottom of her petticoat, rendering it even shorter, and then took a moment to fossick through the stolen saddlebags. There wasn't much: a tinder box, for which she was grateful, a crumpled letter addressed to one 'George Howarth', some beef jerky, half a flat bottle of whiskey, a pocket knife, a coil of fishing line, a tattered map of California and a pouch of tobacco. Then Nell turned her attention to the bedroll and was delighted to find a slicker tucked into the blanket. She donned it, grateful for the extra warmth, however feeble, it provided, as she was feeling decidedly chilly by this time in her flimsy garb. There was no way she could risk a fire, though.

Inventory completed, and the purse she'd stolen shoved into a pocket of the slicker, she wrapped herself in the blanket, and curled up to sleep for a few hours, the stolen pistol close to hand. She'd checked the chamber and she had four bullets left, so whatever happened, be it human or animal that came at her, she'd go down fighting. Before she nodded off, she looked up at the night sky, found the Big Dipper, and used it to locate Polaris, the North Star. When she was a child, Pap had taught her how to find direction from wherever she was and she thanked him silently, now. Come morning, she'd head north. She'd bought her own map in Sacramento and before she'd lost it like everything else, she had taken the time to study it carefully. She recalled a mining town about fifty miles north of Placerville called Nevada City*. Nevada was

Spanish for 'snow-covered', which had made her think nostalgically of Yreka with its dramatic backdrop of pines and mountains. Maybe she could set up there, for a while anyway. Of course, she thought bitterly, her money belt was gone now along with all her other belongings, like Nick's beloved Navy Colt, his Hawken rifle, and, worst of all, her miniature of baby Nicholas. She still had the bulk of her money and possessions she'd left with Kitty, though, and she could send for them. Thinking of Kitty made her feel suddenly alone, vulnerable, and a long way from any place she could call home. Then she reminded herself that she was Nell Hardy. Hardy by name, hardy by nature. *As long as it takes, Jarrow, and if I can get through the next while without being ate up by a bear or catamount, scalped by Indians, or havin' an accident, I will get even with you, you sonofabitch.*

.

*Another gold mining town in California, not to be confused with the state of the same name.

****

In the morning, having slept longer than she intended, Nell woke feeling stiff and sore but, for which she thanked God, still in one piece. She couldn't see it, but she imagined she must have a pretty large bruise on her backside from when she'd leaped off the saloon balcony and landed so gracelessly in the street. It sure throbbed, and her face ached, too. Rubbing the tender patch on her buttock ruefully, she hobbled around in a circle, taking care where she planted her bare feet, to loosen up her limbs and get her blood circulating. Once she'd warmed up a bit, she saddled and bridled the pony, taking time to run an eye over him in the new light of day. He was a plain bay, a homely, wall-eyed animal, but he seemed docile enough and had proved his mettle the previous night. Nell stroked his muzzle, clicking her tongue gently at him, and he responded with soft blowing through his nostrils. Chewing on some of the beef jerky, she studied the map she'd found in the owner's saddlebags, noting the position of Nevada City, and firming her decision to make the town her destination. Pistol tucked securely into her waistband, Nell mounted up and took a moment to look back over the terrain she'd traversed during the night. She was blessed with eyes like a hawk, and she couldn't see any sign of pursuit. Perhaps Jarrow had written her off since he had all her money and possessions, anyway, and he was just as guilty of breaking the law as she was, kidnapping her and forcing her into prostitution. Well, she didn't have time to fret about being hunted. She had to get going.

"Hah!" She dug her heels in hard and the pony leapt forwards, headed north.

The California gold rushes had done much to provide trails across the terrain, but Nell did not stick to the clear track north once she located it. Instead, she ghosted it, moving swiftly and silently, and noting the changes as she climbed – the hills with their stands of pine and aspen, the air beginning to thin and the temperature cooling. The pony proved surefooted once again, and Nell made sure she looked after his welfare, resting him at regular intervals, letting him graze and drink before moving onwards. He was her most important asset right now, the one thing standing between life and death. She was light-headed with hunger herself, but reassured herself that if she covered a good distance today, she could reach the town by the morrow. Breathing a prayer to her lost loved ones, she pressed on.

****

The aroma of fresh coffee and the smell of breakfast bacon being cooked somewhere nearby tormented Nell, making her mouth water. Her stomach felt like a shrunken, flaccid sac plastered to her backbone. Clothing, though, was a priority. Reaching across the rickety picket fence to grab the gingham dress pegged to a drooping line in the small back garden of a single storey clapboard house, Nell froze, arm outstretched, when she heard the unmistakeable sound of the hammer being drawn back on a handgun. The metallic 'click' was ominously magnified in the still, early morning air. Remaining motionless, the next thing she heard was a male voice drawl, "Put your hands up, lady, and turn around real slow." Swallowing hard, Nell complied. *Good work! The first person you meet is a trigger-happy vigilante!*

Once she was about face, she saw a man standing in casual pose on the porch opposite, his pistol trained on her. Light as a cat, he jumped down into the alleyway and she got a better look at him. Nell blinked and blinked again. Even without getting close, he was easily the most handsome man she had ever seen. Mam had always said it was rude to stare, but she couldn't help it. Of course, he had a gun trained on her, too, which served to rivet one's attention somewhat, but even so… Nell had had some nice-looking men in her life; both Pap and Nick had been good lookers, but this man now in front of her was in another league altogether. She realised her mouth was agape and clamped it shut. The man came a couple of steps closer, face expressionless as he took her in from head to toe. Her state of semi-undress was clearly displayed through the open flaps of the slicker and Nell tensed, blue eyes narrowing as she watched him. He was a man after all, and she was showing quite a lot of tantalising, albeit grimy, flesh. Add to this the fact that her recent experience of men had not been very positive and it was hardly surprising that she felt vulnerable. She was aware that her heart was beating hard. "I know what you're thinkin', but I ain't no whore," she said with some feeling. "I had the bad luck to fall in with some bad people, is all." Her lips trembled and she fought back tears, blinking furiously. She was so tired, and so hungry.

The man's response was a peremptory nod. Then he pointed with his free hand to the pistol Nell was carrying, the butt visible forward of her right hip.

"Using two fingers, remove that gun from your waistband and set it down gently. Her captor adjusted his own pistol slightly, pointing it squarely at her head. "Do it slowly." He took a smooth sideways step so that he was perfectly aligned in front of her.

The way he moved was easy, almost graceful, but even so there was a coiled menace about him. Nell knew instinctively that you did not mess with such a man as this. She removed the pistol with thumb and forefinger as he bid and bent to place it at her feet. Then she raised her arms again.

"Good. Push it towards me a little with your right foot. Careful. You have no shoes."

Oddly touched by this unexpected concern that she not hurt herself, Nell deftly slid her toes under the gun and moved it closer towards him, a small shudder of emotion shaking her weary frame. He dropped on to his haunches, retrieved it, and eased it carefully into his belt as he stood again, eyes never leaving hers. "What's your name?"

"Nell Hardy."

"John Tuttle."

"Nice to make your acquaintance, Mr. Tuttle."

The man tipped his head to one side as he studied her. Then he glanced over at the tired pony. "Where have you ridden from?"

"Placerville."

"Were you going to steal Maisie Wilmot's dress?"

"I don't know the owner, but yes. It looked a good fit. She a friend of yours?"

Ignoring her question, Tuttle eased aside his coat to re-holster his gun, and Nell saw the badge on his chest twinkle as it caught the early morning sun. Sheriff! Oh joy. Thief and murderer, she had delivered herself straight into the arms of the law! She felt oddly relieved.

"Well, I can see why you might need a dress." His tone was laconic as he thrust his tongue into his cheek, raising an eyebrow. He glanced again at the pony, which Nell had tethered to the low-hanging branch of an apple tree growing in the same garden that contained the saggy washing line. "That horse belong to you?"

"Yessir. I mean, no sir."

"Well, which is it?"

"I stole it. The tack, too. I think the owner is a George Howarth." Pap had always insisted that if you told the truth, no harm would come to you.

The sheriff nodded. "I see." He drew himself up. "Nell Hardy, I'm arresting you for, on your own admission, horse theft, proposed dress theft, and, er, indecent exposure in a public place. Come with me."

Sure talks fancy.

He gestured for her to walk ahead of him along a narrow alley connected at right angles to the one in which they stood. Nell sighed. She was too exhausted and weak with hunger to argue. They emerged on to what looked like the town's main thoroughfare. "Turn left," instructed the sheriff, and Nell climbed the steps on to the boardwalk. "You can put your hands down, now."

As she walked, Nell gazed around her. In the early morning sunshine, the town of Nevada City, nestled in the Sierra foothills, was an attractive, nay, enchanting place: sturdy buildings that boasted a defiant permanence, a backdrop of deep green pine covered hills, the air as heady as a fine vintage wine. Unlike the other gold towns she'd known it had a gentler, more refined and more established ambience about it. Nell felt her spirits soar. Being arrested aside, she had a good feeling, a feeling of possibly coming home. That's if they didn't hang her.

The sheriff had advanced and was walking alongside her. "Lots of brick," said Nell, identifying the source of the town's attraction.

"Fire," answered the sheriff.

Man of few words.

The sheriff walked a couple of paces ahead and paused outside the door to a small building flanked by others in the town's commercial centre. Nell saw the words 'Sheriff's Office' emblazoned in white letters across the window. A wooden bench sat beneath the sill, facing the street. The sheriff unlocked the door, making a little brass bell tinkle, and ushered her into a neatly furnished room that had an austere, masculine feel. He opened the shutters, gesturing towards a desk positioned in front of a wall to their right and Nell moved towards it, glancing apprehensively around what she now assumed would be her place of incarceration. On the wall behind the desk was a locked gun rack containing several rifles, to its left some shelves with books and manuals, and beside those a cluster of faded posters bearing images of wanted outlaws pinned to a bulletin board. A deerskin was the only floor covering. The sheriff fetched one of a pair of bentwood chairs tucked under a small table against the opposite wall, placed it in front of the desk, and drew out the captain's chair behind it. Removing the pistol he'd taken off Nell from his gun belt, he checked the chamber, slid open a drawer and dropped it in before closing the drawer again. Nell continued to look about her, heartbeat quickening again. She'd never imagined herself being on the wrong side of the law. Mam and Pap had raised her with solid Christian values. Just as well they couldn't see her now – dirty, dishevelled, penniless, under arrest. Her gaze fell on an open doorway in the middle of the back wall and through it she could see dingy, barred cells. There didn't appear to be anyone in them. Well, she soon would be, she surmised. Suddenly, she remembered the stolen pony.

"My horse? The horse? He needs feed n' water."

"My deputy will see to it when he arrives momentarily." Tuttle removed his hat and jacket and hung them on a coat stand in the corner by the window, then gestured towards the chair. "Sit down." He moved the oil lamp on the desk further to the side.

Nell did as he bid, trying to compose herself in something approaching a ladylike fashion, drawing the flaps of the slicker across her body and dirt-stained, mostly bare legs, pressing her knees together and sweeping back her greasy, tousled mane of hair. She caught her breath when a glance down at her feet revealed their shockingly filthy state and she tried to tuck them back under the chair as far as she could. Tuttle lowered himself into his own chair before assuming a quiet composure, hands clasped on the desk before him; neither spoke as they took a good long look at each other. Now that he wasn't pointing a gun at her, Nell felt more relaxed about sizing him up. Up until this moment she hadn't considered the word 'beautiful' could be applied to a man, but she was revising that particular prejudice. He had short, wavy brown hair, ice-blue eyes and a finely sculpted nose and mouth, the lips defined by a deep rose colour and unusual on a man. There was nothing effeminate about him, though. His cheeks were clean-shaven leaving his cheekbones subtly defined. The overall effect

ERIN ELDRIDGE

was one of a beautifully proportioned face that was both strong and humane. He was not tall; about five feet ten, Nell guessed, but his body was like his face – slender and perfectly proportioned. Conscious of the fact that she was unashamedly drinking him in with her eyes, Nell lowered them in a belated attempt to appear demure, only too aware that, given the state of filth and undress she was in, this was unlikely to impress her captor.

Nell was jerked from her reverie when the doorbell jangled and a young man entered. He closed the door behind him, eyes flickering from Nell to Tuttle and back to Nell again. He also wore a badge on his chest. And he looked very surprised as he took in the scene before him. Sheriff Tuttle steepled his fingers, resting his elbows on the desktop.

"Will, this is Nell Hardy. She's under arrest. Miss Hardy, this is my deputy, Will Mothershaw."

Prisoner and officer exchanged polite greetings before Will, a pleasant looking young man with a long, homely face, excused himself, muttering that he had to light the stove. Nell assumed that he meant the potbelly stove that stood on a tiled plinth in the corner of the sheriff's office. A coffee pot and a frying pan rested on the hot plate. Above the stove, a shelf held tin mugs, plates, condiments, caddies, and a small pottery crock from which cutlery protruded. There was a woven basket of kindling and old newspapers next to the stove, along with a barrel Nell assumed contained water, a dipper

414

hanging from a hook on the wall behind it. After he'd removed his hat and coat and as he set about his task, Will stole frequent curious glances at Nell. She didn't mind. In her bizarre garb, dirty knees, scratched legs and feet on show, and almost certainly with traces of a tart's face paint still smeared across her cheeks and lips, she knew she must be a pretty unique sight, even for the frontier. *I surely do look like a whore that's run off from a whorehouse. Well, that's mostly true. Just not the whore bit.*

The door jangled again, making three heads swivel, and a woman came in carrying a tray, the savoury smells that wafted from it making Nell salivate once more. Glancing briefly at Nell, who was instantly fixated on the fragrant tray, she placed it on the sheriff's desk, smiling warmly as she addressed him. "Extra bacon this morning, John, and the rolls are fresh from the oven."

Nell valiantly fought down an urge to fall on the tray like a starved wolf, cramming as much of the food into her mouth as she could before they beat her off.

The sheriff smiled at the tray's deliverer, and Nell felt her heart fluttering. What a smile! Her grubby knees suddenly felt weaker than the rest of her. Then her eyes slid downwards to the tray again.

"I'm obliged, Audrey. May I ask you a favour?"

"Anything, John." Audrey, too, was by now staring curiously at Nell, hands clasped in front of her abdomen. She was a tall, slim, middle-aged woman of dignified bearing with faded dark hair parted in the middle and swept back into a woven mesh snood. She wore a grey silk dress with a lace fichu about her shoulders, clasped at her throat with an eye-catching cameo brooch. Her expression was firm but kindly, her blue eyes friendly.

"This young woman here is in need of a bath, some fresh clothes, and victuals, in that order. I wonder if you could accommodate her? The deputy will escort her to make sure she doesn't escape. She is a prisoner under arrest."

Audrey did not bat an eyelash as she surveyed the tattered apparition before her. "Of course, John. Enjoy that breakfast now, while it's hot. Come along with me, miss. I'm Audrey Russell."

"Nell Hardy, ma'am." Nell shot to her feet, weariness forgotten by the mention of victuals. Will had got the stove going, and already there was an aroma of coffee filling the room. *Oh, please, let them have coffee wherever I'm goin'!* Nell followed Audrey and Will followed her. The town was coming to life, and folk stopped what they were doing to watch the odd little procession cross the street.

****

Nell was on her second helping of beans, bacon, eggs and biscuits, accompanied by a third cup of coffee, when Sheriff Tuttle came into the kitchen of Audrey Russell's boarding house to return his tray, and give Will, who'd been witnessing Nell's relentless appetite with something akin to awe, instructions on where to find the stolen pony.

"Ask Reuben to board the animal for now and I'll stop by later to check the saddlebags."

After Will left, John accepted Audrey's invitation to join her for a cup of coffee and drew out a chair at the table. The kitchen was busy with the morning shift, the serving maids bustling about and the cook, a big-boned woman of ruddy complexion, sweating over the stove, but no one took any notice of their temporary guest. As Nell met the sheriff's eyes over the rim of her cup, she saw frank appreciation for her transformation. One of Audrey's maids, who'd introduced herself as Trudy, had helped to scrub her clean in a wonderfully hot bath, washing her hair as well. They'd found her a shift and knickers, along with a simple white calico dress, stockings and shoes, and brushed her hair 'til it shone before pinning it up. Not having looked in a mirror for some days, Nell was shocked to see that most of the left side of her face was one big purple bruise. That weasel had sure hit her with some force behind it. No wonder they'd all been staring at her so. Trudy had cheerfully informed her that she had a bruise every bit as spectacular as the facial one on her right buttock. Nell smoothed her hands over her clean dress and wiggled her toes luxuriantly in the comfortable shoes. Her personal dignity, always so important to her, had been restored. She closed her eyes and drew in a deep breath before slowly releasing it. Her arrest aside, this town was making a very good first impression.

Apart from the slicker, her filthy clothes had gone into the fire. Then they'd fed her until she could eat no more, her abdomen tight as a drum. Nell sat back in her chair, blissfully replete, smiling at her benefactors. Then she remembered she was still in deep trouble with the law and the smile faded. As if he read her thoughts, John replaced his cup on its saucer and pushed himself to his feet.

"I'm obliged to you, Audrey. You have to come with me now, Miss Hardy."

"She may need to rest, John."

Nell stood up. "I'm fine, ma'am. Thank you for your hospitality, which I hope to repay."

"That won't be necessary. But you know where to find me, dear if you need anything."

Nell nodded, once again deeply grateful for the kindness of strangers, which life seemed to juxtapose with inexplicable cruelty from others, and followed Sheriff Tuttle out the door into the brilliant sunshine.

****

With a transformed Nell once more seated in front of him, Sheriff Tuttle drew a leather-bound ledger from a draw in his desk, a pen and ink well from another, opened the ledger and smoothed the pages, then rested his hands on them as he addressed his prisoner. Nell had already deduced that he was a man who was very neat and orderly in his habits.

"Now, Miss Hardy, I need you to tell me the full story of how you ended up in Nevada City in a poorly state, on what you have already admitted is a stolen horse." He tapped the ledger. "Everything you say will be recorded in here and signed by you, so I strongly recommend that you tell me the whole truth, as it will affect what happens after that."

Nell nodded. "Actually, I'm Mrs. Ellen Hardy, but I'd be obliged if you just called me Nell. That's what I'm used to."

The sheriff blinked. "You are married?"

"Widowed." She held up her left hand. "My wedding ring was stolen."

"I see. Very well…Nell. Shall we begin?"

"By all means." Nell cleared her throat, leaning forwards a little. "First, I want to thank you for…for this." She brushed her hands over her new attire, and swallowed hard, feeling suddenly emotional.

Tuttle turned his gaze to the window as the tired girl blinked away tears. "You're welcome…Nell."

Nell cleared her throat. "Where shall I start?"

"Wherever you want to." The sheriff unstoppered his ink well, picked up his pen, dipped it, shook the excess ink from it, poised it over a clean page, and fixed his ice-blue eyes on the young woman in front of him.

Sometime later, the sheriff poured them both cups of coffee from the pot simmering on the potbelly stove, placed Nell's in front of her, and resumed his seat, running his fingers through his hair. For a moment or two, silence reigned. The sheriff had a lot to process. He had gone very quiet.

"So, you do not know if your assailant is dead or alive?"

"Nope. I didn't stick around to find out." She silently reprimanded herself for her sarcasm. The sheriff had noticeably winced. "But last I seen of him he was bleedin' like a stuck pig. I shot that gentleman in the balls, sir."

Sheriff Tuttle cleared his throat, and Nell grinned inwardly as she observed, through the desk's archway, an almost imperceptible clenching of his thighs. *Men. So protective of their man parts.*

"Yes. And you said you detected no signs of pursuit."

"I did not. Maybe they thought I was makin' for Sonora, to the south." Despite the coffee, Nell could feel her eyelids drooping and she suppressed a yawn. She was very, very tired, quite indifferent at this point as to whether or not Sheriff Tuttle believed her.

The sheriff must have noticed this, too, and was not insensitive to her mood. He closed the ledger and pushed to his feet. Nell looked up. "I haven't signed."

"We'll take care of that later. You are no longer under arrest, Nell. Come with me and we'll find you a place to rest."

Nell rose unsteadily to her feet, stifling another wide yawn as she murmured her thanks. Relief flooded her exhausted body and the thought of rest, sleep, in a real bed, was headily enticing. "Oh, I almost forgot." She took a purse from her pocket and placed it on the sheriff's desk. "I stole that, too, from the man I shot. Oh, an' the pistol you took off me is his as well." She gave a rueful little chuckle. "In fact, nothin' I arrived with belongs to me."

****

Nell had no idea how long she'd been asleep, but the small housemaid's room at Audrey's that had been allotted her to rest in was dark when she awoke, save for a thin strip of light at the bottom of the door. Nell continued to lie quietly for a while, letting her eyes adjust to the dim light, reflecting on the events of the day, from her initial encounter with Tuttle to sinking into the gloriously soft bed at the Russell boarding house, where she'd fallen asleep the moment her head hit the pillow. It certainly could have been a lot worse, and she breathed a prayer of thanks for her safe deliverance. No sooner was that done than she realised she not only badly needed to use the chamber pot but was also exceedingly hungry again. Throwing back the covers, she clambered from the bed to relieve herself and search out her borrowed frock, stockings, and shoes. Once dressed, she opened the door and glanced up and down the passageway before she decided to follow her nose. Half way along the hall, a housemaid intercepted her and showed her into Audrey's private parlour, a cosy, tastefully furnished room, where her benefactor sat before a cheerful fire, reading a book.

"Nell! I hope you had a good rest, dear. Lord knows you needed it." Audrey closed her book and laid it on the side table next to her, placing her eyeglasses on the cover. "Come and sit with me. Trudy, be so good as to bring a supper tray for Nell."

"Yes, ma'am." Trudy bobbed and left.

Nell sat down opposite Audrey, smoothing her skirt and gazing appreciatively into the fire. "Thank you, ma'am. This is so nice."

"Please, dear, call me Audrey. Everyone does, except the staff." She smiled, lowering her voice and leaning forwards a little. "I have to keep some distance, since I am the boss. It doesn't pay to be over-familiar with one's employees."

Nell smiled as she recalled the warm, close-to-family atmosphere in The Shamrock. "No, ma'–, Audrey, I sure do understand." She gazed around the room. "This is a real nice place you got here."

"Thank you, Nell. I've worked hard and I love this town. I have two grown children in San Francisco. My husband passed a few years ago now and I miss him, but I have good friends here and I make a comfortable living."

When Nell had finished her supper of cold cuts, bread and pickles, and Trudy had removed the tray and been dismissed for the day, Audrey poured them each a nightcap of apple brandy, which

Nell felt was a fitting ending to what had, after a shaky start, been a blessed day. She noticed that Audrey had put out a third glass from a sideboard set of fine crystal tumblers and the reason for this was made clear when a gentle knock on the door was followed by the entrance of Sheriff Tuttle, who was warmly welcomed in by his hostess. He greeted both ladies politely before settling himself in a chair and accepting his glass of brandy. Nell rather got the impression that this was a regular ritual. The young man and the older woman were clearly close. Then he turned those ice-blue eyes on Nell and once again she felt her heart flutter alarmingly.

"I trust you enjoyed a good rest, Nell."

"Yes, thank you, Sheriff. I've only just come to and, I'm ashamed to say, have eaten a great deal more than I should have yet again." She patted her midriff and chuckled.

Tuttle grinned. "Please, call me John."

Nell dipped her head. "I will."

Their eyes locked and held. Audrey broke the spell by topping up glasses and wittering on about this and that until John finally drained his tumbler, bade them both goodnight and left on his rounds, albeit with an air of reluctance. Audrey left the room briefly to see him out, and Nell could hear their low voices in the passageway before the front door closed.

On her return, Audrey, cheeks nicely aglow, insisted she and Nell be 'wicked' and have a third glass, which Nell was feeling far too pleasantly mellow to refuse. As they settled back to their libations, Audrey broached the subject of what had brought Nell to Nevada City. After all her kindness, Nell could hardly refuse, so she recounted to her rapt listener the abridged version of what she had told the sheriff.

In the silence following Nell's disclosures, Audrey rose and, despite Nell's protests, refilled their glasses with yet another shot of apple brandy. As she resumed her seat, she raised her tumbler and said, "I salute you, Nell. You are truly a brave young woman to have survived and overcome such a terrible ordeal." She shook her head. "The frontier is really no place for women. I suppose that's why there are so few of us. It's a hard place for females, Nell. What you have faced is more than any woman should have to endure."

Nell gave a wry smile. "I'm not sure the sheriff believed me. I was supposed to sign my testimony, but in the end he did not press me."

"He believed you, or you'd be in a cold jail cell right now. For all his quiet ways, John Tuttle is a shrewd judge of character, with a good nose for the truth and a dedication to the letter of the law. He wouldn't have asked me to take care of you if he didn't think you were worth it."

"You know him well?"

"He stayed here when he first came to Nevada City." Audrey tossed back her dregs. "I'll tell you his story, but not tonight. It's late and I need my bed." She placed her empty glass on the side table. "You'll stay with me for as long as you're happy to. I gave John my word. That room is yours."

"I'm real obliged to you. I got to earn my keep, though. There must be chores I can help with. My late husband and I ran a restaurant in Yreka. I know about cookin' and caterin'."

Audrey smiled. "Well, Pandora, my cook, could use the help, I'm sure, and I know she'd be delighted if she could have some more rest breaks. Like me, she's not getting any younger. I'll introduce you tomorrow." Audrey fixed Nell with what could only be described as a sly look. "Perhaps you could take over the preparation and delivery of John's daily breakfast." She leaned forwards with a conspiratorial air. "He is unattached, you know."

Nell shot her a sharp look. "I'll help with whatever suits," she replied keeping her face impassive. *Oh, I would love to deliver his breakfasts! Lunches and dinners, too, come to that! Does he, perhaps, take morning and afternoon tea?*

Audrey rose, clapping her hands together. "Excellent! It will be so nice having you around. My, I declare my head is quite woozy." She giggled girlishly. "So lovely to enjoy a glass or two with good company. Good night now, Nell dear, and sleep well."

****

The days that followed were pleasant ones for Nell. With rest and good food her resilient young body healed well and her spirits were much restored. After an initially chilly response, Pandora quickly thawed once she could see that Nell was no threat but a genuine asset to her culinary domain and she reverted to the warm, affectionate soul she truly was under the bossy cook façade. The two housemaids, Trudy and Greta also became firm friends as they were close to Nell in age. Nell served in the dining room, too, when it got busy, and she enjoyed the cheer and banter with the varied clientele.

The sheriff seemed more than happy for her to deliver his breakfast tray every morning, and usually waylaid her to enjoy a cup of coffee with him, to which invitations Nell was delighted to acquiesce. He still called at Audrey's most evenings to share a nightcap, and Nell was increasingly amused by the way Audrey would frequently leave the pair alone while she set about doing something she 'suddenly remembered'. Nell had to admit that she loved every moment she spent in John Tuttle's company, especially when she had him to herself.

Audrey found extra clothes for her – two dresses, another shift, a night rail, two more pairs of bloomers, and a nice pair of slippers. Nell wrote to Kitty to let her know where she was and that she was safe and well, skipping over the traumas she'd suffered. She asked her to despatch a promissory note from the bank in Yreka for her monies and to send on her chattels at her earliest convenience, making sure to reimburse herself for any costs involved. Kitty replied quickly, expressing her joy that Nell was settled and happy and promising to fulfil her requests forthwith. To Nell's delight, a note from Toby was included in the letter. Nell also wrote to Marianne and Sholto with her new address and a request for news of baby Nicholas. She did not mention the lost portrait.

Meanwhile, Nell enjoyed immensely her evenings with John, especially when Audrey disappeared and she had him to herself without a chaperone making things awkward. There was only one fly in the ointment, and it began to niggle at her: while she wanted only to snuggle up to him on the sofa, he frequently steered the conversation around to what had befallen her at the hands of Jarrow, events she would prefer to forget. One evening, to Nell's exasperation, he even took out a small notebook and began to make jottings with a stub of pencil, frowning as he concentrated on recording the details Nell supplied, not seeming to notice that her answers were becoming increasingly clipped and terse. When at last she didn't answer a question, he paused, pencil poised, regarding her questioningly.

"Nell?"

Nell's exasperation breached the walls of containment. "John, don't you believe me? Is that why you haven't asked me to sign the confession? If you think me a liar, just say so!"

John drew himself upright, looking more than a little wounded by this outburst. "It is not a confession. It is a record of events. My personal record."

"Then why must you keep quizzing me so? I am weary of it! Goin' over what happened grieves me no little!"

John looked at her for a long moment, then shoved the notebook and pencil into his vest pocket and rose to his feet. "I'm sorry if I upset you, Nell. I'm sure I have what I need, anyway. I'll take my leave. Good night."

Without another word, he crossed to the coat stand, retrieved hat, and jacket, donned both, and exited, closing the door gently behind him. Nell remained staring at the door in a state of perplexity.

The next morning, as Nell laid the sheriff's tray out on the big kitchen table, smoothing a clean white cloth over it, and thinking about how she must make her peace with him, Audrey suddenly appeared and placed a restraining hand on her arm.

"Not this morning, Nell. John's not here."

Nell felt the room swim and gripped the edge of the table. *I was a fool to hope. Oh, I am truly fated!*

CHAPTER TWENTY-EIGHT

Nell cradled her coffee cup in shaking hands, bewildered by her emotional response to the news that a man she barely knew had left town. Seated opposite her at the table, Audrey watched her closely. Pandora and the girls were getting on with the breakfast shift, to all appearances indifferent to what was taking place behind them but, in fact, acutely attuned, ears straining to hear any conversation.

"It's my fault," declared Nell at last.

Audrey stirred sugar into her own coffee. "What is?"

Nell looked up, tears brimming in her eyes, lips trembling. "We had words last night and now he's gone. It's my fault." A tear spilled down her cheek.

Audrey dropped the spoon into her saucer with a clatter and rolled her eyes. "Land sakes, Nell, will you stop being such a drama queen? When I said John's not here I meant he has left on some sheriff's business. He'll almost certainly be back by the end of the week, so absolutely no need to go swooning on me. I thought you would faint clean away."

Nell blinked, looking at her dumbly. "Business?"

"Yes, his job. Will's gone with him, and he's left Sam Green and Howdy Dickson holding the fort." She chuckled. "What did you have words about?"

Nell explained the reasons for her flare up at John, concluding with, "so I got a bit cross, feelin' like he didn't believe me, is all. Then he left."

Audrey chuckled again. "Nell, is that why you think the sheriff wanted so much specific detail, because he didn't believe you? I thought I cleared that up for you, dear. Have you really no idea where he's gone?"

Nell brushed away a tear, frowning. "No. Why would I?" Then her cup crashed down on to the saucer as she straightened out of her slump, eyes open wide. "Oh my god! You don't mean he's gone to…no he wouldn't! Why would he do that? He's gone to find Jarrow, hasn't he?"

"Yes, Nell, he has. He took that pony you arrived on as well. He wants to find the owner and forestall any accusations of horse theft made against you. He asked me to tell you that."

Nell buried her face in her hands. "He's gonna get hisself killed, an' that'll be my fault." The words were muffled, but Audrey heard them well enough. She chuckled heartily, and Nell dropped her hands, glaring at her. Pandora and the two housemaids were laughing, too.

"What's funny 'bout getting' hisself killed?" Nell's voice had gone up a notch.

Audrey leaned across the table and patted Nell's hand. "Nell, there is no way John is going to be killed." She sat back, narrowing her eyes. "But I wouldn't want to be in that man Jarrow's boots."

"But he's huge, like a bear."

Audrey smirked. "Won't matter a damn."

Behind her Pandora and the two girls murmured assent, heads nodding vigorously, smiling broadly.

****

"I should have gone after him," said Nell firmly. She was seated on one side of the fire in Audrey's parlour, sipping her evening glass of apple brandy.

Audrey lowered her embroidery hoop, peering at her over the rims of her pince-nez. "You should have done no such thing. I believe you've done enough wandering around in the wilderness for one lifetime, young lady. Lord alone knows how you're still alive. Besides, John will be back any day now."

Nell smiled. "I'm sure you're right." She put down her glass and leaned forwards, resting her forearms on her thighs, hands clasped. "Why would he risk hisself for me? I ain't nobody. He hardly knows me."

Audrey put down her embroidery and picked up her glass. "John has a strong sense of justice. Some might say he has an over-developed sense of justice. And once he puts his mind to something, there's nothing can stand in his way. That's just the way he is."

"I kinda picked that. So he'd be the same way for anyone, not just me?"

"I didn't say that. I think he was particularly, um, affected by your circumstances, not to mention impressed by your outstanding courage and honesty." Audrey gave an exasperated 'tsk'. "Nell, have you really no idea of his feelings for you? It's clear as day to everyone else."

"His feelings for me?" Nell felt a flush creep up her cheeks.

"John Tuttle is in love with you. And unless my skill in reading people has taken a downswing, you feel the same way."

Nell did not reply. She sat back in her chair, picked up her tumbler, took another sip of applejack, and said softly. "You said you'd tell me his story. Maybe it's time."

Audrey smiled. "It is time indeed." She rose, placed another log on the fire, and then resumed her seat, retrieving her glass. "John was born back East, into a wealthy family. He's an educated, cultured man, but also a fine marksman and a very proficient boxer. He has trophies for both. His mother died when he was young and his father remarried, to a woman with whom John formed no bond. He left home early and lived with an uncle and aunt while he studied law. He fell in love with a girl from a good family and they planned to marry. Mere days before the wedding, she eloped with someone else, one of his close friends. Later he heard she had died in childbirth. He was broken-hearted and wanted to get away from all the bad memories, so he came west, worked around the gold diggings for a while, learned the necessary survival skills, and made a pleasing amount of money, some of it from boxing contests. The fact that his features remain unblemished is testament to his skill.

When he arrived in Nevada City, the town fathers just happened to be looking for a brave, honest man to enforce law and order. John applied for the job and got it. He has proved to be outstanding and has done much good for our town. I think he likes it here, loves to lose himself in the forest and mountains, hunting and fishing. He keeps to himself, a deep, thoughtful man, and I count myself fortunate that he regards me as one of his few close friends. I miss my dear boys so he is like another son to me." Audrey paused to take another sip, and looked over at Nell, but she remained silent, staring into the fire. "John Tuttle is a very fine man, Nell. I would dearly love to see him happy. Lord knows, you are overdue for some happiness, too."

Nell stirred from her trance and smiled at the older woman. "Well, I ain't educated nor cultured, but just the same it seems John an' me have quite a bit in common. I guess that's a good start." She frowned. "He's a good-looking man. Must've been lotsa women trying to win his affections."

Audrey nodded. "Yes indeed, and failing in the face of his indifference." She flashed a sly smile. "He is no longer indifferent, though."

"So, I turn up, lookin' like somethin' the cat dragged in an' he falls in love with me?" Nell shook her head. "I confess, I'm mystified."

Audrey chuckled as she topped up their glasses. "Rest assured, Nell. I'm sure John will explain that one to you, for your ears only."

****

For the rest of the week, Nell kept herself very busy to take her mind off John Tuttle. The furious pace she set herself alarmed Audrey and didn't really serve to distract her, but at least the hectic days followed by nights of leaden sleep helped time pass quickly. One morning, exactly seven days since John's departure, she was furiously beating the dust from a rug suspended over a line in the garden behind the boarding house when she heard a commotion coming from the street. Dropping the beater, she ran along the hallway, out the open front door, and on to the boardwalk, to be confronted by a memorable sight. To her joy, John Tuttle was riding towards her along the main thoroughfare, at the head of a small procession, while onlookers clapped and cheered, dogs raced back and forth yapping, and small boys capered about in the roadway, waving their caps and yahooing. Audrey drew up alongside her.

"Didn't I say he'd be back?"

"You did!" Nell spontaneously flung her arms around the surprised woman, hugging her tight, then gathered up her skirts, flew down the steps, and raced towards John. He rode a horse with the same easy grace that characterised all his movements: reins held loosely in one hand, the other resting on his hip, next to the heavy 'horse pistol' holstered there. He grinned around at the townsfolk who made up the boisterous welcome party, nodding his head in acknowledgement. Then he saw Nell racing towards him and reined in, lifting a hand to alert Will behind him. Will pulled up. He was trailing another mount on a lead rope, and there was someone astride the animal. But Nell didn't really register any of that. She only had eyes for John. As she halted in front of him, breathless, face aglow, neither spoke. The townsfolk went quiet as they watched the tender scene. Their sheriff's attraction to the bedraggled young waif who'd turned up in their town was common knowledge.

Clasping her hands under her chin, her elfin beauty aglow, Nell said breathlessly, "Welcome home, John. I'm glad you're safe."

John touched the brim of his hat. "Thank you, Nell. It's good to see you. I have some things for you." He swivelled in the saddle to look behind him and now Nell followed his gaze.

"Whiskey!" The pony nickered his recognition of her voice. As Nell took a step towards him, she stopped, staring in disbelief at the clean, neatly clad child on his back. "Wart! Oh John, you brought Wart!"

The townsfolk had no idea who Wart was, but clearly his presence was a cause for celebration, so they all cheered lustily as Nell dashed over to child and horse, planting a kiss on Whiskey's muzzle before reaching up for Wart. Wearing a grin that stretched back to his ear lobes, the little boy swung one skinny leg over the pony's back, and dropped into Nell's waiting arms. Everybody cheered again. John dug in his heels and the little procession continued on its way, Nell now bringing up the rear with her arm around Wart's thin shoulders. They halted outside the sheriff's office where, alerted by the commotion, his two deputies stood waiting, thumbs hooked in their gun belts and clearly pleased to see their fellow lawmen safely home. The crowd broke up and drifted away.

Sam and Howdy took charge of the horses, while the others filed into John's office, Wart gazing around in awe at his hero's spartan headquarters. On John's orders, a tired Will headed off to clean up and rest up. No sooner had he left than the door jangled again, and Nell turned to see Ben and Lily Abernathy, a well-liked young couple who ran the General Store, standing hesitantly on the threshold. They greeted John and Nell before they fixed their eyes firmly on Wart, smiling shyly.

"We heard you was back, John." Ben fingered his hat nervously.

John welcomed them in, then dropped on to his haunches beside the child, who was shrinking into Nell's skirts, his big eyes, reflecting fear and suspicion, fixed on the newcomers. "Wart, this is Ben and Lily Abernathy. You're going to be staying with them."

Wart looked at him in dismay. "I thought I was going to stay with you."

"I have to work, and I couldn't take proper care of you. You need to be with a family, have a normal life, go to school, and I promise I'll come see you as often as I can."

"So will I," said Nell, dropping on to her knees on his other side. "Do you trust us?" The little boy nodded. "You're safe now, Wart; nobody's gonna hurt you ever again. Now you say hello to Ben and Lily 'cos that's good manners."

Wart looked up at the smiling duo, who had drawn closer. "Hello," he said softly.

In unison they replied. "Hello, Wart."

"We're very pleased to meet you," added Lily. "If you come along with us, I got johnny cakes with syrup for your lunch, and lemonade."

Wart's eyes lit up at the thought of impending nourishment. Lily extended a hand and he grasped it. Ben took the other one. Smiling back at John and Nell over their shoulders, they led their new charge away. "'Bye, John. 'Bye, Nell," he called.

"'Bye, Wart," they chorused, and then the door closed and they were alone.

John chuckled. "Way to a boy's heart; through his belly. Lily called that right."

Nell smiled. "God bless you, John Tuttle. When I told you about Wart I hardly thought you took notice, but you did, didn't you? An' you arranged things with Ben and Lily fore'n you left, right?"

John nodded. "They have no kids of their own, although they've been married four years. Lily's as broody as a mother hen. That little boy is going to be spoilt rotten."

Nell nodded. That situation certainly resonated with her.

John removed his jacket and hung it with his hat on the coat stand. "Take a seat, Nell. I have some things for you." He lifted his saddlebags off the back of his captain's chair and placed them on his desk. Nell sat down and watched as he unbuckled the straps on the first. By the time he'd unbuckled and emptied the second, there was quite an array of items spread before her. Nell was speechless as she did an inventory of all the things she thought she would never see again.

Her money belt, which seemed to bulge with more cash than was there originally.

"Compensation," said John as she prodded it.

438

Her wedding ring. The Navy Colt and holster. Her precious old journal. The silver framed portrait of Nicholas. Then John removed the saddlebags from the desk and replaced them with a war bag, opening it to remove her clothes, laundered and folded, her boots, jacket and hat.

As Nell continued to gaze in wonderment, he said, "Will has your Hawken rifle, saddle, saddlebags, bridle, and bed roll. He'll return them tomorrow."

Nell reached over and picked up the daguerreotype of her son. Clasping it to her breast she wept freely. "John. I don't know what to say. How can I ever thank you?"

John lifted her to her feet, brushed the tears from her cheeks with the balls of his thumbs and said softly, "I had an ulterior motive, Nell. Will you marry me?"

Nell slid Nicholas into her pocket and flung her arms around him. "Oh yes! Yes, I will!"

John whispered in her ear. "Then I have my thanks."

He kissed her, and Nell felt as if her whole life had been a preparation for that single moment of ecstasy.

When they finally came up for air, Nell asked, "The wall-eyed pony?"

"Returned to his rightful owner, who has withdrawn the charge of theft against you."

"The man I shot?"

"Gilbert Rouncey. He lived. I doubt he'll be troubling any more ladies with his attentions, though. I returned his purse and firearm. And I gave him back the bruise he gave you as well, but with a little, uh, interest."

Nell chuckled.

So there was only one last question remaining. "And Jarrow?"

John looked over her head, sucking on his bottom lip, face serious. Then he looked into her eyes. "Last time I saw him, he was in jail, and somewhat recovered. He was most co-operative."

Nell lifted his right hand and studied the knuckles. The scabs were healing well. She kissed the abraded knuckles, dropped his hand, and pressed herself close to him. "Oh, I wish I'd been there," she whispered. Then she seized a startled John by his ears and kissed him again.

****

When Nell told Kitty she was getting married again, the little Irishwoman wrote back expressing her deep joy and emphatic about her intention to attend the nuptials, making the journey to Nevada City with her faithful Billy, whom, to Nell's delight, she had recently wed. The wedding was held in a packed Trinity Church followed by a reception at the National Hotel, before the happy couple left town to honeymoon in a riverside cabin of secret location, where for five days they lazed, ate, fished, swam, and spent a lot of time in bed. When they returned to Nevada City, they moved into the house John had built with his own hands, the house from which he'd been making his way to his office on the morning he'd apprehended Nell.

The time that followed her marriage to John was the happiest and most settled in Nell's life since the day she'd returned home from school to find her mother dead in childbirth. She took great pleasure in making a home for her and John, in being a wife, cooking, cleaning, gardening, and just spending time with her man, whom she loved deeply and devotedly. For the first time since leaving the farm in Iowa she had a fine vegetable plot, fruit trees, herb garden and, best of all, chickens. There were no more boarding house breakfasts for her husband. She rose every morning to set him up for the day with a sumptuous spread. In the evenings, after a comparable supper, she accompanied him on his rounds, clad once more in her familiar pants, flannels, boots and hat, shotgun broken across her arm. If John had to deal with any trouble, Nell had his back, and many a troublemaker who disrespected her ability to fulfil that role was subsequently sharply enlightened.

When they enjoyed leisure time together, Nell loved nothing more than to have John read to her from his collection of books that included history, law, and the classics. They would debate points raised for hours at a time, and Nell felt she was achieving an even better education than the one she'd missed out on as a child. John made it clear that he sincerely appreciated her insightful contributions, and under such supportive tutelage her confidence soared. A corollary was that her speech and manners became more refined as she matured into womanhood, but with no compromise to her indomitable spirit, which, along with her fierce intelligence, always shone through and was what had won John's heart in the first place. For his part, John enjoyed reading her journal, which, after initial shyness, she allowed him to peruse, and they opened up about their lives to each other, deepening their bond.

The one thing that blighted their happiness was that, not for want of trying, they remained childless. John knew about Nicholas, but had never queried Nell's decision to give him up. He enjoyed hearing about his progress when Nell read Marianne's letters out to him and was happy to have his baby photograph prominently displayed on the mantel. It was all Nell had, as Marianne had not fulfilled her original promise to send milestone photos of her son. Nell generously thought this may have been a ploy to spare her feelings, but she often daydreamed about what he might look like now. The number of letters had dwindled, too, and their content had become more of a recount of Marianne's active social life than anything else, but Nell harboured no bitterness. She had given up her son unconditionally and did not consider she had any special claims on his adoptive parents. Clearly, the synopsis was that he had enjoyed a wonderful life, been raised well with abundant love, and been given every opportunity to pursue his interests and advance himself. She could ask no more.

They saw a lot of Wart – now named Luke – and the robust, happy youngster he'd become filled the void somewhat. He frequently dined with them, stayed over, and loved fishing trips with John, all with his parents' blessing. They agreed with the old adage that it takes a village to raise a youngster. But it grieved Nell just the same that she had been unable to give her beloved husband a child. Her family had never been big breeders, but Nell wondered if some damage had been done at Nicholas's birth when she was just a child herself. It never occurred to her to question John's fertility. If a couple did not conceive it was just assumed the woman was barren, as was the case with the Abernathys.

For his part, John insisted that they were blessed to have each other – and got a dog.

The Civil War passed them by in the main. California supported the Union they'd joined in 1850 with men and gold. There were some southern dissenters among them who raised their own funds for the Confederacy by robbing stagecoaches and freight wagons, and John had to participate in more than one posse to catch the offenders, leaving Nell in a fretful state, which was always supplanted by joy when he returned home safely.

The years passed, and when John fell ill with the wasting sickness, Nell nursed him with unflinching devotion until he passed away in her arms, leaving her widowed again at the age of thirty-nine. Nell, already a local legend widely celebrated for her skill with firearms, was subsequently invited to be the first female sheriff of Nevada City and was only too happy to assume John's mantle, becoming a figure of widespread fame, which she shunned.

One morning, as Nell settled behind the desk in her office preparing to deal with some paperwork, she found herself riveted by an article she'd come across in the day's edition of the town's newspaper, the *Nevada Journal*. She enjoyed browsing through the paper most mornings, feet propped on her desktop, while she sipped a cup of coffee before commencing her duties. What captured her attention was a story about a young woman identified as Emily Dearhurst who had been rescued after a long captivity with the Arapaho Indians. The accompanying halftone photograph depicted a slender, dark-haired woman of about thirty with a striking tribal tattoo on her chin, wearing European clothing and looking directly into the camera with big, luminous eyes. Nell knew her instantly. "Chickabiddy," she whispered. The article went on to say that the young woman had been unable to adjust to life with white people and had returned to live with the Indians, where she was apparently quite content. Nell closed her eyes, leaning back in her chair. "Oh, my sweet chickabiddy. At least you're alive. At least you have a family again."

The doorbell jangling made her look over to see a young man entering, removing his hat as he did so. First glance indicated he was a gentleman.

"Good morning, ma'am." He mustered a hesitant smile.

Nell swept her feet off the desk and stood up, folding the paper and putting it aside. "Good morning. How can I help?"

The young man closed the door and stepped further inside, clearing his throat, his expression earnest. He was tall, good looking, nicely dressed in a suit and matching vest, long blond hair curling around his collar, his eyes a deep blue. He reminded Nell of someone.

"My name is Nicholas Beaumont. I'm a reporter with *The Boston Globe*." He fumbled in a vest pocket and drew out a small white card, holding it towards Nell. "I should probably have written you first, but I prefer face to face dealings." He flashed a sheepish grin. "I've been given a three month commission to find stories of local colour on the western frontier that will engross our readers back east. I was hoping you might make an exception and that I might get an interview with the famous lady sheriff of Nevada City." He blew out his cheeks, exhaled, and raised his eyebrows enquiringly.

Nell thought her heart would leap out of her chest. She took the offered card with trembling fingers and studied it. Finally, she found her voice. "Nicholas Beaumont?"

"Yes." He grinned. "My father wanted me to follow him into the army, but all I ever wanted to do was write. I was lucky that I had Mama on my side." His face became serious. "I'm determined to make a name for myself in the literary world." He lowered his eyes. "Sorry. That must sound arrogant."

"Not at all." Nell felt the need to sit down. She indicated the chair in front of her desk and Nicholas took it with murmured thanks. Pap. His grandfather, Nathan. That's whom he looked like. Nell could not stop staring at him. "How old are you?"

Nicholas looked a little taken aback. "I'm twenty-three."

Nell no longer had any doubt that she was looking at her son. She assumed a stern expression. "You've probably heard that I don't accommodate newspapermen. Not even the local ones. Not with any personal stuff, that is."

Nicholas looked pained. "Yes, I heard that." He added with a hopeful air, "I came on the railroad, a marvellous journey, quite exceptional. Have you ridden it? It's…" His voice trailed off into a resigned sigh as he hung his head.

Nell smiled, drinking him in. He'd indeed come a long, long way. "Well, I'm gonna make an exception for you, young man."

Nicholas's head shot up, huge grin wreathing his face. "Really? Oh, that's great, Mrs. Tuttle, just great. I…"

Nell pushed her chair back and stood up, cutting off the delighted young man in mid-gush. "How are you with a shotgun?"

Nicholas looked momentarily surprised and then leaped to his feet, tossing his hat on to his chair. "I'm all right, quite good, in fact. Father taught me to shoot. Not wanting to boast, but I'm fast and accurate with both rifle and handgun."

Took after me an' his grandpappy, then, not his daddy.

Nell crossed to the gun rack, unlocked it with a key from a bunch she extracted from her hip pocket, removed the shotgun and held it out to him, watching him closely. He took it confidently, as one used to handling a firearm, judged its heft, sighted along the barrels, checked the breech, and finally broke it over one arm with practiced ease, hugging it close to his body. He grinned at her. "Nice weapon."

Nell nodded her approval. "Belonged to my husband, John. I'll get you some shells and a badge, and then we'll go do the rounds. I'm short on deputies this mornin' so you'll fill in nicely." She cocked her head. "That's if you're up for it."

"Oh yes, ma'am. Honoured." He plucked up his hat and donned it at a rakish angle, clearly delighted with his new role.

"Call me Nell, Nicholas." She rolled his name off her tongue as if she were reluctant to let it go. He was too excited to notice.

Once the shotgun shells and badge had been respectively handed over to and pinned on her visitor, Nell took her coat and hat from the coat stand and buckled on her holster, adjusting the gun, a Colt 45 Peacemaker, to rest comfortably on her right hip. As she reached the door, she turned towards her newly deputised assistant, who was reverently fingering his badge with a dreamy look in his eyes. "We can talk as we go, an' then we'll have lunch at the hotel an' you can ask me 'bout anything we missed. We could get a photograph as well. You okay with that?"

"I sure am! Thank you, Nell."

"You can tell me all about yourself while we're at it."

"You want to know about me?"

"I do. Interviews work both ways."

"Well, I'm sure I won't be anywhere near as interesting a subject as you, ma'am, – Nell. Happy to oblige, all the same."

Nell nodded as she put on her hat and opened the door. "Let's go, Deputy. Look sharp there."

"Right here, Sheriff," said a voice behind her. "I've got your back."

Nell grinned.

ABOUT THE AUTHOR

I'm a retired English/Special Needs teacher living in Christchurch New Zealand. I started writing in 2014 and *Nell's West* is my ninth book. The others are *Immortal Longings, The Ivan, Ravening Heart of the Wolf, Days of Insult, The Wolf in Winter, The Siren Se*a, *Rain Doesn't Fall on Angels* and a personal memoir, *Distillation is Beautiful*. I have also published a short story in a collection titled *The Heart of the Matter*. I have plans to finish my 'Wolf' fantasy trilogy and to complete a memoir of my time working and living in Africa and Borneo.

Made in the USA
Middletown, DE
10 July 2022